out Karen

karenbooth.net

Jayci Lee writes poignant, sexy and laugh-out-loud romance every free second she can scavenge. She lives in sunny California with her tall, dark and handsome husband, two amazing boys with boundless energy, and a fluffy rescue whose cuteness is a major distraction. At times, she cannot accommodate reality because her brain is full of drool-worthy heroes and badass heroines clamouring to come to life.

Because of all the books demanding to be written, Jayci writes full-time now and is semi-retired from her fifteen-year career as a defence litigator. She loves food, wine and travelling, and, incidentally, so do her characters. Books have always helped her grow, dream and heal, and she hopes her books will do the same for you.

Discover more at millsandboon.co.uk

RANCHER AFTER MIDNIGHT

KAREN BOOTH

ONE NIGHT ONLY

JAYCI LEE

MILLS & BOON

First Published in Great Britain 2022
by Mills & Boon, an imprint of HarperCollins*Publishers* Ltd
1 London Bridge Street, London, SE1 9GF

www.harpercollins.co.uk

HarperCollins*Publishers*
Macken House, 39/40 Mayor Street Upper,
Dublin 1, D01 C9W8

Rancher After Midnight © 2022 Harlequin Enterprises ULC
One Night Only © 2022 Judith J. Yi

Special thanks and acknowledgement are given to Karen Booth for her contribution to the *Texas Cattleman's Club: Ranchers and Rivals* series.

ISBN: 978-0-263-30394-0

This boo

For n

Printed

RANCHER AFTER MIDNIGHT

KAREN BOOTH

For my fellow Mills & Boon Desire authors
and the editorial team at Mills & Boon.
You make me feel like a member of
the coolest romance club ever!

One

The entire population of Royal, Texas, thought Heath Thurston was a bullheaded jerk. Or at least it seemed that way. They talked about him like he was a mean dog with a bone. A veritable thorn in everyone's side. Heath did not care. Not one whit. They could call him names until they were blue in the face. He wasn't about to let go of his mission, especially not on account of public opinion. If he had to scrap and fight until his dying breath, he'd have some semblance of justice for his mother, Cynthia, and half sister, Ashley. They were no longer on this earth to fight for themselves. And no one else seemed to care that they'd both been wronged while they were alive.

Even his twin brother, Nolan, was shrugging off what the Grandins and Lattimores, two of the biggest and most powerful families in the town, had done to

Cynthia and Ashley. *Let it go*, Nolan had said. *It's time to move on.* But that was easy for Nolan to say. He'd hardly been around at all over the last fifteen years after heading off for greener pastures and leaving Heath to take care of everything at home. Sure, Nolan had finally returned to Royal, but that was only to turn around and be blinded by love—the love of a Grandin, no less. Chelsea. The woman he'd married. Heath could hardly believe the state of affairs. Nine months ago, he'd started his crusade against the Grandin and Lattimore families. And now he was related by marriage to one of them.

To make things worse, it was snowing. "What in the hell is going on?" he muttered under his breath. He peered out the windshield of his Ford F-150 Limited, a truck that was tough as nails on the outside and pure luxury inside. This was not typical weather for Royal, not even a few days after Christmas. It had never occurred to him to check the forecast before he headed out to Ruby Rose Bennett's house so he could talk to her about the oil survey she'd done on the Grandin and Lattimore properties. Her report's ultimate finding was "inconclusive," which Heath found unacceptable. An old report had said there wasn't oil, but he didn't trust it. So either there was oil on that land or there wasn't, and it was her job to find the answer. If there was oil, his mother and half sister had been entitled to it when they were alive. Since they were no longer here to fight for themselves, Heath was going to have to continue to do it for them on his own.

He would not fail. Even though he could admit to himself that things were looking bleak, he was also sure that he was not out of chances. He still had a few cards tucked up his sleeve. And he hoped that Ruby Rose Bennett might be able to help him play a winning hand.

His GPS told him that her driveway was ahead on the right, so he slowed down and made the turn. He was well beyond the city limits of Royal, out in a quiet rural area where there weren't many homes visible from the road and the parcels of land were vast. He started up the winding gravel road and drove up and over the crest of a hill, then began crawling along through a stand of trees that became more dense with every passing minute. He had to wonder what Ruby Rose Bennett was doing living this far out, in such an isolated and remote location. Perhaps she was a loner.

He'd never met the woman, but he imagined her to be in her late fifties or early sixties, possibly with a head of gray hair. Land surveyor was a rugged vocation, especially in Texas, where the terrain could be as unforgiving as it was beautiful. *Surveyor* conjured images of an ornery old man, so he could only envision that a woman in that line of work might have a similar aesthetic. Her email address, their main mode of communication, tipped him off to her age as well, since it suggested someone who did not keep pace with technology. The final hint had been their one phone call. Ruby Rose had a gruff voice that made her sound like a woman who'd been through a lot. He could relate. He'd been through the wringer as well.

The snow seemed to be coming down faster with every passing minute. It really was the most bizarre sight. Heath had lived in Royal his entire life and could count on one hand the number of times they'd had this sort of winter weather. He tried to take it as an omen that things were changing. Hopefully, that included his luck. He was tired of battling the Grandins and the Lattimores. He wanted them to turn over what they'd promised so he could begin the process of moving on in his life. What that might look like, however, he wasn't sure.

Eventually, he spotted the house he presumed to belong to Ms. Bennett. A paved driveway led him to the cute and tidy cottage, painted deep blue with crisp white trim, a high-pitched roof and a stone foundation. Window boxes sat at the sills of leaded-glass panes, overflowing with Christmas greenery of cedar, pine and holly, which now had a frosty coating of fresh snow. Perhaps old Ruby Rose Bennett kept herself busy during her leisure time by decorating for the holidays.

He parked his car off to the far right side, near a cluster of tall trees he hoped would shield his vehicle from any heavy accumulation of snow. He killed the engine and climbed out, bracing for the icy air. He stuffed his hands into his coat pockets and marched up the steps and onto her front porch, his cowboy boots thumping on the wide decking boards. Heath knocked on her door, which was adorned with a rather elaborate holiday wreath. After several moments, there was no answer, but he could see a light on inside, so he knocked again. *Must be taking her some time to get here.* Perhaps that was the problem with the survey Ruby Rose had done. She might not be as able-bodied as the job required. If that was the case, he'd have to find someone else to do it.

When the door finally opened, it felt as though the air was knocked right out of his lungs. Before him stood a stunning woman. Scratch that—she was drop-dead gorgeous. She was tall and willowy, with wavy blond hair, bright green eyes and full pink lips that, unfortunately, weren't saying a thing.

"Yes. Uh, hello." He glanced down at his feet, just to take a breather from her considerable beauty. "I'm looking for Ruby Rose Bennett. Is she home?"

"You're Heath Thurston, aren't you?" The woman eyed him up and down, making him incredibly self-conscious. And if he was being honest, a little turned on. Still, he was taken aback by the fact that she knew who he was. Had his reputation preceded him?

"That's me. I hired Ms. Bennett to do some survey work for me and I need to speak to her about it." He peered into the foyer for some sign of Ruby Rose.

"Okay. Although, I'm hardly dressed to discuss business." The woman looked down at herself. She was wearing a white sweater that hung off her shoulder, revealing a particularly enticing stretch of very touchable skin. Her somewhat beat-up blue jeans fit her like a glove. "A call or an email to set up a meeting would've been nice."

"Wait. What?" It felt as though his brain was fighting him as he struggled to reconcile his assumptions about Ruby Rose Bennett's appearance and the reality of the person standing before him. "You're Ruby Rose?"

"Most people call me Ruby. Add in the Rose and it sounds a little old-fashioned. Although, there's nothing wrong with that, and I do like the name. It was my mother's."

Heath wanted to laugh at how he'd jumped to the wrong conclusion about her. He was normally on the mark when summing up people. This time, he'd been more than a little off base. "Okay, then, Ruby. We need to talk."

"And as I just said, a call or an email would've been nice. At the very least, a text."

"I did call. And email you."

"When, exactly?"

Heath did not appreciate her attitude. He had a legitimate reason to be here. "Yesterday. And this morning."

"It's Saturday. Two days after Christmas. I take time off at the holidays, Mr. Thurston. Curl up with a good book. Drink a mug of hot cocoa. Maybe even with a shot of rum in it. Relax. Perhaps you should try it."

Heath narrowed his vision on her. Dammit, she was pretty, but he did not like the words coming out of her mouth, or more specifically, the condescension with which she delivered them. "I don't need a lesson in how to conduct myself, Ms. Bennett. I hired you to survey the Grandin and Lattimore properties for oil, and I'm not happy with the results. 'Inconclusive' is not an answer."

"I'm sorry about that, but just like the sun coming up in the morning, I have no control over some things. Either Mother Nature spent millions of years creating crude oil on that property, or she didn't. And although I'd love to give you the exact answer, the terrain doesn't allow for it unless you want to spend a whole lot more money."

"More money? You haven't given me what I paid for in the first place, which is a yes or no answer."

"Unfortunately, it's not as simple as that." As if Mother Nature herself was on Ruby's side in this argument, a fierce and bitter wind whipped over Heath's shoulders and straight into her foyer. She wrapped her arms around her midsection. "My gut is to tell you to go home, Mr. Thurston, but with the weather the way it is, you should come inside if you still want to talk about this."

Heath didn't appreciate that her inclination was to send him on his way, but he was thankful she was willing to reconsider. "Yes. That would be great. Thank you." He stepped inside and stomped his feet on the rug.

"Take your boots off."

"I'd prefer to keep them on, if it's all the same to you." Heath didn't walk around in his socks, especially not in front of a beautiful woman when they were about to discuss business.

"Well, it's not all the same to me."

"Excuse me?"

"Have you ever refinished wood floors, Mr. Thurston? By yourself? By *hand*?" She punctuated her question with an artful arch of her eyebrow.

"No."

"Well, I have, and I don't intend to undo my hard work. So take off your boots. Please."

"I'm not staying for long."

She laughed quietly, shaking her head. "You are exactly as bullheaded as everyone says you are, aren't you?"

There it was. Ruby Rose Bennett was on the same side as the rest of Royal. Like everyone else, she thought his stubbornness was a flaw in his personality. When in truth, it was only out of love and a thirst for justice that he was on this crusade. "If that's what you want to call it, then sure. I am."

Ruby was sure of one thing—Heath wasn't going to take off his boots no matter how hard she argued with him. She'd seen Heath's type before. He was rich and entitled, and wound entirely too tight as a result. She had little admiration for any of those qualities, but in his case, she sure could appreciate the appealing package they came wrapped up in. He was temptingly tall, a good five or six inches on her, just enough of an advantage to make her raise her chin and take notice. His hair was touchable and thick and such a dark brown that it was like night, set off by a pair of the most intense and stormy eyes she'd ever seen. For the first time in years, her pulse quickened because of a man. Did that mean she was finally coming back to life? After the loss she'd endured, she'd had every reason to believe she never would.

Despite Heath being a serious case of eye candy, she had to wonder if it had been a mistake to take a job from him. The first whiff of trouble came the day she'd gone out to the Grandin and Lattimore properties to do his survey and she was stopped by a man she knew to be Vic Grandin. Vic had been deeply suspicious of her presence. Enough to make her uncomfortable. Days later at the Royal Diner, she overheard some chatter about a paternity saga in the Grandin family. She didn't have many ties to Royal, but people talked, and this seemed to be a big topic of conversation. She'd heard some real mouthfuls about Heath, too, about his greed and vindictiveness. Was her assignment really about finding oil? Or was there something else at play? She didn't like getting mixed up in other people's affairs.

"Can I get you anything to drink?" Ruby asked as she led Heath down the hall to her living room and kitchen, an open and airy space she'd created when she knocked down the wall between the two rooms soon after buying this cottage three years ago.

"I'm good."

"You sure? Something hot, like coffee? It's not long before dinnertime, but I'm happy to put on a pot."

He shook his head. "I think it's best if we discuss business, so I can leave you to the rest of your day."

As much as she enjoyed looking at him, perhaps this was for the best. "I don't think the weather's supposed to improve anytime soon, so probably a good idea. What do you want to know?"

"I don't see how 'inconclusive' is an acceptable result from an oil survey. Either there's oil or there isn't."

"As I said when I answered the door, it's not that simple, especially in this part of Texas. There are trace amounts of oil almost everywhere. As for the Grandin and Lattimore properties, I did my best with the budget you provided."

"What does that mean?"

"It means that I did what the fee allowed for. I examined any and all surface rock formations. Most contained shale, which can sometimes indicate the presence of oil. Then I did low-level seismic readings, which produced zero evidence of oil. Hence the term 'inconclusive.' It was all in my report."

He pressed his lips together tightly. "Which is more reliable? The rocks or the readings?"

"The readings. By far."

He grimaced. "Are they ever wrong?"

"No. But not all seismic tests are created equal." She wandered around to the other side of her kitchen island, which acted as a natural separation in the great room, and grabbed the mug of cocoa she'd been drinking before he arrived. She took a sip. It was lukewarm, but still delicious, a recipe she'd perfected in the last few years. "If you want to know with one hundred percent confidence, we would need to bring in some serious heavy machinery and do some blasting. We're talking tens of thousands of dollars, or more, and a lot of time. I'm happy to do it if that's what you want." Despite her reticence, she'd take a second job from him. Or a third. Money was tight. "That is, after you convince the families to let you do it."

"I have the deed to the oil in my possession. It gives me the right to do whatever I want on that land in order to get to what's below the surface. And I can sell those rights to an oil company tomorrow. They can start bringing in drills right away."

"I hate to break this to you, Mr. Thurston, but no oil company is going to buy those rights without first verifying the presence of what they're after. And from the available evidence, I doubt you'd be able to get them interested." She'd dealt plenty with oil companies. She knew how they worked and they most certainly did not throw their money away on useless land. "Plus, the Grandin and Lattimore homesteads are beautiful. You really want to go out there and start tearing them up? For nothing?"

He dismissed her comment with a toss of his head. "Maybe that's what they deserve."

Now, *that* sounded like a grudge. Heath wasn't a particularly sympathetic man. He was gruff and quick to make assumptions. Still, there was a part of her that felt for him. He seemed desperate, with a serious case of tunnel vision, both of which could make a person do unreasonable things. "I assume you know about the original survey of the land years ago. There was zero evidence of oil."

"You saw that?"

"I did. I went back and looked up any old surveys after I completed mine. I don't like the word *inconclusive* any more than you do. I wanted to be sure I hadn't missed anything."

"Well, I'm not sure I believe what it said, considering the source."

"Because it was paid for by the Grandin and Lattimore families? It's their land. How is that any different than you having oil rights and wanting them verified? They wanted to know what was on their property. Seems perfectly reasonable to me."

"They have every reason to lie."

"Well, I don't know about that, but I can tell you that Henry Lawrence, the original surveyor, would never do that. My father was a geologist and he was friends with Henry. He's incredibly well respected. One of the best in the business. If he found no oil, then there's likely no oil. He wouldn't put his name on any report that lied about what was on that property."

"If you believe so strongly in what he found, then why not say that in your survey?"

"Because I wasn't able to do the tests that he did. I can't copy someone else's work. It wouldn't be ethical."

He laughed, but there was a sharp and dismissive tone to the sound. "*Ethical.* That's a funny word to throw around when we're talking about the Grandins and the Lattimores. I don't think a single one of them is familiar with the term."

Heath was clinging to bitter doubt like it was the only thing he had going for him. She wanted to understand why. "Can I ask a question? Is this a dispute over oil rights? Or is there something else to it?"

"Very astute observation. This *is* about more than oil. It's about two rich and powerful patriarchs trying to silence a single mom because they didn't want to take responsibility for the child one of their sons fathered. That child was my half sister, Ashley."

Bingo. So this *was* about a paternity case. The one people in Royal had been talking about. "And the single mom is your mother?"

"Was my mother. She's deceased. As is Ashley. Both of them gone too soon. Ash's birthday was last week. She would've been thirty-eight. She had so much life ahead of her."

Ruby suddenly understood what this was really about—loss and grief. Ruby had wrestled with that for more years than she liked to admit. Trying to escape the pain had brought her to Royal. Doing a quick calculation in her head, and understanding what Heath was going through, was the only reason she was about to bring up one detail she'd noticed when she'd gone over the paperwork relating to oil rights. Before, it didn't matter, but now it might give Heath some clarity. "Did you happen to look at the date on Henry's original survey?"

"I never saw it. I was only told about it. By my lawyer."

"We should confirm it, but going by Ashley's birthday, I'm pretty sure Henry's survey was done a full year before they granted rights to your mother."

Heath froze while white-hot anger rose in his face like a flash flood. "Seriously?"

Ruby swallowed hard, understanding what this meant. "Yes."

"So those bastards knew all along that it was worthless. They have piles and piles of money and they purposely looked for something of no value to give to my mother, just to shut her up." He dragged his hand through his hair, then frantically scrubbed his jaw, seeming frustrated and in some ways at war with himself. "They not only lied to her, they tricked her. Of all the low things someone could do, this might be the lowest."

"I'm sorry. I didn't want to be the bearer of bad news."

"I need to go. Now. I'm sorry I bothered you." He stormed out of the room.

For a moment, she hesitated. Did she really want to get involved with this? No. But she hated the thought of two rich and powerful families taking advantage of a struggling woman. "Heath. Wait!"

"Thank you for your help, Ruby. I'm sorry if I interrupted your day." He flung open the front door and slammed it behind him.

"Wait!" She grabbed the knob and opened it again, but she couldn't run after him with nothing more than thick wool socks on her feet. She grabbed her boots, noticing that the snow was coming down sideways and the wind had picked up significantly. There was little to no visibility. She wasn't sure how fast he was walking, but he was already nothing more than a shadowy figure out there. He was a fool for wanting to ride off in this. "Heath. Please stop." She worked her feet into her boots, grabbed a coat and stomped out onto her front porch.

He must have heard her footfalls on the wood planks, because he turned back to her. "I've got to be somewhere. Just let me go. Please go back in the house." He waved her off with his hand.

"No. Don't rush off when you're angry." She scrambled down the stairs and shuffled across her driveway, which was now slippery in spots. The snow was not only still coming down fast, it was incredibly heavy. The branches of the trees surrounding them strained in the wind, weighed down with the winter precipitation, swaying and bobbing like a drunken man. "The weather is too bad. I don't think it's a good idea to be on the ro—" A deafening crack sliced through the air. It was wood splitting. Ruby startled and keeled back on her heels. She backpedaled, but there was no grip. Her feet flew out from under her. *Thud.* Her butt hit the driveway. Pain blinded her. It sizzled down her legs and up her back. More cracks came, then a loud boom, followed by the ground shaking.

Heath lunged for her, but it only made it worse. He landed on his knee and grabbed her shoulder, but the momentum flattened Ruby against the pavement with Heath practically on top of her. His eyes were even wilder and untamed this close, his lips slack as they both struggled to catch their frosty breaths. "What the hell was that?" he asked. "It felt like an earthquake."

"The tree," she answered, trying to ignore how much she liked having his body weight against her. She gestured behind him with a nod. A bald cypress, which had to be more than sixty feet tall, had come down, landing across the road and blocking all access to her house. That thing had shown signs of deterioration a few months ago. She should have had it removed, but it was too late for that. "It fell. You aren't going anywhere."

He turned away from her and shook his head in disbelief. "This doesn't make any sense. We don't get this kind of weather in Royal."

She laughed. She couldn't help it. She could not believe Heath Thurston.

"What?" he asked, seeming indignant.

"You're arguing with what is right in front of you. Snow. A thousand-pound tree blocking your way off my property." She looked skyward and squinted as fat, icy flakes landed on her face. It was really coming down. Yes, she preferred the heat of a Texas summer to a snowstorm. But it was a change of pace, and she appreciated that. She lowered her head and settled her sights on Heath again. He was nice to look at, even when his hair was wet from snow and his cheeks ruddy and red from the cold. "A little help?" she asked.

He blinked and nodded like her words had shaken him awake. "Of course. Sorry. Are you okay?" He threaded his arm under hers, wrapping his hand around her waist and helping her to stand. He held her close once they were on their feet.

For a split second, she thought about kissing him. It would be amazing to get lost in the sheer pleasure of a kiss. But enough outlandish things had already happened in the last five minutes. She didn't need to add to the list. "I'm okay." She took a step back from him, just to break the allure of being in his strong arms. "We should get inside. I should call someone about getting that tree hauled off or we'll be stuck here forever." She was wet and cold, and one side of her ass was throbbing.

"But I really need to speak to my brother. Now." Deep creases formed in his forehead, as if he was not yet convinced that he was stuck there. He raised his cell phone in the air and peered up at the screen. "There's no phone service either."

"Guess that means no one is coming to remove that tree anytime soon."

"But I have to go."

"Is this a matter of life or death?"

"To me? It's the most important thing."

She was tired of talking in circles with this man. Handsome or not, he was going to drive her up a wall. "But will anyone die if you come back inside with me, warm up and let the weather pass?"

He grumbled quietly and tossed his head from side to side as if he was weighing his options. "No. I suppose not."

"Okay, then." She turned and started for the house, being careful not to slip and fall again.

"Okay, then, what?"

She kept going. Hopefully he had enough sense to follow her inside. "Okay, then, get back in my house before we both end up as icicles."

"Do I have to take off my boots this time?"

A breathy laugh escaped her lips as she took the first step up to the porch. She wasn't sure how long Heath Thurston was going to be at her house, but she had a feeling this was going to be a long visit. "Yes. I'm not letting you off the hook this time."

Two

Heath was frustrated, cold, and his knee was killing him. But at least he was inside with a beautiful woman.

"You can't turn me down for a drink this time. I won't let you." Ruby removed her boots, then slid him a stern sideways glance that said the other thing he'd better not refuse was removing his boots.

He planted a hand against her front door and pulled off his boots one by one. "Bourbon?"

She cocked an eyebrow. "Going straight to the hard stuff?"

"It's almost five o'clock and my knee is about to swell up to the size of a basketball." He wasn't the only one who'd been injured out in her driveway. "I'm guessing your…you know…*backside* isn't doing much better."

"My *ass*? Oh, I'm going to end up with a nasty bruise.

I'm sure of it." She enticed him closer with a wave of her hand, then turned to walk down the hall.

He followed, smiling, loving that she was not a woman who tried to hide from anything. He was also a big fan of the view as he studied the hypnotic sway of her hips. It was hard to keep from imagining what her ass looked like when it wasn't wrapped up in a pair of jeans. "Sorry about everything outside. I get a little…" *A little what? Self-possessed? Irrational?* He didn't want to think about words like that when describing himself. His actions made sense to him, and no one else had walked in his shoes. But he could imagine how outward appearances might show him in a less flattering light. "Overly determined."

"So that's what you call it."

"For now, yes."

"Got it." Ruby trailed through her cozy living room, which had tall ceilings accented by hewn wood beams and a stunner of a fireplace with a surround of hand-placed river rocks. Flames danced and flickered, casting a glow and warming up the room, which was decorated in shades of white and cream with the occasional bit of pale pink. These were feminine surroundings he wasn't quite accustomed to anymore, but when his mother and half sister were still alive, these softer touches would have felt as familiar as anything. Ruby came to a stop before the only dark piece in the entire space, an antique mahogany bar cabinet. She opened one of the doors, revealing a jaw-dropping array of bourbon bottles.

Heath had to step closer, if only to examine the many brands and ages of bourbon she had on hand. "I'm not speechless very often, but I am right now. I'm impressed. You're a serious collector. I consider myself a connoisseur, but even I don't have this extensive an assortment at home."

She looked at the bottles and quietly sighed. She even reached out and touched one with the tip of her finger. "I actually don't drink it. I'm more of a wine person. But I can't bring myself to part with these."

"You definitely should *not* part with them. If you're ever thinking of doing that, call me first. I'll happily buy the entire collection from you."

She turned to him, but only held eye contact for a moment. "It's not for sale."

Now Heath was confused—she didn't drink it, but she also didn't want to get rid of it? "Did it belong to someone special?"

"It did." She cleared her throat. "Which one would you like to try?"

Heath found himself even more confounded. Clearly, the previous owner of the bourbon was not someone she cared to discuss. Or at least not now. After all, they barely knew each other. "I'll try the Willett. The twenty-four year. I've only had it once. It's exceptional."

"Sure thing." She took a highball glass from a shelf inside the cabinet. "Here. Pour yourself as much as you like. Can I get you any ice?"

"Absolutely not." Heath popped the cork from the bottle and slowly poured the deep amber liquid into his glass. "This is meant to be enjoyed as is." He carefully put the bottle back in place and rolled the liquor in the highball, smelling the fragrance and admiring the color. "Are you going to join me?"

"I'll have a glass of wine with dinner. For now, I'm going to go heat up the mug of cocoa I was drinking when you got here."

Heath looked out one of the windows along the back side of the house. Impossibly, the snow seemed to be coming down even harder. "I suppose I will be here at least that long, huh?" He finally took a sip of the bourbon, which was even better than he remembered.

"At least until there's cell service and I can call someone to get that tree out of my driveway." Ruby strode to the other side of the open space and rounded a butcher block peninsula, into the heart of her kitchen. She placed a ceramic coffee cup in the microwave and hit a few buttons.

"If I had a chain and a chain saw and an extra hand or two, we could slice it up and haul it out of there with my truck."

The microwave beeped and she retrieved her drink, wrapping her hands around the mug and closing her eyes to smell the steaming liquid inside. Damn, she was beautiful. She was enough to make him forget why he'd come here in the first place. Her eyes slowly opened and she took a sip, looking at him while she did it. It was a penetrating glance, one that seemed to get right down to his core. "Don't take this the wrong way, but you don't really strike me as a man who does that sort of work for himself."

For the first time in a long time, Heath found that his first reaction to that kind of probing or inquisition was not to put up his guard. It only made him more curious about her. What was going on behind those mysterious green eyes? "I own and run a sizable ranch. Now, granted, I don't do a lot of the day-to-day work. I have a whole crew working for me. But I know how to do it all. I *have* done it all, and I'm not a man who's afraid to get his hands dirty." Despite the considerable revenue and income his ranch generated, Heath still thought of himself as a working man. He hadn't come from old money like the Grandins or Lattimores had. And even though he'd inherited the ranch that eventually earned millions, it hadn't been much when he'd started. In fact, the ranch had been in such disrepair that his brother, Nolan, had wanted no part of it.

"Can you saddle a horse?" Ruby returned to the living room and took a seat on the comfortable sofa nearest the fireplace.

Heath followed her lead and joined her, sitting at the opposite end. "Of course."

"Rope a steer?"

"It might not be pretty, but I can get it done."

"Ever birthed a calf?"

"Again, might not be pretty, but I can hold my own."

That made her smile and her eyes twinkle. "You're not quite what I expected, Heath Thurston."

"You aren't quite what I expected, either," he said. That was the understatement of the century. This whole day had come as a complete surprise. "How does a young woman become a surveyor?"

"Not easily. It's such a male-dominated field, but I can't imagine doing anything else. It was my dad's influence. He was a geologist. My mother passed away when my brother, Joe, and I were young. Dad had to travel for work all the time, all over the state of Texas, so he brought us with him." Ruby pulled her knee up onto the couch and turned to face him directly. "We were a very tight little family, and he was an amazing dad. So it was only natural that I wanted to go into something along the lines of what he did. My brother did the same. He's an environmental scientist."

"Is it hard to make a living as a surveyor?"

"It's not pretty, but I can get it done."

He laughed at the way she'd effortlessly tossed his own words back at him. She was quick, with a very appealing spark. "Like I said a few minutes ago, you definitely aren't what I expected either."

"I'm not really sure what that means, to be honest."

He cleared his throat, thinking about what had been running through his head as he'd driven up her driveway. "Your appearance. Your, uh, age."

"I'm thirty years old. Or I will be next week. Why?" Her eyes scanned his face, zipping back and forth like she was looking for clues. Or answers. "Hold on a minute. How old did you think I was?" She ended the question by reaching over and pushing on his shoulder with her fingertips. Damn, she was sexy when she confronted or questioned him, which seemed to be often.

"It doesn't matter."

"You don't want to tell me, do you?"

"Really. Let's talk about something else."

"Heath… I'm going to drag it out of you one way or another. We are stuck here for the foreseeable future. I have nothing but time on my hands right now."

He swallowed hard, fighting an urge to smile or maybe even laugh. "Fine. It's just that I pictured a much older woman. In my defense, even you said that your full name is a bit old-fashioned." He watched as a look of horror crossed her face. Heath was prepared to do anything to make it go away. "I'm not saying I don't love your name. I do. It's beautiful. Just like you."

Any offense she'd taken quickly melted away, replaced by skepticism. A woman as gorgeous and beguiling as her had surely heard hundreds of men tell her something similar. "I think the bourbon's getting to you."

"It's not." *You are. Somehow.* "Plus, the one time we talked on the phone, your voice sounded pretty rough-and-tumble."

"Like a woman who'd been through a lot?"

"Yes. Exactly."

"Well, I had a nasty cold when we talked. If my voice was scratchy, that's why."

"So you haven't been through a lot?" He didn't want to pry, but he was genuinely curious to know more, especially about whoever had once owned that bourbon collection.

"I've been through plenty." She sipped from her mug again. "But we've all been through the wringer in one way or another, haven't we?"

Heath's breath hitched in his chest as her words rang clear in his head. If only she knew how strongly that statement resonated with him. It was like having someone shine a light on his soul.

Ruby was well aware she was deflecting by saying that everyone had gone through hard times, but it was her instinct to keep her memories and her pain to herself, especially as those things related to her fiancé, Lucas. She didn't know Heath very well, and although she'd had nearly three years to process the loss of her fiancé, she liked to keep the anguish from bubbling up to the surface when she was around other people. It was easier that way. But that didn't mean she wanted to skirt all serious subject matter with Heath. She wanted to know more about what he'd been through. Everything people in Royal said about him wasn't holding true for her. He didn't seem vindictive. He seemed like a strong man hiding his vulnerability. Those two things were *not* the same.

"Do you want to tell me about your mom and sister?" she finally asked. "They're at the heart of this dispute over the oil rights, aren't they?"

Heath rolled the bourbon around in his glass, studying the liquid and drawing attention to his hands, which were admittedly amazing, a perfect marriage of strength and grace. "What do you want to know?"

Ruby was surprised he was so willing to share. She shrugged and sat back in her seat. "I'm not going anywhere and neither are you, so tell me everything."

Once again, his vision was trained on what was in his glass and not on her. She didn't know him well, but she could tell that the gears in his head were turning. She wanted desperately to know what he was thinking, making her hope just as hard that he would spill at least a few of the secrets he must be keeping tucked away in his mind.

"My dad died when my twin brother, Nolan, and I were far too young to understand the magnitude of losing him. My mom had always been a melancholy person, but after he died, the sadness she went through was profound. And it never went away. It was very hard."

"I'm sorry. I lost my mom when I was seven. I know how difficult it is to lose a parent, especially when you're too young to process it. The older you get, the farther away they are. And you question your memories of them all the time."

He nodded and looked over at her. "That's so true. All of it." He drew in a deep breath—so deep that it made his shoulders rise up near his ears. "And for me,

I have so many memories of wondering if I was some-how responsible for my mother's sadness. Like it was up to me to make her happy. I don't know where I got that idea from, but it was always with me. A sense of re-sponsibility. It was always there. Maybe I got that from my dad. From the time I could walk, I followed him, learning everything it took to keep the ranch running. Our half sister, Ashley, had to step up, practically be-came a mom to Nolan and me. We were always fighting her on it. We thought we were old enough to take care of ourselves, but she was five years older. She knew more than we did. Either way, we all had to grow up quickly. Our dad had run the ranch, so I took over and was determined not to fail him or my mom. Nolan tried to help for a while, but his interests were elsewhere."

Ruby was taken aback by the idea of Heath and his siblings trying to tackle such a monumental job. "How did you manage?"

"Our dad had some great ranch hands who all stayed on out of a sense of duty to our mom. I always sensed that they knew she'd been through a lot. It wasn't until recently that I figured out that her sadness went well beyond losing our dad. It was because of the way the Grandin family had treated her and Ashley."

"Ashley being half Grandin, right?"

"Yes. Her dad was Daniel Grandin. He had a fling with my mom when she was young and then took off. He lives over in France now. He claims he never knew Mom was pregnant. His father, Victor Grandin Sr., knew and wanted it kept a secret. By all accounts, my mother really struggled when Ashley was a baby. She was broke and all on her own. And then there were the

Grandins, without a care in the world, sitting on their piles of money."

Ruby was starting to appreciate where Heath's bitterness came from. "How did the Lattimores get involved?"

"Those two families have been thick as thieves for generations. Augustus Lattimore and Victor John Grandin were best friends, and their properties are adjacent to each other. Now that you've told me about the date on the old survey, I believe the rotten bastards conspired to buy off my mom with the phony oil rights so she'd never tell anyone Ashley was half Grandin. They were deathly afraid my mom would talk and tarnish the Grandin name, which would have negatively impacted their family fortune, which then would have trickled down to the Lattimores. Rich people like their friends to be rich, too. They figured a worthless piece of paper was enough to shut my mother up."

"You'd think they would have worried about her claiming the rights. Eventually their lies would have caught up with them."

"I think they knew that she didn't have the strength or resources to do anything about it, so she'd never find out they tricked her."

"Augustus Lattimore is still alive, isn't he?" Ruby had heard people in town talk about him. Apparently his health was declining, but he had to be in his nineties, so that was no big surprise. "Can't someone ask him?"

Heath shook his head. "Both families clammed up as soon as I discovered the paperwork for the oil rights in my mother's effects and started looking into it. That's part of why I asked my brother, Nolan, to come back to Royal. To help me try to crack the case of those two families. But that opened up a whole new can of worms."

"In what way?"

He sighed. "Nolan had left Royal when he was eighteen. He was tired of feeling responsible for so much. But that left me here, taking care of the ranch and my mom and helping Ashley. A lot of resentment has built up between us, and it's getting better, but we've still got a ways to go. He came back to Royal to help, but then he fell in love with Chelsea Grandin, and now they're married. So of course he thinks I should drop the whole thing. But I'm not ready to do that. I still feel like I need to make things right for my mom and Ashley."

"What about Daniel Grandin? Ashley's father? Have you met him or talked to him?"

"No. The family has closed ranks and won't let me anywhere near him." He ran his hand through his hair, seeming frustrated again. "Basically, I have a whole lot of questions and not enough definitive answers. I know people see me as a bitter villain, but all I'm trying to do is get some justice for my mom and sister. I know they're gone, but it's hard for me to let it go. Sometimes I feel haunted by the whole situation. By them." His voice quaked as it trailed off. He avoided looking at Ruby, seeming embarrassed by the show of emotion.

"When did your mom and sister pass away?"

"It's been a few years now. Car accident. A truck driver ran a red light."

Ruby sucked in a sharp breath as her heart physically ached. Her biggest strength—or weakness, depending on the situation—was empathy. She had no problem putting herself in other people's shoes and feeling their pain, but everything Heath had been through hit impossibly close to home. "I am so incredibly sorry. I understand everything you're feeling." She reached out and touched his shoulder, trying to ignore the electricity that zipped through her fingertips and up her arm.

"Because of your mom?"

She hesitated for a moment, unsure if she wanted to talk about Lucas. But the pain of losing her mom was decades old. It wasn't as raw as the pain of having lost her fiancé. And she wanted Heath to know she'd struggled greatly with this, too. "My fiancé, Lucas, died. Nearly three years ago. It was an aortic aneurysm. We had no warning. It was like a light switch was turned off and he was gone."

Heath turned to the bar cabinet, then back to Ruby. "That's where the bourbon came from?"

She nodded eagerly, smiling at her good memories of Lucas. "Yes. He was the collector. Absolutely loved it. It keeps me company, even if I don't drink it."

He looked down at his glass. "And you shared it with me? We hardly know each other. I feel terrible now."

She shook her head and dared to touch him again. "Oh, no. Don't. He would want you to have it. He would have wanted someone to appreciate it."

"Are you sure?"

"I'm positive. Absolutely." Before she could say more, the lights overhead flickered. She caught a glimpse of the weather outside. "I didn't think it was possible, but it looks even worse out there. I really hope we don't lose power."

"Yeah. That would not be fun."

"Although, there's plenty of bourbon. And firewood. And I have a gas stove, so we could still eat. It wouldn't be entirely bad." *Cooped up all alone. Just the two of us.*

Their gazes connected, and for the first time, one corner of his mouth turned up in an off-kilter smile. "I know I don't know you that well, Ruby, but I have to say that you are a remarkable human being."

Heat flooded her cheeks. Her heart started pounding. She didn't deserve such praise, but it felt good. "*Remarkable* is a pretty strong word."

"It absolutely applies. You're strong. You're smart and you seem to have great intuition. And if it's not too forward of me, you're so beautiful."

It wouldn't be a stretch to kiss him. In some ways, it would be the easiest thing in the world. But also the scariest. Who was she kidding? Any guy was a leap for her, even after three years. But a man like Heath? He was too much—too handsome, too rich and definitely too complicated. She could see her way past the first two, but that last one? If she was going to get involved with someone, she wasn't ready for serious, and she was certain that "serious" was Heath's middle name. "That's sweet of you to say, but I'm just being me. I don't know another way to be."

The lights flickered again, and they both looked up at the ceiling. A second later, the room fell into darkness. Outside, the wind howled. Inside, Ruby was painfully aware of her proximity to Heath and the way her heart was fluttering.

"I'm sure it'll come back on soon," Ruby said. "I'm on the same grid with the public works department and the animal shelter. They don't usually let them go too long without power."

Heath nodded in the direction of the fireplace. "You've already got a good amount of firewood inside, but we should grab some more, just in case the power company isn't able to get a team out here quickly. The roads can't be in good condition."

"Right. That's smart." Ruby got up from the sofa. "I'm on it."

Heath grabbed her arm. "No. I'll do it."

They both stared at the vision of his hand on her arm. She'd touched him several times in the last hour or so, but this was the first time he'd returned the favor. He didn't let go and she didn't budge an inch. Between them, there was a distinct charge in the air. It was more than electricity. It was attraction…and sex. And for the first time in what felt like a lifetime, Ruby was seriously thinking of hopping on board.

Three

Heath trudged through the snow and battled the wind until he reached the woodpile at the side of Ruby's house. He was all for equality between the sexes, but he also believed in being a gentleman, and that meant he wasn't about to let her go outside in a blizzard for firewood. That seemed like his job.

Plus, he needed to cool off and collect his thoughts. It'd felt so good to drop his guard and tell Ruby his story. He hadn't realized how much he'd needed a sympathetic ear until he had one, and she was nothing short of that. It was hard to wrap his head around such a generous nature. After months of battling with the Grandins and the Lattimores, and having everyone in town think he was an asshole, it was a revelation to have someone simply listen and sympathize. And damn if she wasn't more gorgeous and sexy than any woman he'd been in the company of in recent history. He hadn't dated in more than a year. The only woman he'd kissed during that time was Caitlyn Lattimore, but he preferred not to think about that. She'd used him to make her boyfriend Dev jealous.

The curious thing about Ruby's brand of beauty was that the more he talked to her, the more potent it became. Her generous interior matched her pretty exterior. As far as Heath was concerned, there was too little of that in the world. Most people cared about superfluous things like money and power. Appearances. That was what had driven the Grandin and Lattimore families to deceive his mother and deny his sister her birthright. Heath cared about right and wrong. And Ruby seemed to be cut from the same cloth.

He finished stacking firewood in the canvas log tote Ruby had given to him, loading it up until there was simply no more room. There was no telling how long the power would be out and he didn't want either of them to be cold. Granted, there was a fair amount of heat between him and Ruby—at least, as far as he was reading it. But he was so far out of practice when it came to sex and romance, mostly because he'd shut himself off from the world when his mom and Ashley died. Grief did that to a person.

He made his way back around to the front door, following the path he'd made on his way to the woodpile. He was quick to close the front door when he stepped inside, not wanting to let out any trapped heat. Immediately he noticed a faint glow coming from the living room and kitchen that hadn't been there before. He worked his way out of his jacket and tugged off his boots, then toted the firewood down the hall. When he stepped into the great room, Ruby was busy in the kitchen.

"How was it out there?" she asked with her back to him as she used a flashlight to check the contents of a kitchen cabinet. She'd lit candles, which were everywhere. It was romantic. Dangerously so.

"Cold. And windy. It's a whole lot nicer in here." That was an understatement. Ruby's cottage was a cozy retreat. It might be small and quaint, but it felt like a real home. He carried the firewood to the hearth and first grabbed some of the older, dry logs from a metal rack and carefully placed them atop the fire. Then he unloaded the cold, wet wood he'd brought in from outside so it could dry out.

"Thanks for braving the storm. I appreciate it. I raided the fridge while you were gone. I had some homemade pasta sauce in the freezer, so I'm heating that up now. It won't be fancy, but you'll at least get a hot meal."

"Sounds amazing to me." Heath poked at the fire as the logs began to smolder and catch flame. He shut the screen, then walked over to the kitchen.

She turned and smiled at him. Had she somehow managed to get prettier while he was outside? "Red wine okay? I've got a cabernet and a merlot."

"Cabernet, if that's all right with you."

"Nice. You like something with a little more body?" She pulled out a corkscrew and began opening the bottle.

"I suppose I do." Heath cleared his throat, trying to keep from thinking about Ruby's body and how spectacular it was. Her gentle curves were exactly his speed, and if he spent too much time imagining what she looked like from head to toe, he might be tempted to do something rash, like ask if he could convince her to part with some of her clothes. "Is there anything I can do to help?"

"You can grab some glasses. Top shelf of the cabinet next to the fridge."

Heath rounded the kitchen peninsula and pulled out two stemmed wineglasses, then turned and placed them on the counter. This was the closest they'd stood to each other, aside from that moment in the driveway when he'd had her in his arms. He liked being near her. She smelled amazing, the softest floral fragrance he'd ever breathed in. Her hair tumbled over her shoulders in soft waves, begging to be touched. Her eyes were so full of sincerity and honesty that they simply took his breath away. He was drawn to Ruby in a way he couldn't explain. He felt like a lonely planet being pulled into a new orbit, one that left him revolving around Ruby like she was the sun. Between the weather and being with her, it felt as if he'd arrived in a whole new world.

She poured the wine and handed him his glass, then lifted hers to toast. "To being inside. Because I sure as hell wouldn't want to be outside right now."

He grinned and clinked his glass with hers. "As the person who went to get the firewood, I'm in complete agreement." As he drew in a slow sip of his wine, he found himself overcome by the most unfamiliar feeling—optimism. He not only hadn't felt that way in quite some time, he wasn't sure what exactly it was that he had to feel optimistic about. On paper, his life was a mess. He spent his days trying to find justice for his sister and mother, and his nights all alone and wondering how he could continue this battle as a one-man army.

His brother, Nolan, was certainly of little help. For now, he only knew that he was looking forward to spending the night in this cottage in the woods. With her.

"Will your animals be okay out on the ranch?"

Thankfully, he and the few ranch hands working the week between Christmas and New Year's had taken care of it earlier that day, at the first sign of bad weather. "Yes. They're all tucked away in their respective barns and stables. I had solar panels installed a few years ago, so even the power outage won't impact the heaters that kick in when it gets cold."

"That's good to hear." Ruby turned to look at the stove. "Oh. Water's boiling. Time for pasta."

"You do that. I'll go give the fire another poke." He took his wine and headed for the fireplace, wondering how tonight was going to play out. Dinner was a given. They'd finish that bottle of wine. Then what? He was clearly staying over, but if the power didn't come back on, the smart thing would be for the two of them to sleep as close to the fire as possible. And if they were really smart, they'd cozy up next to each other. But as for how he was going to bring that up, he did not know. He crouched in front of the hearth and poked at the fire as it warmed his face and kept his mind racing. If anyone had told him that morning that his trip to visit Ruby would turn into this, he never would have believed them.

"Pasta will be ready in a few minutes," Ruby said, startling him. She'd walked into the living room so quietly that he hadn't even noticed. "I'd love to eat at the table like grown-ups, but I think it's best if we stay close to the fire as much as possible. Even with the stove on, it's starting to get a little chilly in the kitchen. So let's eat right here, if that's okay with you." She set her wineglass down on the floor near the hearth.

He turned and looked up at her as he remained crouched in front of the fire. "I'm not formal or fancy, Ruby. I'm happy to eat wherever you think we should."

"Okay. Great." She started for the kitchen again, then turned back to him. "Are you coming? I'm going to need help."

Heath straightened and followed her. "What can I do?"

"There's a tablecloth in the top drawer of the buffet near the bar cabinet. Grab that and spread it out on the floor in front of the fireplace. We'll have a picnic." She pulled a pair of pretty cloth napkins and some silverware out of the drawer. "And then you can set these out. And maybe see if there are more candles in the buffet?"

"Got it." Heath did exactly as she asked, soon finding himself rummaging through the contents of the vintage cabinet. The tablecloth was easy enough to find, but the candles were proving more difficult. In the bottom drawer, he came across something that stopped him dead in his tracks. A thick notebook labeled "Wedding Plans." It had been one thing to hear about her fiancé passing away, but it was quite another to be confronted by evidence of their relationship and the future she'd once thought she'd have with him. He closed the drawer quickly. "I don't see any more candles."

"Okay. I think I have more in the front closet. We can look after dinner."

He turned to see her standing in the living room, holding two bowls of steaming pasta. "Sorry." He rushed over, and with a snap, he shook out the tablecloth and allowed it to settle on the floor before the fire.

She handed him his bowl and they both took a seat. "This smells absolutely amazing."

"Thanks. I hope you like it." She took her glass in hand, then raised it for another toast. "To surprises."

Heath reached up to take his glass from the end table where he'd placed it earlier. He looked deeply into her eyes and he toasted her in return, wondering what exactly he'd done to deserve an opportunity to spend time with such a gorgeous woman. "Absolutely. To surprises."

"Speaking of surprises, I never imagined we'd sleep together on the first date, but I don't see how it makes any sense to do anything but that." She twirled the noodles on her fork and popped the bite into her mouth.

Heath froze. "Uh…"

She swallowed her food, then reached out and knocked his shoulder with the back of her hand. "Oh, my God. You can wipe that look of horror off your face, Heath. I'm just giving you a hard time again. I was only trying to say that we're going to have to sleep in here tonight. And if we're smart, we'll keep each other warm."

He exhaled, feeling grateful that she'd taken the time to clarify what she meant. They were on the same page. It was definitely the smartest solution to their predicament, aside from keeping the fire stoked. But exactly how much of a trial would it be to keep this a platonic arrangement? "I was thinking the same thing earlier. I just wasn't quite sure how to bring it up. I didn't want you to think I'm not a gentleman. Or that I was trying to take advantage of the situation."

"I realize we don't know each other very well, but you seem like the perfect gentleman to me."

He laughed quietly. "There are a few dozen people in this town who would like to disagree with you."

"Maybe they just don't know you. Or understand where you're coming from."

"Or maybe they simply care about their own interests more than they care about right or wrong."

She took a long sip of her wine, not taking her eyes off him. "Nothing you can do or say will convince me that you aren't a perfect gentleman."

Well, that certainly took all sexy thoughts he'd had earlier off the table. But maybe that was for the best. After seeing that notebook in the bottom of Ruby's buffet, Heath was starting to think that, as much as he wanted Ruby, it might not be a good idea to get involved with a woman who was living with what was likely a very fragile heart. Instead, he might just need to devote himself to protecting it.

Ruby was at war with herself after she'd made that boneheaded comment about sleeping together on the first date. Why did she have to turn things into a joke? Probably because it was her defense mechanism. Humor was a great way to deflect, and she was a champion at it.

But still, sleeping close was a practical solution to their predicament, right? It was the sensible thing to do. Then why did it make Ruby so nervous? Why did it make her feel so self-conscious to have suggested it? *You just told a sexy and handsome man who you hardly know that you think it's a good idea to sleep in the same bed as him. That was a bold move, Ruby Rose Bennett. Incredibly bold.*

They ate in near silence, nothing but the quiet crackle and pop of the fire to fill the void between them.

Heath finished eating first. "That was delicious. Thank you."

"You're so welcome." Ruby set aside her bowl, leaving the few remaining bites. She was too filled with nervousness to eat any more. She decided she was not going to circle back to the subject of keeping each other warm that night, so she asked about anything else she could think of, like his ranch and growing up in Royal. Heath reciprocated, inquiring about her career. They steered clear of more serious topics, like the death of his mom and sister, or Ruby's own loss, of her fiancé. She marveled at how easy it was to talk to Heath. He might be stubborn and a bit single-minded, but at his core, he seemed kind and thoughtful.

"It's getting late. We should probably revisit the question of sleeping arrangements," Heath said several hours later.

"Right. We don't have to do what I suggested earlier. Unless you're okay with it." She swallowed hard, daring to look into his eyes, even when a single glance made it feel like he was hypnotizing her.

"I think it only makes sense. We have to sleep and we have to stay warm. That's the smartest idea."

Her stomach flipped at the thought of being that close to him. "Great. Good. I was thinking we could drag my mattress in here and put it in front of the fire. That'll be more comfortable than the floor."

"Sounds good. No time like the present." Heath got up, then reached for her to help her stand.

She was perfectly capable of getting up on her own, but she wasn't about to protest. Instead, she put her hand in his, relishing this bit of male attention. It felt so good, like she was her old self. That person she'd been three or four years ago. "My bedroom is just down the hall."

Heath followed Ruby to her room.

"I guess we'll grab the bedding and pillows, and then we'll carry the mattress into the living room. I've got a bunch of extra blankets we can use, too," she said.

"The hall is pretty narrow. Let me take the mattress. You can take the smaller things."

"You sure?"

"Positive."

There it was again—Heath and his gentlemanly ways. She admired that he was like that.

He walked around to the other side of the bed and playfully tossed a pillow in her direction, smiling.

Ruby entertained a fleeting thought—crashing into him and kissing him and pulling him down on top of her right here and now. They could make their own fire. Together. In this bed. "Sounds like a plan."

They followed Heath's suggestion, and a few short minutes later, he had the mattress perfectly situated on the floor in front of the fire, right where they'd eaten. Ruby handed him one end of a clean fitted sheet, then dropped down to her knees to put it on.

Heath followed suit, but he recoiled the instant he reached the floor. "Oh. Ow." He popped back and landed on his butt next to the bed. "That wasn't very smart of me. I forgot about my knee."

"Would you like me to get some ice?" Ruby crawled across the mattress to where he was sitting.

"I'm okay. Really. It's just a little tender. How's your butt doing?"

She grinned. "Are you flirting with me?"

He looked at her and their gazes connected. "Of course. You're so beautiful it'd be stupid for me not to."

Her heart pounded frantically. She was painfully aware of every breath. "So, you're not flirting. You're kidding."

"I'm not. It's the truth."

She bit down on her lip, hard, if only to keep herself in the moment. "You're not half bad yourself."

"Now who's the flirt?"

She shrugged. "I learned from the best."

"Me? Am I the best?"

"Believe it or not, you are." It felt as though she was perched on the edge of a cliff and something was telling her to jump. In truth, all she wanted was a kiss. It had been so long since she'd kissed a man. Since she'd been able to get lost in someone. But was she ready for that? Logic said that three years was more than enough time. But that was the funny thing about loss—logic didn't matter. It was all up to the heart. And right now, her heart and body wanted Heath.

She leaned closer, closing her eyes halfway. She wanted to see the moment when he decided to give in, but she was also scared. Despite his flirting, she still felt so unsure of herself. Mercifully, one corner of Heath's lips quirked up into a smile, and she felt as though she had the green light to go for it. So she did, grasping his shoulder and pressing her mouth to his. There was no hesitation from him, only warmth and strength, exactly what she wanted from a man. When his lips parted and his tongue met hers, heat prickled across her skin, so swiftly that it made her dizzy. Her heart made a happy flip and she used her other hand to pull him closer, until his chest was pressed against hers. His fingers threaded into her hair and he gathered it at her nape, gently tugging on it and causing her to moan with pleasure. She responded by deepening the kiss, their tongues winding in an endless circle, effortlessly. He shifted to his knees, a sure sign that he didn't care at all about discomfort. She pushed her hips to meet his, relishing the moment when he got harder.

He eased them down onto their sides. She slept on this mattress every night, but it had never felt so luxurious, even though it was now supported by nothing more than the hardwood floor. Heath was all firm muscle and a capable grasp, and he rolled to his back, with Ruby on top of him. She really liked weighing him down. She liked the power of it. She liked knowing that this man who aroused so much fear and suspicion in the people of Royal wanted to be under her control.

She pressed harder against him, stomach, chest and lips. His fingers combed up through her hair, and he cupped the back of her head. His hand encouraged an even deeper kiss and the erasing of all space between them. She spread her legs wider, her knees slipping to the mattress so she was straddling his hips. She rocked into him and he groaned fiercely, slipping his warm hands up the back of her sweater and sending a brilliant and shiny thrill through her. This was not only escalating quickly, it was barreling toward somewhere she'd thought it might not go. She wanted him so badly that the need burned inside her, even hotter than the fire so nearby. Heath might end up making her spontaneously combust.

She sat up, looking down at him, marveling at how handsome he was. "I want to see you, Heath." She slipped her fingers beneath his sweater as he raised his arms to let her push the garment past his head. Inch by inch, his incredible chest and shoulders were revealed. She spread her hands across his stomach, feeling the muscles twitch beneath her touch. Every inch of him was hard, chiseled and perfection. But then she remembered how soft his lips were, so she dropped down to seek his kiss again, just to see if it was as heavenly as she remembered.

"This really isn't fair." He broke the kiss and whispered into her hair with a hot huff of breath. "You saw me. I haven't seen any of you. And it's killing me."

Ruby gnawed on her lower lip, filled with this implausible mix of desire and defensiveness. No man had seen her in recent history. Was she ready for this? She wasn't sure, but she'd come this far and she wasn't ready to stop. Not yet. She sat back and Heath followed. Then they shifted until he was leaning against the couch and her legs were wrapped around his waist. His hands curled under the hem of her sweater as she drew in a sharp breath, knowing what was coming…knowing how vulnerable she was about to be. He raised it slowly, lifting the fabric up and away, leaving her exposed to him. She was thankful for the soft glow of the fire. It made him look so amazing. He gently tossed her sweater aside, and then he reached around to the center of her back. He kissed the top of her breast, blazing a trail along the edge of her bra cup as he unhooked the clasp, then dragged the straps down her shoulders. They entered a new level of familiarity as he cast aside the bra and her breasts were left naked.

Their gazes connected as he lightly teased her nipple with his fingertips, rubbing up and down. The skin drew impossibly hard and tight, making her breasts feel warm and full and sending her body temperature spiking. He gripped her rib cage with one hand, pushing her breast higher with his fingers. Then he leaned down and drew her nipple into his warm mouth. She wanted so badly to watch him touch her like that, but it felt so impossibly good that her eyes automatically clamped shut. She rocked her center against his crotch, relishing the unbelievable tension between them. She wanted him. So badly it hurt.

"Do you have a condom?" she asked.

"I don't."

All the air seemed to escape the room. Just like that, her dream of letting go with a man disappeared and reality came back into sharper focus. "Oh."

"I'm, uh, sorry. I… I…" he stammered. "I don't exactly walk around with condoms in my pocket. I thought we were going to have a business meeting."

Ruby wondered what in the hell she'd been thinking. This was Heath Thurston. He was practically her boss. And being with him was like playing with fire. Yes, he was sexy, but if she wasn't careful, all that heat could get out of control and she'd be burned. "Right. Of course. That makes perfect sense. I don't know what I was thinking."

"It was a perfectly suitable question."

"I feel like I started something with that kiss and now it can't happen."

Heath shook his head. "Look. We were having fun and now it's time to be responsible about it."

She reached down for her sweater and clutched it to her chest. She had a deep need to cover herself. Possibly to disappear. She was embarrassed by the way she'd been so forward with him, and then by the way she'd stomped on the brakes. "I shouldn't have kissed you first. I'm not sure I was really ready for this anyway." It was miserable to admit the truth, but she couldn't be anything less than honest.

He reached over and picked up his own sweater, which Ruby took as her cue to climb off his lap. "It's okay, Ruby. Really."

She let out a frustrated sigh and grabbed her bra to put it on. "And now I feel even worse because you're stuck here for the night. And there's no heat." With every passing word, she felt her frustration grow. What a mess. And it was all of her making. She threaded her arms through her sweater and pulled it over her head. "You're just so damn handsome and nice. I'm sorry there's nowhere for you to go to get away from me."

He grinned and sat back, leaning against the sofa and shaking his head. "Ruby. I have had more fun tonight than I've had in the last several years. Please don't apologize. Let's just finish that bottle of wine, climb under the covers and say good-night."

Four

Heath woke to the sound of a chain saw and the feel of Ruby in his arms. He remained impossibly still, waiting to see if the noise outside would wake her while desperately hoping this moment wouldn't end. He closed his eyes, inhaling her smell, wishing the world away so he could have a little more time. He didn't need much. Hell, he hadn't realized he'd needed any time away from the stresses of his life at all, but now that he'd had a taste of setting aside bitter betrayal for something completely different, he wasn't ready for it to end. They'd had a magnificent night, even without sex. Still, he didn't know what to expect now that it was the morning after.

The power had come back on at some point—the house was warmer and what was left of the fire wasn't throwing off enough heat to have accomplished that feat. Judging by what he heard coming from outside, someone was clearing the tree that was blocking the road up to Ruby's cottage. Less than twenty-four hours ago, he would have been incredibly grateful for that. It would have allowed him to race off in his truck and hunt down his brother, all so he could resume his fight against the Grandins and the Lattimores.

Ruby stirred. "It's warm in here," she muttered into his chest.

"It is. Power came back on, but we both slept right through it."

"So, technically, we don't *need* each other's body heat."

A ribbon of doubt worked its way through Heath. He felt like he'd been caught red-handed. They no longer had the pretense of needing each other for survival. "No. We don't. You're right." He let go of her and distanced himself.

She raised her head and looked him in the eye. One glance and it was like she could see right through him. "I'm just giving you crap, Heath. I liked being in your arms. It was nice."

A wide smile bloomed on his face as relief washed over him, followed quickly by a wave of raw attraction. He didn't act on it, though. He was fully committed to following her lead. "I thought so, too."

From outside came the sound of a truck beeping as it backed up. "I wonder if that's Sam out there, hauling off the tree."

"Sam?" Heath wondered for a moment if he had competition for Ruby's attention.

"He works for public works. He checks on me every now and then. I think he might have a crush on me."

A crush. Heath didn't have to wonder if he had a

crush on Ruby. It was full-on infatuation and he'd spent less than a day with her. This realization didn't scare him. It brought him the first blips of happiness he'd experienced in months. Possibly years. But he sure as hell wasn't going to go around sharing that information. "Do you want me to go check?"

"I should go. It's my house. And if it is Sam, he's going to want to talk to me anyway."

"I'll come with you."

Ruby sat up and pulled on some socks over the ones she was already wearing. Her hair was a sexy mess and Heath took some pride in knowing he'd contributed to that, if only for a few minutes. He rolled off the mattress and ducked down the hall to use the bathroom while Ruby put on her boots and jacket. By the time he was done, Ruby was already out on the porch, so Heath grabbed his coat and joined her. It was a brisk morning, but the sun was bright and the snow on the tree branches was already starting to melt. Sure enough, two men were tossing chunks of that big tree into the bed of a pickup that said Royal Public Works on the side.

"There's Sam," Ruby said, pointing to the taller of the two men. "I'll be right back."

"I'll be here. I'm going to check if there's cell service. Might call my brother if there is." He watched Ruby approach the two men as he pulled his phone out of his pocket. Sure enough, the bars had returned. He dialed Nolan's number.

His brother answered after only a few rings. "How about this weather, huh?"

"Is this not the weirdest thing ever? So much snow in Royal? I can't think of another time that it was this bad."

"We would have loved this when we were kids. I

felt like we always wished for snow at Christmas and we never got it."

Heath wasn't able to look back fondly at all of his childhood, but he did have a few amazing memories of Nolan from when they were younger. Being a twin was a singular experience—everyone assumed he and Nolan were impossibly close, but they'd always wanted different things. The times they found something they agreed on, those were the times Heath cherished. Nolan had gotten sick of Royal and the responsibility of the ranch, left right after high school and stayed away for most of fifteen years. So much for the solidarity of being a twin. "Hey," Heath said, "I need to talk to you about something."

"Uh-oh. Your voice just got significantly more serious. Is this about the oil rights? I told you that I'm staying out of it. I helped you when you first found the paperwork, but that's all behind me now. My relationship with Chelsea is my first priority. You know I can't get involved. You need to move on, Heath. I've told you that one hundred times."

Move on. A day ago, Heath would have thought that was impossible. Hell, even as recently as the conclusion of that first conversation with Ruby, he was ready to redouble his efforts and wage full-on war against the Grandins and Lattimores. But standing out here on this crystal clear morning, looking at Ruby, with her messy blond hair and a laugh that rivaled anything the birds in the trees were singing, he had this glimmer in his head and his heart—a very vague feeling that his life could be better. "It's just that I had a meeting with Ruby Bennett, the surveyor, yesterday."

"A meeting on a Saturday? Two days after Christmas?"

Funny, but that was the same thing Ruby had said to him. He supposed he had been pretty irrational with his timing. "I know. I got a little carried away. But she pointed out something very damning. Something that says that the Grandins knew—"

"Stop right there. Please don't say another word."

"I'm trying to tell you something. Something that is not insignificant. Something major."

"And I told you, Heath, that I want to be closer to you. I want to keep rebuilding our relationship. But I can't do that if you're going to hold on to this grudge. The only way for me to have a happy marriage with Chelsea *and* be close to you is for this entire thing to go away. You hold the key to that."

Heath grumbled under his breath, but then Ruby turned, waved at him and smiled. He felt like his insides were turning to pudding. "It's more than a grudge, Nolan. It's about right and wrong. We're talking about our mother. And our sister. Where would you and I be right now if Ashley hadn't stepped in after Dad's death? If she hadn't cared for us? Mom sure as hell wasn't capable of much. And I think we both know who's responsible for that."

"I realize all of that, Heath. And there's no question that it's sad and unfortunate. But as for the rest of it, there are no real answers because it's all in the past. Ashley and Mom knew that we loved them. And we know that they loved us. We all did our best during that time. That's got to be the end of it."

"The end?" The thought of that made something in Heath's heart twist into a tight knot. "So you want me to walk away right now? Call our lawyer and tell him we're done? It's over?"

"He's your lawyer, not mine. But if it were up to me, yes, that's what I would do."

"I've got a few more days to make that decision." Heath's lawyer, Albert Cortez, an old family friend, had asked for an update on their working relationship. If Heath no longer required his services, Albert preferred to know that before the end of the year. It made things easier from an accounting standpoint. But Albert apparently hadn't made the connection between the dates on the original oil survey and the deed to the oil rights given to Heath and Nolan's mom. That was going to require a conversation.

"Look, if you want to talk about finding ways to fund Ashley's foundation, I'm all ears," Nolan said. "But if it's going to be anything else pertaining to oil, I don't want to hear it. I love you, but I will not hesitate to hang up on you."

Maybe his brother was right. Maybe he needed to find a way to look ahead. Ruby sure made him want to. "Okay. Can we talk about the foundation, then?"

"We can definitely talk about it. Not now, though. Chelsea and I are about to go for a walk in the snow."

"Well…when, then? Don't put me off on this."

"And don't get surly with me. Chelsea and I are newlyweds. We're entitled to spend time together, especially over the holidays."

Heath felt like a heel. This was another example of him getting too wrapped up in his own head. "I'm sorry. You're right."

"It's okay. I understand. Maybe we can get together. What are you doing for New Year's Eve?"

"Nothing."

Nolan laughed. "Why does that not surprise me?"

"I never do anything on New Year's. I don't see the point. So we flip the calendar? It's just another day to me."

Nolan let out a dismissive tut. "Chelsea and I are going to the party at the Cattleman's Club. I think you should join us. There will be music and dancing and amazing food. And I think you should bring a date. It'd be good for you to have some female companionship, Heath. I worry about you all alone in that big house, working harder than any person needs to and stewing in your own juices about Mom and Ashley."

"I don't know. I'm not big on parties." And frankly, going to the Texas Cattleman's Club was a minefield in waiting. He'd been a member forever, but there was a good-sized chunk of the membership that was not a fan of his at the moment. Many people had sided with the Grandin and Lattimore families in the dispute.

"Then do it for me. I want you and Chelsea to spend more time together. My twin brother and my wife should know each other better. We didn't even get to see you at Christmas."

"I know." On paper, he welcomed the idea of being closer to Nolan and finally returning to a true family dynamic after so many years of being apart. But what was Heath supposed to talk about with Chelsea? He sure as hell couldn't ask how her family was doing.

"Then come to the party. Do you have someone you can ask?"

Heath cleared his throat. "I have an idea of someone. Yes."

"Who is it?"

"A woman. A woman I know. Or actually, a woman I know who I just met for the first time in person."

"You're talking in circles. She must be something."

Heath couldn't keep his eyes off Ruby. She was laughing as she talked to the two men, who were clearly enthralled with her. That came as no surprise. She was mesmerizing. "You could say that."

"Who is she?"

"I told you a few minutes ago. Ruby Rose Bennett."

"The surveyor? You want to bring a surveyor to a New Year's Eve party?"

"Hey. What's that supposed to mean?"

"Nothing. I'm just not really envisioning someone who wants to put on a cocktail dress and drink champagne."

Heath had no earthly idea what Ruby might wear. He'd only seen her in jeans and a sweater, but he was a huge fan of what he saw. He'd also seen a little bit more, and he would have been lying if he said he didn't want to see all of her. "For the record, she's stunning."

At the end of the driveway, one of the men closed up the back of the truck while the other climbed into the driver's seat and started the engine. The warm exhaust billowed in clouds from the tailpipe. That loud *beep beep beep* sounded as he backed up the vehicle to turn it around.

"Where are you? It sounds like a garbage truck."

"I'm at Ruby's. A tree fell across her driveway from the storm. The public works guys are here to haul it away."

"Hold on a minute. What time did you meet with her? And where?"

Dammit. Heath shouldn't have divulged where he was. His brother was going to give him a hard time about this. "I came over around four or five yesterday."

"Exactly when the storm started to get bad."

"Yes, Nolan. So what?"

"How did you get home? The roads were horrible. And then you went back this morning?"

"I stayed here. What's your point?"

Nolan laughed. "Well, I'll be damned. Now you really have to come on New Year's Eve. I want to meet Ruby the surveyor. And I won't take no for an answer."

Ruby was making her way back up to the house now that the truck was slowly heading back down her driveway.

"Fine. We'll come. I have to go. I'll talk to you later."

"I'll text you the details."

"Yeah. Sure." Heath was desperate to end the call so he could talk to Ruby. As to how he was going to broach the subject of New Year's Eve with her, he wasn't sure.

"I hope you know how happy this makes me," Nolan added.

"Goodbye, Nolan." Heath ended the call and stuffed his phone back into his pocket. "Hey," he said to Ruby as she climbed the stairs. "All taken care of?"

"Yes. Sam is such a sweetheart. He was worried about me because he knew that the power had gone out. He drove up to check and that's when he saw the tree. He went back to get help and, well, that's how you ended up with a clear passage to civilization."

Heath then realized that, aside from the folks he paid to take care of his ranch, absolutely no one would check on him or his welfare. Not even Nolan would. He'd be too busy worrying and thinking about Chelsea. That was the difference between Ruby and him. She was kind and people clearly adored her. He was a monster who people despised. "That's really nice."

"So, yeah." Ruby looked down at the porch floor. "You're free to go whenever."

Heath wanted to take Ruby's hand, but he wasn't sure that was what she wanted, so he didn't. "I need to ask you something, but let's go back inside, okay?"

"Sure." Ruby followed him back into the house and closed the door. "Were you able to talk to your brother?"

"I was."

"What did he say about that little detail I pointed out about the old survey?"

"I didn't get that far. He didn't want to hear about it."

She nodded. "Because he's married to a member of the Grandin family."

"Right. And he said I was living in the past. He also pointed out that I can't really fix what happened because my mom and Ashley aren't here."

She drew in a deep breath through her nose. "What did you say?"

He shrugged. "There wasn't much I could say. He told me he was going to hang up if I kept talking about it."

"Okay, well, then how do you feel about it?"

Heath wasn't particularly good at talking about his feelings. Emotions were too abstract. Too unpredictable and entirely impossible to control. But Ruby made him want to try, even if he was fairly certain he wouldn't do well. "It makes me mad. He's shutting me down without listening."

"Sounds like you need to say that to him, then."

"Maybe. We'll see."

"It doesn't make him wrong. There is probably some truth to what he's telling you about not living in the past and letting things go." She reached for his arm and

stepped closer. "But I also understand why you're struggling with that. Between my mom and Lucas, I've been
through a lot of loss. I know what it's like to feel like
the past is holding you back, but you don't know how
to do anything other than cling to it because it hurt so
much to lose everything you did."

It took Heath a minute to wrap his head around that.
She was right. Of course. And she understood what he
was going through, which helped him digest her words
a bit better. But was he really clinging to the past? Or
was it just that somebody, somewhere, had to right this
wrong? Simply so a bit of order could be restored and
he could finally sleep? And if that was the case, he was
clearly the only person who could do the job. No one
else had the mettle to continue with the charge. No one
else cared as much as he did. "It feels good to know that
you understand. It helps."

Ruby leaned against the wall and smiled softly.
"Good. I'm glad. Hopefully that will help you move
forward."

"I do want to figure out how to fund my sister's foundation. Maybe I need to focus on that."

"That sounds like a great idea. Having a project is
good. What kind of foundation was it?"

"She wanted to open a horseback riding center for
kids and adults with cognitive and physical impair-
ments. Horseback riding can be incredibly therapeutic.
Ashley learned about it when she was a teaching assistant in a classroom for autistic children. She saw what
it did for their development, both physical and mental.
And the kids tended to form very special bonds with
the horses. It's an all-around wonderful thing."

Ruby grinned even wider now. "That sounds so

amazing. I would love to help. If you're going to need volunteers or anything like that."

"Really?"

"Of course."

Up until that moment, Heath hadn't considered that anyone might help with this, aside from Nolan chipping in some money and possibly some volunteer time. "That would be so great. It was just an idea when Ashley was still alive, but I'd like to make it happen. I'm thinking I can house it on my property, and I've got money set aside to build the infrastructure, but there will be staff and ongoing maintenance, which could end up being sizable. If I can fund an endowment, it could run on its own forever and no one would ever have to pay a penny for the services. That would be the ultimate goal."

Ruby stepped closer and took his hand. It brought him immense relief to have that physical contact with her, to know that she wanted it, too. "You're a good man, Heath. A really, really good man."

He saw a tear roll down her cheek. He couldn't help but reach out and wipe it away with the back of his hand. "Do you have any idea how long it's been since someone said that to me?"

She shook her head and pressed her lips together tightly as if she was fighting back more tears. "I don't. But if it's been a while, I'm glad that I had the chance to say it."

As physically frustrated as he'd been last night that he and Ruby hadn't had sex, he was thankful for it now. There was something growing between them, and if he'd had to chalk it up to lust, he might doubt how real it was. "I need to ask you a question."

"Sure. Anything."

"Do you have plans for New Year's Eve?"

"I don't. I usually don't do anything other than put on my pj's, pop some popcorn and watch a movie."

That sounded like sheer heaven to Heath, but he did want to forge that stronger bond with Nolan. It felt like an essential on his to-do list. "My brother wants me to go to the party at the Texas Cattleman's Club. It's not really my speed, but I need to spend more time with him and my sister-in-law. I was hoping that you might come with me."

She grinned and the tears evaporated, making way for the shine of her incredibly bright eyes. "I would love to go. I've never been to the TCC. I've heard it's amazing."

"It can be fun. It can also be a runaway train if you're the subject of town gossip. But I'm going to hope for the best, and honestly, I think I can endure anything if you're with me."

"Perfect, then. I guess it's a date?"

He placed a hand at her waist, still unsure of what degree of physical contact was okay with her. He didn't want to cross any lines. "It absolutely is."

She leaned closer. "I'm sorry about last night. I'm sorry that I wasn't ready."

He shook his head. "Don't apologize. I'm happy to take things slow."

She placed a finger on his shoulder, then drew it down his chest. "I don't need things to go too slow. I just needed some time to wrap my head around it. That's all. I didn't expect a sexy man to show up on my doorstep yesterday."

Heath couldn't hide the wide grin that spread across his face. "That's going to go straight to my head, you know."

She leaned in closer, flattening her other hand against his chest. "I hope that's exactly where it will go." Her lips met his in the softest kiss he'd ever experienced. It was sweet and sexy and exactly what he needed. Everything he wanted.

And everything he hadn't taken the time to dream of.

Five

Ruby had nothing to wear to a New Year's Eve party in Royal, especially not one at the Texas Cattleman's Club. Although she'd never been, she'd heard plenty of stories. The TCC had a reputation. It was where the wealthy and powerful players of Royal gathered to make deals, hammer out problems and celebrate, usually on a very large and lavish scale. There was no way she was going to attend what had to be one of the biggest parties of the year at the club without looking spectacular. Even more to the point, she wasn't going to be Heath Thurston's date without looking perfectly put together. And sexy. If she still had it in her.

The day after the tree had been removed from her driveway and Heath had left her by herself, the snow in Royal was mostly melted and the roads were clear. She hopped in her SUV and headed for the heart of downtown to go shopping at the Rancher's Daughter. She owned plenty of cute, feminine clothes—fun summer dresses, flirtatious skirts and formfitting tops—but she'd worn almost none of it since Lucas had died. It had felt unnecessary to present herself to the world in a way that suggested she was a woman who desired any attention or felt free. After all, Ruby had felt neither of those things when she'd suddenly found herself all alone. But Heath had awoken something in her, a part of her that she'd feared might never come to life. It was time to dress herself up and remind herself that it was okay to move on. It might not be easy, but it was okay.

A chime sounded when Ruby opened the door to the boutique, which was full of some of the cutest and most stylish clothes Ruby had ever seen, all of it artfully displayed. If money wasn't always a bit tight, she could see herself going on a real shopping spree here. As she slowly strolled past the racks and shelves, she was drawn to so much, it was hard to know where to start, except that she knew she hadn't yet seen anything dressy enough for New Year's Eve.

A woman with fair skin and striking red hair stepped out of the back room, talking on a cell phone. She made eye contact with Ruby and held up a finger. "Hey, Zanai, I need to call you back. I have a customer," she said into the phone. "Okay. 'Bye." She pressed a button on the screen and placed the device on the counter near the register. "I'm so sorry. It's my best friend. We start talking and I swear it could go all day long."

Ruby smiled, thinking that she needed more friends. She'd essentially locked herself away in her cottage since Lucas had died, refinishing floors and taking down walls. If she wasn't doing that, she was working.

She had almost no social life. That had to change. "Oh, don't worry about it. I was just taking it all in. It's such a beautiful store."

"Well, aren't you sweet? I'm Morgan Grandin. This is my shop. What can I help you with today?"

Ruby froze for a moment. *Morgan Grandin.* If she had the family members straight, Morgan was the youngest of the Grandin siblings. "It's nice to meet you, Morgan. I've actually been out on your family's property. I'm a surveyor." Ruby saw no reason to hide from this fact. In her experience, it was best to be open and honest with people. It could pay big dividends.

Morgan's eyes went wide as she seemed to make the connection. "Oh, okay." She nodded eagerly and wagged her finger. "I heard about you. I think you met my older brother, Vic, when you were out there. He was out on his horse and saw you."

"Yes. I was finishing up my survey."

"And you found nothing, right?"

Ruby hesitated to answer. She not only worked for Heath, she liked him quite a lot. Hell, she was about to be his date for New Year's Eve. Would divulging this information betray him in any way? Her immediate tendency was to protect him, however short their acquaintance had been. "The survey was inconclusive."

"Ah. I'm guessing you were hired by Heath Thurston?" Morgan reached out and straightened a blouse on a hanger. "What's he really like? I can't get a good read on him. Everyone says he's a jerk, including my fiancé. But I really like Nolan, Heath's twin. He and my sister Chelsea got married before Christmas and they're ridiculously happy. You should see the way he looks at her. You'd think she hung the moon. Identical twins are basically the same people, aren't they?"

Ruby was having a hard time keeping up. Morgan really liked to talk, and apparently she didn't have any qualms about discussing potentially sensitive matters in front of strangers. "I've never met Nolan, so I'm not sure I'm qualified to chime in on that. I do think twins can have different personalities. Especially if they've been through different things." Heath had mentioned that Nolan left Royal when he was eighteen and had stayed away until recently. She surmised that the brothers had grown apart even more during that time because Heath had hinted at efforts to mend their relationship. Her gut told her that Heath and Nolan were not identical in every regard. She'd have to assess that when she finally met Nolan on New Year's Eve.

Morgan tilted her head to one side. "I'm sorry. I'm rambling when I should be helping you. Are you in for something special today?"

"Actually, yes. I need a dress for New Year's Eve. I'm going to the party at the TCC."

"Oh! Nice!" Morgan's face lit up as she eyed Ruby from head to toe. "Girl, I've got a couple of things that would look amazing on you. Come on." With a wave of her hand, she invited Ruby to follow her back toward the front of the store.

In the corner, right in front of one of the large windows overlooking the street, was a sizable section of special occasion dresses. Ruby wasn't sure where to start, so she was glad Morgan was there to help her. "What do you suggest?"

"Something sparkly, of course. You've got to sparkle on New Year's Eve. It's like a rule." Morgan pulled out a silver-and-white sequined dress with a plunging neckline. It seemed like a huge leap from what Ruby was currently wearing—a pair of jeans, cowboy boots and yet another of her cozy sweaters.

"I'm not sure I feel like a sparkly person. At least, not now. Maybe something a little more subdued?"

Morgan shot Ruby a questioning glance. "We live in Royal, Texas, honey. You're going to the Texas Cattleman's Club on New Year's Eve. They might not let you in the door if you don't sparkle. Sparkly is the order of the day. Plus, you put on one of these dresses and you will see how amazing you look and you'll be ready to hand over your credit card. Trust me."

Ruby took in a deep breath. "Okay. But maybe not white. Maybe something darker?"

"Want something a little more mysterious?"

"I'd like it better if I wasn't visible from space."

Morgan laughed. "Got it." She flipped through the rack of dresses. "How about this?" She pulled out a deep emerald green full-length gown. It had skinny straps and the same plunging neckline of the previous dress, but Ruby felt like this one was a little more doable.

Ruby reached out and touched the fabric, which was surprisingly soft and silky in her hands. The sparkle came from threads woven into the cloth, rather than sequins. "I think this could work."

"Perfect. Let's try it on."

Ruby followed Morgan to the dressing room with a mix of excitement and nervousness. She hoped she was up to wearing this dress. It would make her night with Heath far more fun if she could pull it off. After their false start the other night, she really wanted to show him that she could be comfortable in her own skin and completely on board with him touching hers.

Heath had most meetings with his lawyer, Albert Cortez, at Albert's office in downtown Royal. Albert always said it was better to discuss delicate matters in person, where all parties could be more open about their opinions and no one had to worry about a paper trail. After Heath's chat with his brother yesterday, the question of whether to keep Albert on retainer seemed even more urgent to answer. Heath had to make a choice one way or the other.

"Heath, come on in. Have a seat." Albert eagerly waved Heath into his office. He was a stout man with a thick mustache that reminded Heath of a scrubbing brush. Heath had known him forever. Albert had been friends with his parents and was a strong tie to the past. "What can I help you with today? Have you made a decision?" Albert had a warm personality, but he didn't engage in much chitchat. It was always right down to business.

Heath parked himself in one of the leather armchairs opposite Albert's desk. "I'm afraid I don't know. Not until we talk about the one detail I think you missed."

Albert cocked a thick eyebrow at Heath and plopped down into his seat. "I'm all ears."

"It's the date on the original oil survey on the Grandin and Lattimore properties. Did you not notice that it was completed one year before my mother was given those oil rights?"

Deep creases formed between Albert's eyes. "Are you sure?"

"Ruby Bennett, the woman who did my survey, told

me. I haven't seen the original survey. I only heard about the results, and I heard about them from you."

"Well, let me see." Albert hoisted himself out of his chair and ambled over to an old wood filing cabinet. He flipped through the files in the top drawer, humming as he went. "Hold on. Your file is here somewhere."

That was not entirely reassuring, but Heath couldn't bear to give Albert a hard time. The man was kind and had a near encyclopedic knowledge of the law, especially as it pertained to oil rights.

"Here we go." Albert returned to his desk, put on a pair of reading glasses and flipped through what was a remarkably thin file. Had Heath made something out of nothing? Judging by the paltry number of documents, he was certainly wondering. "It's right here. And yes, you're right. One year. Almost to the day."

Heath blew out a frustrated breath, then sat forward and reached for the file. He needed to see it himself, but the confirmation only made him that much angrier. All he could do was imagine Victor Grandin Sr. and Augustus Lattimore signing that worthless piece of paper and presenting it to his mother as though it was of great value. "What do you suggest?"

Albert sat back in his chair and shrugged. "It really depends on your goals. And before you reply, let me remind you that revenge is not a goal. At least, not from a legal standpoint."

"I know that." Heath shifted in his seat, feeling uncomfortable. "What about a lawsuit, though? Based on the merits of those documents?"

"What are you going to do with more money, Heath? I already know you don't spend it on yourself, aside from maybe buying a new car every year."

"I'd like to fund an endowment for Ashley's foundation and get a therapeutic riding center off the ground. I've spoken to Lexi Alderidge-Bowden over at Alderidge Bank. She works extensively with nonprofits and she walked me through the specifics. It would mean that I could not only set it all up, but it would outlive me. I would never have to wonder whether Ashley's dream had been fulfilled."

"That is completely doable. And realistic. Although, I also know that you could fund an endowment on your own, right?"

"Well, sure, but I plan on paying to build everything. And it's the principle of the thing. Ashley spent her entire life being a good person and trying to make the world a better place. She could have done even more good if the Grandins had acknowledged that she was part of that family and given her everything she was entitled to."

Albert nodded. "Of course. Whatever you decide to do, I'm here for you. I just need you to give me the go-ahead and I'll start drafting a suit."

Heath glanced out the window. The sun was shining as bright as could be. His mind immediately went to Ruby. She was an unexpected bright spot. Despite his bluster when they'd first met in person, Ruby had been patient with him. She'd listened. And she seemed to understand what he was struggling with. That alone had been enough to dial down his anger and frustration about the oil rights. And then she kissed him, and, well, that had been enough to make him think harder about what he wanted for himself. Everyone in Royal assumed that he was hounding the Grandins and Lattimores because he enjoyed stirring up trouble. That couldn't be further from the truth. He longed to leave it all behind and move forward. Ruby only made that desire feel a bit more urgent. "Let me think on it, okay?" Heath rose from his seat and reached over to shake hands with Albert.

"Of course."

"I'd like to extend your retainer for another three months, if that works."

"Anything for you. And I appreciate the business. Just let me know what you decide to do."

Heath walked outside and decided to take advantage of the beautiful weather with a stroll down the main drag of Royal. Every step was another reminder of the past, especially when he passed people and they shot him glances and mumbled under their breath. Funny how this town had been home for his entire life, and he'd always been content here. He'd never had a desire to get away. He'd spent years completely dumbfounded by his brother's decision to leave Royal behind. Now that he'd been forced to wrangle with some of the more unpleasant forces in this town, he could understand a little better why Nolan had stayed away.

A block or so into his walk, he caught a glimpse of something out of the corner of his eye that made him stop dead in his tracks. A blonde woman. Was that Ruby? In the Rancher's Daughter? The woman in question wasn't fully visible—he could only see a sliver of her between the clothing displays, and the view was of her back, but the hair looked to be the same. Her height, creamy skin and posture all made him think it was definitely her. But the dress this woman was wearing was the sticking point—it was so sexy it made his head spin, clinging to every inch of her appealing frame. It was also far more formal and dressy than anything he'd seen Ruby wear.

He stepped closer to the shop window for a better look, and that was when she turned to the side and he definitely knew it was her. His heart broke into an inconvenient sprint, making his pulse race. Why was he feeling like this? He'd only known her for a few days. Of course, it didn't take a rocket scientist to figure it out. She was smart, beautiful and kind—everything Heath admired in a woman. It would be so easy to get lost in her. His vision went fuzzy at the thought of touching her again. Kissing her.

Just then, another woman popped into view, and his stomach sank. He would've known that red hair anywhere. It was Morgan Grandin, the youngest of the Grandin kids. It wasn't a big surprise that she was there—it was her shop, after all. But it still put Heath on edge. Like every other time he'd seen Morgan, her mouth was moving at full speed. What in the world was she saying to Ruby?

He sucked in a deep breath, wondering about his next step, when Ruby turned toward the window and spotted him. Her eyes flickered and an effortless smile bloomed on her face. She waved. And that left Heath with no choice. He had to go talk to her. He pulled on the door and an electronic chime sounded as he walked into the boutique. He immediately headed in Ruby's direction.

"Speak of the devil," Ruby said, standing next to Morgan. "We were just talking about you."

Dammit. His worst suspicions were true. Morgan had been running her mouth about him. He could only imagine what she'd said. *You're going out on New Year's Eve with Heath Thurston? He's bad news, Ruby. Pure evil.* It wasn't a stretch. Her family not only hated him, Morgan's fiancé, Ryan, had gotten downright ugly about Heath's crusade over the oil rights. He'd confronted Heath at Chelsea and Nolan's wedding, for God's sake. These people were so predictable—if money and pride were involved, they'd drop down into the dirt and fight like hell rather than admit they'd done something wrong.

It would have been so easy to tear into Morgan. Heath had real ammunition against the Grandins now. But he wasn't ready to show his cards, and he certainly would not sink to the level of a Grandin. Not today. Not in front of Ruby. Heath sidled up to her. To his great surprise, Ruby gripped his biceps and kissed his cheek. It was a sweet gesture, but it made his blood run hot. "So that's why my ears were burning." He nodded at Morgan. "Hello, Morgan." It took everything he had to keep the venom out of his mouth when he said her name.

"Hey there, Heath. Funny that you should show up. Have you ever been in my store before?"

"I have not."

"I'm just doing a little shopping." Ruby's eyes darted back and forth between Morgan and him as she clearly tried to assess whether somebody was about to kick up some dirt. "I need something to wear for the New Year's party at the TCC. I don't have anything that's good enough for a place like that." She turned back to face the mirror, turning and twisting in front of it and eyeing herself.

Heath was blown away that she was making plans for their date, and so soon after he'd asked her, although he supposed the clock was ticking. The thirty-first would be here in two days. "I don't know what else you've tried on, but that dress looks spectacular."

"This is the first one. Morgan picked it out. I can't believe how perfect it is."

Morgan slid him a smile, which on the surface gave him some far more positive feelings about her, but he also had to wonder if she was happy merely because his approval meant she'd make a big sale.

"The dress is great, but you're what makes it special." Heath swallowed hard, wondering if he was laying it on too thick. He didn't want to mess things up with Ruby. Or put any undue pressure on her. She'd been through a lot.

Ruby looked down at herself, then turned her attention to him. "Do you really like it?"

Like was a wholly inadequate word. "I'll be with the most stunning woman in the room."

"Oh. Wow," Morgan said. "Okay. *Now* I'm putting the pieces together."

Ruby turned to her. "Pieces?"

Morgan cleared her throat and looked down at the floor for a moment. "I'm sorry. Sometimes words just fly out of my mouth." She stepped closer to Ruby and adjusted one of the straps of the dress. "I didn't realize that Heath was your date for New Year's. I thought we were just talking about him."

Heath's instinct to get into it with Morgan returned with a vengeance. He knew he was the subject of gossip in town, but the fact that Morgan was so willing to engage in it while fulfilling her role as shop owner? Apparently some members of the Grandin family saw dragging his name through the mud as an everyday activity, like casually chatting about the weather.

"I'm sorry. I thought I'd told you," Ruby said.

"Don't worry about me. It's none of my business,"

Morgan said. "For what it's worth, I do think you two make a very cute couple."

Heath watched as Ruby's face flushed with pink, which was a pleasant distraction as he wondered if he was letting paranoia get the best of him. Or was Morgan simply buttering them up? Once again, the motivations of the Grandin family made him question everything.

"Thank you," Ruby said, then looked at Heath in the reflection of the mirror. "Well? Do you think I should get this one?"

"Even if you didn't have a big party to attend, I think it'd be foolish to not buy it. You look gorgeous."

From across the shop, a phone rang. "Oh, shoot. I left my cell by the register," Morgan said. "Please excuse me. I'm waiting on a call. I'll leave you two to talk about the dress." She bustled away.

Ruby took the price tag in her hand and looked at it, then once again peered into the mirror. "I'm not sure this is the best choice. Maybe I should be a little more sensible and buy something that I can wear more than once. I don't know where I would ever wear this after New Year's Eve."

He could hear the depth of her inner struggle in her voice. Something told him this was about more than the dress. It was about her feeling unsure of herself. Heath so identified with that. There was something about loss that made you question everything you did. Everything that you were. "Then let me be the insensible one." He stepped closer to her. Everything in his mind and body made him want to touch her. Pull her into his arms.

"No offense, but I really don't think this dress would look good on you." She jokingly arched both eyebrows at him. "You don't have the hips to fill it out."

Heath laughed. "You know that wasn't what I was saying. Let me buy it for you."

"You haven't even looked at the price. This thing is expensive."

"I don't care about that. I care about you feeling good about yourself at this party. I care about you having fun that night. With me."

"That's so sweet."

If only she knew the thoughts that were going through his head right now. Not all of them were sweet. He wanted to wish Morgan away. He wanted to pull Ruby into the dressing room, lock the door, and kiss her and touch every inch of her until neither of them could see straight. "Is that a yes? Will you let me buy you the dress?"

"I don't know. It's a lot to ask."

He shook his head. "Trust me. You'd be doing me the favor."

"How, exactly?"

"It'll let me show a Grandin that I'm not a jerk. And it'll let me show you that, even though we haven't known each other for a very long time, I care."

She smiled softly and nodded, but it was clear that his words were still running through her head. "Okay, but on one condition. You let me take you out for lunch at the Royal Diner after this."

Heath's day was getting better at every turn. "Pie?"

"Of course," Ruby said.

Morgan returned. "Well? Do we have a decision?"

Heath pulled his credit card out of his wallet and handed it over to Morgan. "Sold."

"Yes, sir," she said in response. "Is there anything else you need, Ruby? Shoes? A handbag? A wrap?"

Heath didn't wait for Ruby to respond. "Whatever she wants."

Twenty minutes later, Heath and Ruby were leaving the Rancher's Daughter with two large shopping bags full of everything she needed for their night at the TCC. They walked down the street to the Royal Diner and popped inside. Heath hadn't crossed that threshold in quite some time. In general, he avoided it. The diner, with its red faux leather booths and black-and-white checkerboard floor, was an immensely popular spot in Royal, but that also made it a hub for gossip. He hoped they could have lunch in peace.

They were seated at a booth in the back, which gave them some semblance of privacy. "Thank you. For the dress and everything else. You really didn't have to do that." Ruby reached across the table and touched the back of his hand. "I appreciate it."

"I wanted to do it. Don't think twice about it." Heath perused the menu, realizing that one thing was still bothering him. "What were you and Morgan talking about before I got there?"

"You mean about you?"

He knew exactly how paranoid it made him seem, but he had to know. "I'm curious."

"It didn't take her long to figure out who I was. As soon as I told her that I'd been on her family's property, she knew that I worked for you. That's how we got on the subject. I assure you that I didn't simply pop into her store and start talking about you."

"Of course not. I wasn't thinking that you would do that. I assumed she was the instigator."

Ruby dropped her head to one side, admonishing him with a single glance. "If you want to know the truth, she said that she's not sure how you could possibly be the bad guy everyone makes you out to be."

"That's not a huge comfort."

"You don't actually care what people think, do you? If you did, it seems like you would drop the whole thing."

He had to think about that for a moment. He'd told himself all along that he would never drop it. That it would be *wrong* to let it go. But that had been when he was walking around town with a big wall around himself, a wall that Ruby had managed to breach in short order. Now he was doing things he wouldn't have done a few months ago, like going to the Royal Diner and a New Year's Eve party at the TCC. He *did* care. At least a little. "Popular opinion isn't a reason to walk away from something that's difficult."

"Heath, you really should tell people about the foundation. Tell them how much good you want to do for others. And for this community. That will turn around their opinion of you."

"Why? Does that somehow make this battle morally correct?" He leaned closer so he could whisper. "The two women I cared about most in this world were deceived and tricked by powerful people who had nothing to lose other than a bit of money and pride. That gives me plenty of moral high ground." With every word, he felt his blood pressure rising and his face growing hot. His anger hadn't lessened because of Ruby. It had only been blurred. "It's the Grandins and the Lattimores who need to think about what's good and bad. More often than not, they're on the wrong side of that equation."

Ruby scanned his face, her eyes sweeping back and forth. "Okay."

Her tone of voice told him everything. He'd gone too far. "I'm sorry." He willed himself to calm down. Maybe everyone in town was right. Maybe he really was a jerk.

"I understand, Heath. I do. My guess is you're going to have to find a way to put all of this to rest."

He reached across the table and took her hand, marveling at how soft her skin was. "Let's talk about New Year's Eve. And you in that dress."

"What's there to say about that?"

"Only that I can't wait for the moment when we walk in the front door with you on my arm."

She smiled. "You really are a total flirt. I need to run to the ladies' room. Order me a cheeseburger when the waitress comes."

"Got it." He watched her walk away from the table. Her words were still tumbling in his head. *Put all of this to rest.* He needed to do that. For himself. For the sake of his growing relationship with Ruby. He just needed to exhaust the one detail that wouldn't go away. Then he could wash his hands of the whole thing. He'd know in his heart that he had done everything he could to make things right for the memories of his mom and sister. He pulled his phone out of his pocket and sent a text to Albert. Send the letters. Let them know that I know.

His response came quickly. You sure?

Heath imagined what would come next—surely drama, especially from the Grandins. But it would pass quickly, they would finally pay, and then he could move on. Yes. I'm sure.

Six

Ruby was filled with a mix of nerves and optimism. It was an odd cocktail to kick off her New Year's Eve, but she couldn't do anything about the way she was feeling. The reality was that she still didn't know what to make of Heath. She liked him so much that it scared her at times, but there was a temper locked up inside his handsome head and she didn't like the way it came out when she wasn't expecting it. Case in point, their conversation at the Royal Diner two days ago. One minute, everything was fine, and then the next minute, he was spewing vitriol about the Grandin and Lattimore families. It wasn't good for her to be around that kind of negativity, and she wasn't sure what it would take for him to move beyond it.

But she also felt as though she'd gotten through to him. He'd listened to her. He seemed to appreciate that she understood him on a deeper level. They had both been through so much. That commonality had forged their connection from the very beginning. How rare a thing that was—to feel a real bond so soon after meeting someone. She couldn't cast that aside or ignore it. Something in the very center of her heart told her that she had to explore where this might go, even if there might be moments that made her nervous.

For now, Ruby was standing in her foyer, looking out through the sidelights next to her front door, waiting for Heath to pick her up for the party. As soon as she saw the headlights coming up the driveway, she gathered her evening bag, draped her faux fur wrap around her shoulders and walked out onto the front porch, then locked her front door.

"Ruby!" Heath called from behind her. "You should have let me come to the door to get you."

She turned and watched as he stepped into the glow of her porch lights. Good Lord, the man could rock a tuxedo like no one she'd ever seen. The relaxed and genuine smile on his face told her that everything she'd been worrying about earlier was silly.

"I'm fine," she said as she descended the staircase.

"That's not the point." He held out his hand for her. "Call me old-fashioned, but I feel like I owe it to you to pick you up at your door."

She hooked her arm in his as they walked across the driveway. He hadn't driven his truck this time, but had instead brought some sort of fancy sports car. "Next time I'll wait inside. How about that?"

"As long as there's a next time, I'm happy." He opened the passenger's-side car door for her. "You look stunning, by the way," he said as she slid into the seat.

"You don't look half bad yourself."

"Perfect. That's exactly what I was going for. Not half bad." He closed her door and rounded the back of the vehicle, then climbed into the driver's seat, turned on the car and started down her driveway to the main road. "So, tonight. I want you to know that we can leave anytime you want. If this isn't your scene or you aren't having fun, just tell me. I don't have any strong feelings one way or the other as to how long we stay."

"It sounds to me like you do, though."

"You know how it is in Royal. People talk. And I'm sure a few people are going to choose to talk about me tonight. That might not be fun for you, and I want you to have a good time. It's the only thing I really care about."

Ruby reached over and touched his arm. "Don't worry about me. I'm looking forward to meeting your brother and sister-in-law and getting to know each other. That's all *I* really care about."

He slid her an approving glance. "You are amazing. I hope you know that."

She grinned and settled back a little more in her seat. "Thanks. That's really nice to hear."

About twenty minutes later, they pulled into the parking lot of the Texas Cattleman's Club. There were already hundreds of cars there, and the windows of the sprawling single-story slate-topped building were all lit up. Outside, dozens of couples were approaching the entrance to the imposing dark stone-and-wood structure.

"Wow," Ruby said. "I've driven past here, but only during the day. I've never seen it at night. It really is impressive."

Heath pulled into a parking space and killed the

engine. "I suppose it is. I guess I never gave it much thought."

"Have you been a member for a long time?"

"Our family have been members my entire life. My father became a member before Nolan and I were born. It helped him network when he was trying to put the Thurston ranch on the map."

"Huh. Interesting."

"Why is that interesting?"

"Because you always talk about yourself as a Royal outsider. But being a member of the Texas Cattleman's Club for your entire life sort of disproves that theory, doesn't it?"

"It's a club. A way to do business."

"Well, sure, but not everyone belongs, do they? It's still an elite and exclusive circle."

Heath looked off through the windows of his car. "Interesting. I never thought of it that way."

"That's what happens. We get used to something and don't think anything of it. But to someone else, it might seem like a big deal." She clapped him on the shoulder. "I, for one, am excited that you're a member. It means I finally get to experience it for myself."

They climbed out of the car, and Ruby hooked her arm in Heath's as they strode through the parking lot. There was excitement in the air as he opened one of the tall doors for her and they stepped inside to the impressive entry, with its soaring ceilings and opulent furnishings. Hunting trophies and historic artifacts seemed to adorn every wall. The space was abuzz with the sound of celebratory conversation, filled to the hilt with people. Ruby's first impression was that the Texas Cattleman's Club was a place built on money and longevity, much like Royal itself.

As they made their way toward the reception table, Ruby immediately spotted Nolan, who was impossible to miss given that he was the spitting image of Heath. Standing next to Nolan was a tall and willowy woman with flowing dark brown hair, wearing a strapless black dress, who Ruby could only presume was Chelsea.

Nolan spotted Heath and Ruby as they approached and waved. "Well, well, well. You actually showed up." He extended his arm and shook hands with Heath, then immediately turned to Ruby. "You must be Ruby. I've heard a lot about you."

She eyed Heath, who looked embarrassed. "Really? I wasn't aware there was much to say."

"Don't be modest," Heath interjected, then turned to his brother. "And don't make me look bad, okay? It's our first real date."

A wave of heat rushed across her skin. She liked hearing him describe their night out as a date. She offered her hand to Chelsea. "Hi. I'm Ruby. You must be Chelsea."

"I am. I heard a lot about you, too. From my sister, Morgan." Chelsea shook Ruby's hand and smiled warmly, putting Ruby at ease. "The dress is fabulous, by the way."

"Thank you." Ruby wasn't used to having so much focus on her. "Can we go inside and get a drink?"

Nolan looked at Heath with sly regard. "I like her already."

The four of them filed into the grand ballroom where the party was set to take place. Straight ahead, there was a large dance floor, which was already filled with people enjoying themselves. Black, silver and gold metallic streamers hung from the ceiling for festive effect, while dozens of large round tables dotted the perimeter of the room.

"Our table is over here." Chelsea led them through the crowd of people and to a spot on the far left. It was a bit quieter in this part of the room, but only by a slim margin. The party was definitely in full swing.

A waiter stopped by their table, delivering four glasses of champagne as they each took a seat. "I'd like to suggest a toast," Nolan said. "To new beginnings."

"Hear, hear." Ruby raised her glass and clinked it with everyone else's while she tried to gauge Heath's reaction to his brother's words. She hoped that he would soon start to realize that he could give himself his own new beginning, simply by looking forward.

Chelsea took a second sip of her champagne, then set her glass on the table. "Here comes my brother, Vic. Ruby, I believe you met him that day you were out on my family's property."

Ruby turned and instantly recognized the man, with his solid build and penetrating brown eyes, much like Chelsea's. She remembered very much the way he'd reacted when she'd been out on the Grandin property and hoped greatly that he wasn't about to confront her about it.

As if he understood what she was feeling, Heath reached over and gently grasped her forearm. "If he's a jerk to you, please let me take the heat," he whispered in her ear.

"I can handle it on my own," she muttered in return.

"I have no doubt about that. I'm only saying that I'm willing to take the bullet."

"Hello, everyone," Vic said, leaning down to kiss his sister on the cheek.

Nolan stood and shook hands with Vic. "Happy New Year, Vic."

"It'd be a little happier if you hadn't brought your twin," Vic said.

"Vic. Please don't start this," Chelsea pleaded, getting up from her seat.

Heath got up, too. "Chelsea, you don't need to defend me. I know Vic doesn't like me."

"And yet that has done nothing to change your behavior," Vic shot back.

Ruby watched the two men stare each other down, her heart pounding.

"I don't need your approval," Heath said. "But I'm sure you've figured that out by now."

Vic glanced at Ruby, then directed his stare at Heath again. "I see you brought your surveyor this evening. I still can't believe you sent a woman to do your dirty work."

"Shut the hell up," Heath blurted, then lunged for Vic.

Nolan got between them in the nick of time. "Hold on, you two." He was facing his brother, with Vic at his back. "It's a party. Please don't ruin this. Let's try to get along."

"Talk to your brother," Vic groaned. "And don't worry about me. I'll spend the rest of the night on the other side of the room." He turned to Chelsea. "'Bye, sis. I'll see you later." Just as quickly as he'd arrived, Vic stalked off.

Chelsea rushed over to Ruby. "I am so sorry. My brother can be a real hothead."

Ruby shook her head. "It's okay. Honestly, I'm only mad that I didn't have a chance to tell him off. I realize you're related to him, but that thing he said about being a woman was pretty sexist. I can hold my own."

Chelsea blew out a frustrated breath. "Yeah. He can be extremely misogynistic. I usually call him on it, but I was hoping tonight could have a minimum of family drama."

Heath was right at her side, eyes full of concern. "Are you okay?"

His question made her want to laugh. It also made her want to kiss him. "Are you? You're the one who nearly got into a fight."

He stroked her arm up and down with the tips of his fingers, bringing her entire body to life. "It's not a big deal. I'm fine. I only want to be sure that you're okay."

Ruby smiled and leaned in to kiss his cheek. His concern and protective nature were so endearing. "I promise you that I'm more than okay. I'm great."

He planted his hand on her hip and curled his fingers into her bottom. "Oh, I already knew that."

She laughed quietly. "You're flirting again."

"I'll keep doing what works until it stops being effective."

"Hey, Ruby," Chelsea said. "I'm going to run to the ladies' room. Do you want to come with me?"

Ruby felt torn. What she really wanted was to fall into Heath's arms. But maybe it was a good idea for her to cool off. It was going to be a long night. "Sure thing." She turned to Heath. "We'll be right back."

"I'll be waiting."

Heath watched as Ruby and Chelsea left for the ladies' room. "Any clue what they're going to talk about?" he asked Nolan.

"Us, of course." Nolan flagged down a waiter. "Any chance we can get two bourbons, neat?"

"Absolutely, sir. I'll be right back." The waiter disappeared into the crowd.

"Smart thinking," Heath said, taking his seat again. "I could use something stronger than champagne."

Nolan joined him. "I figured as much. I'm sorry that happened. Vic can be a great guy, but he can also be a jerk."

Heath shrugged. "He's protecting his family. Just like I am. So I figure we're even."

Nolan nodded and drew in a deep breath through his nose. "I'm glad you decided to come tonight. I feel bad that I shut you down the other day when you called and you wanted to talk."

"Really? What happened to being absolutely sure that you didn't want to talk about the oil rights?"

"I don't want to talk about it. Ever. But I feel stuck. Between you and Chelsea."

Heath let that tumble around in his head. He didn't want his brother to suffer, but maybe it was good for Nolan to feel stuck. Heath had felt that way for his entire life. "Chelsea and I are fine. I like her. She likes me. We don't talk about her family. It seems to work."

Nolan leaned forward and rested his elbow on the table, casting Heath a serious look. "I have to wonder how long that's sustainable."

"It'll go away soon. And then we can all move on." Heath hadn't told Nolan that he'd asked Albert to file the suit against the Grandin estate. His brother had made it clear that he wanted to be kept in the dark when it came to that matter, and Heath was committed to keeping that promise. Still, he eventually wanted Nolan to know about the timing of the original survey and the issuance of the oil rights to their mother. A lawsuit, or the threat of one, might be the only way to bring that final and crucial detail to light.

A slight smile broke across Nolan's face. "I'm glad to hear you say that. Really glad."

"I'd like to talk about Ashley's foundation. About the riding center. I've contacted an architect and he's set to come for a site visit in a few days."

"That's fantastic you've gotten the ball rolling." Nolan knocked Heath's shoulder with his fist just as the waiter dropped off their drinks. He slipped the waiter a ten, then raised his glass. "To making Ashley's dream come true."

Heath clinked his glass with his brother's. "I'd really like you to be involved. In all of it. It will mean more if we do this together."

"Absolutely. You can count on me. Whatever you need."

"Count on you for what?" Chelsea asked as she and Ruby appeared back at the table.

Nolan stood and took her hand. "A trip around the dance floor, of course." He turned back to Heath and Ruby. "We'll see you two in a little bit."

Ruby eased into her seat. "They're adorable together. They seem really happy."

They did seem happy. Heath wondered if he would ever feel like that. Ruby certainly made him believe that it was possible. "Would you like to dance?"

She winced and made a funny face. "I sort of have two left feet."

"It's okay. We'll go slow." He stood and grasped her hand, tugging her closer to the dance floor. He wound his way through the crowd, ignoring anyone who cast him a disparaging look. He was going to dance with his date and that was all there was to that. As soon as they were out there with the other couples, Heath wasted no time pulling Ruby into his arms.

"You don't really seem like the dancing type," she said.

He laughed, noticing how easily she pressed into him and warmed him from head to toe. "I'm not. But I love music, and I would have to be a fool to not want everyone in Royal to see me with the most beautiful woman at this party."

She shook her head. "You heap entirely too much praise on me."

"Not true. In fact, I get the distinct impression that you don't get enough praise and attention in your life. I worry about you living down that road, all by yourself."

"I know. It wasn't that smart for me to buy my place, but I wanted a fixer-upper and that was the cheapest thing I could find."

He disliked the thought of her having to worry about money, but he supposed that was part and parcel of being in her line of work. It certainly couldn't be lucrative. "So you fixed up the whole thing by yourself?"

"I did. I worked through my grief by knocking down walls and ripping up old tile and putting in new light fixtures. The whole nine yards."

"I can't believe you didn't hire someone to do it."

"It was a learning experience. I wanted to push my limits. So I sanded those floors on my hands and knees, chipping away at it a little more every day. It took forever. Which is why I was so mad when you wouldn't take your boots off."

"I eventually succumbed to your requests."

Her eyes had a sexy glimmer. "And my kiss. You succumbed to that, too."

He turned her in a circle, and the whole room fell away. Despite the negativity that had been aimed at him this evening, none of it came close to matching the positive charge of being with Ruby. "Of course I did. I'd been thinking about it for hours."

"You had?"

"Pretty much from the moment I laid eyes on you."

She swallowed so hard that he saw the motion in her graceful neck. "What were you thinking?"

He pulled her even closer and swept her hair aside so he could speak right into her ear. "I was thinking that if I could convince you to kiss me, I would be the luckiest guy in the world. I was thinking that I wanted to touch you and taste you and explore every inch of your beautiful body."

Ruby audibly sighed. "And I disappointed you."

"No. You didn't. It's not possible for you to disappoint me. I'm glad we waited. And we can wait as long as you want to." It wasn't an easy thing to say, but he meant it. He was fully committed to following her lead.

"What if I said that I was thinking about you from the moment I met you?"

That admission made everything below his waist draw tight. "Really?" His voice came out raspy and raw.

"Yes, really. I almost kissed you in the driveway when I fell."

"Seriously? I was acting like a person with half a brain."

She shrugged. "It was endearing. That you cared that much. Most people don't care about anything outside themselves. You do. It's very sexy."

"When else did you think about kissing me?"

"In my room, when we went to get the mattress. I almost pushed you down on the bed right then and there and begged you to take me."

Not only was this conversation making Heath's blood run hot, it was making him feel so damn lucky. That instant attraction he'd felt went both ways. "I would never make you beg."

"Not even a little?"

A lustful groan rumbled around in the base of his throat, and he found his head drifting closer to hers. He wanted to kiss her so bad it hurt. "I'm not saying it wouldn't turn me on." *Just like this whole conversation. Just like everything about you.*

Ruby leaned in and nudged his cheek with her nose, her breath hot against his skin. Then she inched closer to his ear. "Please tell me you want me. Tell me now."

"I want you," he muttered. "Now."

"You're going to have to wait. We're at a New Year's Eve party and it's not even eight o'clock. Don't you want to ring in the New Year?"

Heath felt as though his head was swimming. He couldn't see straight. All he could think about was being alone with Ruby. "Here's the problem."

"Okay…"

"We wait until midnight. Which is going to be hard for me because, right now, I want you so bad that I can barely form coherent sentences."

"I don't know. You're doing pretty well for yourself right now."

He laughed, which at least helped to loosen the tension in his body. "Just listen a second." He pulled her even closer, flattening his hand against the center of her back and holding her flush against him, if only to soak up more of her body heat. "The problem is that I'm going to kiss you when the clock strikes twelve. And once that happens, I'm not going to want to stop. And as much as I would love to give this town some more to say about me, they'd start saying those things about you, too, and I can't live with that."

She bit down on her lip, staring up into his eyes. "You are a mystery to me, Heath Thurston, but I do love watching your mind at work."

"So? Can I convince you to skip the countdown to midnight and come back to my place now?"

She unleashed half a grin, eased up onto her toes and planted a soft, wet kiss on his lips. "I've been waiting all night for you to ask."

Seven

Ruby felt as though her entire body was on fire. Heath was that hot. And she wanted him that badly. At any other time in her life, this might have been the perfect time to start thinking about nonsexy things, if only to force herself to cool down a bit. But she didn't want to douse the flames inside her. Not this time. They made her feel alive. She didn't want to keep pressing Pause on her own existence. So, for tonight, she'd focus on kindling the blaze.

"This is us," Heath said as he turned off the main road. They were far away from where Ruby lived, in one of the parts of Royal where the parcels of land grew impossibly large, cattle roamed the rolling hills, and the sprawling homes were often as grand as they were expensive. This was a place of permanence, reminding

Ruby of Heath's ties to this town, which was ironically where Ruby had gone when she needed to start over.

As they got closer to Heath's place, the house came into view. It was an impressive property, clad in river stone with a tall pitched roof above the center porch and entrance, which hosted double glass-paned doors and a circular wrought-iron chandelier. It struck her that this was where almost all of Heath's history had been written, the past that still haunted him. She hoped that crossing the threshold would mean that she could better understand him. "It's beautiful, Heath. Absolutely gorgeous."

"Thanks," he said as he clicked a button on the dash of his car and eased the vehicle into the three-bay garage. "It's home. The only one I've ever known." He shut off the engine and turned to her. "Ready to see it?"

"It's so wonderful that you've lived here your entire life. I've moved around too much over the years."

"Staying in one place isn't all it's cracked up to be." He led her inside, through a mudroom and into the kitchen, which was nearly the size of Ruby's entire cottage. It had beautiful black Shaker cabinets, white marble countertops with gray veining, and a wide porcelain farmhouse sink with a window above it overlooking the property. "And I'm sure you've been to all sorts of exciting places. You've probably traveled more than I have."

"I doubt it. I've never even been out of the state of Texas." It was a little embarrassing to admit, but she couldn't help but be honest. She took this chance to set her handbag and wrap on the kitchen table, which was situated in a large bay of windows.

"You should let me take you somewhere." He reached

for her and ran his fingers down the back of her bare arm as he admired her, which made her feel as though she was floating above the floor.

"Like where?"

He shrugged and clasped one of her hands. Then the other. "Anywhere you want."

"New York?"

"Sure." He slyly grinned and tugged her a little closer.

"San Francisco? Miami?"

"Of course."

Heath was offering to open up the world for her, which was such a generous gesture. If only he could understand how she felt about it—part of her wanted nothing more than to strike out on an adventure, but there was another part that craved the reliable comforts of home. A home like this one that felt as though it was never going anywhere. "Your bedroom?"

A low groan left his throat and he pulled her closer. "I thought you'd never ask." His lips fell on hers and there was this magical moment where she lost all sense of time and place, and nothing else existed other than Heath, his strong hands caressing her back, and the way his tongue sought hers in a warm and giving kiss. She did not have a care in the world right now and it buoyed her like nothing she'd experienced in a long time.

She popped up onto her tiptoes, stretched out her arms onto his shoulders and dug her fingers into his thick hair. She deepened their kiss, and he countered, making her whimper with desire. He wrapped his arms tighter around her, but then one hand dropped to her hip and gathered the skirt of her dress upward, taking a fistful of the garment. His fingers reached her bare thigh, and she gasped as though he'd just burned her, but it was the most pleasurable feeling she'd experienced in an eon. A man's touch. She needed more of it.

"I thought we were going to your bedroom," she said, breathless.

"Where are my manners?" With that, he reached down and swept her into his arms, holding her tight.

She wrapped her arms around his neck and set her head against his chest, craving his warmth and relishing the safety of his arms.

He wasted no time walking through the house and to his bedroom. He planted a knee on the bed and set her down gently. She kicked off her heels, then reclined and swished her hands across the duvet, which was soft and silky. "This feels amazing."

"You're amazing." Heath worked his shoulders out of his tuxedo jacket and yanked off his tie, not taking his eyes off her for so much as a second.

She couldn't stop looking at him either. The raw need on his face was fuel for her own desire. Knowing he wanted her gave her so much confidence. It made her feel bold. She propped up on her elbows and raised her knee, allowing the skirt of her dress to slide down her thigh to her hip. He responded by unbuttoning his shirt at lightning speed.

"I like watching you take your clothes off," she said, surprised she had the guts to do so.

He tossed his shirt on the floor. "I'm going to enjoy taking *your* clothes off." He stretched out on the bed next to her and kissed her like his life depended on it. He flattened her against the bed and she dug her fingers into his back, hitching her leg up over his hips and taking the back of his thigh with her foot. He was nothing but muscle, surely made from countless hours working on the ranch. She slipped her other leg between his and pressed against his crotch, feeling his erection and prompting a groan from the depths of his belly. The heat inside her was building like a wildfire on a hot and windy day. This was an all-new level of longing.

He pulled one dress strap off her shoulder and she clamped her eyes shut, relishing his touch as he tugged down the other. "My zipper," she muttered.

Heath eased to his side and took Ruby with him, then drew down the metal closure until it was all the way past her waist. He tugged down the layers of fabric, and luckily, she didn't have to ask him to unhook the strapless bra the dress required. He did that all on his own, then cupped one of her breasts with his hand and rubbed her nipple with his thumb, which was deliciously rough and calloused. He lowered his head and flicked his tongue against the tight bundle of nerves, and she felt heat surge in her body, rushing to meet his lips as he drew her skin into his mouth. She moaned, rubbing her leg even harder against his steely length.

He lowered his hand and raked her skirt higher. When he reached her hip, he moved across her belly, and then his fingers slipped down into the front of her panties. He took his time reaching her center, teasing with a delicate touch that made her arch her back. One skilled loop with his fingers and she was digging her nails into his biceps, needing him to keep going. As he artfully rolled his fingertips over her clit, the pressure in her hips started building, and she knew it wouldn't take much for her to give way. She clamored for his belt buckle, unhooking it and unzipping his pants. Without so much as an instant of hesitation, she slipped her hand inside, molding her fingers around his erection, loving how hard and hot he was. All she could think about was what it would be like to have him inside her, to experience every magnificent inch of him.

Thankfully, he led the charge by scrambling off the bed and shucking his pants and boxers. Ruby quickly shifted to her knees and wriggled her dress and panties past her hips. Heath climbed back onto the mattress behind her. He took her hair in his hand and pulled it aside, wrapping his other arm around her waist and pulling her snug against his body. He ground his hips against her bottom as he kissed his way from the nape of her neck to one shoulder, then back to the center. Needing more of him, Ruby turned in his arms and planted a hot, wet kiss on his lips. Then she did what she'd never imagined herself doing. She pushed him back onto the bed. The shock on his face was its own reward. She loved the thought of surprising him.

Heath could not believe his own eyes. Hovering above him was naked Ruby, a curvy and sumptuous feast for every one of his senses. She dragged her hand down his chest and stomach, then shot him a white-hot look before gripping his erection, lowering her head and taking him into her mouth. His eyes clamped shut, his mouth so agape with pleasure that he wasn't sure he'd ever be able to close his jaw again. The tenderness of her tongue, the firm and careful grip of her lips, and the warmth of her mouth felt so impossibly good. It would've been amazing to have this treatment from any woman, but from Ruby, it went so far beyond physical gratification. He was a lucky man and he knew it.

Heath caressed Ruby's shoulders and combed his fingers through her silky hair over and over again, matching her steady rhythm. He let go of as many thoughts as he could, the things that worried him and stressed him out, and instead allowed himself the luxury of the pleasure Ruby was lavishing on him. But when she gripped his hips more firmly with her hands and rolled her tongue over the tip of his length, he knew he couldn't last too much longer. As heavenly as this was, it wasn't everything he really wanted.

He grasped her arms and tugged her closer. "Come here, Ruby. I need to kiss you."

She carefully relinquished her hold on him. "I'm right here." She began to crawl up the length of his body, pressing her lips along his midline, inch by inch. Heath smoothed his hands over the velvety skin of her butt, then along her spine, until she reached his neck and they could finally fall into the kiss he so desperately wanted. He cupped both sides of her face as their tongues wound in an endless loop. He could have kissed her forever, but then her knees dropped to the bed, bracketing his hips. That left her slick center riding along his dick as she ground into him. His mind became a hazy place. His belly drew tight and he was right back on the precipice of release.

"Condom," he muttered. "Let me get one."

One more kiss, then Ruby rolled off him, allowing him to get up from the bed. As he opened the nightstand drawer and pulled out the box, she sprawled out on the bed, leaving him with the visual of her glorious body. She was slowly killing him, that was all there was to it, and that was a good thing. He didn't need much more in life than her right now. He tore open the foil packet and rolled it on himself quickly, never allowing himself to look away from her beauty.

She had the goofiest grin on her face, and in that moment, he fully appreciated just how much she already trusted him. He wished he could be like that, always seeing the good and looking away from the bad. He placed a knee on the bed, and she responded by spreading her legs wider, welcoming him as he positioned himself at her entrance and drove inside.

With that first stroke, Heath needed an instant to grapple with how perfectly they fit together. Her heat and grip on him were everything he could have asked for, and it made it hard to breathe. Made him work to think. He settled his weight on her and she wrapped her legs around his waist, dragging her heels along the backs of his thighs. He focused on every little noise she made, wanting this to be a mind-blowing experience. He not only needed to please her, he wanted to give himself the best chance at this happening again.

Their kisses were slow and deep while the pressure was coiling tightly inside him. He drove harder, listening to her breaths as they became choppier and the way she countered his strokes became more insistent. The pleasure was mounting, becoming impossible to resist, but he waited until her body clutched and she arched into him. Then he tumbled into his release, his shoulders and hips freezing and relaxing over and over again as he allowed the waves to wash over him.

A million kisses followed, and even then it didn't seem like it was enough. Eventually, Heath got up to use the bathroom, getting rid of the condom and washing his hands. Ruby took her turn right after him, and he waited in his bed for her, eager to wrap himself around her when she arrived.

"So, is it really true that you've never been out of Texas?" he asked. "You've never even taken a step over the state line?"

Ruby snuggled closer to him. "Why? Does that make me sound pathetic?"

"No. Of course not. I just want to know more about you. And, I mean, if you had to pick a state to live your whole life in, Texas would be a great choice."

"I guess I just never had the chance to go anywhere else. Either work was getting in the way, or money. Or sometimes, both."

He cleared his throat, wondering if it was wise to bring up the topic that was so present in his mind right now. It was the thing that had made her hold back the first time they were together. "Was Lucas from Texas?"

She paused for a moment, making him wonder if he'd made a grave mistake. "He was. Born and raised in Abilene. We met on a job site."

He considered asking for more, but discussing her former fiancé wasn't the best pillow talk. "I wasn't kidding when I told you that I'd take you someplace. We'd have fun traveling together." Heath couldn't even remember the last time he'd been on a vacation.

"How do I choose?" Ruby pushed up on her elbow and propped her head up with her hand. The moon outside was so bright that it cast her in the most mindblowing glow. She really was so beautiful.

"Make a list. We'll do them all."

"How many places can I pick? I'd like to go to California. San Francisco and LA. I really want to go to New York City and Washington, DC, and Miami. And of course, I'd really love to go someplace like the Grand Canyon. It would be so much fun to go geek out on rocks for a week."

"I've been to a few of those places. Some are great. Some aren't all that. I loved New York the few times I've been. It's very, very different from Texas. Totally different from Royal."

"You've spent your whole life here, haven't you?"

"I have. Born and raised. Nolan was the one who got out, but not me. Someone had to stay and look after the ranch."

"Does that bother you? That you stayed and he took off?"

Just thinking about Nolan's departure made him sad. They were only eighteen at the time, and Heath already knew the ranch was his life. "It bothered me a lot when he first left. I was furious because he took off without warning. I couldn't understand how he could leave or why he wanted to. But we've talked a fair amount since he came back to town. I think I get it now." He drew in a deep breath. "You know, even though we're twins, we can be very different. I always felt like the one who had to be responsible for everything. I love the ranch, but there was always the pressure of making it into a success because I knew my dad was counting on me to look after everything and everyone."

"So when Nolan left, it felt like your fate was sealed?"

Heath drew his fingers up and down Ruby's spine. "I suppose I did. I definitely felt like a door closed." Had feeling stuck fueled his quest against the Grandin and Lattimore families? Had it given him too much time to think? Ruby made him ask himself these questions, but he kept it all to himself.

"I'm glad you stayed here. We might not have met otherwise. And I can't wait to see the ranch."

"I'll gladly give you a tour." The thought filled him with even more optimism. It was one more thing to look forward to, spending time with her and showing off the product of his hard work.

"I'd like that. I'd like to learn more about you, too."

Heath pulled her closer. "What are you going to do for your birthday?"

Ruby reared her head back. "How did you know my birthday was coming?"

"You told me the day I came to your house."

"I did?"

"Yes. Remember when I was trying to explain how I thought you might be older than you are?"

Ruby laughed quietly. "Oh, right. I forgot about that."

"Good. I keep playing that moment over in my head, hating myself for making the mistake."

"To answer your question, I don't have any plans. I honestly haven't done anything for three years. My brother tried to convince me to visit last year, but I just wasn't in the mood for celebrating."

"Would it be okay if you and I celebrated? I think it's a good idea." He wondered if he was pushing her too hard. He knew how much he disliked it when someone pressured him about anything.

"What did you have in mind?"

"Whatever you want. It's your birthday."

"Maybe dinner?"

"Of course. Where would you like to go?"

"Sheen? Is that too much to ask?"

Heath hesitated for a moment, because he knew exactly what going to Sheen involved. It was the hippest restaurant in all of Royal and, because of that, immensely popular. He'd been a few times, and it'd been packed to the rafters on every occasion. Would he receive the same treatment he'd just endured at the TCC? Would someone like Vic decide to take issue with him? Every passing day made it more likely. It wouldn't be long before the Grandin and Lattimore families would receive the letter from his lawyer, and then it would be their turn to put up or shut up. "Nothing is too much to ask. I'd love to take you to Sheen. I'll make a call and get a reservation."

Eight

Ruby was finally starting her last house project, a complete rework of the closet in her bedroom. Closets in older homes were notoriously tiny, and hers was bursting at the seams. The hanging clothes were so jam-packed that it took an extraordinary amount of upper body strength to pull a single hanger off the rod. The shoes were even worse—the entire floor was littered with a mountain of cowboy boots, sneakers, sandals and heels. Starting the project had created its own mess. Ruby's entire wardrobe was piled on the sofa in the living room to keep it away from the construction dust.

Her first task was to remove the drywall at the back of her closet, which gave her access to the same space in the guest room. It wasn't a load-bearing wall, so she planned to knock down the framing between and double the square footage for her wardrobe. It was a big undertaking, but completing it would mean that she was done with transforming her house. Unless she thought of a new project. There was always something that could be done to improve things. And on some days, like today, she simply needed to stay busy. It was her birthday, and although Heath was taking her out tonight, it was still going to be a difficult day. Lucas had always gone the extra yard for her birthday.

When she'd first started working on this little cottage, it was a way to keep herself busy while she mourned Lucas's death. She'd needed something truly immersive, and it had to be physical. There was a lot of cathartic release to be had from smashing down walls with a sledgehammer and ripping up floorboards with a crowbar. Of course, she'd been sobbing through a lot of it, an actual sea of tears. She'd never known it was possible to cry so much. She kept waiting for the day when her grief would finally dry up and go away. But that was the biggest lesson she had waiting for her—it didn't work like that. The struggle didn't travel a straight line. It was a roller coaster. A string of good days would be followed by an unexpected descent back into sadness. Then the sun would come up and she'd heal for a few days. Maybe a few weeks. Then the cycle would start again.

Sometimes it was prompted by a memory, like of planning her wedding with Lucas. She'd thought her whole life was ahead of her then. She'd had no idea it was about to feel like it had come to an end. Right after Lucas was gone, she used to sleep with one of his shirts and the wedding planner notebook she'd been using to stay organized. A few months in, she'd realized how much she was torturing herself, and so she'd tucked away the notebook in the buffet. And she made the shirt into a pillow, but she put it on the bed in the guest room. It was a comfort to know that it was there if she needed it.

She kept an eye on the clock as she swept up the mess from the drywall and readied herself to start cutting two-by-fours for the framing. She was supposed to be at Heath's at five o'clock. Their dinner reservations for Sheen were at seven. He was adorable for having remembered that she'd mentioned it the first time he'd come to her house. He was even more adorable for insisting he take her out. He really was a generous person, and she couldn't see why others didn't see that in him. Maybe it was because he was so good at hiding it. He definitely wouldn't go out of his way to take or receive credit for anything. She had to admire that. Most people had too big an ego to not get every bit of credit they felt they deserved. But not Heath. People were free to take him or leave him. He didn't seem to care too much either way.

Around three thirty, she decided she'd better knock off for the day and hop in the shower. But before she could do that, her phone rang with a call from Heath. "Hey," she said. "I was just thinking about you. What's up?"

"I have a huge problem."

Ruby's stomach sank. She really hoped this didn't have anything to do with the Grandin or Lattimore families. "What's going on?"

"One of the horses got out of the barn, and I let my ranch hands leave early so they could go to an NBA game in Dallas. Normally, I'd wait for Lucky to come back. The whole property is fenced. But it's going to be dark soon and this horse is old, and she can't spend the night out in the cold."

"I was just about to get ready for our date. Do you want me to come over now and help you look?"

"I hate asking. I hate that this happened at all. It's your birthday and this is not how I wanted to spend it."

"I know that. It was your idea to celebrate at all. I'll come over now. But fair warning—I look like a wreck. No makeup, my hair is in a ponytail, and I probably smell pretty bad, too."

"I'm sure that, however you look, you're perfect."

"Famous last words, mister." She glanced at the gaping hole in the wall and decided that she'd have to clean up later. If she had any hope of salvaging her birthday date, she needed to help Heath now.

"Bring whatever you were going to wear tonight. If we find Lucky in time, we can still make it to Sheen. Or I'll call over there and ask them to move our seating time."

"One problem at a time, okay? I'll be there as quick as I can." Ruby hung up and quickly packed a bag with her clothes for their date, plus some makeup and her hair dryer. Feeling optimistic, she added an outfit for tomorrow. Maybe he would want her to sleep over. Maybe she and Heath could spend the entire day together.

She grabbed her coat and rushed outside, then raced to Heath's ranch, doing her best to not break any traffic laws, although she did run a yellow light at what could have been considered the last second. When she pulled up to his house, he was standing next to his truck, which was on one of the access roads that wound through the property. His vehicle was already running. She could see the billowy puffs of exhaust in the cold.

She parked her car and left her things inside, jogging over to his truck. "I told you I look like a wreck."

He smiled wide and pulled her closer, pressing a soft kiss to her lips. "You're more gorgeous than the last time I saw you."

That had been only a few days ago, and she'd been freshly showered at the time, so she was positive that wasn't true. "You're a pretty good liar."

"Not really." He opened the passenger's-side door of his truck. "Let's go. It's getting darker."

"And colder." Ruby climbed inside, thankful that Heath had the heat blazing.

"I already made one pass with the truck and I can't find her anywhere. We might have to go out into some of the pastures on foot, so I brought some flashlights. I know some of Lucky's hiding spots."

"She must be a pretty special horse. What breed is she?"

Heath laughed as he put the engine in Reverse. He made a quick three-point turn, and then they were on their way. "Not sure. She was a rescue. She was Ashley's horse."

Now Ruby understood why this was so urgent, aside from the animal's age and the dropping temperatures outside—he couldn't allow his sister's horse to suffer at all. "We'll find her."

"The whole thing was so stupid. I got distracted when I was putting her back in the stable late this afternoon. Pretty sure I forgot to double-latch her stall." He kept his eyes trained on the terrain as the truck bounced over the rough road and the headlights shone on their path. "She's mischievous. She sometimes makes a break for it. It's so bad that I keep a breakaway halter on her all the time. She actually has a tag like a dog."

"You'd think she'd get one whiff of how cold it is and head right back inside."

Heath glanced over at Ruby. "Yeah. Well. She hasn't been the same since Ashley died. It's like she misses her, which I know probably sounds a little unhinged."

Ruby looked out the passenger's-side window, scanning the landscape. "No sign of her over here. If you've already done one pass in the truck, maybe we should just accept that we'll need to go on foot. You mentioned that she has hiding places. Should we check those?"

"That's probably the best way to do this. Unfortunately, the most likely spot is also the least accessible. Are you sure you're up for this?"

"I already look like hell, so yes."

"No, you don't. But I'm going to agree with you about this approach." Heath took a sharp right and started over a long series of rolling ridges. About ten minutes later, he slowed down and pulled off to the side, gravel rumbling under the tires. A wooded area was to the right, with a small stand of bare hardwood trees with evergreens mixed in. It had to be a quarter mile away, down an incline and into a small valley. "There's a watering hole down there. She loves it." He zipped up his coat. "I can check it out if you want to stay in the car."

Ruby had come this far. She wasn't about to let him go on his own. "I'd like to go with you."

"Are you sure?"

She nodded eagerly. "Never been so sure in all my life."

Heath and Ruby started down the hill. He led the way, wanting to be sure he was there to catch her if she tripped. The sun had nearly dipped beneath the horizon, the temperature was dropping, and he was filled with a mix of emotions—worry over Lucky, appreciation for Ruby and regret that this had happened in the first place. "I hate that you're spending part of your birthday doing this."

"Well, the first part of my day was spent tearing out drywall."

"Another house project?"

"Yeah. I'm expanding my closet."

Heath remembered what she'd told him when they were dancing at the Texas Cattleman's Club, about what had sent her on her home improvement journey—working through her grief. "I hope that doesn't mean you were having a hard day because it's your birthday. Milestones can hit hard when you've lost someone."

"Actually, today was a good day. Right now, it's just about finishing up the house. Having that sense of accomplishment."

Heath really hoped that was the case. Off in the distance, he heard the distinct sound of a horse's whinny. "That's her. That's Lucky." He picked up the pace. "Come on. She's probably down by the water."

"I'm right behind you," Ruby said.

Eventually, the slope eased up and flattened out, and they were able to run. He knew exactly where they were going and led Ruby into the trees, where it was far colder than out in the wide-open spaces. Even these bare trees had sheltered the area from the warmth of the sun. "Lucky! Lucky!" he shouted, dodging rocks and trees.

"There she is!" Ruby, who was running alongside him now, pointed off to the left.

Heath stopped dead in his tracks, realizing that

Lucky wasn't at the water. She was in the spot where Heath had scattered some of Ashley's ashes. What could have possibly drawn Lucky to that particular place? A well of emotion rose up inside of him and he had to close his eyes to keep it at bay. He wasn't about to break down in front of Ruby.

"Are you okay?" she asked, breathless.

"I'm fine." He opened his eyes and shook his head in disbelief.

"Heath. Get real. You're obviously not okay. I can see it on your face."

How did she see right through him? "It's just that Lucky is in the exact spot where I left some of Ashley's ashes." He started walking toward Lucky. Ruby was right at his side.

"This must be a special place."

"Ashley showed Nolan and me this hiding spot. After our dad passed away. When the three of us needed to get away and just goof off. The watering hole isn't very deep, so we'd swim in there sometimes. Bring food or sneak some beer and talk. About the future." Just saying that word out loud—*future*—made him realize exactly how much he'd clung to the idea of better days ahead when he was younger. It was the only thing that kept him going. All of that hope went away when his mom and Ashley had their accident. And now Ruby had given him a reminder of how powerful even a drop of optimism could be. He still had hope that the Grandin and Lattimore families would own up to their mistakes so they could all move on.

Lucky whinnied again, making it even easier to see her as the warm breath rose from her nose in the frigid air. She rubbed her head up against a tree fitfully.

"How amazing is it that she came here?" Ruby asked as they closed in on the beautiful animal, sable brown with tufts of white along her nose and on her belly and tail. Ruby didn't hesitate to go right up to Lucky, although she was gentle and careful with her approach. Lucky warmed to her immediately, nudging at her arm as Ruby caressed her head and shushed her when she whinnied again.

"After all this time. I don't understand," Heath said, struggling to wrap his head around the idea that, on some level, Lucky knew that some of Ashley's ashes were here.

"Animals are amazing. They know things. They understand when we're in pain. They love just like we do." Ruby looked into Lucky's eyes, and they seemed to share a special moment. It was the exact sort of connection Ashley had had with horses. They trusted her, and she adored them.

It was Heath's turn to give Lucky a rub behind her ears. "Today was not really the day to remind me about Ashley, Lucky. I'm supposed to take Ruby out for her birthday. Now we're going to have to rush to get to dinner." He turned to Ruby. "I can ride her back to the stable if you want to take the truck. And I'll meet you there?"

"You can ride bareback?"

"That's how I learned. And she'll do fine with her halter on. We're not going to be running at top speed."

"You need some serious core strength to stay up on a horse like that. Although, I've seen your abs, so I suppose it makes sense." Ruby laughed. "You amaze me."

You amaze me. Heath had pretty well ruined her birthday plans and Ruby was being nothing less than a very good sport about it. "I can hoist myself up there if I get on that rock." Ahead was a sizable boulder, probably three or four feet high. It would be just enough of a boost. He led Lucky over with her bridle, and sure enough, it gave him just the right angle to swing his leg over and mount the horse. "The keys are in the truck. Will you be okay?" he asked, looking down at Ruby.

"Yes. I'm going to drive slow, though, so I can keep an eye on you two."

"Probably a good idea."

Heath did his best to urge Lucky along, but she was showing her age and it was slow going. It took nearly twice as long to get back to the stable as it had with the truck. Every step of that ride gave Heath another minute to think about where he was in life and the women who had been so important to him. First Ashley and his mom, but now Ruby. In very short order, she had become an integral part of the puzzle that was his existence. She understood him on a level that very few people did, and she appreciated the losses he had endured. He hoped that when and if his push against the Grandin and Lattimore families came to light, she would know he had only done it out of love. During their lunch at the Royal Diner, she'd urged him to do what he needed to do to put it all to rest. Well, that was exactly what he'd set in motion.

Heath got Lucky settled back in her stall in the stable, which was toasty warm and comfortable. Surely the horse realized now that this was a far better place to be than out on the ranch, with no refuge from the cold. "Thank you for coming out," he said to Ruby, looking at his watch. "We have about a half hour until our reservation. We can hurry up and try to get ready, or I can call the restaurant and ask them to move our time. What do you think?"

Ruby shook her head. "You know, I don't really feel like going out at this point. I'd rather stay here. With you."

"Really? I feel like I've ruined your birthday."

"This is exactly my speed, to be honest."

He pulled her closer, wrapping his arms around her waist. He was so relieved that she didn't want to go to Sheen. Running into a Grandin and Lattimore and having them yell at him in the middle of a crowded restaurant would really ruin her birthday. Of course, he wasn't about to share his worries. That was his burden to bear. "That's what I like about you. Aside from the part where we froze our butts off finding a lost horse, this is my speed, too. Do you want to go back to the house so I can show you something?" he asked.

She smiled, the corner of her mouth quirking up adorably. "Is it something of yours? Because I've seen it all, but I wouldn't mind looking again."

He laughed and planted a kiss on her lips. "I love that your brain immediately turns to sex, but I'm actually talking about something else."

"Lead the way."

Heath and Ruby hopped in his truck and were back at the house in a few short minutes. Inside, he led her to his home office, which was right off the living room. "I just got the preliminary drawings for the riding center. No one else has seen them. I texted Nolan about it, but he hasn't gotten back to me." Just then, Heath's phone beeped with a text. "Speak of the devil," he said as he consulted the screen. "He wants to know if we'll have dinner with Chelsea and him at their place. I can bring the plans over then."

It sounded like a fabulous evening to Ruby, but she did worry that things were moving fast. She and Heath were spending so much time together. *Take a breath. You like him. It's okay to like him.* "That's sweet. Yes. I'd love to go."

Heath tapped away on his phone, then looked at her. "Friday okay?"

"That should work."

Heath finished one more text, then set his phone down and unfurled the first set of plans. "This is all very early. Just a few elevations to give me a sense of the direction for the project."

Ruby stood closer to him, peering down at the scroll of architectural drawings. "What's that?" she asked, pointing to a large building. When she'd been thinking "riding center," she'd only considered the corrals.

"That will be the main building, for administrative duties, a small visitors' center and classrooms." He peeled back a page to show a sketch of the rest of the center. "There will be three corrals. One fully enclosed, with seating for a crowd if we choose to do any shows. One will be open-air and the last one will be covered."

"This is a serious undertaking. How are you going to pay for all of this?"

"I have the money myself. But I'm working on some local contributions. I'd like the community to be invested in it." He turned to her and the soft lighting in his office lit him from the side, making him even more handsome. Or maybe it was the way this subject matter made him light up from within.

"I think that's a wonderful idea. You should do everything you can to make sure it's an integral part of Royal."

He put his arm around her shoulders and snuggled her closer, then planted a kiss on top of her head. "I love the way you think. You're always looking for ways to make things better. Which is ironic since you do that all on your own."

She turned to face him and they naturally drew each other into an embrace, one where they could still look at each other. "I'm not sure what that means."

"It means that you are an actual ray of sunshine, Ruby. You shine a light on things, good or bad, and try to figure out a way to make everything better." He cupped both sides of her face with his hands and peered into her eyes. From anyone else, this gesture might make her feel entirely too vulnerable. But his touch always made her feel safe. Protected. Adored.

"Do you know what I like so much about you, Heath?"

He grinned as he rubbed her cheek with his thumb. "Is this a trick question?"

She laughed quietly. "No. I'm trying to pay you a compliment. You're always saying nice things about me. You need to let me take a turn."

"Okay. Go for it."

"I like that you think about and consider everything. You have this rugged handsome exterior, but you are a very cerebral guy. It's very sexy."

"So you're saying I'm handsome…" He lowered his head to go in for a kiss.

She tugged him closer and raised her chin. "What I'm saying is that you're the whole package." He kissed her and all she wanted was to melt into him. She definitely wanted to rip off his clothes and spend the entire night going to town on each other. When he reached down and palmed her thigh, then hitched it up, she knew that was exactly where this was going. She broke free from the kiss. "Heath, I'm a wreck. I'd like to clean up before things go any further."

"Me too. I think we can kill two birds with one stone and have a whole lot of fun while we do it. Come on." He grabbed her hand and led her through his bedroom, into his luxurious bathroom. There was masculine slate tile and a long vanity topped with Carrara marble. The glass shower enclosure was built for two. Absolutely perfect.

Heath wasted zero time turning on the water in the shower while Ruby pulled out her ponytail and removed the small gold stud earrings she was wearing. He pulled off his boots and stripped off the rest of his clothes in record time. Her breath hitched when she saw how hard he was already. She wasn't sure what she'd done to be so lucky. Heath turned his attention to her, pushing her sweater up over her head. She loved the way he looked at her, the way his eyes got stormy and dark with each new item of clothing removed. Her boots and socks, jeans and bra, and finally, her panties. Standing there, completely naked, she had every reason to feel too exposed. Too vulnerable. But she felt nothing but turned on, which was a feat in its own right since he'd hardly touched her.

He opened the shower door and she stepped into the warm spray, her muscles immediately relaxing. Heath joined her and closed the door, then positioned himself behind her. He pressed his erection against her bottom and placed his hands on her hips, caressing them as he kissed her neck. His touch was soft and sensuous, all while the steam rose around them. "Your skin is so damn soft, Ruby. I could touch you forever."

Forever. In her recent history, that was a word that had become meaningless. Then she'd met Heath and things started to change. "I love having your hands all over me."

He reached past her for a bar of soap and rolled it in his hands, his arms threaded under hers. He spread the creamy lather up her stomach, then over her breasts, his hands slowly working in circles, rubbing her nipples with the palms of his hands. Ruby reached above her head and clasped her hands back behind his neck, giving him complete access to every inch of her torso. She pressed her bottom harder against his steely length, wagging her hips back and forth. Heath groaned his approval into her neck, then rinsed off one of his hands. He caressed her belly, then slid his fingers lower, spreading her delicate folds until he found her center. He rubbed in languid circles while he cupped one of her breasts with his other hand. The pressure was building so fast in her body it was hard to think straight, especially as the hot water streamed down her thighs. Heath started to move faster. Harder. And that made the tension tighter, winding and winding, completing a circuit between her clit and her nipple, until finally it all peaked. She knocked her head back against Heath's shoulder and cried out.

He slowed his hand between her legs, then turned her in his arms. She kissed him deeply as the waves of pleasure were still rolling over her. "That was amazing."

"Think of it as the first course."

"I don't care how good the food is at Sheen, it's definitely not *that* good."

Heath chuckled. "Let me get cleaned up and we can see exactly how good it can get around here."

Ruby grabbed the bar of soap and spread silky bubbles across his firm chest while he worked shampoo through his hair. Even after that dizzying orgasm, she still hadn't had enough of him. She needed everything. He rinsed off the soap, then turned off the water. As they stepped out of the shower, the bathroom felt just as warm, so they didn't bother with towels and instead wrapped up in each other's arms. Their slick wet skin rubbed together as he walked her backward to the vanity.

Ruby reached back for the counter, but Heath went one better, cupped her butt in his hands and lifted her. The cool stone counter made her arch her back, which only left her closer to him. She coiled her legs around his waist, dug her hands into his wet hair, kissing him as their tongues wound together and water went everywhere. "Condom?" she had the presence of mind to ask.

"Yes. Right here." He opened a cabinet and pulled out a small box, then rolled the condom onto himself. He wasted no time, grabbing her hips and pulling her to the edge of the counter, then guiding himself inside. Their gazes connected while he did it, and the intensity of that moment overwhelmed her. There was nothing else in the world other than Heath at that moment. His first strokes were slow and deep, and she dug her heels into his ass, wanting him even closer. She could tell from his breaths and facial expressions that he was already close. His eyes kept drifting shut and his lips were slack. She pushed against him harder with the motion of her hips. She didn't want him to be gentle, caring Heath. She wanted him to unleash whatever it was that drove him to do some of the things he did. The things people hated him for. He read her intent and drove into her faster, sending her barreling toward her second peak. She leaned back and flattened her hands on the vanity, if only to counter the force of his thrusts. She smiled when she noticed how he was momentarily hypnotized by the bounce of her breasts.

Ruby was so close to the brink that she could taste it. She could *see* it. And then, finally, with one more stroke, her torso jerked forward and Heath followed, his breaths choppy and torn as he pulled her chest to his and they rode out the waves together. All that was left was quiet, warmth, and the *thump thump thump* as his heartbeat matched hers. They were in sync. Blissfully so. And she knew then that she had fallen right off the cliff and into the waiting arms of Heath.

Nine

With every passing day, Ruby was growing closer to Heath. She was getting in a little deeper. At her strongest moments, when she was in his arms and the sun was shining and she saw the promise of a new day, it felt wonderful. It felt right. He was not only a surprise in her life, he was a gift. He made her remember how amazing it was to laugh with someone, so hard that your legs went weak and your stomach hurt. He reminded her how incredible it was to glance at another person, lock eyes and have an entire conversation without a single word exchanged. Those moments almost always ignited the passion between them. Time and place ceased to mean a thing. All that existed for Ruby was Heath and she wanted to think he felt the same way.

But there were times, usually in the middle of the night when she couldn't sleep, that her feelings scared the hell out of her. It had hurt so much to lose Lucas. It changed her forever. Was she really ready to be all in with Heath? She truly wanted to be, but she shuddered to think how badly it would destroy her if things didn't work out. That would feel like it had before. Like she was having her heart ripped out. She couldn't live through that again. It almost killed her the first time.

Her biggest concern when she'd first met Heath had been his crusade against the Grandins and the Lattimores. She could not be with a man who was living a life that kept him looking backward, or at the very least always looking over his shoulder. Her only path was forward. It had taken her three years to figure that out. It was only after months and months of desperately longing for what had been that she'd learned that some things were gone forever. And there was nothing anyone could do about it. Some things simply had to be let go, with a reluctant uncurling of fingers as you allowed that person or vexing situation to simply slip away. It didn't mean that you didn't care. It didn't mean that your love for someone wasn't strong. It meant that your strength and energy needed to go into living.

Thankfully, Heath hadn't brought up his dispute with the families since their night at the TCC, or if he did, it was only to crack a joke or make a dismissive comment under his breath, something that could be quickly cast aside. Ever since the day they'd run into each other in downtown Royal at the Rancher's Daughter and they had lunch at the diner, her approach had been to keep him focused on Ashley's foundation and the riding center. It genuinely excited him. It made him optimistic and enthusiastic. That was the Heath Thurston she adored. That was the man she had fallen for.

Tonight, they were going to dinner at Chelsea and Nolan's apartment. In Ruby's mind, this was going to be a big test. She really wanted to see how he interacted with Chelsea in a more intimate setting. The only other time she'd been with them both had been New Year's Eve at the Texas Cattleman's Club. They'd been congenial toward each other, but that was easy in a crowded celebratory setting with champagne flowing.

"I didn't realize Nolan and Chelsea lived downtown," Ruby said as she and Heath walked hand in hand from the spot where Heath had parked the car.

"Yep. They have a pretty cool loft, but it's just a rental. They're planning on breaking ground on a house in the spring. Chelsea was gifted twenty acres of the Grandin property on her twenty-first birthday."

Ruby had to wonder if that was a hard pill for Heath to swallow. He'd spent so much time raging against the Grandin family, particularly about their property, and now his brother was going to go live on it? Plus, inheritance was at the core of what Heath had been pursuing all along. If Ashley was still alive and the Grandins had acknowledged her place in their family, she should have been given a similar birthday present. That couldn't be an easy fact for Heath to accept. "Building a house from the ground up sounds exciting."

"It is. They've got their whole lives ahead of them." Heath pointed ahead to a door near the corner. "This is it." He pressed a button for the intercom and moments later they were buzzed into the building.

"Building a house also sounds like a lot of work," Ruby added as they entered a stairwell and headed upstairs. "I can't imagine having to pick everything out.

Tile, flooring, paint colors, appliances. It would be exhausting."

"So says the woman who redid her entire home. On her own. Most people would say that was impossible. I still can't believe you did that."

"It helped me move ahead. Just like you have the riding center and Ashley's foundation. It's basically the same thing."

"I suppose you're right. It's good to focus on something positive."

It warmed Ruby from head to toe to know that Heath was focusing on the good. It helped her believe that they could have a future together. A few weeks ago, that would have been a scary thought, but so much had happened since then. Every day was another step toward something more lasting.

When they arrived at Nolan's door, Heath gave it a knock, but never let go of Ruby's hand. Nolan was quick to answer with Chelsea at his side. They both erupted in an eager welcome, ushering Ruby and Heath inside.

"Oh, wow," Ruby said as she got her first glimpse of their apartment. As Heath had mentioned, it was a true loft, with an open space containing a living room area at its heart, an open kitchen on the far wall, and a bedroom area in one corner, complete with a king bed. It had a casual sophistication to it that Ruby really liked—a blending of comfort, color and style. "What a cool space. I love it."

"Thank you," Chelsea said. "We won't be here too much longer, but it works."

"Heath mentioned that you're about to break ground

on the house you're building on your family's property. How exciting."

Chelsea and Nolan looked into each other's eyes with nothing less than pure adoration. "I can't wait," Nolan said. "We can't start a family living here. And we're really eager to get pregnant."

Heath cleared his throat. "Wow. I wasn't really expecting that bit of news." His voice wobbled with surprise.

"Are you surprised?" Nolan asked.

"I suppose I am," Heath answered. "It wasn't that long ago that you were the guy running all over the world. It's a big change."

Nolan eyed Heath. "Love has changed me. Chelsea has changed me. I don't need the things I used to chase. All I care about is our relationship." He turned back to Chelsea. "All I need is you."

"That's so sweet, babe," Chelsea said. "Really. I love you so much."

"I love you, too," Nolan replied, then kissed her on the forehead.

Ruby felt as though her heart was going to pound right out of her chest and not in a good way. She couldn't read Heath's reaction at all and she worried that this might upset him. After all, his war had been waged against the Grandin family, and now his twin brother was not only married to a Grandin, he was ready to start having children with one.

"What are you thinking?" Nolan asked Heath.

"Honestly?" Heath let a breathy laugh escape his lips. "I'm happy. I love the thought of you and Chelsea becoming parents. I love the idea of being an uncle, and especially since you're going to stay in Royal, where

I get to be a part of it. I never thought this day would come, Nolan."

Heath's voice was truly breaking with a mix of elation and raw emotion. He reached for his brother and the two embraced. Ruby looked over at Chelsea through watery eyes, noticing that Chelsea was crying, too. It was then that Ruby realized exactly how much of Heath's crusade had been about nothing more than needing the love of family. Who could possibly fault him for that? Surely not Ruby. She needed it, too.

"You two are going to ruin my mascara," Chelsea said, wiping the tears away.

Nolan and Heath stepped out of their hug, but held strong eye contact for a few moments. It was a powerful image—two identical men having a conversation only they could have, without words. "I love you," Heath said. "I'm so glad you're back in my life."

"It's good to be back. I love you, too," Nolan replied.

Ruby hadn't realized until right then that she'd been holding her breath. How could so much healing possibly be packed into such a short amount of time? She wasn't sure, but she was thankful she'd been there to see it.

"Okay, then." Nolan looked at Ruby and smiled, then turned back to Chelsea. "I think we could all use a glass of wine."

"Great idea. Dinner will be ready in a few minutes, and then we can sit down and talk and eat and enjoy," Chelsea said.

"Did you bring the riding center plans?" Nolan asked Heath.

"I didn't. The second round is almost ready. I didn't

want to show you plans that would change in a few days."

"Okay. Let's get together when you have them," Nolan replied.

Chelsea turned to Ruby. "Want to help me get the last few things ready?"

"Absolutely." Ruby followed Chelsea into the kitchen while Heath and Nolan wandered over to a tall wine rack in the corner of the apartment.

"Do you want to go ahead and toss the salad?" Chelsea asked. "Everything's ready to go in that big bowl on the island and the dressing is in the fridge door."

"Sure thing." Ruby followed Chelsea's directive. "That was pretty intense," she said as she removed the top from the dressing and lightly drizzled it on the greens.

"It was. But it's been a long time coming. They've been getting closer since Nolan returned to Royal, but some scars run pretty deep. I'm not entirely sure either of them truly trusted each other. I think it has helped that Heath seems to have dropped his crusade against my family and that Nolan is going to help with Ashley's foundation."

Ruby tossed the salad, feeling fortunate that she'd witnessed that momentous exchange between the brothers. It was one more positive note in the case she was making for herself, one that said she and Heath Thurston belonged together.

Dinner was amazing, even though Chelsea hadn't prepared it. She admitted that she wasn't much of a cook, but she'd ordered a heat-and-eat meal from a local chef that included a hearty pasta dish with braised pork, tomato, fresh herbs and lots of Parmesan. It was flat-out delicious. Even so, the real highlight was the four of them at that tiny dining table, talking, laughing, eating, and drinking wine. There was no negativity or acrimony, only genuine affection and good feelings. They were making memories, and for the first time in a long time, they were happy ones.

Heath had never imagined such a scene would be possible with a member of the Grandin family, but clearly it was. He was also now convinced that his brother had absolutely made the right decision in marrying Chelsea. They were perfect for each other, which made Heath realize that there was another perfect fit in the room—he and Ruby. How had she so effortlessly folded herself into his life? How had they become so impossibly close in such a short amount of time? He wasn't sure of any of the answers. He only knew that he considered himself lucky. Very, very lucky.

After dinner, Heath and Nolan volunteered for cleanup duty while Chelsea and Ruby hung out in the living room and talked about decor choices for Nolan and Chelsea's new house.

"Fatherhood. It's a big step," Heath said to Nolan, taking a clean plate from him to dry. "I'm proud of you."

Nolan glanced at him and smiled. "Thanks. I guess it just feels like the most natural thing in the world. And that's something I never imagined myself saying."

Heath laughed and put away the dish, then took another. "You know who would be really happy about this?"

"Ashley?" Nolan asked.

"Yes. Exactly."

Stillness settled over them for a moment. "She would

have made such an amazing aunt. And Mom always had her troubles dealing with us, but I'm sure she would have been a proud grandmother."

"Oh, God. Yes. They absolutely would have loved it." Heath was surprised to realize that although the sadness over their mother's and sister's untimely deaths might never go away, he could actually talk about them now without getting angry or upset.

"It's okay. They're going to get the best uncle in the world."

Heath laughed, but he had to think about that for a moment. Would the best uncle in the world ever threaten to sue his sister-in-law's family? No. Nothing had come of the letter Albert had sent other than an eventual response from Victor Grandin Jr. and Ben Lattimore, which asked for more time, but it was still out there in the world, like a land mine. How long before someone, probably him, would step on it? It was probably time to put it all to an end. Everything tonight had been so wonderful. Why would he want to ruin everything that was ahead for the four people in this room? He didn't want to do that. He didn't even want to risk it.

"Thanks a ton for inviting us over tonight. This was so much fun. Ruby and I have both had a great time," Heath said.

"Hold on a second. Let me go grab my phone so I can record you saying that you had fun." Nolan's devilish grin said that he was joking around, but Heath was still a little hurt by it.

"Hey. I like to have fun as much as the next person."

Nolan nodded and looked across the room. "You've definitely been inching toward that since you met Ruby.

Which is part of the reason we invited you two over to-night. Chelsea and I will do anything to encourage this relationship."

"She's pretty amazing, isn't she?"

Nolan looked back at Heath and shook his head. "Yes. She is. But it's not just her. It's the two of you together. Heath, you have so much good inside of you and it's been hidden away. I'm really glad to see it all come back out. I look at you and see the brother I used to know."

"I can admit that I do feel more like my old self. I got lost there for a pretty long time."

"It's not surprising. Mom's and Ashley's deaths were a shock to us both. It was horrible. But…" Nolan stared down at the floor, seeming weighed down by something.

"But what?"

He raised his head and made eye contact with Heath. "I hate to say this."

"Whatever it is, come out with it. You can tell me anything and everything."

"Of course I'm heartbroken over the accident. I always will be. But I have to wonder what would have happened between you and me if that hadn't happened. What if they were still here? How would things be different?"

Heath had pondered this scenario a million times. He'd thought about what would have happened if they'd left the house five minutes earlier or five minutes later. It was the cruel twist of fate that really ate at him. "You and I wouldn't be having this conversation. I know that much. Our relationship would still be strained. Or non-existent. Which is probably more accurate."

"Right. Exactly. Now, the old me would have seen the whole situation in black and white, but Chelsea has helped me see the shades of gray. Losing Mom and Ashley was terrible, but it brought us back together. We're all going to die someday. That was their day. And as tragic as that was, good still came out of it."

"I never really looked at it that way." Nolan had just blown Heath's mind. It might take him a long time to wrap his head around the concept.

"Anyway. That's one of those things that popped into my head in the middle of the night when I couldn't sleep because I was worried about you. About us."

"I've had those same sleepless nights." Too many to count.

"I bet you have."

"I don't want either of us to have those anymore, Nolan. We're moving forward, okay? You and I, together, as brothers."

"That is music to my ears."

"Hey, Nolan," Chelsea said. "Can you come over here and explain to Ruby that thing you want to do with the flooring in the kitchen? I still don't really understand it."

"Sure thing." Nolan glanced at Heath. "Do you want to come and see?"

"Actually, I need to send a text real quick. I'll be over in a minute." Heath watched as his brother crossed the room. Then he turned his back to them, pulled out his phone and tapped out a quick text to Albert. Changed my mind. Tell them there will be no lawsuit. Whatever you need to do. It felt like an eternity passed as he stared at his phone, waiting to hear back from Albert. Eventually, a few moments later, he got a reply.

You sure?

Heath had to smile at the question. He'd never been more sure of anything in his life. Yes. Kill it.

Right away.

"Everything okay?" Ruby asked, coming up behind him and placing her hands on his shoulders.

He turned and pulled her into his arms. "Everything's perfect."

She rested her chin on his chest and peered up at him. "Want to get out of here?"

His body responded with a wave of warmth that only Ruby could bring about. It was amazing that she had that sort of effect on him. "I do. Are you and Chelsea all done?"

"Yep. And guess what? Chelsea and I made a date to go shopping together at the Rancher's Daughter next weekend. Morgan will have all of the new spring clothes then."

"That sounds like fun."

"So maybe you and Nolan can get together to talk about the riding center then."

"That should be perfect. I should have the full plans by then." He took her hand and they walked over to Chelsea and Nolan in the living room area, where they were seated on the couch, looking over their house plans. "Hey, Nolan. Ruby and I are going to head out. Do you want to go over the riding center plans next week when Chelsea and Ruby are shopping?"

"Sounds good," Nolan said as he and Chelsea got up

from the couch and made their way to the front door. "I'll talk to you soon?" he asked Heath.

Heath loved that everything was coming together so well. The woman he was head over heels for had already become close with his brother, the person he cared about most in the world. And as for Chelsea, Heath's opinion of her had softened considerably. Seeing her interact with Ruby so effortlessly certainly helped. "Yes. And thanks again to you both for dinner. It was an amazing night. I hope we can do it again."

Nolan opened the door for Ruby and Heath. "I'm counting on it."

Ten

Ruby was excited by the prospect of her shopping trip with Chelsea, and not just because Heath had given her his credit card and instructed her to buy whatever she wanted. Chelsea had quickly become a good friend, which really helped Ruby feel more connected to Royal. Before she met Heath, she'd felt like a stranger in this small town, but as he introduced her to the people in his life, her social circle was widening, and she realized how much she'd cut herself off from everything and everyone after Lucas died. It was nice to be a part of something once again, and Chelsea was definitely a big piece in that puzzle.

"Are you sure you want to pay?" Ruby asked Heath as they stood outside of the Rancher's Daughter, waiting for Chelsea and Nolan to meet them. It was a chilly morning, and she and Heath had their arms wrapped around each other, although, to be fair, that was the case most of the time.

"I'm positive," Heath said. "Buy whatever you want. I don't care how much it costs."

"I have my own money, you know."

"I'm aware of that. But your birthday wasn't everything I wanted it to be. So let me do this one nice thing for you, okay?"

Ruby peered up at him, admiring his handsome face and also getting warm and fuzzy feelings about his generous nature. "You do nice things for me all the time. You were more than nice to me last night." Ruby had been staying over at Heath's all week long. Every night was an exploration of the heat and passion between them, but Heath had really outdone himself a mere twelve hours ago. Just thinking about it sent a thrill along her spine.

"Hey. I enjoyed it, too. Trust me."

"Jeez, you two. Get a room." Nolan's voice came out of nowhere, making Ruby jump. He placed his hands on her shoulders, giving her a gentle squeeze.

"Good morning to you, too," Heath said.

"Hey, guys," Chelsea chimed in as she appeared and patted Heath on the arm before directing her attention to Ruby. "Are we ready to do some serious damage in my sister's store?"

Ruby grinned. "Absolutely." She slid Heath a look of reassurance. "Well, not too much damage."

"You guys are going to go grab a late breakfast at the diner?" Chelsea asked.

Heath nodded eagerly, holding up the cardboard tube that contained the architect's plans. "Yes. I've got the drawings and the preliminary budget for the riding center. I want to go over all of that with Nolan, and we'll talk about funding the endowment."

"I'd love to volunteer when it's up and running."

"Thank you." Heath leaned closer to Ruby and kissed her. "Have fun."

"I will."

Chelsea and Nolan gave each other a quick kiss. "I love you," Chelsea said.

"Love you, too," Nolan replied.

The exchange between Chelsea and Nolan played in her head, and Ruby realized the one thing missing from her otherwise perfect relationship with Heath were those three little words. She looked at him and their gazes connected, but she could only imagine how odd she must look because Heath seemed puzzled. If only he knew the confusion between her head and heart. Was she really ready to tell Heath that she loved him? The idea felt surprisingly natural. What a revelation that was. When they'd met, she couldn't have imagined she'd ever say it again to anyone.

"See you guys in a little bit," Chelsea said, opening the door to the shop.

Ruby followed Chelsea inside, still a little dazed by her realization that she was ready to tell Heath she loved him. It had come hard and fast like a bolt of lightning during a summer thunderstorm, although she supposed she should have seen it coming.

Morgan looked up from her spot behind the register and rushed out to greet them. "I'm so excited for you two to see all of the new stuff. I pulled a bunch of things for you both to look at. It's all back by the dressing rooms."

Chelsea and Ruby followed, and sure enough, there

was a vast array of cute warm-weather clothes waiting for them on a rolling rack. There were summery dresses, adorable sleeveless tops, several different types of skirts, and Ruby's favorite, blue jeans. Just seeing the clothes made her excited for summer. She was officially *over* winter.

"I guess we'd better get to trying some of this stuff on, huh?" Chelsea asked.

"Get your butts in there," Morgan said. "I've put enough stuff for you both to get started in the dressing rooms. Ruby, you're on the right. Chelsea, you're the left."

"I can't wait to see what you picked out," Chelsea said.

"It's a lot more fun now that you've expanded beyond blue jeans," Morgan replied with a laugh.

Ruby and Chelsea took their respective rooms. Ruby zipped the curtain closed and put down her purse, then pulled off her sweater to try on the first top.

"Let me know if any of the sizes are off," Morgan called. "I'll be sitting here, checking my email."

Ruby was turning in the mirror to admire this first item of clothing, a gauzy sleeveless black blouse with lace trim, when she heard Morgan's voice shrieking with panic.

"Oh, my God. Chelsea. Get out here. Right now."

"What's wrong?" Chelsea asked with a similarly frantic tone.

"Are you even listening to me? Please. Get out here. Now."

Ruby ducked out of her dressing room to see what was going on. Chelsea was a step ahead of her.

"Look at this." Morgan thrust her phone in her sister's face.

"What is it?" Chelsea asked.

"The county attorney just announced his reelection campaign. And at the same time, he announced an investigation and pending charges against our family and the Lattimores. He's saying that he believes both families have committed fraud. He used the word *conspiracy.*"

Chelsea took the phone, and although Ruby was scared to look, she stepped closer to see what all of the fuss was about. She instantly recognized the design of the local newspaper's website. There on the screen was a still image of an important-looking man named Nelson Redfield. The story was beneath it. Chelsea began scrolling, shaking her head. A few paragraphs in, Chelsea looked up at Morgan. "It says he was tipped off by *private* legal actions against the families, brought forth by another member of the Royal community. And it specifically mentions oil rights."

Ruby's mind immediately went to one person— Heath. Her stomach sank to her feet. "You don't think it could be…"

"It has to be Heath. Who else could it be?" Chelsea's voice was spilling over with distress. "Nolan worried that he'd do something like this. We need to go talk to both of them. Right now."

"I'm calling Vic. Maybe he knows what this means." Morgan took her phone from her sister and stalked back toward the register.

Chelsea rushed back into her dressing room, presumably to change her clothes, leaving Ruby standing there in shock. Her first instinct was to run down the street to find Heath and warn him that the Grandins, or at least Chelsea and possibly Morgan, were ready to blame him for all of this. There had to be another explanation.

Just as she was about to return to the dressing room, she caught sight of Nolan and Heath charging into the store. Nolan was leading the way, with Heath close on his heels.

"Where's Chelsea?" Nolan asked Ruby. All color had drained from his face.

"I'm here," Chelsea answered, bursting out of the fitting room. She flew past Nolan and headed straight for Heath. "What in the hell did you do?"

Heath froze. "I'm as confused as you are. I don't know how Nelson Redfield would have found out about anything I did. It was all between me and my lawyer."

Ruby rushed to Heath's side. "Between you and your lawyer? You were still pursuing legal action? I thought you decided not to do that."

"He's talking *criminal* charges, Heath," Chelsea blurted. "That means a trial. That means members of my family in jail. We could lose everything. And they're talking about it in the damn newspaper. Our reputations could be completely ruined."

Nolan placed his hands on his wife's shoulders. It partly looked like he wanted to calm her down. It partly looked like he needed to hold her back. "Hold on a second. Let's take a deep breath and talk this through. We don't need to start worrying about worst-case scenarios right away. A whole lot would need to happen before that. There has to be a way out of this."

"Just so everyone knows, I instructed my lawyer to drop the whole thing," Heath said. "All of it. So I don't see how I'm at fault here."

"But when, Heath? What was the timing?" Ruby's mind was racing, running through the chronology of their relationship. That first day they'd met, he'd gotten angry when he understood the timing of the first survey. But by the next day, he'd seemed ready to move on. Although there had been plenty of times he got upset about the Grandin and Lattimore families, he'd backed down every time. Ruby had assumed he was moving on. Moving *forward*. So that they could do that together.

Morgan strode over from the checkout counter and looked straight at her sister. "I just got off the phone with Vic. Mom and Dad were sent a threatening letter by Heath's lawyer on December 30. They didn't tell us because they were trying to keep it quiet until they figured out their next steps." Morgan turned and delivered a death stare to Heath. "They were waiting to see if you might change your mind."

"I *did* change my mind," Heath pleaded. "Why does no one understand that?"

"Hold on a minute," Nolan interjected and faced Heath. "December 30? You and I and Chelsea and Ruby went to the TCC together the next night. We had you over for dinner a week ago. And all that time, you were being nice to my wife's face while you were going after her family? What kind of sick person does that? And when in the hell are you going to finally let this go?"

Ruby saw the moment when Heath was deflated by his brother's words. She could see the conflict buried deep inside him bubbling to the surface. He'd talked a big game about letting go, but he couldn't. The memories of Ashley and his mother were that strong. His need to get justice for them was so powerful that it made him do things he was now ashamed of.

"Heath Thurston, you just won't rest until you destroy my family, will you?" Chelsea asked.

"And I suppose it's perfectly okay that your family destroyed mine," he snapped back at Chelsea. He then turned to Nolan. "*Our* family."

Nolan shook his head. "We have been through this and I've been extremely clear about it. If you make me pick a side, I'm picking Chelsea's. She's my wife, Heath. She's my whole life."

Ruby felt like her heart was being torn in ten different directions. She felt bad for everyone, but she couldn't ignore the other feeling that wouldn't go away. Heath wasn't the man she'd thought he was. All she could do was look back at their time together and realize that every moment she'd thought she was falling in love with him, he wasn't being truthful. What sort of future could they possibly have together under those circumstances?

"Chelsea and I are going." Nolan turned to Heath. "Fix this or I will never forgive you. And just so you know, there's still a good chance I will never forgive you."

Chelsea didn't even say a thing. She stormed back to the dressing room, grabbed her purse, kissed Morgan on the cheek, then walked right out of the store with Nolan at her side.

Heath watched as Chelsea and Nolan walked out of the Rancher's Daughter. *What a mess. What an absolute mess.* He turned to Ruby, needing her touch. Her reassurance. Her confidence in him. "This is not what I wanted to have happen. This was all an accident. A misunderstanding."

"Heath, the thing I'm struggling with right now is the timeline. I feel more than a little betrayed. I... I... I feel like you lied to me."

"Hey, you two." Morgan's tone was biting. "You're going to need to have your lovers' quarrel somewhere else. I'd like to close early for the day so I can go console my parents, who are now completely beside themselves."

Heath had felt plenty bad over the course of his life, but this was a new low—getting kicked out of a clothing boutique in the middle of downtown Royal. "Do you need help getting your things?" he asked Ruby.

"No. I got it. I need to change." She walked off for the fitting room, leaving only Heath and Morgan and the world's most uncomfortable silence.

"I'm going to fix this," he said to Morgan.

"Uh-huh. Right." Her voice dripped with sarcasm.

"Okay. I get it. You have zero confidence in me, but I am going to fix it."

"Let me put it this way. Your words don't mean a whole lot right now. Okay?" Morgan jangled her keys impatiently in her hand.

Of course, Heath had no earthly clue how he was going to fix this. He had no connections with Nelson Redfield, and how in the hell did you go about getting criminal charges dropped? Funnily enough, this news would have made him ecstatic six months ago. He would have been dancing in the streets. Now? He felt nothing less than utter devastation. He'd hurt the people he cared about most in this world, including his brother, just as they'd finally gotten back to a good place with their relationship. Heath might never forget the look on his brother's face when they'd been sitting down to breakfast, and the diner became abuzz with the news story. But even worse than that was the situation with Ruby. She'd used the word *betrayed*. How was he supposed to come back from that?

Ruby emerged from the dressing room, looking dejected. "I'm so sorry, Morgan. I'll come back to shop later."

"That sounds great. I look forward to seeing you. But please tell your boyfriend to stay at home next time. He's no longer welcome in my store."

Heath felt the anger rise up inside him. He had to rush to Ruby's defense, even when he knew that it would be far more advantageous if he held his head up and walked right out of the shop. "Morgan, please don't take it out on Ruby. She hasn't done a single thing to deserve it. You're welcome to be as mean as you want to me."

"I'll take that under advisement," Morgan said.

Ruby walked past Heath, shaking her head. "Please don't make it worse," she said under her breath, then kept going right on through the door.

Heath closed his eyes and pinched the bridge of his nose, then followed her outside. "Ruby. Please," he called after her. "Let me explain."

She was already nearly fifty yards ahead of him, taking hurried strides toward his truck. She didn't respond to his plea. She didn't turn back. Heath was smart enough to know when a woman was angry with him. Hell, he'd just stood there and taken it from Chelsea and Morgan, and it had hurt. But seeing Ruby's anger and disappointment was an entirely different experience. It cut him to the core. And he was desperate to make it stop.

He ran to catch up, but she was already at the truck,

standing at the passenger's door and avoiding eye contact. Heath clicked the fob and waited for Ruby to get in before he did the same. Part of him was worried she'd take off running the instant he climbed in and put on his seat belt. "Ruby, I'm so sorry that happened," he said once they were both inside. "It had to have been horribly embarrassing." He reached for her arm, needing to touch her. It created an ache square in the center of his chest.

She stared down at his hand on her, then shook her head and pulled her arm away, turning toward the window. "Drive, Heath. Just take me back to your place so I can get my car and go home."

Heath swallowed hard. "I think we should talk about this."

"Just drive." Uncomfortable silence filled the cabin of his truck like poisonous gas, making it hard to breathe. Ruby turned to him and their gazes connected. Her eyes were ringed in pink and full of pain. "Please drive, Heath. I'm begging you."

He didn't need any more persuading. Perhaps she was right. They just needed to get to his place. Cool off. Then they could figure out what to do next. He started the truck and headed home. A million thoughts tumbled through his mind. He had a lot of things to fix right now, and although the most logical place to start was with a long conversation with Albert, he was far more concerned with mending things with Ruby. Surely she would understand where he was coming from. She always had before. It was part of what had drawn him to her. Why would now be any different?

As he pulled into his driveway and headed up to the house, he decided that he would let Ruby take the lead on this. He'd done an excellent job digging himself a hole with his words. He didn't need to be in any deeper. He parked in front of the house and killed the engine, then opened his door, but Ruby didn't move. "Are you coming inside?"

She shook her head. "No. I'm going to leave in a minute. But I have a few things I need to say first, and I don't want to go back inside your house, and I don't want to stand outside and freeze to death."

Heath immediately closed his truck door. It wasn't worth arguing that they would be far more comfortable in his living room, sitting in front of a roaring fire with something strong to drink. "Of course. Whatever you want. Why don't you tell me what you're thinking? And don't hold back. Let it rip. I figure we might as well get it all out now."

She took several long breaths in through her nose and blew them out through her mouth, like she was trying to center herself. "You know what, Heath? I know that justice for your mother and sister means a lot to you." Her voice was already cracking with emotion, which made Heath's heart bind up into a tight ball. "But I had hoped that your better nature would win out. That you wouldn't break up another family's legacy just to fulfill your own."

"This isn't about *my* legacy. It's about my sister and everything she can't do because she's not here."

"Listen to what you just said. Ashley isn't here anymore. Neither is your mother. They're both gone. And I'm not sure you've come to terms with that. You can't get real justice for a memory. You can't. Anything you accomplish with a lawsuit will be for you. No one else."

The hurt in her voice was like a knife to the center

of his chest, but he accepted that he had to hear these things, even when he didn't fully agree. "I don't think that's entirely true. The foundation will help people. You've said it yourself. Plus, is it so wrong that it matters to me? I'm here. I'm not a memory. I'm sitting right here with you, Ruby. And I need you to understand where I was coming from when I made one last attempt at getting the Grandins and Lattimores to own up to their misdeeds."

"Do you think I don't understand that you're holding on to more than a memory?" she croaked. "I know the difference between someone being here and not being here. Every minute of my existence is wrapped around knowing the difference. I lived through that when I lost Lucas."

"And that's one of the reasons we grew so close so quickly. We have that shared experience. We are cut from the same cloth, Ruby."

"We are not the same. You have this need to get even. You're vindictive. And it's your vindictiveness that's gotten everyone into this situation. I thought I knew you, but clearly I do not."

At first Heath had no response to that. Ruby's words were still slicing through him. After a few weighty moments, he said, "I hope you realize that being vindictive is not a normal part of my personality. If I ever became that way, it was because of things others did. I didn't start this."

"And I'm so tired of hearing that story, Heath. At some point, you have to let it go."

"I did let it go. I have. I told my lawyer to drop the suit. I don't see why everyone doesn't understand that. I had no way of knowing Nelson Redfield would get wind of any of this. And if the Grandin and Lattimore families committed a crime, that's not my fault."

"That's not what I'm angry about. I'm angry because the whole time we've been together, we had dozens of talks about the importance of moving on. And now I know that you were just saying things that you didn't really mean. That whole time, you weren't actually moving on. How am I supposed to believe that anything between us was real? That it was anything more than sex?"

Heath could not believe what she was saying to him right now. Was her opinion of him really that poor? "You really don't believe that what happened between us was real? Do you have any idea how much that hurts me? I told you about my mom and my sister. I told you my deepest feelings about everything that happened to my family. That was all real to me. Just like it was real when you told me about Lucas."

Pink rose to the surface of Ruby's cheeks and her shoulders drew tight. "But it's not exactly the same, is it? I was going to spend the rest of my life with Lucas. My entire future was wrapped up in him. He took a piece of my heart with him. It will never be replaced. There will always be a part of me that is missing. And it's not coming back."

"Are you trying to say that romantic love is stronger than what I had for my family? I don't see how that makes any sense. Family is the beginning and the end."

"Family is about more than blood, Heath. It's about love and trust. You can make someone your family. You can also send them away."

"Well, that much is true. My brother did that."

"Please don't feel sorry for yourself."

"I'm not. These are facts." The frustration inside was so immense that he could hardly think straight. "You know, Ruby, you told me that you were disappointed in me, but I have to say that I feel the same way about you. You have always understood my side in this. What changed? What's different?"

She scanned his face as if she were looking for answers or deciphering a puzzle. "It's different because I love you."

Heath blinked several times. *That* he had not expected. And he didn't know how to respond. He was incredibly fond of Ruby. His mind and body wanted her. Needed her. But love? Already? It hadn't even been a month. He wasn't ready to say that, especially when she was so angry with him.

Ruby laughed quietly, but nothing about the situation was funny. "Okay, then. This is just like me. To go and fall in love with a man who I thought I knew, only to find out that he's a stranger. It's like I lost you, Heath. Just like I lost Lucas."

"And I'd like a minute to catch up, if that's okay with you." He kneaded his forehead. "Plus, isn't that a little melodramatic? We're having an argument. I'm not going anywhere."

"But I am." She leaned closer and kissed him on the cheek. "Take care of yourself. Please. Promise me that much." She opened her door.

"What are you saying?"

She hopped out of the truck and turned back to him, holding the door and boring into his soul with those brilliant green eyes of hers. "I can't do this, Heath. I can't. I need someone who's looking ahead to the future, not focused on the past. The past is where all of my hurt is.

I need to keep that where it is. Behind me." She closed the door and headed for her car.

Heath wasn't ready for this to be over. He couldn't let her leave. He leaped out of the truck and ran over to her. "You tell me you love me one minute, and in the next, you tell me it's over?"

She opened her car door and climbed inside, immediately turning on the engine. "And you didn't say a damn thing back to me. That told me all I needed to know."

"I need time, Ruby. That's all. I care about you a lot." *So much. More than anyone. Including myself.*

"Now you'll have all the time you need." With that, she closed her car door and sped down his driveway, kicking up gravel.

As Ruby disappeared in a cloud of dust, traveling away from his house and from him, it felt like she was dragging his heart behind her car. Part of him was gone now. It might never come back. It sent his mind into a downward spiral of pure chaos. And the one sentiment it kept circling back to was that the only reason he felt like this was that he loved her. He. Loved. Her. *Dammit. Dammit. Dammit. Why in the hell is my heart on a ten-minute delay?* He wanted to kick himself. If he could have figured out a way to make his boot meet his ass, he would have done it. More than once. He probably wouldn't have felt it, though. His body was too numb. He'd thought he'd experienced loss before, but this was something entirely different. It was like the earth had been yanked out from under his feet and now he was floating in space, aimless, with nothing or no one to rescue him. He'd been on his own before and he did not want to go back to being that man again. Moving forward? He couldn't do that if he didn't have Ruby.

He bent over and rested his hands on his knees, letting the cold work its way through his clothes and wondering what came next. Go inside? What was the point? His whole life had fallen apart, and either he was going to salvage it and piece it back together, or he was going to accept defeat. People had said countless horrible things about him, but one thing no one could dispute was that he was determined.

He climbed back in his truck and wasted no time getting to the main road. When he came to the stop, he had enough presence of mind to carefully look both ways. If he turned left, he'd be headed to Ruby's. But what could they possibly argue about now? He had to move the needle. He had to prove to her that he was the man she'd fallen in love with, not the man who mindlessly sought vengeance. Which meant he needed to turn right. That direction would eventually lead him to a place he did not want to go. A place he'd once been convinced was where pure evil resided. The instant the idea came into his head, he wanted to bat it away like a fly. But there was no other way. If he wanted to fix his relationship with his brother and convince Ruby that he really was the man she needed him to be, he was going to have to go through hell to do it.

With resignation so deep it registered as a burning ache in his belly, he sucked in a sharp breath, flipped on his turn signal and headed in the direction away from Ruby. He went right. Straight toward the Grandin family ranch.

Eleven

Heath's meeting with the Grandins never happened. They wouldn't even let him through the gates. Instead, Vic rode out on a horse and told Heath to get off their property. The *hell* off their *damn* property, to be exact.

So Heath shifted to plan B, which was to convince Albert to meet him on his day off, so they could discuss their options for getting Nelson Redfield to back off. They arranged a call with the man, and that was when Heath met his second roadblock—the county attorney was not playing around. He'd seen the original survey and he'd seen a copy of the oil rights, and although he refused to divulge his source, he wanted Heath to know that he agreed with him. The Grandins and the Lattimores had purposely deceived his mother, and his sister had been denied her birthright.

"You should be happy," he'd said to Heath. "They're finally going to pay for what they did."

To which Heath replied, "Except that I'm not. I don't want the Grandins or the Lattimores to get into trouble over this. What's done is done. It's water under the bridge." He could hardly believe those words had come out of his mouth, but it was his determination, and stubbornness, talking. He would do anything to fix this, all so he had a chance of fixing his relationship with Nolan and getting Ruby back.

"It's an election year, Mr. Thurston," Nelson said. "I can't drop it now. My constituents need to know I'm tough on crime. Any chance you'd be interested in a donation? We can always stand to print more yard signs when the time comes."

"I'm going to forget that you asked my client for money," Albert said right before he ended the call. Then he turned to Heath. "He wants a high-profile case to campaign on. That's all this is. Nelson Redfield cares about justice about as much as I care about losing weight and exercising more."

That gave Heath an idea. "Who's his opponent?"

"You want to dabble in local politics? That's a dangerous game."

Heath shrugged it off. Nothing could make his predicament worse. "I've been playing with fire this whole time."

That had been a week ago, which meant it had been that long since Heath had seen Ruby. Every day had been a test of his mental toughness. It was so hard not to see her, especially knowing that she was so nearby. He'd left a few messages for her, all of which hadn't been returned. He missed her so desperately that it felt like his entire body was hollow. He was a shell of a man, fueled by nothing other than tenacity and a refusal to fail. He would not let the actions of the old Heath steal the future the new Heath wanted, which was to be with Ruby. Forever.

As for that part, although he had left her those messages, he hadn't divulged the full breadth of his feelings. It didn't feel right to say it over the phone. He wanted to say it to her beautiful face. He needed to witness her reaction, if only to know that all of this had been worthwhile. He did manage to gather one piece of intel as to what she was up to—he'd gone to the hardware store to get a new latch for Lucky's stall door, and the woman working the register, who apparently had seen Ruby and Heath together at the Royal Diner, told him that he'd just missed her. She'd been in for some paint and drywall mud. It was nice to know what she was doing, but it also made him incredibly sad. She worked on her house when she was feeling down and lost. He hated the thought of her being unhappy. He knew that he could make things better for her, but the key to that was repairing the damage he'd done.

The real work of that was going to happen today, more than a week after the awful news of the criminal case had broken. He was about to do one more thing he'd never *ever* thought he would do. He was about to welcome the Grandins and the Lattimores to his home. This was not going to be a social visit, but he still felt as though he had to offer refreshments, so he was putting out tea and a cheese board with crackers. Also a bottle of bourbon because he was certainly going to need it. The hospitality was all his mother's doing. She might have struggled her whole life, but she was a Southern woman through and through, and she always offered guests a beverage and a snack of some sort. Always.

Heath hoped to hell this was going to work. No, he hadn't been successful in reaching Ruby and inviting her to come to this event, but he had at least convinced his brother and Chelsea. Although, to be fair, Nolan hadn't needed much persuading. He was desperate for all of this to go away. During the most recent phone conversation they'd had, Nolan had even expressed to Heath that he believed him. Nolan said he'd been angry when they were at the Rancher's Daughter, but it had subsided, which gave Heath something to cling to. Someone was on his side, and that person was immensely important to him—his twin brother.

Chelsea and Nolan were the first to arrive. Nolan offered a handshake rather than a hug, but Heath knew it was going to take time for their brotherly relationship to get fully back on the right track.

"I hope this works," Chelsea said, casting Heath a doubtful look.

"Alexa seemed happy with everything when she and I talked," Heath said. Alexa was a Lattimore, the elder daughter, who was a lawyer and representing the Grandin and Lattimore families.

"I'm glad to hear that. Alexa's a hard nut to crack. If she's happy, that gives me some optimism," Chelsea said, glancing at Nolan. "By the way, do you have a place where we can set up a laptop? My uncle Daniel wants to join us via videoconference."

Now, this was a new development. Daniel was the man believed to be Ashley's father, who lived in France and had very little interaction with the rest of the Grandin family. "Is there something I need to know?" Heath asked.

"Only that he wants to be involved. And I believe he has something he wants to say to you and Nolan." Chelsea reached for Heath's arm. It was a small gesture, but it meant the world to him. "Don't worry. I think it'll all be good. Barbara Lattimore reached out to him after she talked to Alexa. She likes bringing people together."

"Okay. Sounds good. We can set up the laptop on the entertainment center in the living room."

"I'll take care of that," Nolan said. "Have you talked to Ruby?"

Heath shook his head. "I haven't. I called and left a few messages, but she hasn't returned my call. I'm just hoping she doesn't hate me. Although, I would understand it if she did. I messed up. I made a huge mistake and I was wrong. That's what today is for. Apologies. I have a lot of them to make." He glanced out the window and his heart immediately started pounding. Out in his driveway was Victor Grandin Jr., Vic and Chelsea's father, and his wife, Bethany. Heath looked at Chelsea and Nolan. "I guess this is starting. Wish me luck."

Without hesitating, he headed for his front door, opened it and stepped out onto the porch. Ben and Barbara Lattimore, along with their daughter Alexa, were climbing out of their car. It was a surreal moment for Heath, standing there and facing the people who he'd been at war with, knowing that he was about to extend the olive branch and try like hell to make this all go away. "Thank you for coming. Please, come inside and grab a drink, and we'll get started."

Barbara Lattimore led the way, marching right up to Heath with her husband, Ben, right behind her. "Mr.

Thurston," Barbara said. "My husband and I look forward to hearing what you have to say."

Heath shook hands with them both. "Call me Heath. I hope that we can all part ways today with a clear path forward."

Their daughter Alexa joined them and shook hands with Heath. "It's nice to see you, Heath. Are we all good with the plan we discussed?"

Heath nodded eagerly. "Absolutely. Nolan and Chelsea have already arrived." The three strolled past him, leaving Heath to greet Victor Jr. and Bethany. "Mr. and Mrs. Grandin. Thank you for coming."

Victor Jr. glanced at his wife, then turned his attention to Heath, offering a firm handshake. "It takes a big man to do what you're doing."

Heath finally felt as though he could breathe. This wasn't going to be easy, but it was already going far better than he ever could've imagined. He let the last of his guests walk inside. Then he followed and closed the door. Everyone was either helping themselves to refreshments or had already settled in the living room, which was where Heath had planned to talk.

"Game time?" Nolan said, handing his brother a small glass of bourbon.

"I believe so."

"Good. I got Daniel all set up on the laptop. He's on right now. Good luck."

Heath slugged back his drink for courage, then strolled into the room and stood near the fireplace, which gave Daniel Grandin a good view of all in attendance. "I'm going to make this quick and to the point. I'd like to say that I made a mistake, but that's not entirely accurate. I've made dozens." He paused, soaking up the admission. "I led a vengeful crusade against your two families and it was wrong. I allowed my actions to be determined by anger and I didn't listen when anyone tried to point out the harm I was inflicting. And so I'd like to apologize. I am sorry for any and all pain I have caused. I am truly sorry." Heath took a moment to let the relief of getting that off his chest roll over him. A weight had been lifted. Already.

"Thank you, Heath. I think both families appreciate that," Alexa said.

"Well, I hope so. And if anyone needs to speak to me privately after this, please don't hesitate to ask." He drew in one more deep breath. "Which brings me to my plans to get Nelson Redfield to back off." With that announcement, everyone seemed to lean in to listen more closely. Heath went on to explain the complications of it being an election year and that he believed the county attorney's motivations were purely political. "Running for this office is all about holding on to power. Nelson Redfield has held this position for over twenty years, and I think everyone in this room knows that he really only surfaces when it's time to be reelected. No one has made a serious run at unseating him, but there's an amazing candidate named Lucia Vega up against him. Alexa speaks very highly of her. She's smart and young and she's hungry to go after real crime in our county. I'd like to encourage everyone in this room to throw their support behind Ms. Vega. It will be one part of the two-pronged approach I devised to get Mr. Redfield to drop his case."

"What's the other half of it?" Barbara asked.

"The other half is a PR campaign. Your two families are beloved in this community," Heath said. "Believe me. The ire I received by going after you was fierce. So let's let Nelson Redfield know that his plan is not going to be a popular one. We do that by publicly reminding everyone of your importance to Royal. Which is why I'd like to invite you to partner with my brother and me in the development of the Ashley Thurston Therapeutic Riding Center." Heath explained the mission of the center, as well as its financial needs. "I think it's a win-win for everyone. And of course, any donation will be fully tax-deductible."

Barbara looked at her husband and they both smiled. Then Ben turned to Heath. "We're in. You can count on the full support of the Lattimore family."

Victor Jr., who had been silent up until this point, cleared his throat. "We are, too. Of course." He directed his attention to Nolan and Chelsea. "I mostly just want Chelsea and our new son-in-law to know that we care and want to be a part of making things better between the families."

Heath breathed a huge sigh of relief. "This is fantastic. And I think it's the right call. My mother and sister might be gone, but this is the right thing to do in their memory." It was an immensely difficult thing to say. For as many times as he'd said that he was moving on from the deaths of his mother and sister, he hadn't really. That was the crux of why he'd been pursuing all of this. It had been too hard to accept that they were gone. "We have to move forward. This will pave the way."

"I believe my uncle Daniel would like to say something," Chelsea said.

Daniel straightened in his seat and leaned closer to his computer monitor. "Hey, y'all. I won't take up too much of your time. Heath and Nolan, I just want you to know that I truly did not know about Ashley. I had no idea, and I'm very sorry that I never got to know her. By all accounts, she was a lovely human being."

Yet again, Heath was confronted with the other side of the story. Ashley had missed out, but so had Daniel. He'd had a daughter who he hadn't had the privilege of knowing.

"What your mother and I shared was very nice, but it was fleeting," Daniel continued. "I was young and so was she. I honestly thought it was nothing more than a fling, and so I moved on. If I had known that she'd had a child and that she was mine, I would have come back to Royal. I would have proudly taken responsibility. And so I'm happy to contribute whatever you need to make Ashley's riding center a reality. And someday, I'd like to learn more about her from you both, Heath and Nolan. In the meantime, just tell me what you need and I'll make sure you get it."

Heath looked at Nolan and an entire conversation took place in a split second, all without words. Emotion welled up in Heath's eyes, but he kept it at bay.

"I have something that needs to be said as well." Barbara stood and looked at everyone in the room, one by one. She was an admirable woman, someone who did not beat around the bush or mince words. "My husband and I have talked about this a great deal. And I spoke to Miriam about it as well." Miriam Grandin was the matriarch of that family, in her late eighties. She was the widow of Victor Grandin Sr., who had died nine months ago, right before the question of the oil rights had come up. "Victor Sr. and Augustus Lattimore, my father-in-law, may have led the families well for decades, but they were misguided in many of their actions. What they did to cover up the birth of Ashley and her true family lineage was disgraceful. And every last person in this room has had to suffer because of it in one way or another. We can't go back and undo the past, but if we acknowledge it, we can heal. I think Heath has laid out a road map for us to follow, and I think we all need to thank him for that."

Heath was so choked up he could hardly see straight. The last thing he'd ever imagined was that anyone would thank him for anything. "I don't need the praise, but I do appreciate it. Really."

Barbara looked around the room one more time. "Can we toast to it? Because I think we could all use a drink."

Ruby was trying to finish up the last of the painting in her new closet, but she kept making mistakes. "Dammit," she muttered as she once again slipped with the roller and left a big smudge on the ceiling. "I'm going to have so much touch-up to do. It's ridiculous." Of course, it wasn't entirely a case of being clumsy. She was on edge. Chelsea had called her that morning to let Ruby know that Heath was having the Grandins and the Lattimores over to the Thurston ranch today so they could discuss a plan to get the county attorney to drop the case against the families.

Ruby could only imagine what might be going on. Screaming. Yelling. Throwing of sharp objects. Funnily enough, as much as Heath had been blamed for all of this, she didn't see him doing those things. No, she imagined him sitting at one end of one of the couches in his living room, patiently listening and waiting until there was a break in the conversation so that he could tell everyone why they were wrong. He was very good at arguing. So much so that Ruby had thought he might have a future as a lawyer.

She felt bad about everything that had happened. She knew that she'd been particularly hard on him when they'd had their argument in his driveway after the dustup at the Rancher's Daughter. Even so, nothing she'd said was untrue. She did need to move forward, and everything in Heath's actions had said that he wasn't ready to do that. But she still wondered if maybe this had been a stumbling block for him. That although there was a difference between what he did and what he said, it didn't change what he wanted. There was a very good chance that his desire to move ahead was real, but he hadn't known the right way to go about it.

The many messages he'd left for her had hinted at all of that. As reluctant as she'd been to take his calls, she did listen to the things he had to say. More than once. Sometimes she listened to them right before she went to bed, if only to have the comfort of his voice in the dark. He did sound sad. And he did sound sincere. But something was keeping her from reaching out to him. And she wasn't sure what it was.

She finished up the last of the painting, then gathered her supplies and went into her laundry room to wash things up in the utility tub. With that done, she went next to the living room to look at the clothes she'd piled on the sofa. Some of these things probably needed to be donated to the thrift store in town. As she sifted through the garments, she came across the dress that Heath had bought for her to wear to the party at the TCC. And it really struck her exactly how generous it had been of him to buy it for her. What was between them was so new at that point, and although there had been physical intimacy, she had stomped on the brakes, which he'd taken in stride. He had an immense capacity to understand and to be giving, even when the world had not always shown him those positive traits. When she'd told him that he was a good man, she'd been right. And she'd meant it.

The sound of Ruby's cell phone ringing took her by surprise. She flipped through the pile of clothes until she found the device. The caller ID said it was Chelsea. "Hey. Is everything okay? Did anyone end up in the hospital?" Ruby didn't want to sound melodramatic, but considering the outlandish things that had happened in the last month, it wasn't completely out of the question.

"No. Actually, everything is great. I can hardly believe I'm saying that, but it's true. Heath and Nolan are in the other room with my dad and mom, and Barbara and Ben Lattimore. They're chatting up a storm and having a great time."

Ruby struggled to understand how such a dramatic shift could have taken place. "What happened?"

"It's a long story, but the short version is that Heath worked his butt off to come up with a way out of this. And he apologized to everyone in a very beautiful way. He was so humble, and, well, he just basically proved to us all what an incredible man he is."

Ruby was so thrilled to hear this news, but it came at a price. "I feel horrible. He's been trying to reach me all week and I haven't called him back."

"He told us. You didn't want to talk to him?"

"It's not that. Actually, I think I just needed time to process my feelings. I'm a work in progress. There's not much more I can say than that."

"We all are, aren't we?"

"True. Very true." Ruby smiled, but it faded quickly. "And there's one other thing. I told him that I love him and he didn't say it back. It's hard to recover from that."

Chelsea's end of the line was quiet for a moment. "Can I tell you something about the Thurston men? They aren't great at admitting to their feelings. At least, not right away. I have zero doubt that he cares about you a lot. And that he wants to see you. I really think his actions today were motivated so much by his feelings for you. So, maybe give him another chance?"

Ruby really wanted to, but would it work? She wasn't sure. "I should at least talk to him, right?"

"Yes. Get your butt over here and talk to him. I know he would love to see you and it would absolutely make his day. It'll probably make his whole life."

"I just finished a painting job. I need to get cleaned up. It'll probably be an hour or so."

"From the sound of the laughter coming from the other room, I don't think he's going anywhere. Just get here when you can."

Ruby smiled, happy to have a way forward. "I will. And thank you, Chelsea. I really appreciate you reaching out."

"I like you a lot, Ruby. I hope you and Heath can sort it out. Then we can hopefully go shopping at the Rancher's Daughter and not have anything horrible happen."

"That sounds like fun." Ruby said goodbye to Chelsea, hung up the phone and headed straight for her bathroom. She showered as quickly as she could, nervous anticipation running through her body at full speed. She hoped that Heath would talk to her. She hoped that he would give her a chance to apologize, and hopefully that would mean a second chance at them being a couple. She dressed in jeans and the same sweater she'd been wearing the day they met. It was a sentimental choice, harking back to the beginning. As much as she'd told him it was important to move forward, it was okay to look back sometimes. Hair and makeup took a bit longer than she would have liked, but she wanted to look good. A final spritz of perfume and she was ready to go.

She stopped at the front door to pull on her boots, but something caught her eye as she glimpsed the living room—the bar cabinet. Lucas's bourbon collection was in there. Heath was its rightful owner, as far as she was concerned. Lucas would have wanted a true connoisseur to have it. She ran back to the guest room, grabbed an empty cardboard box and started carefully packing up the bottles. With that complete, she felt as though she could leave.

With a click of her fob, she raised the tailgate on her SUV and was sliding the box into the back when she heard a car kicking up gravel on her road. She turned and saw Heath's big black truck coming toward her. She was more than a little confounded. Chelsea had said he was busy socializing at the house. When had he decided to leave? And why had he decided to come here?

He parked right alongside her car and hopped out. "Please don't tell me you're moving, Ruby. Why are you loading boxes into your car?"

A grin crossed her face, and she sighed for good measure. He was so handsome it was worth marking the moment. "Not moving. I was bringing you a gift."

He stepped closer and glanced in the back of her car, then looked at her with pure astonishment on his face. "The bourbon collection? For me?"

She grasped his arm, needing to touch him. "I figured I had to apologize. I shouldn't have gotten so upset with you that day. I should have given you the benefit of the doubt. I'm so sorry."

Heath shook his head so fast it messed up his hair. "No. Ruby. I'm the one who's sorry. And before we get any deeper into this conversation, can I please just tell you that I love you?"

The words went into her ears, registered in her brain, and the next thing she knew, she was flattening herself against his solid chest and wrapping her arms around his waist. "You do?"

He pulled her in even tighter, kissing the top of her head. "I knew that I loved you, but I hadn't admitted it to myself. I think I never thought that you would fall for me. I always thought I would be the one doing the falling."

Ruby reared back her head. "What? Did you really think that?"

He nodded. "I did. I'm not always the sharpest tool in the shed."

A laugh escaped her lips. "Oh, shush. You're brilliant. From everything Chelsea said, you really saved the day today. I can't believe you figured it all out."

"Chelsea called you?"

"She did. I think she feels just as bad about everything that happened that day at Morgan's shop."

"Maybe we should forget the whole thing."

"I think that sounds like an excellent idea."

"Well, we're not out of the woods yet, but I think we have a solid plan, and most important, we're all on the same page. No more warring between families."

She smiled and peered up into his face. It was a

chilly afternoon, but she didn't care. Heath was all of the warmth she needed. "That's so great. I don't want there to be any more war. All I want is peace and happiness. Especially between us."

"Good. Because that's exactly what I want, too." He brushed aside a lock of her hair. "You and I have talked so many times about how hard it is to say goodbye. But I don't ever want to say goodbye to you, Ruby." Pulling her closer, he planted a soft and sensuous kiss on her lips. "Tell me I don't have to say goodbye."

Ruby was nearly floating from the kiss. "From now on, we only say hello."

Epilogue

Seven months later

Heath had hoped for better weather today, but apparently that wasn't meant to be.

"Clouds? How can it be this overcast in the middle of August in Texas?" he asked Ruby as he poured himself a cup of coffee and peered out through the kitchen window. This view out onto his property was especially beautiful this time of year, with the meadow of perennial wildflowers planted by his mother years ago in full bloom. August was one of his favorite months in Royal. He loved the first taste of summer heat, the way the air was sweet and sticky, but not quite suffocating yet. "It's supposed to be a happy day. When I think of happy, I think of sunshine."

"It *will* be a happy day, regardless of whether or not

there are a few clouds." Ruby was seated at the kitchen island, drinking coffee and reading on her phone.

Of course, she was right. And in many ways, she was the only sunshine he needed. "Thank you for telling me to stop being so negative without actually pointing out that I was in fact being negative."

"That's my job. Kindly putting you on notice." She cleared her throat and slid her mug across the kitchen island. "Like now. Refill, please."

He happily obliged her request, then walked the cup around to her. "What if it rains?"

"Then it rains and people get wet if they don't bring an umbrella."

"Should we call everyone and tell them to bring one?"

Ruby sighed and set her phone aside. "I know you want everything to be perfect, but it's not possible, okay? It doesn't mean today won't be great. I promise it will." She ended her long string of assertions with a smile, probably knowing he could never disagree with her when she had that look on her face.

Indeed, he did want the opening of the Ashley Thurston Therapeutic Riding Center to be perfect. But simply the fact that they'd gotten this far was enough. "I'm so glad you're here for this. I couldn't do it without you." He couldn't fathom what today would be like without her. "Now we should probably sit down and look through the to-do list. Just to make sure we don't miss anything."

Ruby dropped her head to one side. "Heath. Do you really think I would let anything go undone? I want you to enjoy today. This is your victory lap. Take it. I promise you that everything will be perfect."

Good God, he loved her so much. She was the one person on the planet who enjoyed taking care of him. It was such a delicious change of pace. He'd spent his first thirty-three years on this earth worrying about others. "Have I told you lately how much I love you?"

She smiled. "Last night before we went to bed, but I wouldn't mind hearing it again."

"I love you, Ruby Rose Bennett. More than you will ever know." Although, Heath had a plan for later today that involved showing her exactly how much he loved her. And he hoped like hell that it would be met with an affirmative response. He didn't know what he would do if she said no.

"I love you, too, Heath. I hope you know that."

"I do, but just like you, I also enjoy hearing it on a regular basis."

An alarm on his smartwatch went off. "Can you at least run me through the schedule for today?"

"Of course." Ruby sipped her coffee. "The caterer arrives at ten. They'll be setting up everything. Lunch, the bar, the tables and chairs out on the back patio. Guests arrive at eleven. The signs are all posted to direct everyone to park at the riding center. You'll give your speech. We'll do the ribbon cutting. Then you and Nolan can give everyone a quick tour of the stables and the riding corrals, and everyone will get to meet the horses, too."

"I still can't believe I have to make a speech."

"After everything everyone has been through, I think it's only fitting that you're the one to finally put the last positive spin on everything."

Heath sucked in a deep breath, fighting back the nerves that threatened his morning calm. "I suppose you're right."

"Then after that, everyone will drive back up here to the house. The caterer will have everything ready, so all we need to do is have lunch and socialize. I think we should be all done by two or three at the latest, depending on how long everyone decides to stay."

As thrilled as Heath was about everything today, he was nervous about the socializing part. It had been about two months since the county attorney had officially dropped the case against the Grandin and Lattimore families, but he still worried about whether enough time had passed for everyone to feel as though they could truly move on. "I can't wait until this is over."

"But you've been looking forward to it for weeks."

"I know. But I also just want to move ahead and get to the business of doing the actual work. You know, getting the people who will benefit from this here onto the ranch and riding. That's all that matters to me."

"And that's why I love you, Heath Thurston. You don't care about the spotlight. You care about getting things done."

"Exactly why I'm not super excited to give a speech."

"Which is why I'm here. To force you to do things you don't want to do. Like go get in the shower. Your brother and Chelsea are going to be here in forty-five minutes."

"You don't want to join me?" he asked with a bob of his eyebrows.

"Normally, yes. But I have things I need to do."

It was probably for the best. If he was going to have that time with her, he didn't want to rush. "I'll go get ready."

"Sounds good."

Heath walked down to their bedroom and got cleaned up, then dressed in a pale blue dress shirt and dark jeans, trying to strike the balance between looking nice, staying cool, and recognizing that he was going to have to show folks around a horse barn in a few hours. By the time he walked back out to the main part of the house, he saw that the caterers had arrived early and had already taken over his kitchen. Outside, they were setting up a tent to provide respite from the August sun, and luckily enough, protection from the rain if they needed it.

"This is a bit of a surprise," he said to Ruby.

"Tell me about it. I guess better early than late, but I still need to get dressed."

"You go. I'll be here if anyone has any questions."

Ruby popped up onto her tiptoes and kissed his cheek. "I'll be right back."

Heath walked out to the back patio. The caterers were setting up tables and bringing in all sorts of supplies for lunch. He kept waiting for someone to ask him a question, but Ruby had apparently done an excellent job in preparing them. They knew exactly what they were doing, so he walked back inside. He stopped at the built-in cabinets in the living room, opened a drawer and peeked inside, just to make sure a very important item was still there. He was about to pull it out when he heard Nolan's voice.

"Knock, knock," Nolan said.

Heath slammed the drawer closed and hustled into the foyer, watching as Nolan closed the door behind Chelsea.

"Hey, you two," Heath said, embracing his brother and then Chelsea. "Ruby should be out in a second."

"I'm right here," Ruby said, emerging from the hall that went back to the master bedroom. She gave Nolan and Chelsea a hug, then stepped to Heath's side.

"So, we have news. And we thought now was a good time to deliver it," Nolan said, looking conspiratorially at Chelsea.

"I'm pregnant!" Chelsea exclaimed.

Heath didn't know who to hug first, but since Ruby immediately descended on Chelsea, that left his brother. As they embraced, Heath was overwhelmed with gratitude and joy, while he was also struck by the feeling that their mom and sister should be here for this. It brought a bittersweet edge to an otherwise perfect moment. "I am *so* happy for you guys," Heath said.

Chelsea smiled and touched her belly. "It's still early. I'm about three months along."

"A winter baby. How exciting," Ruby said.

"We're really happy. Now we just need to get our house going. As you know, we haven't had any luck pinning down our contractor on a start date, and the lease on the loft is just about up. We need to figure out a plan," Nolan said.

"We do *not* want to move in with my parents. I love them, but no," Chelsea added. "And of course, my real worry is that we won't have a place to be settled in when the baby comes."

That gave Heath an idea, but he was going to need to speak to Ruby about it first. "Well, congratulations. It's really amazing."

"We should probably head down to the stables," Ruby said. "We don't want the guests arriving before us."

"Good point," Heath said.

The four of them piled into Heath's truck and rode

down one of the access roads that bisected the ranch until they were at the far end of the property. Heath wasn't sure he'd ever tire of seeing the riding center now that it was complete. There was the welcome center, complete with classrooms, offices for staff and other administrative purposes. The stable was state-of-the-art with full climate control for the horses and easy access for loading in feed. Beyond that were three corrals— one open-air, one covered and another that was fully enclosed so that the center could be used year-round. Heath had spared no expense in making his sister's dream come to life. He hoped it would be standing for a very long time.

Ruby was so full of pride for Heath's accomplishment when they arrived at the riding center that she felt like her heart might burst. It was such an honor to be part of this momentous day.

"It's so beautiful," Chelsea said when they got out of the truck.

"My brother did a fantastic job," Nolan said, clapping Heath on the back.

"We *both* did a fantastic job. It was a joint effort. As it should have been."

Off in the distance, Ruby saw a car turn onto the main access road for the riding center. "It looks like the first of the guests are here."

"That's Ryan and Morgan in that first car. I can't wait to love on my niece," Chelsea said as Nolan and Heath walked toward the main corral.

Ruby hadn't even known that Morgan was pregnant when she first met her, but she was. Morgan had given birth to a little girl named Cora about two weeks ago. Ruby had only seen her a few times, but she had the most adorable head of bright red hair, just like her mama. "There's Alexa and Jackson," Ruby said, referring to Alexa Lattimore and her husband, Jackson Strom. "Hold on a minute. Is that a baby bump I see?"

Chelsea elbowed Ruby. "Yes. Morgan told me Alexa is pregnant. It's a bit surprising. She doesn't seem like the mommy type, but apparently they're very happy."

"That's so great," Ruby said. "Looks like we're about to have a real crowd." She pointed at the growing line of cars pulling up the drive to the parking lot. "I'd better go talk to Heath about his speech."

Ruby found Heath and Nolan down in the spot where they planned to do the dedication, in a lovely grassy spot. Right next to it was the main corral, which was occupied solely by Lucky. Heath thought she should be there to represent Ashley. The brothers were both stroking Lucky's head.

"Everyone will be here any minute."

Heath looked past her. "Looks to me like we've already got a capacity crowd. It's Grandins and Lattimores for days. Even Daniel Grandin flew in from Paris."

That alone was full evidence of just how much things had changed in the last seven months. When she'd met Heath, those names were like poison in his mouth. Now he talked about them like friends, and there was zero controversy in bringing up the topic. It was such a welcome relief. "Are you nervous?"

Heath was wringing his hands. "A little. Like I said earlier, I want to get past this part. So we can get on with our life." He pulled Ruby closer and kissed her cheek. "Thank you for being here today. I couldn't do any of this without you."

"It's my absolute pleasure. And just so you know, I think your speech is going to be fantastic." Ruby strode over to the arriving guests, waving them closer and directing them where to stand. Heath had been adamant about no chairs, since he wanted this to be very short and sweet. After ten minutes or so, it seemed as though everyone was ready. Ruby gave Heath the go-ahead with a nod of her head.

"Thank you, everyone, for coming today as we mark the opening of the Ashley Thurston Therapeutic Riding Center. My brother, Nolan, and I are so happy that you could join us for this important day. As many of you know, this was a dream of our sister's, and it means a lot to be able to bring it to fruition, for the enjoyment of the entire Royal community. It would not have been possible without the generous donations of both the Grandin and Lattimore families. I want to give special thanks to Vic Grandin, who called in many favors with his friends in construction. Vic made our impossibly tight deadline possible." Everyone in the crowd clapped, no one as much as Heath did. He and Vic had actually become friends, which was its own miracle. "So I hope everyone will enjoy a quick tour of the facilities and then join us up at the house for lunch."

Another round of applause followed the end of Heath's speech, and then everyone descended upon him and Nolan. Ruby hung back, letting Heath have his moment in the sun, and just enjoying watching him as he gave tours and talked about bringing Ashley's vision to life. It was so endearing to see the time and attention he gave to everyone he interacted with. One thing no one could accuse Heath Thurston of was being ungenerous.

After an hour or so, everyone drove up to the house, where they all had a lovely lunch of what Ruby had learned was Ashley's favorite midday meal, a chicken Caesar salad with warm yeast rolls and iced tea, followed by his mother's favorite dessert, lemon icebox pie. It all went off without a hitch, exactly as Ruby had planned it. Bellies full and hearts bursting with the loveliness of the day, one by one the guests all said goodbye. Nolan and Chelsea were the last to leave.

"Goodbye, Nolan," Heath said. "We did good today."

"You did good, brother. And I couldn't be any more proud."

Ruby and Chelsea watched as they shared an extended embrace. It was a touching moment, in the midst of a day chock-full of happy times. "I hope you continue to feel well," Ruby said to Chelsea.

"Thanks. I'd love your help picking out baby clothes, if you're ever up for more shopping."

Ruby hugged Chelsea. "Sounds great. Text me."

Heath and Ruby stood in the driveway and watched as his brother and Chelsea drove away. Then they headed back inside. Now that everyone had gone, Ruby wanted a chance to bring something up with Heath, but she was a little nervous about it. He'd been so stressed about today. Unveiling the riding center had been a massive undertaking, right on the heels of building it. Maybe it wasn't best to put a big question in his lap. Would he think it was too soon? Would he think she was moving too fast? "Hey, Heath. I was thinking about something," she said as they walked into the kitchen.

"Oh, no. Not that." He reined her in with his strong arms, the one place she always wanted to be.

"Stop joking around. I'm serious."

He adopted a far more stern look on his face. His forehead wrinkled with concern. "Okay. Go."

"Well, I can't stop thinking about what Nolan and Chelsea said. That the contractor can't start on their house yet. With the baby coming, I know that's got to be incredibly stressful for Chelsea. And let's face it, even if they broke ground today, there's no way a custom home is going to be ready to move into in six months. You had to move heaven and earth to get the riding center built in that time, and that didn't require everything a home will."

"Right. And it's pretty clear that she hates the idea of having to move back home with her parents." Heath pressed his lips together tightly. "I was thinking about suggesting that they come and live here, but I wanted to talk to you about it first. I wouldn't want to make a decision like that without you."

"Well, I actually had a different idea. What if we let Nolan and Chelsea move into my house? It's completely finished and the perfect size for a young family. They could set up a real nursery and have their own space."

A deep crease formed between Heath's eyes. "So you're saying you want to move in here?"

Ruby was confounded by his tone. It was so stern. "I am. But hold on. What did you mean when you said that you wouldn't want to invite them to live here without talking to me first? It's your house."

Heath pinched the bridge of his nose. "I should know better than to plan anything. It never works out exactly

the way I want it to." He started for the living room.
"Come on."

"Heath. What is going on?" she asked, shuffling after
him. "Are you angry? Are you upset with me?"

He stopped in front of the entertainment center, but
didn't turn back to her. "No. Quite the contrary. But I
need you to stop talking and close your eyes."

"Now I'm super confused."

"Like I said, no talking."

"Okay. My lips are sealed." Ruby stood as still as a
statue, unsure what he was doing, but trusting that there
was a reason behind his strange behavior.

"Okay," Heath said. His voice was inches away.
"Open your eyes."

Ruby gasped. There before her was Heath on bended
knee with a small box from a jewelry store in his hand.
"Heath. Is this why you've been acting so antsy today?"

"Yes. The stuff with the riding center was fine. This
was the real thing I was nervous about." He smiled
and encouraged her with a nod of his head. "Please.
Open it."

She took the box from his hands and popped it open.
Inside was a beautiful solitaire diamond, surrounded
by rubies, in a platinum setting. It was so beautiful, she
couldn't even touch it. Nor did she know what to say.

"I don't just want you to think about moving in,
Ruby. I want to know if you'll marry me."

She blinked at him as tears started to roll down her
cheeks. "I… I…" No matter how hard she tried, the
words would not come out.

"Hold on. I just want to say one more thing."

"Before you do that, will you please stand up?"

"I thought you'd never ask. These floors are murder

on my knee." He straightened to his full height and gathered himself, then took her hand. "Today was a chance for me to honor two very important women in my life. But I'm hoping that you'll become the most important woman in my world. My wife. Will you marry me?"

She nodded so many times she was surprised she wasn't flinging tears all over the room. With one hand, she took the box with the ring in it, and with the other, she clasped the side of his head and brought his lips to hers. "I love you so much, Heath. Of course I will marry you. I can't wait to marry you."

He took the ring from the box and slid it onto her hand. She wiggled her fingers, watching the beautiful stones catch the light. "I not only went with rubies because of your name, but you also told me you were a nerd for rocks. These are the best rocks I could find."

She giggled so hard she nearly couldn't stop. "You can be a real goof, Heath. And I love you for it."

He laughed quietly. "I'll take goof over bullheaded any day. And I love you, too, Ruby Rose Bennett. More than you'll ever know."

* * * * *

ONE NIGHT ONLY

JAYCI LEE

In memory of Jae W. Chon.

Prologue

When Megan Han and her sisters performed as the Hana Trio, the sound of her violin, Angie's cello and Chloe's viola came together as one—as *hana*—to create the music of their hearts. The thrill, joy and fulfillment Megan derived from being a part of the trio couldn't be matched. She was living her dream—a dream she shared with her sisters—and she wouldn't have it any other way.

But lately, she felt a restlessness stirring inside her. She didn't know what it meant to stand on her own. A part of her felt transparent, like she wasn't a fully realized person yet. Maybe that was why she had agreed to play rock violin at the Tipsy Dahlia, a seedy nightclub in Hollywood, on the same night the Hana Trio was performing in the Chamber Music Society's last concert of the season. The timing wasn't ideal, but no-name performers—she didn't mention she was part of the Hana Trio—couldn't be choosers.

The electric violin was a recent preoccupation of hers *plus* she wanted to know if she could move an audience without her sisters and the clout of the Hana Trio. She wouldn't necessarily call this a rebellion, since she could do whatever the hell she wanted with her free time, but it did feel like her little secret. Something that was hers alone. She wasn't entirely sure how she felt about that. Probably both excited and scared.

The burst of applause snapped her out of her reverie and returned her to the backstage of the concert hall. Megan clapped along with the audience from behind the curtains. The Chamber Orchestra had performed beautifully.

"I can't believe it's the final night of the season," Chloe said, shaking her head.

"I know. Concert season feels grueling sometimes, but I'm going to miss playing in front of a big audience." Angie sighed. "Nothing matches the energy of these concerts."

"Well, let's go out there and generate enough energy to carry us through the off-season." Megan smoothed her hand down her claret, floor-length dress. "It's show-time, ladies."

She and her sisters were met by resounding applause as they strode onto the stage. Megan put her hand on her chest and smiled at the audience, filled with gratitude. The Hana Trio had gained renown in the last couple of years, due in part to the piece they were performing tonight—the string trio Angie's husband, Joshua Shin, had composed for them. Since they premiered the work last season, it had become one of their signature pieces and a definite fan favorite.

Silence fell around them when they took their seats. Megan brought her violin under her chin and held her sisters' eyes. With a subtle nod, she lowered her bow to the strings, and the first dulcet strains of the string trio filled the auditorium.

The beauty of the piece pulled her under its spell and she swayed with the music, playing the violin with her whole body. Her sisters danced and moved on each side of her, melody and harmony spilling from their instruments. She always imagined that they looked like three lithe trees, waving in the wind—their movements unsynchronized but graceful.

The concert hall remained eerily quiet as the last notes echoed into silence. Then, as though snapped awake by a hypnotist, the entire audience jumped to their feet, clapping in a quick staccato. Megan and her sisters rose from their seats and bowed deeply. Once, then twice. Her heart pounded with adrenaline and euphoria as they walked off the stage.

"I'm so proud of you guys." Angie hugged Chloe, then Megan, balancing her cello with one hand.

"We're proud of you, too." Megan returned her older sister's one-armed hug, holding her violin to the side.

"Don't forget Joshua," her younger sister chimed in. "We should give him some credit for writing that masterpiece."

"Thank you, Chloe," Joshua said, walking up to them. "You three sounded magnificent."

He wrapped his arm around Angie's waist and dropped a kiss on her forehead with tender affection. Megan watched the exchange with a dreamy sigh. Her soul mate would find her someday. She just wished he would stop taking his sweet time about it.

"I know I can't top praise like that from the composer himself." Their dad joined them backstage, beaming with pride. "But you girls played beautifully. It almost takes away the sting of not having any of my daughters follow in my footsteps."

He hugged Megan and Chloe but hesitated in front of her older sister. With a soft smile, Angie wrapped her arms around his waist and embraced him. His eyes closed for a second as though he wanted to commit the moment to his memory. Angie and their dad had been estranged for over six years until they began mending their relationship last year.

"Ahbunim." Joshua bowed from his waist.

"It's good to see you, son." Their dad patted his back before waving over a couple who had been standing a little apart from the group. "Girls, you remember Mr. and Mrs. Werner."

"You three have grown into such lovely, talented women," Anne Werner said with a tremulous smile. "Your mom would've been so proud."

Their dad was the CEO of Jigu Corporation, a thriving electronic components company, and Anne was a member of the board of directors. She had also been a dear friend of their mom's, who'd passed away from breast cancer seven years ago.

"Thank you, Anne," Megan said, squeezing her tightly. Her sisters joined in for a group hug.

"I also wanted to introduce you to our new CFO—" their dad glanced around with a perplexed frown "—but he didn't make it to the concert. He probably got held up at work."

"Such disrespect." Anne snorted with uncharacteristic disdain. "Minsung, I told you that young man is too arrogant for his own good."

"You're mistaking confidence for arrogance," he said evenly. "He's going to take Jigu Corporation to the next level. You'll see."

"Now, Anne." Tim Werner put his hand on his wife's shoulder when she took a deep breath in preparation for a retort. "Don't you think you should save the business talk for another time? Tonight is about the Hana Trio and the Chamber Music Society."

"Well said, Tim." Their dad clasped his hands together. "We should go out and celebrate. All of us."

"I, um…" Megan took a quick glance at the clock. *Crap.* She had less than an hour to get dressed and make it to Hollywood for her rock violin debut. She yawned loudly. "I am *exhausted.* I'm going to turn in early."

"Then, I'll come home with you," their dad said, concern clouding his expression. Guilt twisted in her gut. She hated lying, even when it was harmless. She just wasn't ready to share her rock violin debut with anyone yet, especially since she might bomb and prove once and for all that she was nothing without her sisters.

"Don't be silly. You should go celebrate with them. We drove separately anyway. I'll see you tomorrow morning, Appa." Before anyone could respond, she picked up her dress and hurried away from her family and friends. "Have fun, guys. Bye. Good night."

Alone in the dressing room—while her fellow musicians lingered backstage celebrating the last concert of the season—she stepped out of her formal dress and tugged on a pair of tight, ripped jeans and a black bustier top. Holding a hair tie between her lips, she shook her tasteful curls out as though she had a spider crawling in her head and pulled her tousled hair into a high ponytail. Then she made quick work of applying some charcoal eye shadow and a deep purple lipstick.

Megan smiled at the stranger looking out at her from the mirror. This was too much fun. Not wanting to explain her attire to anyone, she slipped out of the dressing room and made a beeline for her car. By the time she started the engine and drove out to the street, she was down to forty-five minutes. She pushed her candy-red Carrera as fast as she dared, swerving in and out of lanes. She could almost hear her little sister lecturing her that driving like an asshole would only get her to her destination an average of three minutes faster.

Well, she needed every minute she could scavenge. She refused to be late for her first performance. She might have decided to perform on an impulsive whim, but she was a professional musician and she couldn't keep her audience waiting. But two blocks from the concert hall, her car slowed and sputtered. She barely had time to pull over to the curb before it died on her with a soft whine.

"No, no, no." She grabbed and shook the steering wheel as though she could wake her car up. When that didn't work, she stomped to the rear of the vehicle and popped the hood to take a look at the engine. She grabbed her forehead and cursed. "I don't even know what I'm supposed to check."

A black Maserati pulled out of traffic and parked behind her. *Thank heavens for Good Samaritans.* Curious who her rescuer might be, she craned her neck to watch as a man stepped out of the car—a tall, gorgeous man with black hair swept off his forehead, deep coffee-brown eyes and amazing cheekbones. She would literally kill for his bone structure.

Megan belatedly realized his distractingly scrumptious lips were moving. She gave her head a sharp shake and said, "I'm sorry. What was that?"

"Do you need some help?" he asked in a sexy baritone, coming to stand next to her.

"Yes, my car went belly-up." She stared at her engine again to stop herself from ogling the stranger.

"I can take a look." He unbuttoned his dress shirt at the wrist and rolled up his sleeve, revealing a superb forearm. "Do you want to try starting the engine?"

"Yeah. Of course." When she stood unmoving—waiting for him to unveil his other forearm—he cocked his head in question. "I mean, sure. I'm going now. To start the car."

She almost fanned her face when she got in the driver's seat but caught herself just in time. What was she? Twelve? She was practically swooning over the man. *Have some dignity, Megan.* Besides, now was not the time. She had to get to the club. She couldn't be late for her performance. As she reached for the ignition switch, her eyes were drawn to something on the dashboard.

"No." She shook her head in denial. "Please, no."

But the fuel gauge revealed the truth about her predicament. Her car hadn't broken down. She apparently had forgotten to put gas in it. Megan lightly banged her head against the steering wheel. She'd chosen the worst day to fail at adulting.

"Is everything all right?"

Megan sat up with a surprised yelp. Right. The Good Samaritan. She'd been so busy beating herself up that she didn't even notice that he'd come to stand by her door.

"Yeah, um, hi." A fierce blush sprang to her cheeks.

"Hi." A corner of his lips quirked for a split second. "Are you okay?"

"I'm fine." She blew out a long breath. "But I'm an idiot. I know what's wrong with my car. It's out of gas."

His eyebrows shot up on his forehead, but his voice was judgment free when he said, "Well, I'm glad you figured out the problem."

"Yes. Thank you for stopping to help," she mumbled. Too embarrassed to meet his eyes, she grabbed her phone and opened her rideshare app. But she was in Los Angeles past nine o'clock on a Saturday. No driver would arrive in time to take her to Hollywood. "I'm so screwed."

"What's wrong?" That ghost of a smile touched his lips again as he added, "Other than being stranded on the side of the road."

"I'm supposed to perform at a club in Hollywood, but I don't think I'll be able to make it on time." She clicked on another app and sighed. "It's peak time for rideshares."

"I would offer to give you a lift, but I'm supposed to meet someone at the Chamber Music Society performance."

It was her turn to offer him a sympathetic smile. "Sorry, but that concert ended almost half an hour ago."

"Shit." He raked his fingers through his hair, straightening to his full height. After a moment, he said, "I guess that means I can give you a lift to Hollywood."

Accepting a ride from a complete stranger might be the dumbest thing she had done in her adult life, but the musician in her balked at the idea of missing her debut performance. And she trusted the man on a basic level—nothing in her was yelling "run for your life"—and her intuition was never wrong. Besides, tonight was about leaving her comfort zone and embarking on something new.

"I'm going to shamelessly take advantage of your kindness." She caught her bottom lip between her teeth, hoping she wouldn't regret this.

"By all means," he said with a gracious nod.

Megan grabbed her violin and locked up her car. Luckily, it had stopped at a street that allowed parking from 9:00 p.m. to 6:00 a.m., so she could come back with a can of gas after the performance. They walked over to his Maserati and he opened the passenger door for her. She was oddly reassured by the old-fashioned gesture. Whoever heard of a criminal with good manners?

After tapping the Tipsy Dahlia into his navigation app, he maneuvered the car into the street. She took a moment to study his profile from under her lashes, her heart drumming in her chest. She couldn't remember the last time she'd been so attracted to a man—probably because she'd never been this attracted to anyone before. The magnetic pull he had on her was both heady and unnerving.

"You're not an ax murderer or anything, are you?" she asked to curb the lust simmering in her blood.

"Shouldn't you have asked me that before you got in my car?" He arched an eyebrow at her, amusement dancing in his eyes. A delicious shiver traveled down her back. "But no, I've never owned an ax."

She laughed and relaxed into her seat. "I'm Megan, by the way."

"I'm Daniel," he said, glancing sideways at her. His

eyes lingered on her face and she felt heat rising to her cheeks. "Nice to meet you."

"Thank you for coming to my rescue." She looked down at her hands, suddenly feeling shy.

"My pleasure." His deep voice felt like a caress against her skin, and goose bumps spread on her arms. "May I ask what you're performing tonight?"

"Something I've never done before," she confessed. "I'm playing rock violin at the club."

"I'm intrigued," he said in a way that made her wonder if he was talking about her performance or *her*. "Is that your violin?"

"Yes, my electric violin." She patted the case she had tucked to one side of her legs. It was a glorious, edgy beauty—bright, shiny and red.

"I'm looking forward to hearing you play," he said.

"You're going to stay?" She couldn't hold back her grin.

"I can't think of a better way to spend the evening." He smiled back at her. It was a hint of a smile, really—small and slightly crooked—but it made her breath catch in her throat.

She shouldn't read anything into it. He was just curious about what a rock violin performance looked like. Well, she was curious, too, since she had never been to one herself, much less performed in one. Hopefully, she would make it there on time. She was certain she would lose her slot if she was late. The easy conversation in the car trickled to a stop as she anxiously stared at the dashboard clock.

"What time is your performance?" he asked.

"Ten." She squirmed a bit in her seat.

"We'll make it." His reassurance—and the slight lurch of the car as he sped up—eased some of her worry.

They drove up to the front of the club at precisely three minutes before ten. Grabbing her violin, she opened the door and stepped one foot on the sidewalk.

She paused long enough to say, "Thank you so much."

Megan skidded inside the Tipsy Dahlia with two minutes to spare. She wasted a precious minute for her eyes to adjust to the bleary darkness. The club was small but it was jam-packed. She squeezed through the crowd of people, heading for what she hoped was the backstage area.

She made it there out of breath and pulled her violin from the case just as the MC announced, "And here to rock out on her violin with you… Megan."

She felt the familiar course of preperformance jitters and excitement flow through her as she walked out on the stage. Alone. The spotlight was so bright that she could hardly see anything. She looked over her shoulder, but her sisters weren't there to give her a reassuring smile or a warm squeeze of her hand.

Swallowing nervously, she turned her gaze back to the audience. The light was still blinding, but she let the roar of the crowd and the heat of their bodies wash over her. She took a slow, steadying breath. They wanted to hear her music and there was nothing she loved more than sharing it with the audience. She tucked her violin under her chin, her face splitting into a giant grin. She could do this.

Her performance was loud, messy and so damn fun. The energy of the crowd zinged through her like electricity and she wove through the stage with her violin, her ponytail swishing back and forth with every bend and twist of her body. The music swelled around her and reached dizzying heights as she played the highest notes on the violin with frantic speed. Her audience's shouts became frenzied as she held them at the pinnacle for impossibly long seconds—channeling her favorite heavy-metal guitar solos—then she brought them crashing down only to gently lift them up again. When she finished, she threw her arms up to the ceiling, her bow and violin in each hand, and the crowd howled its approval.

"Thank you. You guys are awesome." High on adrenaline, she strode off the stage with her chest heaving and sweat dripping down her forehead.

She did it. She fucking nailed her first solo performance. She pressed an unsteady hand over her mouth as a sound between a sob and a laugh escaped from her. If felt incredible to stand on her own—just knowing that she could centered something inside her. She closed her eyes and took a deep breath to savor the moment.

"You were spectacular."

Megan swung around to find her gorgeous stranger leaning against the back wall with his arms crossed over his chest.

"You stayed," she whispered, surprised by how happy that made her.

"I told you I would." He pushed himself off the wall and walked toward her.

She hurriedly stowed away her violin and straightened to face him. "Why?"

He stopped a few feet away from her, his eyes raking her body with enough heat to burn her panties off. "For you."

Instinct was a funny thing. She had never attacked a man before, but she pounced on the stranger as though she'd done it a hundred times. She pressed her body against him like she wanted to meld with him, and her hands fisted in his thick hair as she crushed her mouth to his.

To his credit, he didn't hesitate before wrapping her leg around his waist, his other hand cupping her ass. Her lips parted on a moan, and his tongue invaded her mouth with swift authority. Her teeth clacked against his as she sucked him in deeper and tangled her tongue roughly with his.

She reminded herself that she'd spoken fewer than ten sentences with the man. She didn't even know his last name. But her body had taken over. She didn't give a damn that she was kissing a stranger as though her life depended on it as long as she got to keep doing it.

He hoisted her up by the waist and she wrapped her other leg around him, and he spun them around and pressed her back against the wall. Her breath left her on a sharp gasp when he cupped her breast with his large hand and kneaded it. She didn't hear the laughter or the clack of footsteps until he set her back on the ground, holding her firmly by her hips.

"Let's get out of here," he said in a gravelly voice, his chest rising and falling with each swift breath.

Megan didn't think she could form words, so she nodded. Something hot and hungry flared in his eyes, then he took her hand and sprinted toward the exit. She ran beside him with a smile lighting up her face. This surreal night would be something all her own.

One

Three months later

"Please don't tell me that's your lunch," Angie said with a disapproving glance at the bag of Sour Patch Kids.

Megan popped another piece into her mouth and chewed, swallowing down a wave of nausea. "Of course not. It's three o'clock. Who eats lunch at three?"

Now that she was nearing the second trimester of her pregnancy, her morning sickness—which was actually all-freaking-day sickness—was finally beginning to let up. She was able to tolerate a few spoons of soup for lunch, then she washed it down with half a can of Coke because water still tasted disgusting. It was better than living solely off Sour Patch Kids and candied ginger like she had for the last couple of months.

"I worry about you. You've lost weight," her older sister fretted.

Megan smiled. She loved being fussed over by her unni. A part of her couldn't wait to tell her sisters about being pregnant so they could fuss their big ol' hearts out. But another part of her didn't want to worry them, because she planned on raising the baby on her own.

An image of the beautiful stranger flashed through her mind, but she pushed it aside. That was all he was. A stranger. Besides, it wasn't like she had any way of contacting him to let him know that she was pregnant. This baby was hers and hers alone.

She breathed to stop the now-familiar panic from taking hold. Having something all her own didn't feel like a sparkling treasure anymore. But she could do this—she had to for her baby. *My baby.* She remembered her performance at the Tipsy Dahlia—how amazing it felt to stand on her own. The thought reinforced her spine with steely confidence. *I* can *do this.*

"Especially since you didn't have any spare weight to lose in the first place," Chloe added. "It wouldn't be as big a deal if I dropped a few pounds."

Angie tsked. "You're lovely just as you are."

"I know." Her younger sister smiled, with her eyes twinkling. She really was very lovely. "I'm just saying Megan needs to start eating better."

"All right. Stop ganging up on me." Megan rolled her eyes. Even before she got pregnant, her sisters had been on her case about her candy addiction. "I'll eat real food. Satisfied?"

"Yes." Angie nodded. "Ready to get to work?"

"Let's do this," Chloe said, lifting her viola to her

chin. "We haven't played this piece in months. It's going to need some work."

Megan and her sisters practiced three times a week in a room they rented at the local community college. With the new season fast approaching, they would need to rehearse even more often. *The new season.* She was going to start showing soon. She couldn't help but wonder if her pregnancy would affect her career in any way. Many of the Chamber Music Society's patrons were quite conservative. Would they frown upon her single-mom status?

And she would have to miss some performances because the baby was due before the end of the season. The Hana Trio wouldn't be a trio without her... She would worry about that when the time came but she couldn't put off telling her sisters much longer.

The rehearsal was a welcome distraction from her cluttered thoughts. Playing with her sisters—even when they were practicing the same few bars over and over again—always made her happy. The music seemed to chase away the lingering morning sickness. By the end of practice, she felt better than she had in months.

"Yup," Megan said while putting away her violin, "this piece definitely needs more work."

"But I think we made good progress today," Angie pointed out.

"Agreed." Chloe stood from her chair and shouldered her viola case. "We'll have it perfected by opening night."

After hugging each of her sisters much longer than necessary, Megan walked out to her car and ventured onto the congested freeway for her drive home. Describing rush hour in Los Angeles as heavy traffic was a gross understatement. *Traffic* implied that there was some movement. No, the freeways felt more like a giant parking lot. Her playlist was the only thing that kept Megan sane through her commute.

While she was a classically trained musician, her playlist consisted mostly of rock and heavy metal. She sincerely believed that her love of that genre made her a better musician, especially with so much classical influence in heavy metal. And it definitely helped her interpret her rock violin pieces more authentically. Not that she had performed at any more clubs since that first night. A wistful sigh escaped her.

It hadn't been possible for her to perform her electric violin with her unrelenting morning sickness. But even before that, she didn't go out of her way to book another gig. She might or might not have been avoiding another chance encounter with *him*. She didn't know what the etiquette of a one-night stand was, but sneaking out of the hotel room in the cover of darkness seemed like a dick move—a dick move she had pulled.

How could she have known that his last name or a phone number would've come in handy a few weeks later when she peed on a stick or two? Fine, five. She peed on five sticks. Regardless, she'd made a decision— mostly out of panic and mortification, but it was still her decision to run away—and now she had to live with the rather significant consequence of raising a child on her own.

But her decision to become a mother at this point in her life was not a *consequence* but a *choice*. She lived in a state where abortions were legal so she had the free-dom to make that important, personal choice for her-self. It infuriated her that she felt grateful for it—that there was a very real threat that such a basic human right could be taken away from her...from every person who could become pregnant. She blew out a long, frustrated breath.

Megan survived her drive home and parked in the garage with a deep sigh. The moment she opened the door leading into the house, the aroma of a Korean feast assailed her nostrils—soy sauce, garlic, sesame oil—and she didn't hate it. In fact, her stomach growled raucously and her mouth watered because everything smelled...delicious. Did this mean her morning sickness was over?

In her excitement over the prospect of eating a proper meal, it slipped her mind that her dad had mentioned having a business associate over for dinner. So when she barged into the living room, she was doubly shocked to discover a stranger sitting on the sectional with her dad—not just any stranger but *her* stranger.

What in the ever-loving hell?

The stranger shot to his feet, his expression a mixture of shock, anger and a hint of something she couldn't identify. Then everything was wiped clean and replaced by polite indifference, making her doubt whether any of the emotions were ever there.

"Ah, Megan. You're home," her dad said, turning to face her. She scrambled to close her gaping mouth but couldn't hide her bewilderment in time. Grooves of concern formed over the bridge of his nose. "Did you forget we were having a dinner guest?"

"Yes...we're so busy preparing for the new season," she managed. *How is this happening?* "Please forgive me."

"I'm Daniel Pak." Their guest walked up to her and extended his hand. "Nice to meet you."

So they were going to pretend to be complete strangers… That was probably a good call on his part. He couldn't exactly say, "Hey, didn't we sleep together a few months ago?" in front of her dad. God, she was unravelling.

"Megan Han." She plastered on a fake smile by sheer force of will and gave him a firm handshake. The jolt of electricity that shot down her spine was hard to ignore and only added to her panic. "It's a pleasure to meet you."

Daniel held on to her hand for a second too long and she wondered what that meant. Was he happy to see her again? Or was it a warning not to tell her dad anything? *Right.* If she could guess what the man was thinking by an extra second of hand shaking then she was in the wrong profession. She felt hysterical laughter bubble in her throat.

"Daniel is—" her dad began.

"I'm going to see if Mrs. Chung needs any help with dinner," Megan practically shouted over him and rushed out of the living room.

In a daze, she climbed the stairs to her room. Who the hell was he? How did he know her dad? *Oh God. Do I have to tell him about the baby?* She closed her bedroom door and leaned back against it. She didn't know what to do.

Her fist clenched around the handle of her violin case, reminding her she needed to put it away. After taking a deep breath, she pushed off the door and set her violin down beside her music stand. Hiding in her room wouldn't solve anything. If she wanted answers, she had to go back downstairs and join her dad and their guest for dinner. Then she could decide how she felt about this chance encounter—their second one.

She walked into her closet and clicked on the light. Both her dad and Daniel were wearing dress shirts and slacks, so she was a bit underdressed in her leggings and oversize T-shirt. She changed into a pale blue blouse and pulled a black pencil skirt off the hanger. But when she stepped into it and lifted it over her hips, she could barely close the zipper halfway up.

"Shit," she muttered.

Even though she'd lost weight over the last couple months, a soft bump pushed insistently from her lower stomach. Soon, none of her clothes would fit her. But her frustration quickly morphed into a tenderness that still surprised her. She placed her hand over her stomach and smiled down at her changing body. How could she love someone she hadn't even met yet?

Her smile faltered and a frisson of nerves ran through her. The baby's father was waiting downstairs for her… and she had to tell him about the baby. How would he react to the news? She shook her head before any disastrous scenarios could take root in her mind. It didn't matter. He had a right to know. With calm resolve, she changed into a cream shift dress and headed for the kitchen.

"Hi, Mrs. Chung," Megan said, her eyes going round at the sight of all the delectable food. Mrs. Chung had been her family's housekeeper for as long as she could remember. With both her sisters out of the house—Chloe had decided to live on campus while she finished her master's—and her dad working long hours, Megan would've been lonely if it hadn't been for Mrs. Chung. "Do you need any help?"

"No, I'm fine. Thank you for asking, my dear," she said, placing bite-size pieces of egg-battered cod on the frying pan. "I just need to finish frying up this last batch of jeon."

Megan snagged one of the fish jeon resting in a wicker platter and popped it in her mouth. Her eyes slid shut at the savory, umami goodness. "Mmm."

"Do you have your appetite back?" Mrs. Chung's eyebrows rose in surprise. "You've hardly eaten the last couple months."

"Yeah, um, it's just been too hot this summer," Megan said, avoiding her eyes. She would have to tell everyone eventually—starting with Daniel tonight—but first, she was going to fortify herself with some food. She popped another piece of fish in her mouth while she schooled her features. "I guess I have more of an appetite now that it's finally cooling down. I should, um, set the table."

When everything was ready, her dad took a seat at the head of the table. Megan studiously avoided staring at Daniel as they sat down across from each other on either side of her dad. The dinner was more relaxed and casual than the slightly stuffy business affairs her dad occasionally held at their home. The two men shared a rapport that would've piqued her curiosity if she wasn't so preoccupied with her own predicament.

Unable to stop herself, she glanced at Daniel from under her lashes. Her dad didn't invite just anyone over for dinner at their house. They had to be of some significance to Jigu Corporation. Who was he? What was his relationship to her dad? Her eyes narrowed as a sudden thought occurred to her. Had he known she was

Minsung Han's daughter when he approached her that night? What game was he playing at?

In all fairness, Daniel wasn't playing any games with her at the dinner table. He certainly didn't send any secret, significant glances her way. He paid her just enough attention not to be impolite but he didn't seem the least bit interested in her. She covered her huff of annoyance by stuffing some bulgogi in her mouth. What did she care about capturing his interest? She had bigger things to worry about. But her eyes kept straying toward him—the darn man was as gorgeous as he'd been the night she'd first met him.

"Daniel joined Jigu Corporation as the new Chief Financial Officer a few months back," her dad addressed her.

She froze with her hand over the japchae, and the slippery vermicelli noodles slid straight off her chopsticks. *You've got to be kidding me.* Her one-night stand worked for her dad? It would've been bad enough if he was some business associate in town for a few days. But him being a long-term fixture at her dad's company made things so much worse. Her pregnancy could wreak havoc on the situation if she didn't tread carefully.

How had someone so young become the CFO anyway? He couldn't be more than a couple years older than her. Then again, she was a twenty-seven-year-old who constantly got carded when ordering drinks. Maybe he just looked younger than he was. Even so, he couldn't be older than thirty.

"Oh?" She hid her surprise and resumed transferring the noodles to her plate. "The same CFO who didn't show up at our last concert?"

"My apologies," Daniel interjected smoothly. "I got detained with an urgent matter at work. By the time I got to the concert hall, the performance had already ended."

"That's a shame," she murmured.

"Yes," he said with a slight arch of his eyebrow, "but I was fortunate enough to catch another performance that evening, which I quite enjoyed."

"Is that so?" She fell miles short of cool indifference as her cheeks flushed with pleasure. She cleared her throat and looked down at her plate. "I didn't even realize the CFO position was open."

"I begged Jerry to hold off his retirement until we found someone perfect for the job." Her dad raised his glass to the young CFO with a playful wink. "He sure was glad when Daniel came along."

Megan's eyes widened despite herself. *Perfect?* Her dad held himself and others to ridiculously high standards. She'd never heard him describe anyone or anything as *perfect* before.

"I'm hardly perfect, Mr. Han," Daniel said with a hint of a smile.

"Don't sell yourself short. You've more than proven your competence during your time at the East Coast office. You single-handedly revamped the business development department in one year. That's no small feat. Jigu needs that kind of passion and vision at the executive level," her dad said, clapping Daniel on the shoulder. "Besides, the board of directors wouldn't have approved your appointment if they didn't believe you were qualified."

She couldn't believe the bromance vibes she was getting. She stared at her dad, but he busied himself piling more food onto his plate, urging their guest to do the same.

"Thank you. I appreciate your faith in me." Daniel regarded her dad with undisguised respect. "But we have to remember that not everyone was thrilled about my appointment as the new CFO."

"Don't worry about that." Her dad waved aside the younger man's concern. "You'll win them over soon enough."

What in the world was going on? It was hard enough figuring out what it meant to have Daniel back in her life. But now she had to contend with the fact that he and her dad had a close connection that she knew nothing about. Megan had a sinking feeling that things were about to get much more complicated.

Daniel tasted nothing as he methodically shoveled food into his mouth, chewed and swallowed. He nodded and chuckled along with Mr. Han's anecdotes without really hearing him. He was too busy *feeling* Megan sitting across from him, with every molecule in his body. Once everything sank in, he knew he'd be more concerned with the fact that she was Minsung Han's daughter—that he'd slept with the CEO's daughter—but for now, he couldn't stop his heart from racing with the thrill of being in the same room as her.

A headache was building up in his temples from all the effort it took to keep his eyes off her. But if he looked at her, he might not be able to hold back the longing and frustration he'd been suppressing for the last three months. She'd probably hoped to never see him again when she snuck out of the hotel room that night. He had convinced himself that he had no problem with that. At least he thought he had. But with her only a few feet away from him, he wasn't so sure anymore.

Daniel finally allowed himself to steal a glimpse of her as they moved from the dining room back to the living room. She was even more beautiful than he'd remembered. Her silky black hair fell past her shoulders and her face was clear of makeup other than the rosy sheen of her lips. She looked thinner, though. His eyebrows drew together.

After a dessert of sliced apples, pears and tea, Mr. Han made a show of yawning loudly. "This old man needs to turn in for the night…"

Daniel got to his feet. "I should head out."

"Why are you in such a hurry to get back to your empty condo?" The older man placed a hand on his shoulder. "You two should chat a while longer. As they say, the night is still young."

Daniel lowered himself back onto the sofa and glanced at Megan. She gaped at Mr. Han as though she was wondering who the hell he was and what he'd done with her father.

"Appa…" she began.

"Keep him company and get to know him a little," Mr. Han cajoled with a wide smile. "He's part of the Jigu family now."

All Mr. Han needed to do was give them an exaggerated wink to make it any more obvious that he was playing matchmaker. Daniel was touched that he would trust one of his daughters to him. And he felt horrible that he had betrayed his trust even before it was given to him. Minsung Han was his mentor and his friend. What would he think if he knew that Daniel had had a one-night stand with Megan?

"Good night." With a wave over his shoulder, Mr. Han walked out of the living room, leaving the two of them alone.

"Do you have any idea what that was all about?" Megan turned to Daniel in a huff.

"No clue." He leaned back on the couch and crossed his arms over his chest. "Now, I have a question for you."

She opened her mouth, then closed it. After staring intently at her lap for a few seconds, she met his gaze. "Not here. There's a café nearby. I'll meet you at the door in two minutes."

He watched her leave the room, unable to stop himself from taking in the sway of her hips and the soft curve of her calves. He couldn't deny that he still wanted her, but she was off-limits now. Getting involved with the CEO's daughter was asking for trouble, especially when he was only good for a casual fling. Experience told him that women didn't stick around, so it was better to not give them any permanence in his life. He swiped a hand down his face and headed for the front door. She joined him shortly with a purse hooked on her arm.

"Do you want to drive together?" she asked, stepping out the door he held open for her. "It's not far. I'll grab a rideshare back home after we chat."

"Sure," he said. She quirked an eyebrow at him as though she knew he had every intention of bringing her home himself.

They arrived at the small café after a short, silent drive—she'd seemed lost in thought and he'd kept his eyes on the road. After ordering their drinks at the counter, they sat at a corner table which allowed them some privacy.

"Okay." Megan wrapped her hands around her mug as though she needed comfort. "Ask me."

"Why did you leave without a word that night?" He allowed his expression to betray no more than mild curiosity even though he was holding his breath, waiting for her answer.

"I, um—" she ran her fingertip around the rim of her mug "—kind of freaked out."

"Freaked out?" he repeated slowly, his eyebrow arching in bewilderment.

"I've never done something like that," she said. When his eyes widened, she clicked her tongue. "Not sex. I've had sex before…although I had no idea that sex could be like *that*. But that's not the point."

How could he notice how adorable she was at a time like this? He overcompensated for the smile he was fighting by drawing his lips down into a grim line.

"The point is I've never had sex with a complete stranger before," she continued. "I didn't even know your last name…"

"Do you usually deal with novel situations by running away?" He didn't like the hint of bitterness in his tone. What was wrong with him? They'd slept together once. He had no claim on her. But as much as he hated to admit it, it stung that she'd been ready to never see him again.

"Judge all you want, but I do *not* make a habit of running away from my problems," she said, tilting her chin up. "My turn. Did you know who I was when we met that night?"

"What? Know you how?" Then he realized what she was asking and his eyes narrowed with a flash of anger.

"Are you implying that I deliberately approached you because you're Minsung Han's daughter?"

"To be honest, I see no reason for you to have done that," she stated matter-of-factly. "I have to believe that this is just a bizarre, unfortunate coincidence."

He pinched the bridge of his nose. He agreed that it was bizarre, but he wasn't sure if it was unfortunate. Even if one night was all he got with her, he didn't regret it.

"Damn it. I offended you." She sighed, her shoulders drooping. "It really doesn't help me to offend you right now. I just needed to make sure you didn't have any nefarious, alternative motives for sleeping with me that night—other than lust. Because I'm fine with lust."

"I'm glad you approve of lust." A corner of his lips twitched against his volition. "But why do you need to rule out…what was it?…*nefarious, alternative motives*?"

"Because I have something to tell you and I can't have you using the information against me or my father."

He paused with his mug halfway to his lips. "What do you have to tell me?"

"I'm pregnant," she said.

His mug slammed back on the table, sloshing hot coffee on his hand, but Daniel didn't feel a thing as her words sank in and his world tilted.

I'm going to be a father.

Two

Megan braced herself for the usual line of questions men asked in these situations. She had no personal experience, but she'd seen enough TV shows and movies to know what to expect. She could handle the angry denials and accusations. She had a third-degree black belt in verbal sparring.

Daniel wiped the spilled coffee off the table with care, then stared intently down at his hands. His quiet contemplation stretched on until she wanted to squirm in her seat. She felt like she'd showed up for battle—loins girded—only to find her enemy pouring tea for them on a linen-covered table. When he looked up at last, her stomach lurched with nerves. What was he thinking?

"Marry me," he said in a low, even voice.

She almost fell out of her chair.

"What?" she shouted before clapping her hand over her mouth. He couldn't have said what she thought he'd said. She glanced around the café to make sure no one noticed and said in a much softer voice, "What?"

"I want you to marry me." He nodded as though his bonkers proposal sounded even better to him the second time around.

"Aren't you… Aren't you going to ask me if I'm sure the baby is yours?" she said weakly.

"Based on your *freak-out*, you're not someone who engages in casual sex," he observed. "And you don't seem like a person who would cheat on someone you're in a relationship with."

"But we used a condom," she argued on his behalf.

"Two condoms. I recall having you twice," he murmured.

Her heart fluttered in response to his barely there smile, and the memory of their night together made heat gather low in her stomach.

"Why are you so calm?" She glared at him, suddenly finding his composure infuriating when she was all aflutter and horny to boot.

"I'm asking a woman I'm meeting for the second time to marry me. I'm far from calm," he said, sounding as calm as could be. "But this is how *I* respond to novel situations. By analyzing the facts and choosing the most logical course of action, which, in this case, is taking responsibility for my actions."

"*Our* actions," she corrected. "But that's not the point. You don't have to take responsibility for anything. This is my body, my baby, my responsibility."

"That makes no sense." His eyebrows furrowed over

the bridge of his nose. "If it's *our* actions then it's *our* baby, *our* responsibility—"

"I'm only telling you because you have the right to know." She cut him off and held up a finger when he opened his mouth. "If you want…you can be a part of the child's life. But a loveless marriage is out of the question."

Icy disdain hardened his features. "Marriage doesn't have to be about love."

"Well, marriage shouldn't be about responsibility and duty," she countered, her voice rising in indignation. A happy marriage was all about love. She'd seen it with her parents and now with Angie and Joshua.

"Responsibility and duty are far more reliable than love," he bit out.

The finality of his statement chilled her. What happened to him to make him balk at the idea of love? Had someone hurt him in the past? It was none of her business. Everyone had their emotional baggage. Besides, it wasn't like she was going to marry him. It didn't matter what he thought about love.

"We'll have to agree to disagree on that one," she said quietly.

He held her gaze for a moment, then nodded once. The hard edge left his expression when he asked, "Does your father know you're pregnant?"

"No." She shook her head. "I haven't told anyone yet."

"He championed me to become Jigu Corporation's CFO, and I repay him by getting his daughter pregnant," Daniel scoffed and swiped a weary hand down his face. "How could I have betrayed his trust like this?"

"It's not like we had unprotected sex." She wanted

to ease his remorse. Neither of them had intended to step into this complicated mess. "Besides, you didn't even know who I was."

"That doesn't change the fact that you're pregnant with my child," he said with a hint of possessiveness that made her stomach dip.

"What do you want me to do?" Her voice was barely above a whisper.

"I already told you." He swooped in like a hawk diving for its prey. "I want you to marry me."

She blinked rapidly. Marrying him would make life so much easier. She wouldn't have to worry about disappointing her dad, being a single mom or the potential censure of the classical music community. But… she couldn't compromise on love. She wouldn't. And she could stand on her own—not only to perform rock violin but in life. She knew that now.

"Please stop saying that. We're not getting married." She smiled to soften her words even though he was only proposing out of a misplaced sense of duty. "Other than that…what do you want from me?"

"Nothing I can have again." There was no denying the heat in his eyes.

Her breath caught in her throat and warmth gathered between her legs. He still wanted her, and if her body's reaction was any indication, she very much wanted him back. But he was right. They couldn't give in to their attraction. Things were complicated enough without them picking up where they'd left off.

"This is a lot for us to process all at once," she said, suddenly exhausted. "Let's take some time to think things through before we decide how we want to handle this. I'll hold off on telling my father anything for the time being."

"Are you finally going to give me your number?" he asked wryly.

She rolled her eyes and held out her hand. When he reached into his pocket and handed her his phone, she tapped in her number and pressed Dial. An East Coast number popped up on her screen.

"There." She returned his phone. "Now we both have each other's number."

"Good," he said, rising to his feet. "Let me take you home."

"There's no need. I'll get a rideshare."

With an impatient click of his tongue, Daniel unhooked her purse from the back of her chair and walked off.

"Hey," she protested, even though she had no choice but to follow.

He waited by his car, holding the passenger-side door open. She caught up with him with unhurried steps. His high-handed stunt annoyed her, but she had a feeling there were many more battles ahead of them. He could have this tiny victory as long as she won the big ones.

After exchanging a ridiculously courteous goodnight with Daniel—she had no idea how to behave with her one-night stand turned secret baby daddy—Megan went straight to her dad's study and knocked. She knew he hadn't *turned in early*. He was a night owl like her.

"Come in," he said.

She pushed open the door and found him typing away on his laptop with his reading glasses perched on his nose. Even by the soft lamplight, she could see how much his hair had grayed in the last few years. He had always worked long hours, but that was all he seemed to do since her mom died.

"Do you have a minute?" she asked, settling down on an armchair.

He responded with a rush of typing, then came to join her in the sitting area. "What is it?"

"I wanted to talk to you about Daniel." She wanted to find out more about the connection the two men shared that she'd detected earlier in the evening. And if she were being honest with herself, she was more than mildly curious about the father of her baby. "Are you guys…close?"

"Why do you ask?" Her dad took off his glasses and wiped the lenses with the end of his shirt, trying to hide the smile playing around his mouth. "Did you have a nice time with him?"

"Appa, I'm being serious."

"And I'm not?" His grin grew wider. "He's a good man. Smart, loyal and decent."

"Hmm." There it was again—the high praise. She pursed her lips. "I just got the feeling that he was more than a valued employee."

"Well, that depends. Are you seeing him again?"

"Stop it." She stood from her seat. Her dad was in an odd mood, and she wasn't getting anywhere with him. "You're a horrible matchmaker."

"I want you to give it some thought." His expression turned serious as he got to his feet. "I'm grooming him to take over Jigu Corporation when I retire. It would be nice to keep the business in the family."

Too shocked to reply, Megan nodded and left his study. She replayed her conversation with her dad as she went through her nighttime routine. He was preparing Daniel to become Jigu's next CEO. He'd dedicated all of his adult life to the company and loved it like an extension of himself. He really must trust Daniel.

She lay down in bed and stared up at the ceiling. Fate must have a twisted sense of humor. Her dad valued loyalty above all else. He would be livid if he found out Daniel had had a one-night stand with her and got her pregnant. He would see it as a betrayal and an affront to their family's honor. But then he would quickly see the situation as his matchmaking dream come true and try to force them to get married. Well, force *her* to marry Daniel since the man was already prepared to embrace matrimony out of duty.

She couldn't allow that to happen.

It was true this baby was unexpected, but that didn't mean she had to give up on love and happily ever after. She placed a gentle hand on her stomach. No, it meant that she had to fight harder for her dreams now because her baby's happiness depended on it, too.

Daniel yawned into his sixth cup of coffee. His week had passed in a blur of meetings. He was relieved when his dinner meeting was canceled—he desperately needed a break from schmoozing—so he could continue familiarizing himself with his actual duties as the CFO. But it was past eight o'clock in the evening and the words on the screen were beginning to blur.

He rubbed his eyes with his thumb and index finger until the stinging subsided and leaned back in his chair. Even in the midst of his hectic week, Megan had never been far from his mind—Megan and the baby. His stomach clenched nervously. *Their* baby.

Marriage and children had not been a part of his plans—even before Sienna's betrayal. He swept aside the intrusive thought. His parents' marriage was a patented disaster, based on his memory of the wreck his father had been when his mother left them. His father hadn't been able to look at Daniel without remembering his mother—his gaze filled with a mixture of loss and resentment. He had wondered countless times whether his father regretted having him. He rubbed his chest as a cold hollowness spread inside him. If his father hadn't loved his mother—and been utterly devastated when their marriage ended—then maybe he would've been able to love Daniel more.

No, marriage and children had never factored into his goals. He wanted to become a formidable figure in his field and earn the respect of his peers. He wanted to prove to the world that he was someone valuable— someone they couldn't toss aside. But planned or not, he refused to bring a child into this world and have them feel unwanted.

Daniel pushed himself away from his desk and paced the length of his office. He wanted to raise his child in a home with both a mother and a father—maybe because he'd never had that. A marriage based on responsibility and duty meant that no one would get their heart broken. Their love for their child would never be tainted by bitterness and resentment. Why couldn't Megan see that?

He dragged his fingers through his hair. He couldn't force her to marry him, but there were other ways for him to be in his child's life. He would make sure they knew that they were wanted and loved. Always.

Daniel retrieved his phone from his desk and texted Megan.

We need to talk.

Fortunately for his sanity, ellipses started rolling immediately after he hit Send.

I agree. When and where?

His thumbs flew over his phone.

In forty-five minutes. At the café we met last week.

He didn't wait for her response and grabbed his jacket from the coat hanger. Even if rush hour was over, it was going to take him at least thirty minutes to get to the café. He had a fifteen-minute cushion, but he didn't want to keep Megan waiting. His phone dinged as he stepped out of his office and headed toward the elevators.

See you soon.

The traffic was heavier than he would've liked and he pulled into the café's parking lot with only five minutes to spare. After he got out of his car, he saw Megan near the entrance and sprinted to catch up with her.

"Megan," he said, grabbing the door handle before her.

"Oh." She placed her hand over her chest. "You startled me. Where did you come from?"

"Sorry." He wanted to smack his forehead. "I was right behind you."

"That's fine. No big deal," she said, walking in through the door.

He followed her inside and headed for the counter. "What would you like?"

"Decaf Moroccan mint tea, please." She came to stand beside him.

"Why don't you go have a seat? I'll bring the drinks over when they're ready."

She shrugged and headed for the corner table they occupied last time. When he joined her with two mugs, she smiled at him. "Thank you."

"My pleasure." He caught himself staring at her and quickly took a sip of his green tea, scalding his tongue and the roof of his mouth.

"I'm glad you reached out to me," she said. "I wanted to talk to you, but I didn't want to bother you. My father said you had a hectic week at work."

He bit back a curse. She'd been waiting to hear back from him. "I'm sorry for taking so long."

"No worries." She blew on her tea before she took a careful sip.

Megan seemed more relaxed than the last time he saw her, and being near her calmed him somehow. The thought of becoming a father still made his stomach flip over, but maybe they could make this work.

"I'm going to take a wild guess," he said. "You still don't want to marry me."

"Bingo." She winked.

His heart stuttered like a needle skipping on a vinyl record. He curled his hands into fists on his thighs to stop himself from grabbing her from across the table and kissing her senseless. She looked expectantly at him as though he was capable of speech. When he continued staring wordlessly at her, she cocked her head to the side.

"I guess I'll go first," she said after a moment. "We can't tell my father that the baby is yours."

"What? That's unacceptable." That did the job of snapping him out of his wink-induced stupor. "I can't lie to your father."

"We won't lie to him." She drew little circles on the table. "We'll just omit the truth."

"Which is the same as lying."

"What are you? A Boy Scout?" She narrowed her eyes at him. "Look, my father can be...hardheaded. If he finds out that I'm pregnant with your baby—as a result of a one-night stand—he will kill you. Then he'll resurrect you and kill you again for good measure."

He couldn't hold back his cringe. "I think you're exaggerating."

Megan arched an eyebrow and silently held his gaze.

"Slightly," he amended, remembering his mentor's hot temper.

"And he'll try to force us to get married." She held up her hand when he opened his mouth. "Uh-uh. No marriage. At any rate, if we refuse to join hands in holy matrimony, he might even fire you."

"Then, so be it," he said, even as his heart sank.

"Look, I know you worked hard to be here." She leaned closer to him and a waft of her sweet scent teased him. "It's not something you should throw away lightly."

His hand tightened around his mug. "I'm not doing any of this lightly, Megan."

Being Jigu Corporation's future CEO was his dream. He'd vowed to dedicate himself to carrying on Jigu's legacy. It would gut him to lose this opportunity, but he couldn't betray Mr. Han.

"I'm not saying we should keep him in the dark forever. I just need time to figure out a way to break the news to him without making him lose his senses." She lowered her voice. "I have a feeling my father won't do anything rash once the baby arrives and captures his heart."

His lips quirked despite himself. "You're going to use our baby to shield us from your father's wrath?"

"*Use* sounds a bit cold… Wait." Her eyelashes fluttered. "Our baby? So you've decided? You want to be a part of…our baby's life?"

"Yes." He swallowed against the tightness in his throat. "I want to be part of their life. Every moment of their life."

"I… I'm glad," she said with a tremulous smile.

"Me, too." His eyes flickered to her lips, but he forced his attention back to the issue at hand. "But about your father—"

"We'll tell him," she interrupted. "Just not yet. Think about it. What will happen if you get fired from Jigu? Can you guarantee that you'll be able to find a comparable job in LA? If you have to move away, you're going to miss so much of the baby's life."

"Hell."

She was right. Losing his position at Jigu Corporation meant he would have to find another job. Depending on the company, that might take him across the country. He didn't like it—he actually hated it—but maybe they should wait to tell her father.

"We'll revisit this issue soon," he said, raking his fingers through his hair.

"Okay." She nodded several times in quick succession. "I promise."

"So…" He blew out a long breath, leaning back in his seat. "How should we do this?"

"Do what?" She wrinkled her nose in confusion.

He waved his hand between them as he searched for the right words. "Be there for the baby. Together."

"Ah," she said with a small smile. "You mean co-parenting?"

"Yes, coparenting." He held back an answering smile. "We would probably need to see each other fairly often."

"I would assume so."

The thought of spending time with Megan appealed to him much more than was wise. He stomped down on the thrill of anticipation and muttered to remind himself, "All behind your father's back."

She shrugged helplessly. "For now, yes."

"Only until we figure out a way to tell him without getting my ass fired," he added. "We're not waiting for the baby to arrive."

"Okay." Megan pressed a hand to her stomach. "Honestly, it makes me sick to keep the truth from my father. I'm all for finding a solution as soon as possible."

His chest constricted at her distress. This wasn't an easy situation for either of them—especially for her. And if they weren't careful, things could get even more difficult.

"We need to acknowledge some things before we proceed," he said, holding her gaze. "I want you."

Her lips parted on a sharp indrawn breath and his groin tightened. Then she nodded with wide eyes, acknowledging his desire or admitting her own—he wasn't sure.

"But we can't act on this attraction." Sleeping with her, knowing who she was, would be a betrayal of Mr.

Han's trust. Keeping the truth from him was betrayal enough. "We can't add more lies to our deception."

"No, we can't," she said in a small voice, her guilt plain on her face. "We...we could be partners. Coparenting partners. Nothing more."

"Agreed." He ignored the bewildering disappointment inside him. "We'll be partners."

They sat in silence for a while, staring down at their drinks. When he glanced up, his eyes caught on her bottom lip, which she worried between her teeth. He swallowed and resolutely shifted his focus to her forehead. As lovely as it was, it seemed safer than staring into her beautiful eyes, which were dangerously close to her plump pink lips.

"Tell me what you need," he blurted. He had no idea how to be there for Megan and the baby at this stage. "I mean...is there anything I can do for you? Do you have any doctor's appointments coming up?"

"It's still a couple of weeks away, but yeah, I do." She cleared her throat. "It's actually a pretty important appointment. The doctor's going to do an ultrasound and...she'll be able to tell us the sex of the baby."

The café spun ever so slightly around him. "The sex of the baby?"

"Yeah, it's pretty wild." She giggled a bit nervously. "It's going to make things feel so...real."

"Do you mind if I go with you?" Truthfully, the thought of seeing the baby for the first time—and finding out their sex—scared the shit out of him, but he wouldn't miss it for the world.

"No, not at all. I could use the moral support," she said shyly.

"I could do that. Give you moral support."

"Thank you." She hesitated before she continued, "If you don't want to find out the sex of the baby, we could wait…"

"Oh." He considered it for a moment. "I think I'd like to know. What about you?"

"Me, too."

They shared a smile. It felt good making decisions about their baby together. It felt really good.

"What else do you need?" he asked, feeling motivated. "Do you have any cravings?"

"Hmm." She scrunched her mouth to one side. "Not really. I'm just glad to be done with morning sickness. Until a week or so ago, I couldn't even drink water."

He wished he could've been there for her. "That sounds horrible."

"Yeah, it was." She wrinkled her nose.

"Well, if you get any cravings, let me know."

"Why? Do you plan on being my personal food delivery service?" she teased.

He chuckled. "If you'd like."

"Well, you asked for it. Don't come crying when I demand potato chips and ice cream at one in the morning."

"Maybe I should set up business hours," he said.

She tilted her head back and laughed. He was surprised at how much he enjoyed the sound. He tore his eyes away from her shining face and swallowed a mouthful of his lukewarm tea. He needed to get his attraction for her under control. They were coparenting partners now.

Even without their *agreement*, he had to remember that she'd walked out of the hotel room—and out of his life—without so much as a goodbye. If it wasn't for the baby, she wouldn't have wanted anything to do with him. He couldn't forget that.

Daniel had to tread carefully. Under different circumstances, he would have avoided spending time with her at all costs. Since that wasn't an option, he had to use every ounce of his self-control to remember that Megan Han was off-limits for him.

Three

After checking her phone for the twentieth time, Megan slapped it facedown on the table and took big gulps of her ice water. Her dad was even later than usual for their dinner date. If she hadn't been dying to try the new French bistro, she might've been tempted to leave. The cozy atmosphere with rich draperies and candlelit tables helped soothe her growing impatience, but if he wasn't there in ten minutes, she was going to order without him.

"Megan?" a familiar voice said from her side.

"Daniel?" She looked up at him in surprise. "What are you doing here?"

"I'm supposed to have dinner with your father, but I got held up at work." He scanned the restaurant. "It doesn't look like he's here yet. Will you be joining us?"

Daniel glanced down at the table with confusion,

drawing his eyebrows together. She was sitting at a table for two. Megan barely managed to hold back her groan. It went against every ounce of the filial piety engrained in her, but she was going to kill her dad when she got home.

"Why don't you sit down, Daniel?" She sighed and picked up the menu. A part of her didn't want to give in to her dad's matchmaking trickery, but she was hungry and she wasn't about to forego the chance to eat at the exclusive restaurant. "It's going to be just you and me for dinner tonight."

His frown cleared as he caught on to Minsung Han's clumsy attempt at playing Cupid. Daniel sat across from her with a bemused smile. "Not very subtle, is he?"

Megan snorted. "Not when it comes to matchmaking, I guess."

His eyes widened as though realizing something. "I kept you waiting for a while. I apologize. You must be starving."

"Apology accepted." She gave a one-shouldered shrug. "You didn't even know I'd be here."

"Even so."

"Everything sounds delicious." She changed the subject, noting that Daniel tended to be hard on himself. "I think I'm going to go for the tasting menu with white truffles."

"I'll have the same," he said, setting aside his menu.

"Good choice. It's nice and expensive." When he cocked his head in question, she explained, "It's going to be my father's treat. I'm whipping out his black card for pulling this stunt."

"Well, thank you for dinner, Mr. Han." Daniel raised his glass in mock salute.

Her phone buzzed and Megan snatched it off the table. It could only be one person. Her missing dinner date.

I'm sorry for the no show, but I sent you a younger, better looking dinner companion. Bon appetit!

"This is so embarrassing," she huffed her outrage and stuffed her phone into her purse with more force than necessary. "I'll have a talk with my father and make sure he doesn't try something like this again."

"Don't worry about it," he soothed. "Let's just pretend we ran into each other by coincidence."

"Sure, why not." She snapped her cloth napkin open and spread it across her lap. "We seem to do that a lot anyway."

"Do what a lot?"

"Run into each other by coincidence." Her face flushed the moment the words left her mouth. Would he think she was alluding to their first night together?

Before the moment could turn awkward, their server appeared at their table and they placed their orders.

"Would you like to do the wine pairing with the tasting menu?" the server asked.

Daniel shot a quick glance at her before answering, "No, thank you."

When their server left, she leaned toward Daniel and said softly, "You could do the wine pairing. I really don't mind."

"Neither do I. I'd much rather offer you my moral support." His full lips quirked at one corner.

"That's very considerate of you," she murmured.

Before she realized what she was doing, she reached

across the table and placed her hand on top of his. Daniel turned his hand over and linked his fingers through hers without missing a beat. Then he looked down at their hands as though he had no idea how that had happened. But he didn't break the contact and neither did she, even as heat spread up her arm and through her body.

"Megan?"

Walter Liu, an old family friend and a member of Jigu Corporation's board of directors, walked up to her. As though on cue, she and Daniel snatched their hands away and hid them under the table.

"Mr. Liu, how are you?" She half stood from her seat to receive his hug.

"Can't complain." His smile turned slightly guarded as he turned toward her dinner companion. "Hello, Daniel. Fancy meeting you here."

"Hello, Mr. Liu," Daniel replied, a look of polite indifference settling on his features.

With a bemused grunt, Walter Liu raised his eyebrows at her in obvious question of her choice for company.

"My father was supposed to join us, but he got detained at work," she explained.

"Minsung works too hard." Mr. Liu clucked his tongue. "Well, enjoy your dinner, my dear. I better head back to my table before my wife sends out a search party."

"It was lovely seeing you," Megan said with genuine warmth. "I'll come by to say hello to Mrs. Liu in a bit."

Daniel waited until Mr. Liu was out of hearing range before he asked, "Do you have every member of the board wrapped around your little finger? Or is it just Walter Liu?"

"Not *every* member," she said with a teasing smile. She liked it when his wry humor snuck past his solemn demeanor. "Many of the board members are old family friends. They watched me and my sisters grow up, so they're kind of like uncles and aunties to us. They were a godsend when my mom…"

"I'm glad you and your family had good friends to support you when your mother passed away." His voice was gentle with compassion.

"Yeah, it helped a lot." Megan took a sip of water to soothe the constriction in her throat. "Especially for my father. I don't know what we would've done if it weren't for Walter Liu and Anne Werner. They were the only ones who could get through to him."

They were sitting in companionable silence when Megan gasped, her hand flying to her mouth.

"What's wrong?" His eyes darted over her face. "Are you okay?"

"Yes, I'm fine," she said, waving away his concern. "I know what we have to do."

"What do we have to do?" he asked warily.

"We both agree that we can't tell my father about our baby yet." She waited for her words to register with Daniel. "But we also agree that we can't keep this… situation between us a secret forever."

"No, absolutely not." He pinched the bridge of his nose. "Mr. Han has a right to know. We have to tell him as soon as we can."

"Right." She nodded curtly, impatient to share her brilliant plan. "So I know what we have to do to allow us to tell my father everything without getting you fired. And I'm not talking about waiting until the baby is born."

"I'm listening." He didn't sound too hopeful. *O ye of little faith.*

"My father heeds the counsel of his friends, Walter and Anne, who also happen to be board members of Jigu Corporation." She gripped her hands together on her lap because she was waving them around too much. She always did that when she got excited. "From what I've seen, neither of them seems to be a huge fan of you."

"Harsh—" he cringed "—but fair."

"Sorry. But that's not the point. Well, that's kind of the point." She shook her head. "The *real* point is that we have to get Walter Liu and Anne Werner to bring you into their fold. As well as anyone else you think is still on the fence about you."

"I plan to earn their trust, but that's going to take some time," Daniel said. "Once they see what I'm doing for Jigu Corporation as its CFO, they'll come around eventually."

"No, we don't have time to wait for them to *come around eventually.*" She gave an impatient shake of her head.

"Then, what—"

She cut him off and blurted, "I can help you become a part of the *in* crowd."

"You're going to make me popular?" Amusement sparkled in his eyes.

"Ha-ha. I'm serious," she said, fighting back a smile. "Walter and Anne have a soft spot for me and my sisters. I can accompany you to some social events to show them you have the Han family stamp of approval and get them to warm up to you. Plus, I know them well so I can coach you on their likes and dislikes."

"And you're hoping that it'll be enough to compel them to hold your father back as he tries to choke the life out of me." He adjusted his tie as though he could feel it tightening around his neck.

"At the very least, they'll be able to convince him that it's not in Jigu's best interest to fire you," she said. "I mean, you're good at your job, right?"

"Damn right, I'm good at my job."

"Hmm." She tapped her index finger on her lips. "Maybe we should start by working on some humility."

Something close to a full-blown smile spread across his face. Before she could become completely mesmerized by it, he said, "Are you sure your plan will work?"

"Have you got any better ideas?" She crossed her arms over her chest.

"If all else fails, there's always good old-fashioned groveling." His expression turned serious, and she wanted to whimper at the loss of his rare smile. "I'll do anything to be a part of our child's life."

Her heart puddled in her chest and renewed determination filled her. "My plan will work. I'll make sure of it."

Daniel knew he should slow down, but he didn't want to be late for Megan's prenatal appointment. He blew out a long breath and adjusted his grip on the steering wheel—his palms damp and slippery. He wouldn't be much use for moral support if he was a nervous wreck, so he shied away from thinking about the ultrasound and discovering the baby's sex.

Did all newly expectant parents feel like they were venturing into the jungle with their eyes blindfolded? *Hell.* It would probably help to admit that he had no idea what he was doing and accept that he would have to learn everything along the way. All he could do at this point was be there for Megan in whatever way she needed him.

He spotted Megan on a bench right outside the medical building. He quickened his pace just as she glanced up and smiled at him. The late-afternoon sunlight shone down on her upturned face and his breath got lodged in his throat.

"Am I late?" He hoped she didn't notice how husky he sounded.

"No, I'm early. We still have five minutes till the appointment," she said, getting to her feet. He hastily reached for her elbow to help her up even though she had no trouble standing on her own. She smirked but humored him. "Thank you."

After checking in, Megan pointed him toward the warm, pink waiting room and disappeared behind a door, saying something about peeing in a cup. Daniel couldn't help gawking a little at the other patients in various stages of their pregnancy. He was still standing where she'd left him when Megan came back to his side. She touched his arm and led them to a set of chairs.

"It's pretty wild, huh?" She placed her hand on the soft curve of her belly. "I'm barely starting to show, but soon I'm going to look like I swallowed a watermelon whole."

A smile tugged at his lips and he gave in to it. "I think all of you in here are heroes—incredibly brave and beautiful."

"I know. We are freaking sacred vessels." Although her words were playful, her voice held a hint of awe.

"I still can't believe I'm growing a teeny-tiny human being inside me."

A teeny-tiny human being that was part him and part her. He coughed into his fist and shifted in his seat. None of this felt truly real to him, but he was certain it was going to hit him hard sometime soon.

"Megan Han?" A nurse in purple scrubs called from a doorway.

"Yes," Daniel answered at the same time as Megan, then felt like a fool.

"Come this way," the nurse said with a kind smile.

They were shown to a room, then told that the doctor would be with them shortly. Megan perched herself on the end of the examination table. The room was quite small, so Daniel stood close by her side.

A tall brunette in her early thirties walked into the room after a quick knock. "Hi, Megan. How are you feeling today?"

"Like a million bucks now that the morning sickness is gone," Megan said. "Dr. Pinkus, this is Daniel."

"Nice to meet you, Daniel." She pulled on a pair of latex gloves. "So this is the first baby for the two of you, right?"

The question seemed directed at him, so he managed a nod.

"How lovely. Well, this is going to be an extraspecial appointment." She smiled brightly at them. "Megan, why don't you lie down and get comfortable? Then we'll get started with the ultrasound."

Dr. Pinkus tucked some paper towels into the top of Megan's leggings and tugged them lower with care, then lifted her shirt to just under her breasts. Daniel forced himself to look away from the sight of her bare midriff but not before he remembered the sound of her breathless laugh as he trailed his lips down to her belly button. He jerked his thoughts back to the present.

"We've warmed this up for you," the doctor said as she squeezed a dollop of clear gel on Megan's stomach. "Here we go."

The sound that soon filled the room reminded Daniel of a steam locomotive speeding down the track.

Megan glanced at him and whispered, "That's the baby's heartbeat."

"All right," Dr. Pinkus said, "and here is your baby. Ten fingers. Ten toes…"

Daniel felt the tips of Megan's fingers brush against his palm. He grabbed hold of her hand and held on tight. At first glance, the black-and-white image on the screen looked like random smudges, until he saw the outline of a baby. His chest constricted and his eyes burned with unshed tears.

He finally looked away from the screen when he heard Megan's choked sob. Tears were streaming down her cheeks, past her smiling lips. He used his free hand to brush back her long hair from her face.

"It's a boy," the doctor said in a gentle voice. "And he is healthy and developing nicely."

"Oh, Daniel." Megan squeezed his hand. "We're having a son."

His son. He didn't trust his voice, so he leaned down and kissed her forehead, letting his lips linger against her soft skin. Such easy affection was out of character for him, but it felt so natural with Megan that it almost felt wrong not to touch her. He didn't give a damn if he was stepping on some coparenting partnership line. Not right now.

"When you're ready, you can pick up the ultrasound pictures at checkout." Dr. Pinkus wiped the gel off Megan's stomach. "I'll see you in four weeks."

"Thank you, Doctor." Daniel finally managed to form words.

He turned away as Megan sat up and adjusted her clothes. His protective instinct tried to overwhelm him as the reality of her pregnancy sank in and took root. If he had his way, he would carry her down to her car. Instead, he took a deep breath and linked his fingers through hers as they walked out of the examination room.

When they arrived at her car, he reluctantly released her hand. "If it isn't too much trouble, could you text me the pictures of the ultrasound?"

Megan's eyebrows sprang up in surprise before a lovely smile blossomed on her face. "It won't be any trouble. I'll send them to you as soon as I get home."

"Thank you." He caught himself staring at her, so he took a quick step back and stuck his hands in his pockets. "I should get back to the office."

"Wait—" she said and grabbed his arm. Blushing furiously, she quickly let go and straightened his sleeve. "I was thinking… Maybe we should attend the Breast Cancer Society's annual charity ball at the end of the month. Anne has been an active member in the group ever since my mom was diagnosed. At any rate, it would be a good opportunity for you to earn some brownie points with her. And—"

"Yes," Daniel said a little louder than he'd intended.

"Oh." Megan blinked. "Okay."

He had no idea when exactly the ball was and whether he had a scheduling conflict. He would cancel or reschedule whatever he had planned. Anything to see her sooner than at her next prenatal appointment four weeks later. He didn't question his desire to be with Megan. It wasn't romantically motivated. She was carrying his child. It was his protective instincts flaring again.

"I'll pick you up—" he began.

"No," she interrupted. "We should go separately. I don't want to give my father any encouragement about setting us up."

"Right." He recalled how adamant Megan was about not marrying him. He pushed aside the black mood threatening to overtake him. "I'll meet you there, then."

He should say goodbye and head to his car, but he stood rooted in front of her. She worried her bottom lip for a second before pushing up to her toes to peck him on his cheek. He sucked in a sharp breath from both the surprise and the heat that shot down to his groin. He somehow hung on to his control and didn't crush his lips against hers.

"Thank you for coming today," she said with an endearing shyness. "I'm so glad our baby—our son—has both of us in his life."

"Me, too," he croaked as desire and tenderness whirled inside him. "Thank you for including me in this journey."

In Megan's presence, Daniel became a man he hardly recognized as himself. The emotions she inspired in him made him feel as powerful as a towering mountain and as vulnerable as a leaf hanging on to a branch through a storm. His survival instincts told him to run, but he was afraid that he would find himself running toward her.

Four

Her sisters sat down on either side of her as the morning sunlight poured into the practice room. Megan was euphoric after yesterday's ultrasound and she couldn't wait to tell her sisters she was pregnant. But they were bound to worry about her single-mom status, so she had to figure out a way to break the news to them gently.

"Which piece should we start with today?" Angie asked, thumbing through her sheet-music folder. "How about the *String Trio Op. 3*?"

"It's too early in the morning for—" Chloe yawned loudly "—Beethoven."

Her older sister gasped with exaggerated outrage. "It is never too early for Beethoven."

"I'm pregnant," Megan blurted, interrupting their argument. That might not have been the gentlest way to tell them, but she couldn't hold it in a second longer.

At least she refrained from stepping onto her chair and singing the words at the top of her lungs.

The silence in the room was eerie. For three whole seconds.

"Oh my God. I'm going to be an auntie," Chloe shrieked, her feet tapping the ground as though her shoes were trying to run away from her. "Wait. Is it okay for me to be happy about it?"

"That depends." Angie angled her body toward Megan. "Are *you* happy about it?"

"I'm so happy." Megan promptly burst into tears. Her older sister wrapped Megan in her arms, and her younger sister patted her head. She hiccuped once and said, "I didn't plan for this to happen, but I feel so blessed."

"Then, we are very happy for you," Angie said, squeezing her tightly against her. "Oh, my goodness. A baby. I can't believe it."

When Megan sat up to blow her nose, she saw her sisters exchange a speaking glance—they wanted to know *everything*. She braced herself to be bombarded with questions.

"Have you been seeing someone in secret?" Chloe nudged Megan with her shoulder.

"No… I met someone after last season's final performance. And…and… I slept with him—a total stranger—then snuck out of the hotel room in the middle of the night." Megan paused as Angie gasped and Chloe snorted. They knew she'd never had a one-night stand before. Her sisters quickly composed themselves and signaled for her to continue. "By the time I realized I was pregnant, I had no way of reaching him because

I never asked for his phone number. We didn't even exchange our last names."

"So the baby's father has no idea you're pregnant?" Angie did an admirable job of keeping her voice even.

"No, he knows," Megan mumbled.

"How?" her sisters asked in unison.

"Do you want the short version or the long version?" Megan rummaged around her purse and pulled out a bag of Sour Patch Kids. She ripped open the bag and stuffed a handful of the gummy goodness into her mouth.

"Short," her sisters said together again.

"Then the long, unedited version right after," Chloe clarified.

"The short version? Jigu Corporation's new CFO, Daniel Pak, is the father of the baby," Megan said with a nervous cringe.

"What the literal hell?" Angie groaned. "Does Appa know?"

"No, he does not know." Megan held up her palms and shook her head. "And he absolutely cannot know. At least, not yet."

Her older sister massaged her temples. "You better give us the long version."

"Ooh, start from how you guys met." Chloe scooted to the edge of her seat.

Megan got the requisite ribbing when she revealed to her sisters that her car ran out of gas the night she met Daniel, followed by plenty of disbelieving murmurs when she told them about their surprise reunion. At the end, she relayed her dilemma about revealing the baby's parentage to their dad and her plans to solve the problem.

"You were one hundred percent right not to agree

to a loveless marriage," Angie said with a firm nod. "Being a single mom will be hard, but you'll have me and Chloe by your side."

"Daniel wants to be a part of the baby's life, too." Megan's voice turned husky with sudden emotion.

Having Daniel at her prenatal appointment—watching their baby on the screen with their fingers linked—had felt deeply right to her. But whatever she was beginning to feel for him had to stop now. He'd made his opinions about love crystal clear that night at the café. If she did something very foolish like fall in love with him, then she was guaranteed to get her heart broken. And that would make coparenting the baby much more difficult—not to mention painful. It would be ideal if she and Daniel could become friends. There was no law against coparenting partners being friends.

"It's a boy, by the way," she announced proudly. Her sisters screamed in excitement, then took turns hugging Megan.

"But I'm not sure about lying to Dad," Chloe said, pulling on her lower lip.

"I don't like it either, but it won't be for long." Megan whipped out the ultrasound picture. "Look at this beautiful baby boy. We have to make sure that he has both a mother *and* a father in his life. Right?"

"Right." Her younger sister smiled and reached for the picture. "How cute is he? He looks like a gummy bear. No, wait. Oh my God. He's a Sour Patch Kid!"

"Let me see." Angie took the ultrasound from Chloe, then doubled over laughing. "Aww, look at our little Sour Patch Kid."

"Yes, it's funny because I eat a lot of Sour Patch Kids," Megan deadpanned. "You guys are hilarious."

"Let's call him SPK until you name him," Chloe cheered.

"We are not calling my child SPK." Megan snatched back the picture of her precious baby. "Don't worry, baby boy. Mommy will protect you from your aunties' mischief."

"You called yourself *mommy* so naturally." Angie covered her mouth with her hand, choking back a sob. "This is really happening. My baby sister is going to be a mom."

Tears streamed down Megan's cheeks once more. "Look what you've done, Unni. It's really hard to turn this off once it starts these days."

"Cry all you want." Her older sisters wiped Megan's face with a tissue. "We'll laugh and cry and celebrate this baby."

"I love you guys so much," Megan said, crying harder.

"We love you, too." Chloe sniffled.

Megan could stand on her own and face anything life threw at her. But it was so much better to do it with her sisters by her side—especially playing Beethoven in E-flat major at ten in the morning.

The ultrasound picture burned a hole in Megan's pocket as she sat down for dinner with her dad. On the one hand, she was dying to show off the image of her baby boy. She had to tell him soon anyway, and she knew he would love the child growing inside her once he digested the news. On the other hand, she didn't want to see the disappointment on her dad's face when she told him she was pregnant as a result of a one-night stand.

In a moment of weakness, she thought about telling him that she had been seeing someone, but it didn't work out. But she was already keeping the identity of the baby's father a secret from her dad and she couldn't handle any more lies. He really deserved better.

"Is everything okay?" her dad asked.

"Yeah. Of course everything's okay." She sat up straight, like she'd been caught doodling in class. "Why wouldn't everything be okay?"

"You've been pushing around that broccoli on your plate for the past five minutes." He leveled a stern glance at her. "Do I have to remind you to eat your vegetables?"

Megan laughed and popped the broccoli in her mouth. "I was just lost in thought."

"You and your sisters must be busy preparing for the upcoming season." Her dad took a guess as to her preoccupation.

"We are," she replied truthfully. "But we're excited to perform again."

"You know what you need?" He pointed his fork at her.

"No, Appa. What do I need?" She humored him with a wry smile.

"Golf." He nodded, agreeing enthusiastically with himself. "We should play a round on Saturday. It'll help you relax."

Her dad accepted the fact that none of his daughters would join the company he'd built—he accepted that they were born to be musicians. And it was what her mom had wanted and he would do anything for her. But he'd asked for one thing from her and her sisters. That they learn to play golf. He loved golf and wanted to share his passion with his daughters. She and her sisters had become competent golfers—Chloe was actually rather good—but Megan mostly enjoyed the conversations she shared with her dad on the green.

"It *has* been a while since we played a round," she said thoughtfully. They would talk and bond, then she would tell him she was pregnant. "It's a date."

Daniel stood outside the clubhouse, scrolling through some work email on his phone. Most could wait until Monday, but he would answer some later tonight. For now, he was determined to spend his Saturday like an actual weekend, playing a round of golf with Mr. Han. The familiar guilt that accompanied his thoughts about his mentor settled uncomfortably in his stomach. With a sigh, he pulled up the sonogram and traced the curved silhouette of the baby with the tip of his finger.

Keeping the truth from Mr. Han was in everyone's best interests, even though Daniel felt shitty about it. He couldn't risk being miles away from Megan and the baby, and Jigu Corporation needed him. Mr. Han would regret it if he fired Daniel in the heat of the moment. He was sure of that.

"I'm going to kill him," a melodic voice seethed from behind him.

He spun on his heels and came face-to-face with a furious Megan. "What are you doing here?"

"I can't believe he pulled this shit again," she railed, ignoring his question. "I told him he was embarrassing all of us."

He blew out a breath and rocked back on his heels. "So Mr. Han has struck again?"

"Yes." She paced back and forth in front of him with her fists on her hips.

Megan was obviously fuming, but she looked beautiful nonetheless. She wore a white sleeveless dress that flared around her hips, then fell inches shy of midthigh. Her ponytail bounced under her white cap as she continued to wear a groove on the pavement.

He glanced at his watch. "It's almost tee time."

She stopped and glanced quizzically at him.

"Well, it wasn't easy carving out the time to be here," he said, rubbing the back of his head. "And it would be a shame to waste such a beautiful day…"

He wasn't secretly glad that Megan had showed up instead of Mr. Han. And he definitely wasn't excited to spend the next several hours with her. There was no particular reason why his heart was racing.

"You're right." A rueful smile spread across Megan's face. "If you're anything like my father, I bet you rarely see the sunlight, being stuck in your office all day, every day."

"Guilty as charged." He raised his hand like a doofus, relieved she wasn't about to stomp straight off to go yell at her father.

"Can I make a confession? I actually don't enjoy golf very much. Don't tell my father. He'd be heartbroken if he found out. I only golf to spend time with him." Daniel felt himself deflate a little. *So much for spending a day in the sun with Megan.* But she continued, "Can I offer an alternative way to take advantage of this gorgeous day?"

"Please. Offer away." *Offer away?* He sounded like an eager pup.

"Why don't we go miniature golfing instead?" A mischievous light entered her eyes. "Maybe play a round of Skee-Ball? I'm a Skee-Ball *fiend*."

"Skee-Ball?" His eyebrows drew together.

"Didn't your parents take you to arcades when you were little?" He was saved from answering—neither of them needed to have a conversation about his bleak childhood—because she went on to explain, "You roll this hard, heavy ball down a lane…"

"You mean like bowling?"

"No, no. There are no pins and the balls are baseball-sized." She cupped her hands to show him how big a baseball was since he obviously knew nothing. "Anyway, you roll the ball down a lane and into these small holes with different points. The harder to score, the higher the points."

"That sounds…fun?" He kept his face straight with some effort.

"Yes." Megan slapped his arm. "It is *the* best game in the world. Ooh, and we should definitely eat some greasy arcade pizza."

"Definitely." He gazed longingly at the clubhouse where they served the most delicious Monte Cristos. "Greasy pizza sounds fantastic."

"Oh, come on," she chided. "It's going to be fun. I promise."

"I'll hold you to it," he said, even though he would've happily watched paint dry with her. "Should we drive together? I'm not sure what we should do about your car…"

"No worries. My father had to go in to work this morning. He sent a car over to pick me up so he and I could drive home toge—" She gripped her forehead with her hand. "He deliberately left me stranded here so you'd have to give me a ride."

"How devious of him," Daniel said solemnly, biting the inside of his cheeks.

"I promise this won't happen again," she said with a pained expression.

He snuffed out the disappointment inside him. What was wrong with him?

Nothing good would come of indulging Mr. Han's matchmaking efforts. The longer they let it go on and got his hopes up, the more disappointed and betrayed his mentor would feel when he found out the truth—that Daniel and Megan had no intention of getting married even though he was the father of the baby.

And nothing good would come of indulging in his attraction to Megan. It would only complicate an already difficult situation. That was why they'd agreed to be coparenting partners and nothing more. His head understood that well enough, but his body was having a hard time remembering their agreement.

"It's not your fault." He dragged his fingers through his hair. "But it'll be wise to put an end to his matchmaking scheme soon."

"I was going to tell my father I'm pregnant after we golfed," she whispered, leaning close to him. "He won't keep pushing me on you if he thinks I'm pregnant with another man's child."

"Yes, you're probably right." The necessary omission twisted his gut with guilt, but it would only be until he won over key members of the board of directors. "How…? What will you tell him? About the baby's…father?"

"I'm going to stick as close to the truth as possible." She shrugged a bit helplessly. "I'll tell him I had a one-night stand with a stranger and that we parted without exchanging any contact information."

"I see," he murmured, more than a little concerned

for Megan. It was the twenty-first century, but there was no denying that Korean-American culture remained rather conservative. Mr. Han was a good man, but he would no doubt be disappointed in his daughter. "Are you going to tell him tonight?"

"Yeah. There's no point in putting it off any longer."

"Will you be okay?" he asked even though he knew what her answer was going to be and that it would be a lie. She wasn't going to be okay. At least, not at first.

"Yes." She smiled tremulously, and a vise tightened around his chest. "I'll be fine."

"Well, we better fortify you for the showdown with some arcade pizza," he said, rubbing his hands together.

"And nachos. The processed cheese will coat me with a layer of protection."

He couldn't hold back his cringe. "Processed cheese. Of course."

Megan laughed and reached for her golf bag, but he snatched it away from her and hefted it onto his shoulder before pulling his own bag onto his other shoulder. "Shall we?"

They walked the short distance to his car, and Megan stood beside him typing into her phone as he loaded their golf clubs into the trunk.

"Okay," she said. "I found our place. Let's go."

Family Fun Palace was showing its age but was relatively clean, and the people who worked there seemed friendly and eager to help. The Western-themed miniature golf course was overrun by small kids, but their conscientious parents redirected them to focus on the game so the line didn't grow unbearably long.

Daniel didn't mind the short wait for the last hole as he watched Megan carefully jot down their score with a stubby pencil, munching on some Sour Patch Kids. She held out her hand and he dropped several more colorful pieces onto her palm. Her golf dress didn't have pockets, so he was the designated candy carrier. She plopped all of it into her mouth.

"We're tied," she mumbled morosely around a mouthful. "We can't end on a tie. This isn't freaking soccer."

"Who says I'm going to let you win?" He smirked and popped a piece of candy in his mouth. "Holy shit. What is in this stuff? It's disgusting."

"How dare you?" She snatched the nearly empty bag of Sour Patch Kids from his hand. "This is the single most perfect food in the world. And it was the only thing I could eat for the first trimester of my pregnancy."

"Then I'm grateful for its existence." Before he could stop himself, he reached out and ran his knuckles down her cheek. "I'm sorry. It sounds like you had a hard time."

"It was awful, but it's so worth it." She leaned into his touch before she pulled back suddenly. "Um, I think we're up."

Daniel cursed under his breath for acting on his impulse and followed Megan's brisk steps to the putting area. She stood back to let him set down his neon-green ball on the tee.

"Par nine," he read from the sign by the ninth hole, wanting to scatter the awkward air between them. He arched an eyebrow in challenge. "I'll do it in five strokes."

"Good luck with that," Megan said, crossing her arms over her chest. "Why don't we make this a bit more interesting? The loser buys the winner a slushy."

"You're on," he said, pointing his index finger at her.

Never mind that he would not drink the blended colored water to save his life.

He maneuvered the ball for the final putt in three strokes. Megan stood beside him with her hand on her forehead. He couldn't remember the last time he'd had so much fun—quite possibly never. He turned to her with a shit-eating grin. "You must be tired. I don't see the point of you even taking your turn."

Megan held up a finger with a neatly trimmed nail painted in a deep, vibrant purple. But considering which finger she chose to raise, he didn't think it was meant for him to appreciate her edgy manicure. She dumped the last of the vile candy into her mouth and tossed the empty bag in the trash. Then she positioned her putter by her fluorescent pink ball. He shook his head. She was going to need at least three more strokes to finish. He should be a nice guy and give her the slushy she was going to buy for him.

Her putter met the ball with a sweet clang, and he watched with his mouth agape as her ball bounced and banked impossible curves and edges.

"Oh my God." She jumped up and down. "It's going in. *It's going in.*"

"No, no, no." He prayed for the ball to lose momentum, but it kept rolling and rolling, straight into the hole.

Megan screamed and threw herself into his arms. With a huff of startled laughter, he lifted her off the ground before holding her close to him, pressing his cheek against her hair. She slowly quietened in his embrace but made no move to step away. Her tantalizing sweetness teased his nose, and her warm, soft curves pressed against him. Daniel couldn't deny how much he had longed to hold her like this—ever since he found her again.

She leaned back just enough to meet his gaze and he felt himself falling into the depths of her soft, brown eyes. He swept a strand of hair behind her ear with an unsteady hand and lifted her chin with the crook of his finger. Their faces were mere inches apart—so close he could feel the heat of her breath against his lips. He had to taste her. There was a reason he shouldn't, but he couldn't remember what. The need to kiss her consumed him and nothing else mattered. He slowly lowered his head…

"Ektuse me!" said a ringing voice with a childish lisp. "I hit ball. Hit ball fast and go potty."

Megan pushed away from him so abruptly that she nearly stumbled. He steadied her by her arms, then promptly dropped his hands. "You all right?"

"Yes. Yup. Mmm-hmm." She nodded as though her answer wasn't clear enough.

"I'm so sorry." A woman who appeared to be the toddler's mom waved her hand. "Please take your time."

"No, we're all done here," Daniel said, picking up Megan's putter off the ground where she'd dropped it before she flew into his arms. "I got my butt handed to me."

"I think I'm going to get an extralarge cherry slushy. No. Half cherry, half cola," Megan mused. He sneaked a glance at her and she was all smiles again. "I hope you learned an important lesson today. Never go against a Han when a slushy is on the line."

"Yeah, sure. Feel free to steal the Sicilian's line," he said with a teasing grin.

"You recognize the line?" Her eyes widened with pleasure. "I didn't peg you for a fan of *The Princess Bride*."

"As you get to know me, you'll discover that I'm full of surprises." He blinked and turned to stare straight ahead. He had never uttered a cornier sentence in his entire life. More importantly, was he flirting with her?

"Looking forward to it," Megan murmured.

His gaze shot back to her, but she wasn't looking at him. Was she flirting back? Did he want her to? He felt so completely turned around that he didn't know his right from left anymore. This wasn't like him. He always knew what he wanted. He always chose his path with deliberate care. With Megan, he felt as though he was hurtling down a grassy hill on a sunlit day. He couldn't deny that it was fun and exhilarating, but he felt out of control and more than a little scared.

Megan was intoxicating and that made her dangerous. He had to rein in his emotions before they got out of hand. He had enough riding on their partnership without risking his heart on top of it.

Five

Megan sat down at the dining table, glancing warily at the place setting for two. Her dad had been taking his dinner in his study for the past three nights, since she told him that she'd gotten pregnant from a one-night stand. He was understandably angry and disappointed in her. She sighed and smoothed her napkin on her thighs. It probably had slipped Mrs. Chung's mind that he wouldn't be joining Megan for dinner.

She was reminded that nothing ever slipped their housekeeper extraordinaire's mind when her father walked into the dining room and joined her at the table. She'd always prided herself in being brave and bold, but she couldn't meet her dad's eyes. Other than thanking Mrs. Chung when she brought out their dinner, neither of them said a word to each other for a long while.

The rice and soup in front of her blurred as her eyes

filled with tears, but she inhaled deeply through her nose to hold off the ugly crying. When her dad reached out and placed a piece of grilled fish on her rice, she lost her perilous grip on her emotions and a choked sob escaped from her.

"You need to eat well," he said gruffly.

"I'm so sorry, Appa." She finally met his eyes as tears slid down her cheeks.

Her dad nodded solemnly and said with quiet menace, "When I find the bastard who took advantage of you, I'll tear him apart limb by limb."

"No one took advantage of me," she insisted, alarm jolting through her. "It was my choice. This pregnancy is an unexpected outcome, but I love this baby so much, and…and…"

"Now you understand how much I love you." He squeezed her hand.

"I love you, too." Megan pushed back her chair and knelt by her dad's side, resting her head on his knees. "I know this isn't the way you envisioned becoming a grandpa."

"I'm an old man set in my ways, but I need to learn how to roll with the punches. I lost so much time with Angie being an obstinate fool. When Umma was diagnosed with breast cancer, I would have moved mountains to save her—and to protect you girls from the heartache—but there was nothing I can do. I let my fear of losing her consume me and I became an overbearing tyrant. I forced Angie to leave the love of her life. I thought I was protecting her… I thought I knew best." She raised her head to look at him, taking his hand in hers. He smoothed her hair away from her face with his free hand and said, "I'm not going to repeat that mistake with you…especially with the little rascal on his way."

"Rascal?" She crinkled her nose at him. "He's going to be a perfect angel baby just like I was."

Her dad snorted loud enough to startle her. "When you were two, you thought you could fly. Umma and I seriously considered tying you to a chair after an exceptionally adventurous day."

Umma. What would her mom think if she knew that Megan was keeping the identity of the baby's father a secret from her dad? Guilt threatened to strangle the relief she felt at having her dad finally forgive her.

"The baby and I… We're going to be happy," she said to reassure her dad as well as herself. "You don't have to worry."

"Oh, my dear girl. Parents never stop worrying." His chuckle sounded melancholy. "But yes, you and the baby will be happy. I'll do everything in my power to make sure of that."

She believed him. And if he knew Daniel was the father of her baby, he would do everything in his power to force them to get married. She couldn't let that happen. She had to keep him in the dark for now. This was the only way for all of them to be happy. But knowing the secrecy was necessary didn't do anything to ease her guilt. Her dad's love and acceptance made her feel much, much worse about lying to him.

She managed to keep her unease to herself through dinner, then excused herself. She paced the length of her bedroom while wringing her hands. When that did nothing to make her feel any better, she stopped and shook out her hands, arms and legs. It felt as though ants were crawling all over her body. She had never lied to her dad before. Not like this. She wasn't sure how long she could keep it up.

She wanted to talk to her sisters, but she couldn't involve them in this charade any more than she had to. They'd promised not to say anything to their dad until Megan was ready to tell him herself. Even so, they didn't feel too great about it. No, she couldn't burden them with her turmoil. But who else could she talk to?

The answer was obvious. Still, she hesitated. Not because she didn't want to talk to Daniel. She hesitated because she desperately *wanted* to. They had met all of five times. He was a virtual stranger. But he didn't feel like one. She trusted him in a way that was all but impossible to explain. And she wanted his understanding and solace more than anything. She wanted *him*.

She grabbed her phone off her nightstand and stood with her thumbs poised over the keyboard. He felt bound to her by duty. He was attracted to her, but he didn't want anything *real* with her other than to coparent their child together. Reaching out to him tonight would be emotional self-sabotage.

She nearly dropped her phone when it pinged with a message from Daniel.

How did your talk go with your father?

Was this a courtesy text? If he was really worried, why didn't he text her three nights ago after their miniature golfing adventures? By the time they parted ways that evening, he'd grown quiet and distant. She chalked it up to him being tired or preoccupied with work after spending a rare day away from the office. But in all honesty, she'd instinctively understood that he was reinforcing the do-not-cross line between them. So why was he texting her now?

While she studied his question from all sides, her phone lit up with a new message.

I don't mean to intrude but... I wanted to make sure you were okay.

The truth. She could just answer his question with the truth. There was no need to overthink it.

He didn't speak to me for three days. Tonight, he told me he loves me and that he would do anything to make sure the baby and I are happy. That breaks my heart more than anything. I pretty much made a mess of everything.

Ellipses immediately began scrolling across her screen. She waited, nibbling her bottom lip. His message popped up at last.

Can I see you tonight?

Her heart stuttered in her chest. God, she wanted to see him.

Tonight? Like right now?

She stared at her phone.

I can be at your place in twenty minutes.

She shook her head as she typed.

No, not here.

But she also didn't want to fall apart somewhere public. She tapped out her suggestion before she could regret it.

I'll come over to your place.

His place turned out to be in one of the high-rise condos in Downtown LA not far from Jigu Corporation headquarters. She valeted her car and was shown to the penthouse elevator. He must've already added her to his guest list because keys were turned and buttons pressed without delay. The ride up to the top floor was smooth and fast, and the doors slid open before she felt ready.

Daniel stood a few feet away from the elevator with his hands in his pockets. He was still in a pair of slacks and a dress shirt, but with the top couple buttons undone and his sleeves rolled past his elbows. He looked gorgeous as hell. But that wasn't what had her throwing herself into his arms. The undisguised concern and sympathy in his eyes crumbled her defenses, and she couldn't hold herself back any longer.

His strong arms circled around her and held her close. She burrowed her face into the crook of his neck and pressed herself against him. She would just stay like this for a minute. There was no need for her to fall apart in front of him. She would accept the support he offered with dignity.

"I'm here," he said simply, his warm breath ruffling the hair by her temple.

She wished he'd stayed silent. She wished his words hadn't melted her heart into a puddle.

"No fair," she managed to choke out before she burst

into tears. She was making his shirt all soggy, but she couldn't stop crying. "Sorry. Pregnancy hormones."

"You don't need to blame the hormones." His chest expanded and contracted with a heavy sigh. "Anyone dealing with what you're going through would be having a good cry."

She leaned back to meet his eyes and sniffed loudly. "Please stop saying all the right things."

"I'm saying all the right things?" His eyebrows crested above the bridge of his nose. "I should blurt out the first thing that pops into my head more often."

She huffed a watery laugh and moved to step away from him. He was slow to drop his arms—his hands skimming down her back in a way that made her shiver. Her gaze skittered away from his.

"Nice place," she said, glancing around the foyer painted in muted burgundy and gray. "At least what I can see of it."

"Hell, sorry." He scratched the back of his head. "I obviously don't have people over much. Let me show you to the living room."

She pressed her lips together to keep from smiling. She didn't know why she wanted to smile, honestly. *Who cares if he doesn't have people over often?* She certainly didn't. He could invite women to his place as often as he'd like. It wasn't like they were romantically involved or anything. Megan trudged after him. Suddenly, she didn't feel like smiling at all.

"Make yourself comfortable." Daniel held out his hand toward a dark brown sectional to one side of the large living room, then headed toward the open kitchen on the other end. "Would you like something to drink?"

"Sure." She lowered herself onto the sofa and brushed her hand over the soft leather. "Tea would be nice."

"Yes, of course."

She watched him wander around the kitchen opening a cupboard here and a drawer there. She decided to give him a break when he started cursing under his breath. "Why do I get the feeling you don't come here often either?"

"What?" He spun away from the refrigerator, closing the freezer door. She didn't question why he was looking for tea in the freezer. "I only moved in a few months ago. I honestly don't do much here other than catch a few hours of sleep most nights."

A small frown pinched her forehead. As she'd suspected, Daniel was as much of a workaholic as her dad. But at least her dad had a family to provide some balance to his life. The thought of Daniel being lonely made her heart ache a little.

"On second thought, I don't need any tea," she said, patting the seat beside her. "Come join me."

Daniel felt like an idiot as he sat down next to Megan. He couldn't even give her a cup of tea. But offering her what he had in his freezer instead—and explaining why he had so many cartons of different flavors of ice cream—would be much more mortifying.

"Do you have family back East?" she asked, tucking her legs up onto the couch.

He stiffened reflexively at her unexpected question, but forced himself to relax. "Just my father."

"So you're an only child." She didn't phrase it as a question, so he didn't offer a response. "I can't imagine life without my sisters."

"I got used to being alone. You can't miss something you never had," he said with a matter-of-fact shrug. His mother had left him and his father when he was so young that he didn't remember her at all. It was as if he'd never had a mother.

"I guess that's true." She rested her chin on top of one of her knees. "What about your father? Do you miss him?"

"We aren't...close." He shifted in his seat. The understatement almost felt like a lie, but he couldn't exactly tell her that his father wished he'd never had Daniel.

"I'm beginning to think it's a good thing you have me and the baby in your life," she said in a voice so quiet he wondered if he'd misheard her. But his pounding heart and the slight tremor in his body assured him that he'd understood her correctly.

"I didn't realize I got to have you in my life, too." And why did he say that? She probably didn't mean anything by it. He should've laughed it off instead of hanging on to her words as though they were the only things keeping him afloat.

Her eyes widened and a deep blush rose to her face. He wanted to brush his lips across her cheekbones to see if her skin felt as hot as it looked. "Well, since the baby is inside of me right now, we...the baby and I... kind of come in a package? For the time being?"

"I'm glad you come as part of it all," he said huskily. A jolt of fear shot through him at how happy the package deal made him. They were having a child together, but she didn't plan on being with him. She would leave like the others. As a reminder to himself, he repeated, "For the time being."

She nodded absently and drew circles on the couch

with the tip of her index finger. *Hell.* What was he doing? He'd asked to see her so he could comfort her. The last three days must have been tough for her.

"I'm sorry your father took the news of your pregnancy so hard." He gently picked up her hand. "Was he very angry with you?"

"Very." Her sad smile felt like a punch in the gut. "But I expected that. And when he was angry with me, I felt a bit indignant and self-righteous. I thought to myself 'I'm a grown woman and I can do whatever the hell I want with my body.' The hard part—"

He squeezed her hand when she paused to swallow the emotion swelling up in her.

"The hard part came when he offered me his love and support, because I couldn't hide from the truth anymore. He was only angry because he was worried and scared for me. I can't believe I put him through that." She scoffed and shook her head. "I can't believe what I'm about to put him through by lying to him about who the baby's father is."

"It's not too late to tell him the truth." He gulped. Getting fired from Jigu Corporation was the last thing he wanted, but he couldn't bear to watch Megan hurting. "We could tell him together."

"Daniel, my father respects and trusts you, but if we tell him now that you are the baby's father and we refuse to get married, then he will fire you. My father is a relic from the Joseon Dynasty, when it comes to duty and honor. In the heat of the moment, he would think firing you is the only way to protect our family's honor—my honor." She took a deep breath and squared her shoulders. "His pride and temper often get the best of him, but once he comes to his senses, he'll regret losing you. I can't let him make that mistake. And it's not fair to you or our baby. We have no choice but to carry out our plan."

"I understand." He nodded. She was right, of course. "Is there anything I could do in the meantime to ease your burden?"

"No. Not unless you have ice cream," she said with a wistful smile.

He groaned and placed his head in his hands.

"What's wrong?" She scooted close to him and put her hand on his shoulder.

"What flavor do you want?" he growled.

"What? Oh…" She laughed. "I was just kidding. You don't need to conjure any up for me."

"Just…" He huffed and sat up straight. "Just humor me. Tell me what flavor you want."

"Um, cherry vanilla?" she said hesitantly.

"What else?" He wearily pushed himself off the sofa.

"Butter pecan?" She cocked her head to the side and regarded him curiously. "Are you seriously going out to get me ice cream right now?"

He stomped to the freezer without answering and grabbed a pint each of cherry vanilla and butter pecan. He pulled open a few drawers until he found a spoon and returned to the sofa.

"Ice cream," he announced unnecessarily and plunked down the cartons on the coffee table.

Megan's jaw dropped, and the shock on her face made him feel a little better. "How did you know I was going to ask for these flavors? Wait, how did you even know to have ice cream handy in your freezer?"

He sighed and sat back down on the couch. He might

as well get this over with. "Do you remember how I volunteered to deliver whatever food you were craving?"

"Yes…"

"You mentioned that you might crave ice cream one of these days, but I had no idea what kind you like, so I bought one of virtually every flavor out there." His words ran over each other in his rush to get them out. "I like to be prepared. I didn't want to go jumping from store to store, searching for a particular variety of ice cream. Who wants to keep a pregnant woman waiting? A damn fool. That's who."

He stopped talking because he knew he was rambling like a…damn fool. He thought Megan would be rolling around the floor laughing by now, but she didn't make a peep. He finally turned to glance at her. The tenderness in her expression nearly undid him.

"You did all that for me?" she whispered.

He reached out and ran the back of his hand down her cheek. "I wanted to do something for you… anything. I can't even imagine everything you're going through. How can I help? What can I do?"

She leaned into his touch, cupping her hand over his. "This. I think everything you've done tonight is exactly what I needed."

He couldn't look away from her. She was so close and so beautiful. He felt his head tilting toward her. He couldn't stop himself, but he moved as slowly as he could so she would have a chance to turn away from him. She didn't turn away. Her mouth parted on a shaky breath and her eyes tugged him closer yet.

It was barely a touch—a brush of parted lips against parted lips—but his world seemed to stop. He drew back only enough to search her face, but she gasped with outrage and promptly brought his lips back on hers with her hands buried in his hair. With a helpless, desperate groan, he kissed her the way he'd been starving to kiss her.

He nipped at her full bottom lip, then licked it. He tilted his head to one side, then the other, tasting her from all angles. When she moaned, he plunged his tongue into her hot mouth and wrapped his hand around the back of her neck, steading her against his onslaught. She pushed closer to him, her breasts pressed against his chest. It wasn't close enough.

Daniel leaned back on the sofa until Megan was lying on top of him, kissing him as though she couldn't get enough of him either. Straddling his waist, she sat up long enough to tear her shirt off, then he dragged her back as though kissing her was the only way he could breathe. Their lips moved against each other's, wild and clumsy.

His erection strained against his trousers and he hooked his thumbs into the top of her pants, tugging impatiently. She sucked in a surprised breath and scrambled off him. He rose onto his elbows to find her sitting with her knees drawn to her chest on the other end of the couch. Bewildered, he sat up and clawed his hands through his hair. Shit. He'd gotten so caught up in his desire, he must have pushed her too fast.

"Megan, I'm sorry," he panted, trying to catch his breath.

"No. No, don't be." Her chest was still heaving. "I just…"

"You don't need to explain." He held up his hand. "Shit. I shouldn't have done that. We had an agreement and you're vulnerable right now. I crossed the line—"

"Just shut up and listen for a minute," she commanded. He snapped his mouth shut. She took a deep breath and continued, "I'm wearing maternity pants."

"Why does…? Pardon?"

"When you tugged on my pants, I realized I was wearing maternity garb." She stretched her legs out so he could see them more fully. "It has this stretchy, elastic panel and…it's not very sexy."

His eyes dropped to her waistline and he noticed the soft curve of her stomach for the first time. Emotion rose up to his throat and heat spread through his chest. She was so beautiful. Then a thought made his blood drain from his face. "Oh God. Did I hurt you? The baby—"

"Stop it. I'm fine. We're fine." She buried her face in her hands. "I'm just embarrassed. Okay? It's like getting caught on a date wearing a pair of granny underwear."

Incredulous laughter huffed out of him.

"Are you laughing at me?" Megan's eyes narrowed dangerously.

"I happen to value my life." He grinned and picked up her top from the ground. He pulled it carefully over her head and helped her slide her arms in. He smoothed down her shirt and placed both his hands on her shoulders. "You don't have any idea how beautiful you are, do you?"

"Who looks beautiful in maternity pants?" She turned her head to the side.

He gently grasped her chin between his fingers and made her look at him again. "You."

She stared at him as though she wanted to call his bullshit. He held her gaze because he meant what he said and he wanted her to know that. A soft blush stole across her face. Her eyelashes fluttered and she smiled shyly at him.

"Sorry for halting things so abruptly," she said at last.

"It's for the best." He didn't necessarily believe that at the moment, but he should. Megan was guilt ridden enough without adding another thing to hide from her father. And he knew better than to touch the CEO's daughter when things were quite tangled up as it was. Too bad his intelligence became questionable every time he was around this woman. "We shouldn't do anything we might regret. Coparenting partners, remember?"

Some of the light left Megan's eyes and he wanted to take back his words. But it was for the best. If he told that to himself enough times, he might even believe it.

"Oh, the ice cream," she said, reaching for a carton. "I almost forgot."

"I can get you some different ones if those melted."

"No, they're still good. I like mine a little runny." She scooped up a generous mound of cherry vanilla and licked it off the spoon. "Mmm."

"Happy?" he asked as euphoria filled her face.

"Happy," she said around another mouthful.

"Good." He leaned back on the couch and quietly watched her decimate two cartons of ice cream.

This had to be enough. He would provide her with ice cream, accompany her to her prenatal appointments and offer his support when things got difficult for her at home. If he didn't get greedy, this might be enough for him. It had to be.

Six

Megan's favorite part about the Breast Cancer Society's annual fundraising ball was its venue at the Ebell of Los Angeles clubhouse. The historic two-story building was constructed nearly a hundred years ago in the Italian Renaissance style with a smooth white exterior and dark clay-tile roofing. The dining hall, where the main event would be held, boasted high engraved ceilings and stately columns. With rich wood panels and wrought-iron railings, it felt like a place from another time.

But what made the place truly magical for Megan was the tiled-roof colonnade that led to the manicured courtyard garden. The walkway arches surrounded two sides of the space, draped with silky fuchsia curtains to complement the pink theme, which commemorated the fight against breast cancer. Intricate topiaries lined the street-facing side so the guests could forget that they were idling in a building by a busy Los Angeles street.

Cocktail hour was well underway in the picturesque garden, and guests in tasteful formal wear milled about the ornate water fountain aglow with ambient lighting. Megan walked over to the bar set up in the corner and ordered a club soda with lime. Her Grecian, empire-waist gown effortlessly hid her baby bump, but there was no reason to announce that she wasn't drinking.

"Thank you." She took the glass the bartender extended to her and opened her clutch.

A long arm reached around her and placed a couple twenties in the tip jar. "I'll have the same."

"Daniel." Her voice sounded huskier than she'd like, but she couldn't stop her heart from fluttering at the sight of him. He looked magnificent in a classic tuxedo, fitted to show off his athletic physique to perfection. He wore his hair slicked back from his forehead, adding an irresistible air of sophistication. "You made it."

With his drink in one hand, he placed his other on the small of her back and led her toward one of the draped arches. "Of course. I've been looking forward to it."

"Looking forward to the ball? Or looking forward to seeing me?" She smiled up at him from beneath her lashes.

"I, uh…" He cleared his throat and recovered admirably. "Both. I was looking forward to both."

They hadn't met since the night at his penthouse. He had texted periodically to check in on her but they were more polite than anything else. She wanted to scream with frustration every time she got one, but she sent an equally polite response back. She was biding her time to make her move. And yes…she had every intention of making a move.

Something had shifted for her that night Daniel offered her ice cream in any flavor she could possibly want. His gruff tenderness and vulnerability moved her to the core, and she wanted him. It was foolish and inconvenient. He made it clear that he would regret getting involved with her. Maybe he was right. Maybe they would be sorry. She would loathe having yet another secret to keep from her father. But Megan knew she would regret it more if she didn't at least try to explore the attraction between them. It was something rare and special—at least for her.

"Good answer," she said. "Shall we go find Anne and get you those brownie points?"

"By all means. Lead the way." His hand found its way back to the curve of her back, and shivers of awareness skipped down her spine. "We aren't going to run into your father here, are we?"

"No, it's hard for him to attend these events. Even after seven years, my mom's death is still a raw wound for him." She sighed. "I've been coming and donating on his behalf for the last several years, so we're safe to proceed with our plan."

Anne was in the dining room, adjusting the pink floral centerpieces and smoothing out the bows on the satin chair covers. She looked impeccably elegant in an emerald A-line gown, but a small frown marred her forehead.

"Everything looks absolutely perfect." Megan leaned down to kiss the older woman's cheek. "You can stop fussing."

"Tim stepped out to the garden to get a drink." Anne

laughed and rotated the centerpiece by a quarter turn. "He said I was making him nervous."

Megan wrapped her arm around Anne's shoulders and turned them both to face Daniel. "Look who I found wandering about."

"It's good to see you, Mrs. Werner." His words were friendly enough, but his expression was aloof as he extended his hand toward her. That wouldn't do.

Megan cleared her throat softly. His eyes flitted toward her and she mouthed "Smile," pantomiming a toothy grin.

"Thank you, Mr. Pak." Anne placed her hand in Daniel's with a regal nod. "I'm so glad you could make it."

"You've done an amazing job. The event looks like a success," he said with a hint of a smile. That was better. "And please call me Daniel."

Anne made a noncommittal noise and said, "I didn't realize you two knew each other."

"He came over for dinner one evening and we kind of hit it off," Megan explained. "Call us golfing buddies. We mostly complain about my father to each other."

He held out his hand and hurriedly averred, "I have the greatest respect for Mr. Han."

"Of course you do. We both do. Great man, my father." Megan winked at him and whispered to Anne, "As an added bonus, Daniel is very fun to tease."

"Megan, do be gentle with him." Anne smiled sympathetically at Daniel. "You have to watch out for this one."

"I appreciate the heads-up," he said, his grin widening. "I'll be sure to stay on my toes."

"Look at you two…ganging up on me." Megan was

delighted that Daniel had relaxed enough to let some of his charm shine through.

"We have to even out the playing field somehow," he said, still wearing that beautiful smile. He turned to Anne with humor twinkling in his eyes. "I'll come find you if I need reinforcement."

The older woman laughed, genuine warmth stealing into her expression. "I'll be on the lookout for you."

"Fine. Be that way." Megan wrinkled her nose at them.

"Well, we'll leave you to prepare." Daniel raised his drink and said, "Here's to record-breaking donations."

"Thank you, Daniel. Fingers crossed," Anne said with another fond smile. Then she pulled Megan over to the side and whispered, "Some men look like they were born to wear a tuxedo. Have fun *playing golf* with him."

"Miss Anne," Megan gasped. "We're just friends."

"Whatever you say." Anne wiggled her eyebrows.

Megan cast a quick glance at Daniel, who appeared to be studying the tastefully decorated dining room with interest. "I had to nip my dad's matchmaking fantasies in the bud, so don't you start now."

"Oh, I don't know. You know what they say about the wisdom of elders…"

"I'm going back out to the beautiful garden to enjoy the evening with my *friend*."

Megan hurried off before Anne could continue her teasing. But it was a good sign that she was trying to play matchmaker, too. Her dear friend had taken a liking to Daniel. Now it was up to him to keep the rapport alive.

"Hey, shall we go mingle?" she said, coming to stand next to him.

"Must we?" he drawled dryly. He glanced toward the throng outside with a faint grimace and sipped his drink.

"What?" She widened her eyes innocently. "You don't enjoy smiling until your cheeks cramp, while making small talk with virtual strangers who listen to you with half an ear and silently judge you?"

"It's so delightful. How could I not enjoy that?" He chuckled, the warm sound making her toes curl. She had to try to make him do that more often.

She hooked her arm through his and strolled onto the walkway that led to the garden. "If you pretend that all the people are gone, there's a quiet beauty to this place."

"Maybe we should hide somewhere to enjoy it." He glanced sideways at her and let his eyes linger until her skin tingled as though he'd run his hands down her body. He wanted her as much as she wanted him.

"There may be an alcove at the end of this walkway," she murmured and slowly sashayed her way past the crowd.

The time was ripe to make her move.

The sway of Megan's hips mesmerized him as she glided down the walkway ahead of him. He caught up with her in three long strides and placed his hand on her lower back, his bottom two fingers pressed tantalizingly close to the curve of her ass. His nostrils flared as he caught a whiff of her sweet, floral scent, and reason slipped out of his mind.

He had been determined to keep his distance since the night she came over to his place. He didn't want to betray Mr. Han's trust further by sleeping with his daughter behind his back. And it wouldn't be easy for

Megan to keep another secret from her father. The last thing he wanted was to add to her already full plate. But when he saw her standing in the garden tonight— a vision in her flowing red dress—he knew he would crawl through burning coal to have her again.

She reached for his hand, and he threaded his fingers through hers, and she pulled them into a shadowy alcove and pressed her back against the wall. He placed his hands on either side of her head and stared at her face until his eyes adjusted to the dark. He sucked in a sharp breath when she slid her palms over his chest and wrapped her arms around his neck.

"I don't want to burden you with another secret to keep from your father." He held himself in check even as desire pumped through his veins.

"I think fighting this attraction between us is the bigger burden," she whispered. His head dipped toward her of its own volition, and she wet her lips. "What are you doing, Daniel?"

"Surviving," he said, his voice a low growl. "Because I can't live through another night without having you."

She smiled then—a sensual, triumphant smile— and he was lost. He crushed his lips against hers with a groan and she immediately opened up for him. He plunged his tongue into her mouth again and again, drawing a moan from her. She pressed her body against his, molding his hardness against the softness of her stomach. His hips jerked helplessly as his fingers dug into her hips, pulling her even closer to him.

He cupped her breast over her dress and trailed hot, wet kisses down the column of her neck. Hooking his finger onto her shoulder strap, he tugged it down to reveal more skin for him to taste. His lips dipped to the curve of her breast, flowing above the low-cut bodice. She thrust her chest into his face, rising on her tiptoes. With an impatient growl, he tugged on her bodice because he wanted more…needed more. But the sound of ripping fabric stopped him short.

"Don't stop," she panted when he raised his head and tried to tug him back.

"God, Megan. If we don't stop now, I might take you against this wall." He kissed her hard so she could taste his desperation but pulled back before he lost control again.

"That'll give this fundraising ball a whole new kind of vibe, because I won't be able to keep quiet." She pressed her forehead against his and let out a huff of frustrated laughter. "By the way, did you rip my dress?"

"I might've gotten a little carried away." He grimaced as he slid her shoulder strap back in place. This was so unlike him. He wasn't the type who ripped women's clothes off in a rush to get them naked. He respected buttons and zippers. "I don't think I did too much damage."

"The tear is right under my arm." Megan looked down at her bodice and adjusted it. "As long as I don't wave my arms around, it shouldn't be that visible. It's a good thing tonight isn't a bachelor auction."

His forehead creased with a frown. "Would you be that eager to bid on an eligible bachelor?"

"Well, I *am* a sucker for a burly firefighter." Her eyes twinkled merrily as she teased him.

"Oh?" He arched his eyebrow, not at all amused. "Not into cowboys, are you?"

"Truth be told, I'm sort of into the introverted corporate-executive type." She gave him a sweet peck on the cheek—and wrapped him around her pinkie finger. He bit the inside of his mouth to stop himself from grinning like an idiot.

"I think they're announcing dinner." He frowned as a thought occurred to him. "Will we be seated at different tables since we came separately?"

"Don't worry. I have a feeling Anne made some adjustments on the seating chart to have us sit next to each other."

"I'll have to thank her for that," he murmured as they joined the throng entering the dining room.

"Nothing says thank-you like a big, fat donation," Megan advised. "She'll adore you for that."

"Wouldn't that be buying her approval?" He'd intended to make a generous donation—the fact that breast cancer took Megan's mother away from her made the cause feel much more personal—but he didn't want to use it as a way to get close to Anne.

"Not in the way you think. It won't be the money but your willingness to donate to a good cause—your good deed—that will win you her appreciation."

"This definitely is a worthy cause." He hesitated for a beat, then said, "And I know it was years ago, but I'm sorry about your mother."

"Thank you." The surprise and warmth in her eyes made him glad he'd said something. "We loved her very much, and it was devastating to lose her."

When they reached their table, he helped her into her seat, then sat down next to her. He reached for her hand under the table because he needed to touch her, and smoothed his thumb across her knuckles. He watched as a soft blush stole across her cheeks.

"This dinner is going to feel like an eternity," she said in a low voice.

"I'll be right here with you, slowly going mad, until I can take you home."

"And what are you going to do after you take me home with you?"

"Make you wish our night together will last an eternity." He drew small circles on the sensitive skin of her wrist, remembering how soft she was everywhere.

Tonight, when he had her, he was going to explore every last inch of her and draw a map of her in his head. He didn't know how long he could have her, but he would guard every minute with her.

Seven

Megan could be impulsive, but she rarely regretted her actions. She was an intuitive person, and her intuition never steered her wrong…but there could always be a first time.

She fiddled with the tiny beading on her clutch as the elevator zoomed up to Daniel's place. They hadn't talked much on their drive over, and an odd, charged silence had settled between them. Considering their hot-as-hell kiss in the alcove and the hand orgy they engaged in under the banquet table, she thought they'd be tearing each other's clothes off in the elevator.

She jumped a little when the elevator dinged and the doors slid open onto the penthouse. Daniel held out his arm for her to proceed, so she strode down the hallway and into the living room. If she had been feeling ballsy, she would've walked straight into his bedroom—if she knew where it was—but she was so nervous, her legs bounced restlessly when she sat down on the couch.

Daniel didn't sit. He didn't say a word. He just paced the floor on the other side of the coffee table until she wanted to tackle him to make him stop. Or maybe to kiss him senseless. Apparently, she was capable of feeling both anxious and horny at the same time. Without pausing in his quest to meet his step goals, he loosened his bow tie and threw it on the armchair. His jacket followed suit. When he undid the button at his wrist and began rolling up his sleeve, she almost lost it. *What the hell?* Was this a forearm striptease? And was she expected to sit still and watch? Must. Touch. Forearms.

He finally stopped and knelt in front of her. "Megan, I want you."

"Thank God," she breathed. "I want you, too."

"But I can't… I can't give you what you need…" He ran his hand through his hair.

"You can't give me sex?" She sounded outraged even to her own ears.

"What?" He blinked. "I can give you sex. Shit. I mean I want to make love to you, but I can't give you some rose-tinted fantasy of love and happily-ever-after."

"Oh." A painful pang shot through her heart.

"I…care about you. You must know that," he said haltingly. "But love could consume you…and shatter you. It's not a risk I'd ever wish to take."

He'd told her what he thought about love the night he proposed to her. She already knew that he couldn't give her the kind of love she had always dreamed about. The kind of love her mom and dad had shared—like the love Angie and Joshua had—where they so thoroughly belonged to each other that they didn't know where one soul ended and the other started. Even though she'd known, she couldn't stop the disappointment sweeping through her.

"I don't want to hurt you." He cupped her face with a gentleness she yearned to soak up like sunlight.

Her eyes roamed over his kind, handsome face. He didn't know it, but he was capable of love. She felt it down to her core. Her intuition had never steered her wrong. But even if he could never love her, she wanted this. She wanted the passion, the intimacy, the closeness. She wanted to share those things with this man even if it couldn't be forever.

"I'm not asking you to give me the fantasy, Daniel," she said, turning her head to plant a kiss on his palm. "I want *you*. That's all."

"But—"

She pressed her fingers to his mouth. "I'm *desperate* for you. Maybe it's just lust. Maybe it's something I can get out of my system. Let's just take this day by day. No promises."

Daniel was torn. She could see it in his eyes. He wanted her, but he was a good man and he didn't want to break her heart. If she played it smart, both of them could get what they wanted without anyone getting hurt. All she had to do was not fall in love with him.

"Make love to me, Daniel." She replaced her fingers with her lips. "Please."

She felt the gentle pressure of his hands on her shoulders…pushing her away. Mortification spread like hot water being poured down her head. He didn't want her. Not enough to weather the potential storm. But before she could rush off, Daniel raised her to her feet by her hand and led her through his house. Confused, she tugged on her hand, but he held firm until they reached his bedroom.

The room was minimally furnished with a king-size bed in the center, with two low nightstands on each side and a tufted bench at the foot of the bed. The white-and-gray-color motif could have made the room feel stark, but it actually felt open and inviting.

"Sorry about the mess," Daniel said, gathering some documents and folders scattered on the bed.

When he stood uncertain, with his hands full, Megan walked fully into his bedroom and took the folders from him and placed them down on the bench. "Just focus on why you brought me to your room."

"Are you saying I should focus on undressing you?" The uncertainty melted away from him and a rakish grin spread across his face. "And tasting every last inch of you?"

A thousand butterflies took flight in her stomach. She was suddenly very warm, but she had the where-withal not to fan her face with her hands. "Oh, I thought you brought me here to show me the stunning view of the city."

"I had an entirely different view in mind." He put his arms around her waist and pressed her against his body.

She shivered when he kissed the side of her neck and inched down the zipper on her dress. Reassured of his intent—which she hoped was to fuck her senseless—she slid her hand over the outline of his desire. "I think I remember which view you're talking about. It's quite stunning in its own right."

His throaty chuckle turned into a groan when she gave him a firm squeeze. He trapped both her hands behind her back and stared down at her face. His expression was almost feral with lust and hunger. "You need to behave or this will be over much sooner than either of us want."

"Must I?" She ground her hips against him. "Misbehaving is so much more fun."

He finally caved and captured her lips in a searing kiss. *About damn time.* She wiggled until he freed her hands and went to work on his shirt buttons without breaking their kiss. She had never undressed a man so quickly in her life. She pushed off his shirt and brought her lips to the smooth skin of his chest to nip and lick as she pleased.

When she scraped her teeth over his nipple, he hissed and set her away from him. Her indignant huff turned into a gasp when he ripped her dress off in a single motion, going down to his knees. He helped her step out of the dress and her strappy gold heels until she stood in front of him clad in a black satin bra and matching bikini panties. Teeny-tiny, bikini-style panties worked well for her baby bump because they sat below the curve of her stomach. *Thank the Lord for that.* Daniel stared at her near-naked body with reverence—for just a moment—before he divested her of the scrap of black cloth.

She cried out at the first reverent touch of his open mouth on her—soft, hot and wet. He tilted his head back to meet her eyes before sticking two of his fingers into his mouth, then slowly pulling them out. He glided those fingers through her folds, to open her up, and licked her swollen bud—a flicker at first, then with long, laving strokes.

The quakes started deep inside her lower stomach and gathered at her clit. The pressure built higher and higher, drawing a deep, guttural moan from her. When he took her in his mouth and sucked, she broke with a scream as waves and waves of pleasure crashed into her.

Daniel was on his feet before she could crumble to the ground and picked her up in his arms. He laid her down gently on the bed and stood back to unbuckle his belt and slide the rest of his clothes off. Even limp and languid, her eyes devoured the sight of his naked body and she reached out for him as he joined her at her side.

"You're so beautiful," he whispered, running his hand along her body from her breast to her hip.

"So are you." She tugged on his head until his lips met hers.

The tenderness soon gave way to passion and she squirmed against him as their tongues tangled and their teeth clacked against each other. He dipped his head and drew the tip of her breast into his mouth, and her back arched off the bed. Heeding her silent demand, he slipped his hand between her thighs and plunged a finger inside her. She rode his hand shamelessly as he slid in a second finger.

"Oh God," she panted and reached for his erection. "Daniel. Please."

He groaned and pumped his hips into her fist. "What, baby? What do you want?"

"I want you inside of me." She swirled her thumb over the velvety skin of his tip.

"Fuck," he growled and jerked against her hand.

"Do you want me, too?" she asked with a knowing smile.

In response, he pinned her arms over her head and kissed her until she couldn't breathe. Then he spun around to grab a condom from his dresser and ripped open the packet.

"Wait," she said breathlessly. "Are you… STD free? Because I am. They do all these tests when you get pregnant—"

"Focus, Megan." His laughter rumbled in his chest, but there was desperation in his eyes. "I don't have any STDs…"

"Then, we don't need that." She nodded at the condom in his hand. "It's not like I can get pregnant again. And I want to feel you with nothing between us."

"God, yes."

She opened her legs and wrapped them loosely around his waist. His shoulders taut with control, he entered her with painstaking care, rocking in and out, inch by inch. With a feral growl, she dug her fingers into his ass, tilted her hips and pulled him inside her to the hilt. Her head rolled back and she shouted with satisfaction.

"Megan." Daniel froze over her. "Are you okay?"

"You…feel…so good inside me." She swiveled her hips. "Please take me. I'm not going to break. I want you to take me hard and fast. Please."

A choked groan escaped him before he started riding her with an intensity that took her breath away. It felt glorious. His measured thrusts soon lost their rhythm and he pounded mercilessly into her. She thought she was spent from her last orgasm, but she felt one building inside her again. Her head started rolling from side to side as she met him thrust for thrust.

"Daniel," she moaned as white stars exploded behind her lids, coming even harder than the first time.

He shouted as he reached his own climax and jerked inside her once, then twice. He held himself over her with trembling arms and kissed her hard on her lips before collapsing on the bed beside her. When she could move her limbs, she turned to her side and patted his rock-hard abs.

"Rest up, tiger." She yawned. "Because we're going to do that again."

When he shook with breathless laughter, she snuggled against his side and smiled lazily.

"I'm just going to close my eyes for a second," she said and drifted off to sleep, soothed by the feel of Daniel's hand stroking her naked back. It felt so good and right.

Daniel awoke with a start then smiled and pulled Megan's naked body closer to his. His eyes slid shut again with a contented sigh before they flew back open a second later. He reached for his phone and Megan stirred against him. When he saw that they'd only dozed off for about an hour, he reclaimed his spot and smoothed his hand over her back.

"Shhh. It's okay," he whispered. "You can sleep more."

She stretched languorously, her arched back pressing the front of her more firmly against him. His body responded instantly and his hand traveled down to cup and squeeze her round bottom. The depth of his desire for her made his stomach clench with nerves, but he couldn't stop aching for her even if he wanted to.

"Hmm." She smiled sleepily at him. "Are you sure you want me to go back to sleep? I'm getting mixed signals here."

He would never stop hungering for her, but more than anything, he wanted to wake up beside her in the morning. The thought startled him enough to bolt out of bed. He didn't do sleepovers. He didn't even bring women to his place as a rule. Whatever this was, he had to watch his step.

"I should take you home," he said, gathering his clothes off the floor.

She sat up slowly in bed with the cover held against her chest. A hurt frown flitted across her face, but she said, "Okay."

"I don't want your father to worry," he mumbled, immediately contrite for his brusqueness.

"You're right." She dropped the sheet and got to her feet. Despite his sudden panic and need for space, he stared at her naked body like a man starved.

With her back turned to him, she slipped on her lingerie and stepped into her dress. She held up her hair in one hand and looked over her shoulder at him. "Do you mind?"

He wordlessly zipped up her gown while battling a wild need to rip it off her again. Because he needed to touch her, he rested his hands on her shoulders. After a pause, she turned around to face him, dislodging his hold.

"I can't have you drive me home," she said with a slight arch of her brow. "I don't want my father to know about our...fling. It would be cruel to give him false hope."

"Of course. I understand." He took a step back at her frostiness and stood taller to cover his inexplicable hurt. What had happened tonight was just sex. She didn't really want him. She'd walked out on him once before.

He tamped down on the bitterness churning inside him. He was being unreasonable. How else was she supposed to behave after he'd all but kicked her out of his bed? He followed her as she walked out to the living room to retrieve her clutch. Then he stood indecisively near the edge of the living room as she tapped into her phone.

"My ride should be here soon. I'll go wait down in the lobby." She glided toward the elevator, slipping on her shoes as she went.

"When will I see you again?" He caught her hand before she could press the down button. He had bungled this up, but he couldn't stand the thought of not seeing her again soon.

She twisted her hand out of his grasp and called the elevator. "The Chamber Music Society is hosting an event for its maestro's circle in a couple weeks. Walter Liu will be there."

"Megan," he said helplessly.

"I don't know what's going on with you right now, but you need to figure it out," she snapped. But her voice softened at something in his expression. "Daniel, this was just one night. Well...two nights. It doesn't have to happen again if you don't want it to."

"I want it to." His hands clenched and unclenched at his sides with the need to hold on to her. But he didn't want to *need to* hold on to her. He wanted simple and uncomplicated. It seemed as though that was exactly what Megan was offering him, but he was the one making it complicated. His chest felt taut with tension as though he was being ripped down the middle.

"I'm not sure I believe you," she said with quiet dignity. The elevator dinged and the doors slid open. With a fleeting kiss on his cheek, she stepped inside. "Good night."

The doors closed and he stood staring at his reflection on the polished metal. At least she hadn't said good-bye. That would have felt too permanent. Whatever happened, he would still see her at social events to carry out their plan and for her prenatal appointments. But he knew that wasn't enough anymore.

He thought he'd held himself back from wanting her—from having her—out of respect for Mr. Han and out of concern for Megan…but maybe it had been about himself all along. Maybe he'd been afraid of wanting more of Megan than he could have.

His father had always told him that women couldn't be trusted. Daniel had thought he was a bitter, old fool until… Sienna. She was so beautiful and vibrant. It felt as though he could warm up his cold, lonely existence just by being in her orbit. He couldn't believe his luck when the most sought-after girl in college wanted to date him. She could have anyone.

Daniel understood that only too well and he swore to do whatever he could to give her everything she wanted. But what she'd wanted was his roommate—the son of a wealthy senator. She had just used Daniel to get closer to him. When he confronted her after he found them in bed, she turned on him as though he was the one who had betrayed her.

Don't you want me to be happy for once? Sienna had said.

I could make you happy, he entreated.

I could never be happy with someone like you, she spat.

Women couldn't be trusted. His father had been right. His mother didn't think Daniel was worth sticking around for. Why would Sienna think otherwise? Why would Megan be any different?

He'd kept himself safe since Sienna. He had women in his life after her, but never allowed himself to become emotionally attached. As long as he didn't open himself up, he wouldn't get hurt when they left. It was better for everyone involved. The only thing he ever let himself want was to succeed. And he was almost there. He was the CFO of a major corporation. If he worked hard enough, he might someday become Jigu Corporation's CEO.

But when he had Megan in his arms, he was willing to risk everything he'd worked for to have her. She was still worth the risk—even more so with the smell of her lingering on his skin. But there was no reason to gamble his heart. He was wiser than that. He would only take what she gave him and wouldn't ask for anything more—wouldn't want anything more. They could have the now. *No promises.*

"Fuck," he breathed.

He shouldn't have let Megan leave like that. He'd made her think he regretted sleeping with her, when it was one of the most amazing nights of his life. He jabbed at the elevator button and hurried to retrieve his phone and keys. He ran back when he heard the ping of its arrival and slid between the doors before they closed on him.

Daniel rushed through the lobby and caught sight of her getting into her rideshare. He cursed under his breath and made a mad dash for the parking lot. If he broke some speed limits, he might be able to get to her house before she did.

When he'd arrived at the Han residence, the house was dark except for the exterior lights. He'd parked a few yards away and now stood in the shadows waiting for Megan. It was past midnight, but he didn't want to risk being seen by Mr. Han.

Now that he was here, he didn't know what to do. Had he beat her here? Or had she already gone inside? Would he sound like a lunatic if he called her and asked her to come outside? Just as he pulled his phone out of his back pocket, headlights shone into his eyes. He shielded them with his hand and squinted against the brightness. It was the car that Megan had gotten into.

He stepped toward it as it lurched to a halt—as though Megan had shouted for the driver to stop. She climbed out and walked up to him, looking magnificent in her red formal gown. She tugged him farther down the street, behind the shadow of a tall tree.

"What are you doing here?" Her voice was sharp with surprise.

"I acted like an idiot." He pulled her into his arms and held her close. "I don't regret what happened tonight. I… I have some baggage to deal with, but it's my problem, not yours."

"Daniel—" She held herself stiff against him.

"I want you, Megan," he said before she could continue. "Tell me I haven't blown this."

"I want you, too."

"Don't say *but*."

"But," she said, ignoring his request, "I don't want to push you into something you're not comfortable with…"

He couldn't lie to her. He wasn't at ease with the situation. Not with the secret pregnancy and not with adding a secret affair on top of it. Most of all, he was terrified at how much he wanted her. But none of that mattered if it meant he could have her—just for a little while.

"I don't think either of us are comfortable with lying to your father," he admitted to the half truth, dropping his arms down to his sides. "That's why we have to win over the board members, so we can tell your father that the baby is mine."

"And this?" She flapped her hand between them. "What do we tell him about this?"

"We'll figure that out when the time comes," he hedged.

"I see." A shuttered expression settled on her face. "You're right. Who knows? Maybe there won't be anything to tell him by then."

His stomach lurched with something like dread. He didn't want to think about when he would have to let her go—when she would leave him. He wanted to focus on keeping her by his side for now.

"We'll do this your way." He reached out to cup her face. "Take it day by day. No promises."

"Day by day." She took a deep breath and leaned into his touch. "No promises."

He placed a lingering kiss on her sweet, parted lips. She sighed and pressed herself against him. This was enough. He didn't need more than this. As long as he didn't get greedy, he would be able to let her go without bitterness or resentment. His love for the baby wouldn't be tainted by heartbreak. Everything was going to be just fine.

Eight

"How are you feeling?" Angie whispered to Megan as they took their seats in front of the small audience.

"Barely any jitters," Megan said with a shrug. "The maestro's circle is basically our fan club. They'll love everything we play for them."

"I wasn't asking about that." Her older sister sighed, then stared pointedly at her stomach.

"Ohhh." Megan laughed softly and caught herself before she placed her hand on her baby bump. "We're doing swell."

"Good." Angie's affectionate smile made Megan blink. She looked so much like their mom. "Glad to hear Nephew and Sister are both doing swell."

"Thank you, Unni." Megan turned to include Chloe. "All right, ladies. Are we ready?"

At her sisters' nods, she brought the violin under her

chin and raised the bow. They all inhaled together, held their breath for a second, then Megan dropped her bow to the strings. She and her sisters exhaled as the music carried them away.

Schubert's *String Trio D 471* was both playful and deeply moving—simply beautiful in its complexity. The Hana Trio weaved through the depths and peaks of the piece with courage and vulnerability, the three of them supporting each other and lifting each other up. The trust between Megan and her sisters brought an added layer to the piece that was entirely their own.

As the last note and its vibrations faded, they lowered their bows. There was a moment of awed silence before applause erupted from the audience. Megan smiled at her sisters and the three of them stood and took their bow. The applause didn't die down until another group of their fellow musicians filed onto the stage.

The mezzanine of the concert hall was bustling with the most generous and well-dressed of the Chamber Music Society's donors when the performers joined the party. The royal blue-and-gold carpeting, dark wood trimming and crystal chandeliers gave the event the opulence and elegance befitting their guests of honor, the maestro's circle.

Daniel, while not a member of the maestro's circle yet, scored himself an invite, thanks to Angie. The Chamber Music Society owed Angie and Joshua for their part in revitalizing their organization when it was in dire straits after the pandemic. But even as she craned her neck this way and that, Megan couldn't find the damn man—which only meant one thing. He wasn't there. There was no way she could miss him, even in a crowd.

Then she saw him walking up the staircase with his tie slightly askew. His head swiveled left and right, and he raked his fingers through his hair, obviously not for the first time tonight. Megan was peeved he was late, but decided to give him a break and wove through the crowd toward him.

The frown on his face cleared when his eyes landed on her. "Megan."

"This is the second time you missed our performance," she said, crossing her arms over her chest. "I'm beginning to think that you would do anything to get out of listening to classical music."

"I'm sorry," he murmured. When she continued to glare at him, he moved closer and whispered, "I'm sorry, baby. Forgive me."

She couldn't hold back a shiver at the intimacy of his voice, which made her more cross. "You better have a good reason."

"Charity Hansen wanted to discuss something," he said.

"The board member Charity Hansen?"

"Yes, I thought it would be an excellent opportunity to get to know each other."

"Good thinking." Megan nodded. "We could use her on our side."

"I was hoping you'd say that." The last traces of worry left Daniel's face as he grinned down at her. "But I'm really sorry I missed your performance. Perhaps…you could give me a private one later?"

Her heart fluttered and a blush rose to her cheeks. "Perhaps."

His grin grew broader and decidedly naughtier, but before he could continue, the rest of the Han sisters joined the conversation. Megan's stomach knotted. They knew Daniel was the baby's father, but she hadn't told them about their affair. She didn't want to give them another secret to keep from their father.

"Shouldn't you be over there talking to Walter?" Angie said pointedly to Daniel.

"Nice to meet you. You must be Angie," he said with a smile. At least one of them remembered their manners. "And nice to meet you, Chloe."

"Hi, Daniel." Chloe dimpled prettily at him. "But you should really get over there and charm the hell out of Mr. Liu. Keeping secrets from our dad makes my stomach hurt."

"I'm sorry, Chloe," Megan said miserably.

"Me, too," Daniel said.

"We don't need apologies." Angie jerked her head toward their target. "Go and work your magic, Megan. And Daniel, try not to get in her way. But it was nice meeting you as well."

"Okay." Megan placed her hand on Daniel's arm. "We're going in."

Walter Liu and his wife had broken off from the small group they were chatting with and stood alone, speaking quietly to each other. But when they spotted Megan and Daniel approaching, Walter held his arms wide. "Megan, my dear. You and your sisters were spectacular."

"Thank you, Mr. Liu." Megan hugged him and stepped back. "How are you, Mrs. Liu?"

"Getting old, but that's not something to complain about. It's a blessing." Annette Liu was small in stature but mighty in spirit. "And you are?"

"Hello, Mrs. Liu. I'm Daniel Pak," he said with a polite smile. "It's nice to meet you. And good to see you again, Mr. Liu."

Walter grunted in reply. Daniel was going to have to do better than that. Megan had to coax the charm out of him. "Since my father is out of town, the society invited Daniel as Jigu Corporation's representative. And he conveniently showed up right *after* the performances ended."

The tips of Daniel's ears turned a little pink and he widened his eyes at her. "For which I've profusely apologized."

Walter chuckled. "Megan, stop putting the man on the spot."

"Yes, Megan." Daniel cast a grateful glance at Mr. Liu. "Listen to his wise counsel."

"Don't worry, Mr. Liu," Megan said playfully. "Daniel and I are friends. I won't torment him too much."

"I think I should just stick with Mr. and Mrs. Liu for the rest of the evening," Daniel said, inching closer to them.

Megan couldn't hold back her laugh. Who could resist him when he was so endearing? Walter and Annett exchanged a knowing glance. *Here we go again.* Once her friends saw that Daniel was a decent guy, they immediately thought about matching him up with Megan. She was going to interpret that as a good sign that they would gladly take Daniel into their fold.

Soon. They would be able to tell her dad the truth soon. But not the whole truth, right? Her stomach swooped with anxiety. What could they tell him about what was happening between them? *We don't want to get married even though we made a baby together, but we really like having sex with no strings attached.* That would make any father proud. She cringed inwardly. But daughters didn't have to live their lives to please their fathers. They had to forge their own paths—follow their own instincts.

Despite her confidence in her instincts, Megan wondered if she had any *survival* instincts worth a damn. She knew with everything in her that Daniel Pak was a good man and she wanted him more than she'd ever wanted anyone else before. She could only assume that the teeny-tiny voice inside her, warning her that this wouldn't end well—that she would get her heart broken—was her survival instinct, but the little voice was much too easy to ignore. The drumming of her heart and the rush of blood in her head every time she was near him drowned it out.

The sound of laughter drew her out of her thoughts. With the ice broken, Daniel was winning the Lius with his brand of earnest charm. He always listened closely and responded with solemn honesty. She respected that. Sometimes being honest took courage because it also revealed a part of who you were… It made you vulnerable. She wondered if Daniel knew how brave he was to treat others with such deep respect.

"I'm having lunch with an old friend next week," Walter said. "I think you should join us, Daniel. He might have some wisdom to share with you about the industry. You're young, but you're a leader. You need to surround yourself with good people."

"Thank you so much, Mr. Liu," Daniel said.

"Call me Walter."

"Walter." Daniel smiled and handed him his business card. "This has my direct line. Please call me when you know the details and I'll be sure to join you."

"Good man." Mr. Liu pounded Daniel on the back.

"It was great seeing you, but we should go and make the rounds," Annette suggested, giving her husband a look. When he didn't budge, she tugged him away by his arms. "Give the young people some space, you old dolt."

"Bye, Mr. and Mrs. Liu," Megan said with a wave. She turned to Daniel with a smile. "Look at you. I don't think you even need my help anymore."

"Walter wouldn't have spared me a stiff smile if it hadn't been for you," he said, taking a step closer to her.

She pressed her index finger to his sternum and gently pushed. "Please maintain a friends-only distance. If you get too close, I might be tempted to kiss you."

His grin was blinding as he leaned into her touch for a split-second before he stepped back. "How long do we have to stay?"

"Why?" She glanced at him from under her lashes. "Do you have someplace to be?"

"Yes." His eyes dropped to her lips and she could feel the heat emanating from him even from a respectable distance. "It's rather urgent."

"I have to smile and show my appreciation to all these generous donors." A shiver went down her spine at his frown of displeasure. "Give me thirty minutes and I'll meet you at your place."

"I'll give you twenty," he said with an arrogant arch of his eyebrow.

She would've laughed and teased him about how impatient he was if she wasn't busy holding herself back from jumping him in a room full of people. In the end, all she managed was a small whimper. With a knowing smile, Daniel walked past her, letting the back of his hand lightly graze hers.

She glanced down expecting to see a tendril of smoke wafting up from her hand. *You're in so much trouble*, her survival instinct squeaked.

"Oh, shut up," she muttered. "I have no time for your puny warnings."

Megan had to pull off the fastest smile-and-greet she'd ever done so she could go running into her lover's arms.

Daniel felt his mouth go dry as he watched Megan glide toward him across the lobby in her strapless black dress. Her bare shoulders and sophisticated updo accentuated the alluring line of her neck, and he became frenzied with the desire to nip and lick the sensitive skin there. He'd seen her in a formal dress before, but the simple elegance she exuded tonight made him desperate to *undo* her.

When she came to stand in front of him, he forced himself to glance down at his watch and drawl, "You're late. I said twenty minutes."

Her lashes fluttered and her lips parted. God, she wanted him as much as he wanted her.

"I'm not late," she said in a husky voice. "Your watch is fast."

"Excuses, excuses." He reached behind him and called the elevator to his penthouse.

"I don't need to make excuses." She raised her chin in challenge, but anticipation glinted in her eyes. "You don't get to tell me what to do."

"Is that so?" he crooned softly, even though he felt light-headed with arousal.

He guided her inside the elevator and pushed her up against the back wall as soon as the doors closed behind them.

"You kept me waiting," he said into her ear with his hands planted by her head, imprisoning her with his arms and body. "You're going to make it up to me."

"H-how?" She bit her bottom lip as she waited for her instructions.

"Unzip your dress," he said, leaning back just enough to allow her to reach behind her. Her eyes didn't leave his as she lowered her zipper. "Good girl."

He grabbed the front of her bodice and roughly tugged it down so she was naked from the waist up. Megan's sharp gasp shot straight to his groin. He'd forgotten that they were in an elevator until the doors opened behind them. He wrapped his hands around her waist and spun them around, and marched her backward out of the elevator.

"Take the rest of your clothes off." He stepped back from her and crossed his arms over his chest.

She shimmied the dress past her hips and down to her ankles, and kicked it away from her. She stood proud, clad only in her panties and high heels. Her breasts were fuller than the first night they'd been together and her softly rounded stomach drew his eyes. He was gripped by a dizzying need to possess her.

"Touch me," she said with a hint of impatience.

"Go stand behind the sofa." When she opened her mouth to protest, he cut her off with a command. "Now."

Her cheeks flushed red and her chest rose and fell with every quickening breath. She slowly spun on her heels and made her way to the sofa. The sway of her hips hypnotized him and he stood rooted to the spot until she glanced over her shoulder with a sultry smile. He caught up with her just as she stopped at the sofa and turned to face him.

"Turn around," he said in a gravelly voice he hardly recognized as his own, "and bend over."

A shuddering breath escaped past her lips and she did as she was told. He almost lost it in his pants when she bent over the back of the sofa, thrusting her sweet, round ass toward him. He gripped one side of her waist, his fingers digging into her flesh, and unbuckled his belt with the other hand. Megan whimpered and restlessly bucked her hips.

He drew himself out and dragged his tip through her slick folds before placing himself at her entrance. "Do you want this?"

"Yes," she moaned.

"Yes, what?" He was shaking with his need for her, and sweat slid down his temples.

"Yes, I want you," she said breathlessly. "I want you inside of me. Please."

Daniel thrust inside her and groaned, his head falling back. God, she felt so good. Suddenly, he came to his senses. She was soft, wet and ready for him, but had he been too rough?

"Megan." He smoothed his hands over her waist. "Are you okay, baby?"

In response, she swiveled her hips. "Daniel, please."

He needed no further encouragement. He felt like his mind was splintering with the need to have her, and he said her name again and again as he pounded into her. He was losing control. He couldn't hold on much longer.

"Baby, I need you to come." His fingers found her nub, and he pressed and rubbed her in rhythm with their coupling. "Come for me."

With a low cry, her muscles clenched around him and he joined her in the climax. Waves of pleasure pulsed through him with a force that nearly made his knees buckle. He came back to the present when he felt Megan shivering beneath his hands. He didn't want to leave her warmth yet, but he pulled himself out and lifted her into his arms. He carried her to his bed and collapsed beside her.

As he pulled the covers over her naked body, he realized that he was still fully dressed. He hadn't even taken his blazer off. Shaking his head in wonder, he got up from the bed to undress and joined her again under the covers. He needed to be close to her.

He put his hand on her shoulder and smoothed it down her arm. She had stopped shivering, but she hadn't said a word. Uneasiness shot through him. What had gotten into him? He seemed to lose his mind around her.

"Megan…"

She shifted to her side so she was facing him. Slowly, a wide smile spread across her face and laughter bubbled out of her. "That was fucking amazing."

"I don't know what happened," he murmured almost to himself. "I've never wanted anyone before as much as I've wanted you."

He stiffened as soon as the words left his mouth, but Megan cupped his face and simply said, "Me, too."

A breath he didn't know he was holding left him in a rush and he crushed his lips against hers. He only drew back when his lungs demanded air. She stared at him with wide eyes, her swollen lips parted. Tenderness rushed through him and he ran his index finger down the bridge of her nose, then kissed the tip.

"Are you sure you're okay?" he asked.

"I'll probably be a little sore." She stretched languidly

beside him and lay with her back to him. "But it was totally worth it."

"Good," he said, spooning her snuggly from behind. "By the way, do you really think I don't like classical music?"

"I was just teasing…but *do* you like classical music?" She wrapped his arm firmly around her midriff.

"I love classical music." He nibbled her shoulder. "I even hear it when I make love to you."

"What?" She giggled. "Which piece?"

"Handel's *Messiah*." He grinned against her skin. *"Hallelujah. Hallelujah, hallelujah…"*

"You're such an idiot," she said with a smile in her voice. "But I guess you do love classical music."

He'd always appreciated classical music, but knowing that Megan was a part of that world made the music almost seem like magic now. Having classical music playing in the background throughout his day made him feel close to her. It stopped him from missing her so much that he would drop everything to run to her.

Daniel didn't look too closely at why he wanted to feel close to her. It was desire like he'd never known before. It consumed him. And they had a connection. She made him feel comfortable in his own skin.

When their passion was spent, he hoped they could be friends. Friendship didn't come with any messy emotional entanglement. And even if it ended, friendship would never wreck him enough to tarnish his love for his child. Yes, friendship would be his end goal for this relationship. That would make coparenting that much easier and more enjoyable.

He drifted off to sleep and dreamed of sunny days, picnicking in the park. He was too far gone to think it odd that he carried their son in one arm and had the other wrapped around Megan with his hand resting on her round, pregnant belly. It didn't seem odd at all that they were growing their family. After all, he didn't want his son to be an only child like him. In the dream, he knew he would do anything to keep his family together…even offer Megan his heart. His dream-self threw his head back and laughed at the absurdity of his thought. His heart was already hers.

Nine

Considering how thin Megan was from her morning sickness, it was hard to mistake her baby bump for anything other than what it was, especially in her stretchy maternity pants and fitted shirt with Peter Pan collars. The whispers started the moment she walked onto the stage to join the Chamber Orchestra for rehearsal. She'd been asked to fill in for the second violin, who was away on a family emergency. The conductor hadn't joined them yet, so there was time for her fellow musicians to process their surprise.

"Congratulations, my dear." The principal flutist was the first to approach. She surreptitiously checked her ring finger to make sure Megan hadn't gotten married overnight. "Most of us have an artist's heart, so there's no need to fret about censure. But if you do want me to circulate an official story of sorts, I'll be happy to spread the word to temper the gossip."

"Thank you, Tiffany." Megan smiled warmly at the older woman. She was a talented musician and a professional through and through, but she also had a kind heart. "I'd like that. It would take some heat off my sisters as well."

"Of course." Tiffany looked askance at her when she didn't speak right away.

"Oh, right." Megan shook her head. "The official story. The pregnancy came as a surprise but the baby's father and I are looking forward to parenthood."

The flutist raised her eyebrows at the very brief explanation but nodded and returned to her seat. Megan shared enough to prevent anyone from painting her as the poor little pregnant woman abandoned by her callous lover. Without that bit of drama, the gossip wouldn't be juicy enough to last long.

Megan didn't linger after the rehearsal and headed straight to her car—not to avoid people, but because she had a date with Daniel in a couple of hours. Her heart picked up pace and made a ruckus in her chest. It couldn't be because she got to see Daniel—she'd seen him last night for God's sake—but because she got to see one of her favorite musicians play tonight.

Child prodigy turned virtuoso, violinist Anthony Larsen was only eight years her senior, but she'd watched him perform since she was a little girl. The violin pieces she knew and loved became something new and dynamic with Anthony's energetic and passionate interpretations. As the years passed, his performances only became richer and more nuanced without losing an ounce of passion. She didn't think she'd ever shared her awe of the violinist with Daniel, but to her delight, he had secured them two orchestra seats to Anthony Larsen's concert.

Once she got home, Megan took her time with her bath and styled her hair with loose curls. She applied her makeup with a light touch, using a petal-pink lipstick for both her cheeks and lips. Just as she pushed back from her vanity, she heard a knock at her bedroom door.

"Megan?" It was Mrs. Chung.

"Come in," she said, turning around to face the door.

"I brought you some sandwiches." Their housekeeper strode into her room with a tray laden with enough finger sandwiches for five people. She had been feeding Megan every two hours since she found out about the pregnancy. "You must be hungry."

"You don't give me a chance to get hungry." Megan laughed. "But maybe I am a little peckish…"

A huge smile spread across Mrs. Chung's face as she set out the sandwiches and lemonade on the coffee table in the sitting area. "The little darling is busy growing."

"Yes, he must be. Thank you, Mrs. Chung."

After eating a plate full of dainty sandwiches, Megan walked into her closet and fingered through her dresses suited for an evening at a concert. She opted for a simple boatneck dress in black with enough stretch to accommodate her growing stomach. She added a gold pendant necklace to her ensemble and reapplied the lipstick she'd eaten off with her snack.

Her father wouldn't be home for a few hours, but she had insisted on meeting Daniel at the concert venue. She didn't want to tempt fate by having him pick her up here. They only had a couple more board members to woo, then they could tell her father the truth about the baby's father. She still had no idea how to explain her relationship with Daniel—or if she would tell her father anything about it at all. If it was just a temporary fling, there was no use upsetting him any more than they had to.

But Megan knew that it was not a casual fling for her. It had never been. The question was… Was she going to do anything about it? She'd told him she didn't need promises and she'd meant it. She had wanted him even if it was only for a fleeting moment. She couldn't stop herself from hoping for more, though.

Daniel wanted her. She knew that. But what kept him from opening up to her? Why couldn't something real bloom between them? With a sickening lurch of her stomach, she wondered if he was in love with someone else. Someone back East? An old flame? Maybe someone unattainable. She sighed. Letting her imagination run wild wasn't going to help anyone, especially her.

The drive to the concert felt like an eternity. She needed to see Daniel. When they were together, it felt as though she belonged to him. They were discreet about their relationship, but he couldn't hide the slight quirk of his lips whenever their eyes met, and he couldn't seem to stop himself from touching her—innocuous and light—every chance he got.

Daniel had given Megan her ticket in case he was detained at work, so she went inside and took a seat. She willed her legs not to bounce as she waited for him, but she found herself tapping her index finger on the armrest. She curled her fingers and held tight to the armrest to stop herself from fidgeting.

"Hi." Daniel slid into the seat next to her and offered her a crooked smile. His smiles came much more easily now, and she couldn't help but feel a little responsible for that. "See? I can be on time for classical music."

Her breath left her in a shaky sigh, but she said, "I guess it's only when I'm the one performing that you run late."

"I'm still waiting for that private performance." He chuckled and brushed his knee against hers.

She shivered at the barely there touch, but its familiarity comforted her. The lights dimmed before she could respond, and they turned their attention to the stage. Anthony's music seemed to suck the oxygen out of the concert hall, and Megan watched and listened, holding her breath. But everything in her relaxed as he played Brahms's *Hungarian Dance No. 1*. The beauty of the song brought tears to her eyes and she reached for Daniel's hand in the darkness. His fingers tangled with hers, but his enthralled gaze remained on the violinist.

The music brought her emotions close to the surface and she stared in awe at the beautiful man sitting beside her. No, a short fling was not what she wanted. She wanted Daniel to be hers—heart, body and soul. Was she willing to act on her desire?

Megan couldn't stop to consider whether *her* heart already belonged to him. Then she would be too afraid to act. She wanted him. All of him. She would leave it at that for now. And she wouldn't *say* anything to Daniel. There couldn't be promises without words, right? She would show him that she wanted him by her side with her actions.

Anthony Larsen dove into his rendition of Bizet's "Habanera" from *Carmen*, which brought entirely different emotions to the surface. Megan squirmed in her seat, much too aware of the heat coming off Daniel's body. He ran his thumb over the sensitive skin on her palm. When she turned to glance at him, his gaze focused on her, and everyone else in the room melted away. Her chest rose and fell with each quickening breath as the heat in his eyes slowly burned through her body.

The resounding applause brought her out of the trance, and she rose from her seat and joined the rest of the audience in a standing ovation. Anthony bowed and walked off the stage for intermission and the applause finally quieted.

"Come on." Daniel's hand settled on the small of her back. "I want you to meet someone."

She only had time to quirk her eyebrow as he propelled her through the crowd toward the front of the auditorium. She finally spoke up when he gave his name to a security guard, who opened the door to the backstage area. "Where are we going?"

"Daniel." Anthony Larsen walked up to them and pulled Daniel into a one-armed hug. "It's good to see you, man."

"Good to see you, too." Daniel returned the bro hug before stepping back. "Anthony, this is my…friend, Megan Han."

Something clenched painfully in her chest at the term. She was being ridiculous. Hadn't she introduced him the same way to all the board members? But that had been different. They were her father's friends and they'd agreed to keep their relationship a secret from him. Anthony, it seemed, was Daniel's friend. She shook off her pointless sense of hurt when the violinist beamed at her.

"Megan, it is an absolute pleasure to meet you," he

said, pumping her hand enthusiastically. His light brown hair fell into his striking hazel eyes, making him look boyish and charming. "You and your sisters are incredible musicians. I'm a true fan. I can't believe we haven't run into each other before now."

Her mouth opened and closed several times before she could form proper words. "I've hero-worshipped you since I was four. The pleasure is all mine."

"Okay. Now you've gone and made me feel old." Anthony chuckled a bit sheepishly.

She realized he was embarrassed by her fangirling and decided that she liked him—not the musician but the man—immediately. She was glad he wasn't the superficial playboy the gossip columns painted him to be. Not that she gave them much credence in the first place.

"Hardly," she said with an easy smile. "You were all of twelve yourself."

"We should let you rest and prepare for the second half," Daniel said. "I knew you were going to be bombarded with reporters and fans after the show, so I wanted to come by to say hello and introduce you to Megan."

"I appreciate that." Anthony's gaze turned a bit speculative as it rested on her before he turned back to Daniel. "But you and I should meet up later tonight. I have something for you."

"Yes, right." Daniel nodded quickly. "I'll come by your hotel. Around eleven?"

"That works. See you then." Her idol turned to her with a brilliant smile. "Glad to finally meet you. Will you introduce me to your sisters next time I'm in town?"

"Oh, they wouldn't let me hear the end of it if I

didn't," Megan said honestly. Chloe used to have a huge crush on Anthony Larsen in her tender teenage years.

When they left the backstage, Daniel asked, "Would you like something to drink? We still have a few more minutes until intermission ends."

"No, thanks. I have to pee." Megan crinkled her nose. "I always have to pee these days."

"That must be a hassle." Something tender flitted across Daniel's face as if she'd said something endearing. "I'll wait for you here, then."

"Don't be silly." She felt herself blushing for some reason. "I can find my way back to my seat. Go get settled. I'll be right there."

The line at the restroom was longer than she'd expected and the lights were blinking to signal the end of intermission by the time she arrived at her seat.

"I thought you got lost," Daniel teased, leaning close to her ear as the lights dimmed.

She only had time to stick her tongue out at him before the concert resumed. The only things she was aware of were the music and the warmth of Daniel's hand in hers. When she turned to look at him yet again, he met her eyes in the semi-darkness, as though he felt her gaze on him. She smiled at him with her heart and the corners of his lips turned up in response.

No, she didn't need words to tell him that she wanted him by her side. She would tell him with her whole being.

"Scotch?" Anthony asked him.

"Oh, yeah." Daniel settled back into the plush couch of his friend's hotel suite and accepted the glass of amber liquid. "Thanks."

He'd had a hard time parting with Megan after the concert. Something had shifted between them tonight. He could feel it. He could feel *her*. Her warmth and affection infused him with emotions he couldn't begin to identify—emotions he didn't want to identify. He wasn't sure what he was more afraid of…his own feelings? Or of losing that sense of *rightness* with Megan?

"All right." Nursing his own drink, Anthony plopped down on the sofa next to him. "I'm ready. Spill it."

"Spill what?" He took a sip of his Scotch, enjoying its smooth heat as it went down his throat.

His friend scoffed and aimed straight for the jugular. "Who is she?"

Daniel stopped pretending he didn't know what Anthony was talking about. "She's a…friend."

"You bought a Stradivarius for a *friend*?" Anthony's eyebrows rose high on his forehead.

"She's a friend who is…pregnant with my child," Daniel said quietly. "We're coparenting partners."

"Holy shit. A baby?" His friend took a big gulp of Scotch. "And that's all she is to you?"

"Isn't that enough?" Daniel glanced down at his drink. It had to be enough.

"I saw the way you looked at her." Anthony leveled him with a no-bullshit stare. "She's more than a friend or a coparenting partner to you."

"Think what you want," he said with a shrug.

"She couldn't be the musician that she is if she wasn't strong, dedicated and courageous." Anthony paused for a beat. "She is nothing like Sienna."

"I know that," Daniel scoffed as though he truly believed it. But he knew Megan would leave him just as his mother and Sienna had done. Why would someone like her stick around for him?

"You can't let one bad relationship dictate your life," Anthony pushed.

"Oh, that's rich," Daniel drawled. "We both know you're in no position to give relationship advice."

He immediately regretted lashing out at his friend when Anthony's face paled. He was a dick.

"Shit." Daniel tugged his hand through his hair. "Anthony…"

"You're absolutely right. What would a *player* know about relationships?" Anthony said with a smile that held a tinge of sadness. "Let's not waste time talking about women. We have a lot to catch up on."

Daniel hadn't been able to get Megan out of his mind—the soft brush of her hand against his on the arm of the chair…the warmth of her gaze in the dim concert hall. He'd hardly slept, desperate to have her in his arms. And he asked himself for the umpteenth time what the Stradivarius violin in his closet meant. Damn Anthony and his prying questions.

"Wouldn't you agree?" Walter Liu said, wiping his mouth with a cloth napkin. He'd invited Daniel to lunch as promised.

"I'm sure I do—" it took Daniel two full seconds to realize he'd been asked a question "—but you're going to have to repeat everything you said before that, because my mind wandered for a minute."

Chris Tanner, another longtime member of Jigu Corporation's board of directors, roared with a belly laugh. "Your story clearly bored the man silly, Walter."

"Not at all," Daniel said sheepishly. "I'm running on

less than four hours of sleep. It's making me daydream about my bed."

Everything he said was true except that his day-dreams about his bed usually included Megan. He took a long sip of ice water to cool down his thoughts and wake himself up. He and Anthony hadn't seen each other in close to a year, so catching up—and emptying a bottle of Scotch—had taken longer than practical for a weeknight. Tossing and turning, dreaming of Megan all night, probably hadn't helped either.

"Or you might be being diplomatic by not partici-pating in our roasting of the venerable Minsung Han," Walter Liu said with a good-natured chuckle. The men-tion of Megan's father made Daniel's stomach twist un-comfortably. Guilt was a bitch. "But a word of advice… you're young but you're not invincible. You need food and sleep like any other human being."

"Well, being Minsung's protégé, he's bound to be a workaholic like him," Chris added, pointing his fork at Daniel. "Even so, I agree with Walter about the neces-sity of food and sleep."

"Speaking of food, thank you for letting me join you for lunch." Daniel took a bite out of his club sandwich, hoping it would settle his churning stomach.

This lunch brought him one step closer to telling Mr. Han that he was the baby's father. But would it be the whole truth? He knew, but didn't want to acknowledge, that the only way to truly assuage his guilt would be to stop sleeping with the CEO's daughter behind his back. Even the thought of letting Megan go, however, made his blood run cold. He would rather live with the guilt, even if that made him an ungrateful bastard.

He managed to focus on the conversation for the rest

of lunch, which he enjoyed more than he'd expected. Walter and Chris were wise, intelligent and very much not full of themselves. He had a lot to learn from them. They parted with a promise to get together again soon.

Daniel had left himself plenty of time to make it to Megan's prenatal appointment, so he was sitting on the bench outside the medical building, checking his email, when she walked up to him.

"You don't have to come to every one of my appointments, you know," she said by way of greeting. "This one won't be very exciting. There isn't even going to be an ultrasound or anything."

"It doesn't matter." He got to his feet, pocketing his phone. "I want to hear for myself that you and the baby are doing well."

"What? My word isn't good enough?" she asked, arching her eyebrow.

"You're not a medical doctor, are you?" He took a gentle hold of her elbow and led them inside the building.

Once she'd checked in, Megan handed him her purse and said, "I have to go pee in a cup. Wait for me here."

"I wasn't planning on going anywhere," he said with wry grin.

She walked off with a huff. She seemed cranky today. It was kind of cute, but he hoped nothing was wrong.

They didn't have to wait long to be shown to an examination room, and the doctor joined them soon with a cheerful knock on the door.

"Hello," Dr. Pinkus said. "Good to see you guys. So how are you feeling today?"

"I feel good…" Megan chewed her bottom lip. "But I haven't felt the baby move, yet. Is…is that normal?"

Daniel shot her a sharp glance. She sounded nervous. If she'd been so worried, why hadn't she said anything to him? He held his breath as he waited for the doctor's answer.

"Let's see." The doctor flipped through her chart. "You're at twenty-two weeks, right?"

"Yes," Megan said in a near whisper.

"It's perfectly normal not to feel the baby move yet, especially for a first pregnancy." Dr. Pinkus smiled reassuringly. "There's absolutely no reason to worry. It'll happen sometime in the second trimester. You still have a ways to go."

"Okay." Megan's shoulders slumped with relief. "Thank you, Doctor."

The doctor ran through a series of routine questions and nodded with satisfaction. "You're doing great, my dear."

Daniel finally felt himself relax, but his heart still pounded uncomfortably in his chest. He didn't speak until they stepped into the afternoon sun.

"Why didn't you tell me? If you were worried about not feeling the baby move, why didn't you say anything?"

"You're not a medical doctor, are you?" She mimicked his words, but her eyes were soft with understanding. "I didn't tell you because I knew you would react like this. This way, you were only freaked out for a couple of minutes."

"Next time, you don't need to spare me the worry." He stopped in front of her car and placed his hands on her shoulders. "I told you I wanted to be here for you.

Let me shoulder the concerns with you. You don't need to do this alone."

Her breath left her in a tremulous rush. "Goddammit, Daniel."

His eyebrows rose on his forehead. He didn't know what response he'd expected, but that wasn't it. Neither did he expect her to tug his head down and kiss him senseless in the middle of the parking lot.

When she leaned back and glowered at him, he said, "I'm not sure I understand what's going on here, but could we continue this at my place?"

Her lips quirked up at the corners, but she quickly pulled them down. "Don't you have to get back to work?"

"I'll be useless at the office after that kiss," he said in a low growl.

This time she didn't hold back her smile. "Well, in that case…"

His cell phone started ringing just as their lips were about to meet again. He planned on ignoring it, but Megan put a hand on his chest and pushed him back.

"You'd better get that."

"Shit," he muttered when he saw that it was his executive assistant. "Yes, Terri."

She wanted to know if he could move up his dinner meeting to an hour from now. The investment banker he was scheduled to meet had to fly out of the country for an urgent business matter later in the evening and wouldn't be back in town for at least a week.

"Have him come into the office. I'll be back—" he glanced at his watch "—in forty-five minutes."

Daniel stuffed his phone back in his jacket and sighed. "Megan…"

"I know," she said with a shrug. "Duty calls. You shouldn't have tried to play hooky in the first place."

He grabbed her by the shoulders and kissed her firmly on the lips. "Have dinner with me tonight?"

"Okay. Sure. Dinner sounds good." She sounded a little breathless, and her eyes were glued to his lips.

He couldn't stop the wolfish grin that spread across his face. "After dinner, we'll finish what we started."

"Twice." Her gaze finally rose to meet his and the seductive promise in them sucked the breath out of him.

The power she held over him sang in his blood, and a part of him desperately wanted to answer the siren's call. But a bigger part of him told him to run and hide—to keep himself safe.

He would do neither. He wouldn't let her go—he couldn't—but he wouldn't fall for her. He had to protect himself and remember that he wasn't meant to be loved. She would leave him eventually. That was inevitable. He just had to make sure that she didn't take his heart with her.

Ten

Megan tapped her foot as the elevator climbed to the penthouse. Daniel's afternoon meeting had run long, so their dinner got pushed back. Time had already been crawling at a snail's pace ever since they parted at the parking lot of her ob-gyn's office. Needless to say, she was impatient to see him. She couldn't decide whether to throw herself at him the moment the elevator doors opened or to kick him in the shin for keeping her waiting. She must be very hungry for those to be the only two options she could think of.

But she ended up doing neither when she reached the penthouse, because the smell of meat and butter assailed her nostrils. Plus, Daniel wasn't waiting for her in front of the elevator like he usually did. She followed her nose straight to the kitchen.

He was standing over the stove, barefoot in a plain

white T-shirt and snug jeans. She wasn't sure what was making her mouth water more—the smell of the delicious food or the sight of the gorgeous man in front of her.

"You're cooking?" she managed to get out past her suddenly tight throat.

"It's only steak." He looked up from the pan with a distracted smile. "There's sparkling water in the fridge, if you're thirsty."

"*Only* steak?" She grabbed a bottle from the fridge and poured herself a tall glass. "You didn't even know where to look for tea in this kitchen."

"I still don't know where my housekeeper put the tea," he said, carefully basting the two steaks with what looked like melted butter infused with garlic and rosemary. "But just because I don't know where things are in *this* kitchen doesn't mean that I don't know my away around a kitchen."

"Where did you learn to cook?" She hopped onto a stool and took a long drink of her sparkling water.

"Home." Something in his voice made her frown, but she couldn't see his expression because he had his back turned to her. When she thought he wouldn't continue, he said, "I had to learn how to cook or live off of cold cereal."

Her frown deepened as she felt a painful tug in her heart. "You don't talk about your parents much."

"I never knew my mother." The very evenness of his tone told Megan of the pain hidden behind his words. "In a way, I guess I could say the same thing about my father. I lived at home with him until I went to college, but I might as well have lived alone."

She wanted to go to him, but the stiff way he held

himself told her that he wouldn't welcome her sympathy. Her father had always been busy, but Megan had never doubted that he loved her. And she always had her mom and her sisters. It broke her heart that her sweet, kind Daniel had never known his parents' love—that he had to grow up so alone.

"Okay. It's ready," he said with determined cheerfulness. "I hope you're hungry."

"I'm starving." She forced her lips into a smile and helped him set the table. Once they were seated across from each other, she said, "What? No candles?"

His huff of laughter sounded genuine. "I don't think I have any. Even if I did, I wouldn't know where to find the matches."

"Well, I guess I'll let it pass this time since you did make me dinner." She eagerly sliced into her steak and stuffed a good-sized chunk into her mouth. Her eyes fluttered shut. "Mmm. I think I'd like to have this steak as my last meal."

"*I* think you're just really hungry," he said, but couldn't hide the pleasure from his voice.

Dinner was delicious, but Megan had to admit that her favorite part was the dessert. With a contented sigh, she snuggled against Daniel and tangled their legs under the sheets.

"Thank you for making me dinner." Then she thought it only polite to add, "and for the orgasms."

"Mmm-hmm." He sounded distracted and his fingers drummed against her shoulder blade where he was resting his hand.

"Hey." She glanced up at him. "Where's *my* thank-you?"

Finally, he laughed and kissed the tip of her nose.

"Thank you for the orgasm. Thank you for the privilege of making you come. Thank you—" he leaned back and placed his hand on her stomach "—for carrying my child."

The heartfelt sincerity in his expression silenced the flippant response she had ready. "You're welcome."

"Wait here." He flung back the covers and slipped his jeans over his slim, bare hips.

She rose onto one elbow and watched him hurry to his closet. He reappeared carrying a violin case in his hand. Confusion drawing her eyebrows down, she sat up with the cover held over her breasts.

He carefully laid the violin case on the bed in front of her. His Adam's apple bobbed in his throat before he said, "Open it."

Megan reached out with one hand and unlatched the case. Her heart was pounding so hard she could feel it against the hand she held against her chest. Based on Daniel's expression, this wasn't an ordinary violin. She was almost afraid to see what was inside.

Her shocked gasp filled the room and the sheet she held against her fell to her lap as she reached for the violin with her trembling hands. "Daniel, what is this?"

"It—" he cleared his throat "—it's a Stradivarius."

"I know it's a Stradivarius," she said as she stared down at the violin, slowly turning it over this way and that. "What's it doing in your house? On your bed?"

"I want you to have it," he said simply.

"Why?" Her eyes finally rose to his face.

His expression held no hint of the nervousness he showed a moment ago. The hard line of his mouth and the grim set of his jaws masked his emotions. What was he afraid of revealing?

"I want you to have it," he repeated and shrugged with forced casualness. "You're having my baby and there's so little I could do to help. I just wanted to thank you properly."

Megan hadn't realized she was holding her breath until her chest started burning. She deliberately released it through her mouth. What had she been hoping he would say? That he had been an idiot for thinking that love and forever were a fairy tale that he could never give her? That this precious treasure was a token of his enduring love? Yes, that was what she had hoped he would say, because...she loved him. And she desperately wanted him to love her back.

"A Stradivarius is a bit excessive for a thank-you gift, don't you think?" She forced a lightness to her voice that she didn't feel. "Daniel, this couldn't have costed a penny less than two million dollars."

"It used to belong to Juliet Hannon," he said, watching her face closely.

"*The* Juliet Hannon? The legendary violinist? I thought she was taking a sabbatical." Megan cocked her head to the side. "Why would she sell her violin?"

"She's going to announce her retirement. She has Parkinson's, Megan."

"Oh, no." Her hand flew to her mouth and tears filled her eyes.

"She wanted her violin to go to someone who would love it and care for it just as she had." Daniel sat on the edge of the bed and placed his hand on her knee. "Ms. Hannon is Anthony's friend and mentor. When he shared the situation with me, I immediately thought of you. And they both agreed that you were a worthy successor for the Stradivarius. She sold me the violin at cost."

So many thoughts and feelings were tumbling through her, but she only managed to say, "But that must still be over a million dollars."

"It's not something I could return." He gave her a small smile.

"You should've discussed it with me," she said weakly, still holding on to the violin.

"I wanted it to be a gift from me." He ran his thumb across her wet cheek. She hadn't realized she was crying.

He cared about her. He cared about her enough to buy her a Stradivarius. It wasn't about the extravagance of the gift. He knew what it would mean to her. He knew she would strive to uphold the trust Juliet Hannon placed in her. He knew...her.

It wasn't enough. Megan deserved to be loved wholeheartedly. But it gave her hope—hope that if she fought for his love, she might actually win it.

"I can't accept this..." Something closed off in his expression and she rushed to add, "But I also can't refuse something so precious."

"What are you saying?" He watched her warily.

"I don't have the willpower to stop myself from playing this violin, but you will be the only one to hear me play it. I want to keep this at your place." She put her finger on his lips when he began to protest. "For now. You have to let me think this through, Daniel."

He nodded, so she took her hand back. His face was still carefully neutral, but he looked more or less himself. She didn't know what was in her expression, but

Daniel put his hand on the back of her neck and pulled her in for a hard, possessive kiss.

"I can't believe you gave me a Stradivarius while I'm naked," she said a little breathlessly when he released her. "It's a freaking Stradivarius. It deserves more respect."

He seemed to belatedly realize that other than a thin sheet loosely covering her legs, she was still completely nude. His eyes darkened as they took in her breasts. "You are magnificent naked. The Stradivarius should be honored."

She rolled her eyes even though she felt a blush spread across her chest and face. She gingerly placed the violin back in its case and got out of bed. Without bothering to put on her bra or underwear—the night was still young and Daniel was bound to undress her again—she pulled her oversize tunic over her head and declared herself presentable.

"Make yourself comfy," she said, reaching reverently for the violin.

She was both eager and nervous to try out the Stradivarius, and something about giving Daniel a private performance felt deeply intimate. Like she was baring her soul to him.

Blowing out a shaky breath, she brought the violin under her chin. "Let's see what this baby can do."

Megan had a performance face. It was an expression he'd never seen her make. It was one of intense concentration and immersion. There was a faint groove above the bridge of her nose and one eyebrow was delicately arched. That, of course, wasn't the first thing he noticed, but it was something he cached away in his mental file for everything Megan.

The first thing he noticed—no, felt, with every cell of his body—was the music. She'd chosen a piece lush with romance and passion. The soulful tune vibrated against his skin and bore into his heart. Listening to it while sitting on the edge of his bed, shirtless and barefoot, made him feel powerless against the beauty of the piece—powerless against the talented woman creating such music. By the time Megan opened her eyes and brought the violin and bow down to her sides, his hands were shaking so badly that he had them curled into tight fists on top of his thighs.

"That was just a snippet from a violin concerto…" she began uncertainly when he continued to sit silently.

"Wieniawski," he pushed past his dry throat. *"Violin Concerto No. 2 in D minor, Op. 22."*

"You know this piece." Surprise intermingled with pleasure in her voice. "So you weren't bullshitting me when you said you enjoy classical music."

"No, I wasn't. I like listening to classical music, but I honestly don't know all that much about it. This concerto just happens to be a favorite of mine." He rubbed the back of his head. "I heard Anthony perform it a few years back and something about it touched me."

With a small smile, she lovingly placed the violin back in its case and closed it shut. "Well, if you've heard Anthony play it, then my performance might've been a letdown."

"You were incredible." He clasped his hand around her wrist and pulled her onto his lap. "I feel bewitched."

"Thank you," she said shyly. "For the compliment

and for the Stradivarius. It responds like no other violin I've ever played, and the sound took my breath away."

"You're welcome." Relief rushed through him. A part of him had still been afraid that she would reject his gift. Her acceptance meant that she trusted him—that he was more than a casual fling to her. She wouldn't cast aside without a second thought.

"If you liked the private performance so much, you should come to one of my actual performances." She wrapped her arms around his neck. "I sound better in a concert hall. Your bedroom doesn't have very good acoustics."

"It was the best live performance I've ever heard." He smoothed his hand down her bare thighs. "And you played it only for me so I could claim it as mine."

"Hmm." She spread her legs and straddled his hips. He remembered with a burst of heat that she wore nothing under her tunic. "Do you want to claim my music? Or…me?"

She was just being playful. She couldn't know how desperately he wanted to claim her—to make her his. But he shied away from the thought. Claiming her meant giving himself to her as well, and he couldn't do that. He swore never to make himself vulnerable again—never to put himself in a position to be abandoned again.

"I want to claim your music." He lifted her shirt over her head, and she pressed her breasts against his chest. He wouldn't claim her heart, but her body could be his for tonight. He wouldn't let himself want more than that. They were taking this day by day. Tomorrow she might not be his, and he had to be okay with that. "I want to claim your body."

For a moment, her teasing smile turned sad and he felt his stomach lurch. Had she wanted more? Did she want to be his? But the sadness disappeared from her eyes and her expression turned sultry. Wishful thinking was making him see things that weren't there.

She slid around him and crawled to the middle of the bed, giving him a tantalizing view of her round ass. His chest rose and fell with increasing speed. When she reached the head of the bed, she turned around and beckoned him with the crook of her finger. He jumped to his feet and kicked off his jeans faster than he'd ever moved before. He was on top of her so quickly that she gasped in surprise, her eyes wide and a little intimidated.

The grin that spread across his face felt predatory, but when he leaned down to kiss her, his touch was tender…reverent. She had gifted him with a part of herself tonight. Her music still sang through his veins. Even as his kiss grew hungrier, more frantic, he saw the extraordinary woman in his arms and she deserved nothing less than his reverence.

"Daniel." When he drew back to stare down into her eyes, she cupped his cheek in her hand. "Claim me."

Her words awoke a primal need in him that he'd been trying to subdue. His hand found her center, wet and hot. She was ready for him, but he wanted her to feel as wild as he felt. His thumb drew lazy circles over her nub and she moaned, writhing under him.

"Do you want me?" he asked, inserting a finger into her tight warmth.

Her back arched off the bed. "Yes."

"Yes, what?" He added a second finger and she whimpered.

"I want you." She jerked frantically against his hand. "I want you inside of me."

"I am inside of you." He drew his fingers out and pushed them even deeper inside her. Tremors were running down his spine and sweat dripped down his forehead. Even as he teased her, he knew he couldn't hold back much longer.

"Please."

The raw need in her single word broke his control, and he spread her legs wide and tilted her hips up to receive him. The pleasure that coursed through him when he pushed into her was so intense that it almost felt like pain. He held still to gather himself, but Megan wiggled against him impatiently.

"Please." It was his turn to plead. "If you keep doing that, this isn't going to last very long."

"I don't need long." She moved against him again. "I promise."

True to her words, she fell apart with his name on her lips as he buried himself inside her and rode her with wild, hard thrusts. And as she clenched around him, his own climax wrenched a guttural cry out of him and waves of pleasure wracked through him. When the real world settled around him again, he moved his weight off her and collapsed beside her.

God, she was beautiful. Her face was flushed a delicate pink, and tendrils of hair clung to her damp forehead, but it was the sweet tenderness in her eyes that made his heart perform a somersault. He reached out to tuck her hair behind her ear. He wanted nothing more than to keep her by his side and wake up with her in the morning. *Every morning.* He snatched his hand away from her. The greedier he became, the more it would hurt when this ended—because everything ended…at least for him. The thought washed away his lethargy as effectively as a bucket of ice water.

"Let me take you home," he said curtly and rolled out of bed. But not before he saw the hurt in her eyes. This time, he knew he hadn't imagined it. Still, he did nothing about it…because he was a coward.

Eleven

For every step Megan took toward Daniel, he seemed to take two steps back. The night he gave her the Stradivarius, he'd turned brusque and distant after they made love—just like their second night together. Both nights, it felt as though he was kicking her out of his place. Like he couldn't wait to be alone.

He'd told her that he had emotional baggage and it wasn't about her, but it was hard not to feel hurt by it. Especially when all she wanted to do was fall asleep in his arms and wake up next to him so they would be the first thing the other saw in the morning.

A forlorn sigh slipped past her lips as she stood waiting behind the curtains with her sisters. Thankfully, the Chamber Orchestra was performing onstage, so her sisters didn't hear her. She wished she could spill her guts to them so they could help her figure out what to do, but that wasn't an option. She refused to add another secret for them to keep from their father. It wasn't fair to her sisters.

Besides, Megan already knew what she had to do to win Daniel's heart. She would have to take three steps forward every time he took two steps back. She would back him into a corner and love him relentlessly until he was hers. She wouldn't dwell on how much it stung every time he pushed her away. He had a gentle, kind soul. It would hurt him to know that he caused her pain.

And she instinctively understood that he was distancing himself from her to protect himself—from what, she didn't know yet. Maybe a part of it had to do with his unhappy childhood. She sighed again. It was hard to figure everything out when he shared so little of his past with her.

"We're on, girls." Angie nodded at them with her game face on.

"Let's go have some fun," Chloe said with a cheeky grin and strode out onto the stage first.

Megan followed her with a smile, reminded of what a privilege it was to play with her sisters. They were such amazing musicians and she loved them more than words. As long as she had them—and their music—by her side, she could take anything life threw her way. The thought sounded too much like she was preparing to lose Daniel. No, she wasn't going to let herself give up so easily.

Her unsettled thoughts spilled into her music at times, but her sisters caught her and lifted her up before it could affect their performance. Knowing they had her back and they deserved nothing less than her best, Megan was able to give her one-hundred-percent for the rest of the performance and finished strong.

After bowing to thundering applause, they walked off the stage and Megan breathed a sigh of relief.

Angie put her hand on her back and said softly, "Are you feeling okay, Megan?"

"I'm fine. The doctor said it was normal to have trouble concentrating sometimes." She shrugged as nonchalantly as she could manage. "Pregnancy brain."

"Hmm." Her older sister didn't buy it for a second and gave her a penetrating gaze. "You know I'm always here for you, right?"

"Right," Megan said without hesitation. She knew without a doubt that her sister would always be there for her—would always help shoulder any burden she carried. Even so—or maybe because of that—she had to carry this one on her own. "I know, so stop worrying."

"Okay," Chloe answered instead of Angie. She'd been standing beside them, quietly listening to the whole conversation. "We'll stop worrying for now, but we're going to swoop in the minute we feel like you're in trouble."

"Fair enough." Megan grinned at her sisters. "God, I love you guys so much. I can't stand it."

"Can I join you three and bask in the warmth of sisterly love?" Joshua came to stand with his arms around Angie's and Megan's shoulders.

He leaned down and kissed the top of her older sister's head, and Megan could swear he breathed in the scent of her hair, his eyes fluttering closed for a moment. The love between Angie and Joshua seemed to cocoon them in a sphere of shimmering light. All she wanted was a love like theirs. Megan nibbled her bottom lip as wistful envy swept through her. Suddenly, she missed Daniel with an urgency that nearly brought tears to her eyes.

"You're always welcome to join us," Angie said, snuggling into Joshua's side.

They all turned when someone cleared his throat behind them. Daniel stood a few steps away with three elegant bouquets of calla lilies in his arms. "I hope I'm not intruding."

"Of course you're not." Megan restrained herself from throwing herself into his arms, but there wasn't a damn thing she could do about the giant smile that spread across her face. "I didn't know you were coming."

"I want to kick myself for not attending your concerts sooner. I've been missing out," he said ruefully. "You ladies are extraordinary and it was a privilege hearing you play tonight."

The Han sisters simultaneously blushed with pleasure. Even Angie—with the love of her life standing right next to her—wasn't immune to Daniel's brand of sincerity and charm. They each took the bouquet he held out to them and beamed at him.

"You must be Daniel Pak." Joshua straightened to his full, imposing height and drew his wide shoulders back. His voice could've frozen a lake as he said, "I'm Joshua Shin, Megan's brother-in-law."

"It's a pleasure to meet you," Daniel said evenly, extending his hand.

Joshua narrowed his eyes and paused for two seconds before shaking Daniel's hand. "I'm afraid I can't say the same."

"Joshua!" Angie slapped her husband's arm before turning to Daniel. "Please don't mind him. He's just protective of my younger sisters."

"Come on, Hyungbu," Chloe said with a cringe. "You're embarrassing us."

Deciding her brother-in-law was chastised enough, Megan met Daniel's slightly bemused gaze and shrugged. Glancing around to make sure there was no one close enough to overhear, she said, "That's what you get for knocking me up."

After a stunned second, Daniel and her sisters burst out laughing, dispelling any lingering awkwardness. Even Joshua couldn't hang on to his scowl as he said, "I guess Megan doesn't need me to look out for her."

"No, she doesn't," Daniel said with obvious pride. "I'm no match for her."

"Now that we can all agree on that," Megan said hurriedly when her sisters glanced between her and Daniel with speculative expressions, "should we go out for a nightcap?"

"That sounds like a great—" Joshua began. Angie leaned close to him and whispered something in his ear, and his eyes bulged slightly. He cleared his throat. "It seems Angie and I have a prior engagement. We'll take a raincheck on that nightcap."

"And I have to work on some slides for a presentation tomorrow," Chloe moaned. "It's so hard balancing my duties as a professional musician with my duties as a grad student."

Megan raised an eyebrow. That was an elaborate explanation to simply bow out of a casual get-together. "So what you're saying is that you plan on staying up all night playing League of Legends again?"

"Precisely." Chloe grinned unrepentantly, then she suddenly scowled. "I'm hoping to run into my arch nemesis tonight so I can kick his ass."

"You have an arch nemesis on League of Legends?" Daniel asked with a broad smile. He probably thought her younger sister was as cute as a button, because she really was.

"Yes," Chloe hissed. "I. Hate. Him."

"All right. Settle down," Angie said wryly. "Save that antagonism for the game. You're scaring Daniel."

Which wasn't quite true. In fact, he looked absolutely delighted. He seemed to truly enjoy interacting with her siblings. A pang of sadness ran through Megan as she remembered the lonely childhood he'd had.

"Megan, may I give you a lift home?" Daniel said with impeccable politeness, but there was a glint in his eyes that made her pulse spike.

"Yes, I'd appreciate that, since my sisters are abandoning me," she replied with forced nonchalance.

When it was finally just the two of them as they walked to his car, he took her hand and placed a lingering kiss on the inside of her wrist. "I'm actually relieved I got you to myself."

"Are you now?" The kiss left her a little breathless.

He pushed her up against the passenger door of his car. "I could still feel your music pulsing through my veins. You were magnificent and I feel…frantic."

"Frantic?" she squeaked inelegantly. She could feel his hard length pressing into her stomach.

"Like I would go mad if I don't have you soon," he growled, his lips a breath away from hers.

She closed the remaining distance between them and kissed him with a moan, burying her hands in his hair. She wanted to be everything to him…his love, his family…if only he'd let her. Loving him in secret hurt so much. A sob escaped her before she could push it down.

Daniel pulled back and held her face between his hands. "Megan, what's wrong?"

Her chest rose and fell so quickly she felt light-headed, and for a second—just a split second—she was tempted to tell him everything. That she loved him. That she wanted them to be a family. But the moment passed because she couldn't risk losing him. Not yet.

"We should take this to someplace more private." She couldn't quite manage a smile. "We can't risk starting any rumors that might reach my father's ears. We're so close to having the board members' support secured."

His eyes bore into hers as though he saw through her half-truth, but he merely nodded and opened the car door for her. They drove in silence to his place, their moods subdued. Megan felt his sidelong glances on her, but she stared out the window, not having the energy to pretend everything was okay.

As it stood, what they had between them wouldn't last. No matter how carefully she treaded. So did she want to risk their arrangement for a chance at something real? Something lasting? *Yes.* They would always be in each other's lives in some capacity, because of the baby, but the thought of being cordial acquaintances made her heart bleed. What hurt the most was that it wouldn't be much different from what they were now—casual lovers.

She finally turned away from the window and met Daniel's searching gaze. He reached for her hand and she linked her fingers through his. Megan knew herself. She couldn't settle for anything less than all-consuming love. If she lost him trying to win his love, then at least she would know that she went down fighting. She would have no regrets.

Last night, Megan had made love to him with such tenderness and generosity that Daniel had felt humbled and honored. Then, why did he feel so unsettled? Because it had felt like goodbye. She'd made love to him as though it was for the last time.

He drew several deep breaths through his nose but couldn't fill up his lungs. He listlessly flipped through the documents on his desk before shoving them aside. Leaning back in his chair, he spun around to face the windows of his office. It was past eight and the city below twinkled with lights. But the stunning view looked bleak to his eyes tonight. He spun back to his desk and picked up his cell phone.

Daniel hadn't heard from Megan all day. Even though he'd reached for his device countless times throughout the day, he couldn't work up the nerve to text her himself. He almost dropped his cell when it buzzed in his hand. His breath left him in a whoosh when he saw that it was Megan.

I'm finally cashing in on your offer.

His eyebrows drew together as he typed back.

What offer?

Her response was immediate.

I'm dying for some tiramisu and pistachio cannoli.

Daniel threw back his head and laughed, relief rolling through him. Everything was fine. They were fine.

Where should I deliver them to? Should I park a couple blocks from your house and text you?

He tapped his foot as she typed her response.

I would like front door delivery please. Mrs. Chung is
visiting her daughter and won't be back till tomorrow
afternoon. And as you know, my father is in Austin for
business. Maybe I'll even let you come inside.

Daniel grabbed his jacket and headed out with his
heart pounding. He couldn't wait to see Megan. He'd
seen her the night before, but that felt like an eternity
ago. If he sounded lovesick, he decided not to notice
it. And she was alone tonight. Maybe he would get to
wake up with her in the morning. The thought didn't
plunge him into a blind panic anymore—the *want* far
outweighed the fear. He broke into a run to reach his car.

Besides, it didn't mean anything. He was only curious to see what she looked like waking up in the
morning. Everything about her would be warmed and
softened by sleep—her cheeks rosy, her lips full and
parted, her silken hair tousled around her bare shoulders. He would kiss her awake. First, on her shoulder,
then at the hollow below her throat, then her eyes—one
then the other—and finally her lips, which would blos-
som into a smile underneath his before she opened her
eyes. And he would be the first person she saw in the
new day. He wanted that—desperately—even though
wanting more would do him no good.

He picked up the tiramisu and cannoli from an Italian restaurant nearby. It was fancy, expensive and close.
The food wasn't as good as the hole-in-the-wall Italian
restaurant in his old neighborhood in New York, but it
would have to do. He had to remind himself to ease off
the gas pedal several times as he rushed to Megan's

house. Getting a ticket would take up more time than his speeding would save.

Out of habit, he parked his car a block away and walked to her front door. He rang the doorbell and waited for Megan with blood pounding in his ears. He was being ridiculous, but he was too happy to care. When the door finally opened, the smile she gave him almost convinced him that she was as happy to see him as he was to see her.

"Your delivery is here," he said, holding up the bag of dessert.

"Thank God." She pretended to sag against the door, then stepped back to let him in. "What are you standing around for? Off you go to the kitchen."

She led the way and he followed a few steps behind to admire the view. She was in a silky pink pajama set that slid across her skin as she walked in front of him, hips swaying. She probably put them on for comfort but she looked sexy as hell to him. He wondered if he could have her before they had the dessert.

She looked over her shoulder, opening her mouth to say something, but whatever she saw in his expression made her blush and she turned back without saying a word. When they were in the kitchen, she scooted to the far end of the room, putting the island between them. He took a predatory step toward her and she pressed herself against the counter, holding up a hand.

"Dessert first," she said, sounding breathless.

He continued stalking toward her and she watched him with her hands clenched on the edge of the counter, her chest rising and falling rapidly. His eyes lazily slid down her body, then back up to her face. He stopped inches away from her and placed his hands over hers, trapping her between his arms and his hard, aching body.

"Define *dessert*," he purred, drawing his nose down the side of her face. Her shuddering breath made him smile. His hands circled her waist and he hefted her onto the counter. Spreading her legs, he stepped in between them.

The shyness melted away from Megan as she stared into his eyes and she smoothed her hands over his chest, then over his shoulders. "Dessert is something…decadent. A sweet, rich indulgence. Something that makes you feel a little…sinful."

He crushed his mouth against hers like a man starved. He wanted her so much that a sob lodged itself in his chest. He moaned her name against her lips, which parted for him in invitation. Their tongues slithered against each other, tasting and teasing, and his body caught fire. His need for her was consuming him and he wanted her to burn for him.

But he froze when a sharp gasp escaped her. Both her hands flew to her stomach and her head dropped. Even though her breathing was ragged, she sat still and silent. Fear sliced through his lust-fogged mind.

"God, Megan." He grabbed her shoulders and ducked his head to catch her expression. Was she in pain? "Tell me what's wrong, sweetheart."

"Oh, Daniel. There's nothing wrong. The opposite actually." She raised her tearstained face at last. "It's the baby. He moved. I felt him move."

His knees turned liquid with relief. She was okay. Thank God, she was okay. Then goose bumps rose on his arms as he registered what she had said. The baby— their baby—moved.

"Can I…?" He cleared his throat and tried again, "Do you think I could feel him?"

"Well, let's see." Megan tugged his hand onto her stomach and lowered her head again, as though listening to her body. "It's very subtle. Almost like bubbles rising to the surface."

They both held their breaths and waited. Nothing happened for a minute and Daniel was about to withdraw his hand when he felt it…felt him. The softest fluttering against his palm. He gasped and stepped back, his arm dropping to his side. "Was…was that him?"

"Yes." Happy tears filled Megan's eyes once more. "That's him."

He gingerly placed his hand on Megan's stomach again, and the baby tickled it. "Hi, there."

"Say hi to Daddy," Megan whispered, gazing down at her stomach—her hand placed over his.

The baby fluttered again as though he heard his mother's urging. Heat gathered behind Daniel's eyes and undefinable emotions clogged his throat. Something between a laugh and a sob escaped from him. Then he laughed again because he was so damn happy.

Megan joined in his laughter, tears sliding down her face. He swiped his thumbs across her cheeks and pressed his forehead against hers. Their laughter died down and their breathing evened out as they leaned against each other. Something peaceful and content stole into his heart. This moment. He would never forget this perfect moment for the rest of his life.

"Megan? What…?" He spun around at the sound of Mr. Han's voice, and the older man's eyes widened with shock. "Daniel?"

Daniel's hand was still pressed against Megan's stomach. He didn't remember doing so but he had wrapped a protective arm around her and had pulled her close. She was trembling against him and he tightened his hold on her, cursing under his breath. He couldn't let Megan bear the brunt of her father's anger and disappointment. He had to shield her from it somehow. But how?

"Appa—" Megan's voice shook and when her father held up his hand, she pressed her lips together.

"Are you seeing my daughter, Daniel?" Mr. Han leveled a steely gaze at him.

"Yes, sir," he said. There would be no more lies from this point on. He felt Megan turn to stare at him.

"How long has this been going on?" His mentor's frown smoothed out and hope stole into his expression. *God*. Daniel felt guilt twist in his gut.

"About two months, sir," he answered past his dry throat.

"Two months? So is this the result of my stellar matchmaking skills?" Mr. Han's face split into a full-blown grin as he regarded the two of them. Then his expression turned somber again. "And you are at peace with the fact that my daughter is pregnant with another man's child?"

Daniel felt Megan stiffen beside him and he turned to meet her gaze. She must have seen the grim determination on his face because she slowly shook her head and gripped his hand. She'd worked so hard to protect him from her father's wrath. He gave her a small smile and smoothed back a strand of hair from her eyes.

"Mr. Han—" Daniel looked at his mentor and friend "—Megan is pregnant with my child. I am the baby's father."

Minsung Han staggered back two steps, the shock,

betrayal and hurt plain on his face. Megan scrambled down from her perch on the counter and stepped toward her father with her hand outstretched. Mr. Han drew himself up and pointed a warning finger at her.

"Stay where you are. I don't want to hear a word out of you," her father grit out in an uncompromising tone before he turned to Daniel. "As for you… I presume you wouldn't have kept the baby's parentage a secret—making a mockery out of me—if you intended to marry her."

It wasn't posed as a question, so Daniel said nothing. He didn't say that he would marry his daughter in a hot second if only she would have him, but she'd made it abundantly clear that she didn't want to marry him. Because…because she wanted to marry for love. He couldn't…give her that. If he loved her and lost her, then everything would be tainted…even his love for his son. Something inside him began quaking.

"Appa, please listen," Megan tried again.

"Not. A. Word," he roared.

"Do *not* speak to her that way." Daniel stepped forward, half shielding Megan from her father's rage.

Minsung Han's face transformed into a mask of indifference and he waved a dismissive hand toward Daniel. "You have one week to tender your resignation."

They stood in a cocoon of shock as the sound of Mr. Han's footsteps faded away. Then Megan took a shuddering breath as though she was waking up from a nightmare.

"Daniel, it's going to be okay," she said urgently. "I… I just have to tell my father that you proposed to me—that you tried to do the right thing—but I said no."

"Then we proceeded to see each other behind his

back and didn't tell him that I was the baby's father. We lied to him, Megan," he reminded her gently.

"No, I could explain everything. I'll make him listen." Megan hugged her arms around her midriff. "I'll make him understand."

The only way to appease her father—and to protect Megan from his anger—was for them to get married. His stomach dropped to his feet. He had to ask her... even if she said no again. He had to try.

"Megan, marry me," he said, wrapping his hands around her shoulders. "Marry me. Please."

She raised stunned eyes to his and searched his face. Her voice shook when she asked, "Do you...? Do you love me?"

"Love?" Something inside him seemed to shrivel. He dropped his hands to his sides and took a step back from her. "I told you that I... I couldn't give you the fantasy. This isn't a fairy tale, Megan. What we have is enough. We have a child between us. We respect and enjoy each other. And I will never be unfaithful to you. I promise you that. Isn't that enough?"

A light in her eyes seemed to flicker and die, and a voice inside him screamed. *Coward.* Her bottom lip trembled and she bit viciously down on it. He wanted to reach out and pull her into his arms—hold on tight to her. She breathed in and out of her nose until the trembling eased. She drew back her shoulders, then lifted her chin.

"No, that isn't enough." Quiet strength resonated from her. "I won't marry you, Daniel, because I deserve to be loved. I deserve the fairy tale."

He wanted to shout and rant that fairy tales end. That love was a fickle emotion that faded, leaving pain in its wake. But he said nothing as he watched her walk out of the kitchen and disappear down the hallway. Because even though he had protected himself from the destructive force of love, pain had still found him. Even though he'd known that it was inevitable that she would leave him—abandon him—he still felt himself breaking apart into pieces.

And he said to no one in particular, "But *I* don't deserve to be loved."

Twelve

Megan knocked on her dad's bedroom door, but there was no answer. It might be for the best. She could hardly stand on her own, and her teeth were chattering so hard that her dad wouldn't be able to understand a word out of her. So, leaning against the hallway wall, she dragged herself to her room with halting, faltering steps.

She half fell onto her bed and curled into herself. Her head and limbs were heavy, and she felt like she was sinking deeper and deeper into the mattress. She imagined herself being swallowed up by it along with her loss and sorrow.

An odd numbness had come over her as she'd walked away from Daniel. She didn't know how long it would last—how long it would keep the pain at bay. Anxiety crept into her. She felt like a rabbit being hunted as she hid from the inevitable grief. She jolted up and scrambled back into the headrest, pulling the covers up to her chin. Her breathing grew ragged. She didn't want to face what she'd done. She couldn't face it.

Was he gone? Had he left? Maybe if she ran back downstairs, she'd find him in the kitchen, standing exactly where she'd left him. Then she could tell him that she would marry him. That she would take whatever he could offer her. That she didn't need his love as long as she had some part of him.

What was it he'd said? Ah, yes. She would have his respect and fidelity. That was something. And their passion. There was that. But how long could passion burn without love? An image of their cold marriage bed, where they slept with their backs turned toward each other, flashed through her mind. She shivered and pulled the covers more tightly around her.

Then the baby fluttered in her stomach as though he was saying, "And me. There's me." Yes, they would have their baby. The tears she'd been holding at bay finally started to fall. Would Daniel love their son? She knew he would—that he already did. And how long would it be before Megan began resenting their little boy for having his love—the love that he denied her?

The tears fell faster as sobs wracked her body. It would destroy her to marry Daniel knowing he didn't love her. Her love for him would turn into poison inside her and she would become a bitter shadow of herself. She would lose herself forever. No, she couldn't let that happen. She couldn't do that to her father, her sisters and her baby. She couldn't do that to herself.

So she had to let Daniel go…no matter how much it hurt. Her sobs turned into wails that ravaged her throat, and she clawed at her chest. It was only when her dad wrapped his arms around her and tucked her under his chin that she realized he had come into her room. She wailed until her voice became a husky rasp, then she sobbed until her body went limp with fatigue, and she cried until her tears dried up—until she was empty.

Her dad held her tight against his chest even after she stilled and grew silent. He held her until exhaustion claimed her and darkness edged into her consciousness. At last, in the safety of his arms, Megan allowed herself to fall into a dreamless slumber where she could stop hurting for a little while.

Megan woke up early next morning with her throat raw and her eyes swollen. She knew the damage outside was far less evident than the mangled mess that was her shattered heart. Even so, she pushed back her covers and got out of bed. She showered, dried her hair and dressed in a cozy sweater and comfortable leggings. She had to show her dad that she was okay—that she was going to be okay. It must've broken his heart to watch her fall apart last night even after she'd betrayed him in the worst possible way.

She went downstairs to the kitchen and puttered around to make some tea and toast. Once everything was finished and arranged on a tray, she carried it upstairs and stopped in front of her dad's door.

"Appa, I need you to open the door me," she said, her voice husky but steady. "My hands are full."

The door opened, and her dad's eyes roamed her face for a moment before he stepped back to let her in. He was dressed casually in a pair of khakis and a polo shirt with a cardigan over it. He was planning on staying home—she swallowed a lump in her throat—to look after her.

Megan placed the tray on the coffee table in the sitting area and sat down in one of the armchairs. "Mrs. Chung will be back this afternoon. For now, you'll have to make do with toast."

With a noncommittal grunt, he settled into the chair next to her and spread his toast with a generous pat of butter and strawberry jam. He took a big bite before pouring tea into both their cups. She followed his example and munched on some toast even though she couldn't taste a thing. She took a sip of her tea to help her swallow it down.

"Thank you," she said quietly. "I know I've hurt you. You didn't deserve that. I'm going to apologize for that in a minute. But more than anything, I want to thank you. Thank you for holding me together last night. I don't know what I would've done without you."

"You don't ever have to wonder what you will do without me." He gazed steadily at her. "Because I will always be there for you."

"I know." She sniffed and shook her head. If she started crying again, she didn't know if she could ever stop. "I love you, Daddy."

"I know."

"And now, we've come to the portion of the program where I grovel," she said with a nervous laugh. "I'm sorry I lied to you. I'm so sorry I hurt you."

"You made a fool out of me." His expression turned thunderous in an instant as though he'd been suppressing his rage until he knew she was okay. He rose from his seat and paced with short, agitated steps. "To think I was trying to set you two up."

"I thought I had good reason to keep things from you, but now all those reasons seem nonsensical." She threw her hands up in a helpless gesture.

"There is no excuse for what you did," he said in a low, furious voice.

"You're right. I should have told you the truth as soon as I found out."

"What?" Her dad's eyebrows rose in surprise. He sat back down and wiped his hand over his face. "You didn't know all along?"

"I'm sure you don't want to hear this again, but I really did have a one-night stand with a stranger," she said, swallowing her mortification. "When I found out I was pregnant, I had no way of contacting him. That's all true. It doesn't make what I did okay, but I never told you an outright lie."

"Yes, it doesn't make what you did okay," he snapped, but some of the anger seemed to have seeped out of him. He jerked his chin toward her. "So tell me what happened."

"I didn't know who Daniel was…until that night you invited him over for dinner."

He huffed an incredulous laugh then stared at her with wide eyes. "Wait. You're serious."

"Yes. Imagine my surprise running into my one-night stand—three months after the fact—in my own house."

"And you had another surprise for him…"

"Daniel must have been shocked, but he asked me to marry him the moment I told him I was pregnant. I'm the one who refused him. He wanted to tell you every-thing, but I convinced him not to."

Megan explained her brilliant plan to win over the

board members so her dad wouldn't react rashly to the news. "Daniel wanted to be in the baby's life and didn't want to risk having to relocate far away from me and the baby."

"Thank you for thinking so highly of me," her dad muttered.

"You can't say I was wrong," she said gently. "You asked him for his resignation last night. Remember?"

"I remember." He sat up in his chair. "And I'm standing by my decision."

"But Appa…" He raised an imperious hand and she snapped her mouth shut. She wasn't there to ask him for a favor. She was there to beg for his forgiveness. "Just please remember that I'm the one who refused to marry him. He…he even asked me again last night… and…and I…"

"That's all right. You don't need to continue." He sighed. "I can guess what you said from your state. Tell me, Megan. Why did you say no?"

"Because…" she choked out as every raw crack in her broken heart burned. She closed her eyes to gather herself. "Because I want to marry for love."

"I think," he said quietly, "you *would* be marrying for love."

For a moment, all she could do was blink at her dad. "Am I that obvious?"

"A person doesn't grieve like you did yesterday unless they lost someone they loved." He understood. He'd grieved so deeply when her mom died.

"I do love Daniel—" Megan took a shuddering breath "—but he doesn't love me."

"Are you sure about that? The scene I walked in on last night…" Her dad arched an eyebrow. "You two were drowning in each other's eyes and glowing with happiness. Hell, that sounds like poetry and I'm no poet. There's just no other way to describe what I saw."

"He thinks love is a fantasy..." she said uncertainly, her heart pounding with a terrifying glimmer of hope.

"For a smart man, he does a great job of acting the fool." He clucked his tongue. "Have you told him that you loved him?"

"No." She had planned to tell him. "I... I was afraid of pushing him away."

"Have you ever considered the possibility that he was scared, too?" her dad asked. "Maybe he was afraid that you don't feel the same way—so afraid that he couldn't even admit to himself that he loved you."

"That's just wild speculation," she whispered, but she couldn't dismiss what he'd said. She didn't want to.

"More like an educated guess." He wagged his finger at her. "I know what I saw. Credit your old man with some wisdom. I've lived a lot longer than you have."

She suddenly couldn't talk about Daniel—or even think about him—for another second. She stood from her chair and kissed her dad's cheek. "Thank you, Appa."

"And don't think I've forgiven you, yet," he said as though he meant "you're forgiven."

Megan carried the half-empty tray back to the kitchen, not sure how to feel...not sure she wanted to feel anything at all. Now that she'd made the first step toward making things right with her dad, the guilt that had kept the devastation at bay diminished, and even her determination to appear okay seemed to dwindle.

She shuffled into the living room and lay down on the couch and curled into a ball—or as much as her growing stomach would allow. She did nothing to stop the tears that dripped down from the corners of her eyes until the hair on her temple became damp with them. Her eyelids became too heavy to keep open so she closed them, not caring she'd only just woken up.

In the end, she hadn't fought for Daniel—for them. She'd completely chickened out. So much for being brave and courageous. Her courage had deserted her when everything had been on the line. She'd been too scared to tell him that she loved him. Even so…he'd let her walk away. A sob tore through her throat. Couldn't he have fought for her just a little?

Even if her dad was right, she couldn't risk getting her heart broken for a second time by confessing her love to him. At least, not yet. She needed time to heal—needed time to grow strong again. Only then would she know if she had the courage to fight for him.

Daniel hadn't slept or eaten but he'd consumed quite a bit of whiskey. He was late for work—soon to be his former job—but he stood under the spray of steaming hot water to wash away the stench of alcohol seeping out of his pores. Effectively fired or not, he respected Jigu Corporation too much to go into the office looking—and smelling—like the wreck he was.

He told himself what a close call that had been. If he was like this now, how would he have been if he'd let himself fall in love with Megan? There would've been nothing left of him if he'd lost her after he fell for her. Laughter snuck out of him and echoed hollowly in the shower. His shoulders shook with the force of the laugh and he leaned against the wall for support. When he realized he sounded hysterical, he shut his mouth and clenched his teeth to stop laughing.

He needed to get to the office. He had a week to tie up loose ends and streamline the transition for his successor. Stepping out of the shower, he dried off briskly and wiped his hand across the fogged-up mirror. He scowled at the image staring back at him. He needed a shave, but he couldn't stand looking at himself a moment longer, so he turned around and walked into his room. He carelessly pulled clothes off the hanger and rushed to dress himself. He was desperate to get out of his penthouse, away from his own company. He had to lose himself in his work.

Once he got to Jigu, he nodded curtly to his assistant, making her cheery smile slide off her face, and locked himself in his office. First thing first, he wrote his resignation letter. After typing and deleting a half dozen drafts, he decided to go with the first version he'd written: *Please accept my resignation...* Bland, generic and completely inadequate to express the remorse he felt for what he'd done to Minsung Han.

He printed out the letter, folded it with crisp, sharp edges and inserted it into a pristine white envelope. Then he held and stared at it for God knew how long before he picked up the phone and dialed Mr. Han's extension. No answer. Daniel called the CEO's executive assistant.

"Is Mr. Han in?" he asked more brusquely than he'd intended.

"No, Mr. Pak," she said with cool professionalism. "He said he will be working from home this morning. He might come in late afternoon, but he said to cancel all meetings for today."

Daniel hung up the phone with a mumbled thank-you and stood from his chair. Jigu Corporation's CEO never worked from home and never canceled meetings at the last minute. He wore his professionalism like an armor and sought to be an example for all his employees. No matter how shocked and betrayed he might've been the night before, Mr. Han would not stay home to sulk or lick his wounds.

Megan. Something must be wrong with Megan. Daniel paced back and forth, clenching and unclenching his hands. It couldn't be the baby. The baby was healthy and moving… His mind flashed back to the kitchen and the joy he'd felt in that moment. He closed his eyes and shook his head. He couldn't think about that. He was certain he wouldn't be able to survive dwelling on that moment because it would remind him of what he'd lost. No, the baby was fine. But Megan…maybe she wasn't fine.

Try as he might, he couldn't forget the pain in her eyes when he all but told her that he didn't love her. She would get over it, wouldn't she? They'd both agreed that there wouldn't be any promises. She had to have known that the affair would eventually end. Hadn't she? She would've been the one to leave him. Like they all do. In fact, she *was* the one who'd ended things. She was the one who'd refused to marry him—the one who'd walked away from him.

He cringed with shame. That was a new low for him. He knew exactly what he was doing when he'd told her that what they had was enough—that he couldn't give her the *fantasy.* He was the one who ended their relationship. He was the one who had hurt her. *God, please let Megan be okay.*

To hang on to his sanity, he threw himself into his work. He went from one project to the next, document after document, barking out orders to anyone who might slow him down. He had to keep moving.

When his phone buzzed, he nearly growled, "Yes?"

"Mr. Han would like to see you in his office," Terri said quietly.

He gripped his phone and took a deep breath. "Let him know I'll be there shortly. Thank you."

Daniel raked his fingers through his hair and stood up. He put on his suit jacket and slid his resignation letter into the inside pocket before walking out of his office. He offered a small smile to his assistant as a meager apology for being an asshole all day, then made his way to the CEO's office.

"I'm here to see Mr. Han," Daniel said to the executive assistant.

"Yes, please go right in," she said with a gracious nod.

After a courtesy knock, he walked into the CEO's office, closing the door behind him. Mr. Han kept his eyes on the document he was reading until Daniel stood in front of his desk. When the older man finally met his eyes, he wished the CEO would resume reading. Daniel realized that he had never before seen what Minsung Han looked like when he was regarding an adversary.

Mr. Han's gaze was both ice and fire and 100 percent intimidating. Not that Daniel couldn't hold his own against intimidation, but he was in no position to stare the CEO down. He was there to grovel to salvage whatever he could of his relationship with his mentor, which couldn't be much. But he had to try.

"Here is my letter of resignation." Daniel held out

the envelope, but Minsung Han made no move to take it from him. After an awkward, silent stretch of time, Daniel finally placed his resignation letter on the desk. "I know an apology doesn't mean much at this point, but I still want to offer you my deepest, sincerest apology. I have no excuse for deceiving you…"

"And you have an excuse for impregnating my daughter?" Mr. Han barked.

"I didn't know who she was…" Daniel clamped his mouth shut on the excuse. "No, I have no excuse for that either."

"So you don't want to marry my daughter?"

"No, sir. That's not true. I want to marry her." He swallowed past a painful lump. "More than anything."

"Except you don't love her." Mr. Han's scowl inexplicably softened as he regarded Daniel. "At least, that's what Megan thinks."

"Is she… Is she okay?" He gripped the backs of the guest chairs in each hand as his blood pounded in his ears.

"No." Mr. Han's face closed off again. "She's not okay."

Daniel spun on his heels and took several steps toward the door before he stopped himself. Where was he going? To Megan? He couldn't go to her. He was the reason she wasn't okay. He returned to his spot in front of her father's desk.

"I'm sorry," Daniel said as something inside him cracked. He'd hurt Megan. He'd disappointed his mentor. "I'm going to take the week to get my projects in order and ready to hand off to my successor—"

"You think I could find your replacement in a week?" Mr. Han scoffed. "Get out of my office. I don't want to look at your sorry face anymore. And take that damn envelope off my desk."

"But, sir—" Daniel frowned in confusion.

"I thought I told you to leave." The older man narrowed his eyes into menacing slits. "I also told you to take this with you. Do you think you can manage that?"

Daniel could only nod as he placed his resignation letter back in his jacket pocket. After bowing from his waist, he strode out of the CEO's office. Back at his desk, he spun his chair to face the window and stared unseeingly at the city below him.

There was no doubt that Mr. Han was furious with him. Even so, he'd refused to accept Daniel's resignation. What had changed his mind? He buried his head in his hands with a groan. Not what. Who. Megan must've told her father everything…down to the reason she'd refused his proposal. She had stood up for him even after he'd cast aside her love—

Daniel shot to his feet. *Her love.* Her answer to his proposal had depended on whether or not he loved her, because there was no doubt as to her love. *Do you love me?* He remembered her as she said those words—her eyes too wide for her face as hope and fear warred inside them. She loved him and all she needed to hear was that he loved her, too. She had given him the chance to have her—all of her—but he'd thrown it in her face.

He didn't remember what it felt like to be abandoned by his mother—he'd been too young—he only knew the bone-deep emptiness of her absence. But he did remember what it felt like to find the woman he thought he loved in the arms of his roommate. He remembered what it felt like to listen to Sienna tell him that she'd never wanted him…that he wasn't good enough for her.

Her betrayal had brought to surface the fear he'd
carried with him all his life. That a boy his mother
had abandoned—and his father didn't want—couldn't
be good enough for anyone. He hated Sienna for that.
He hated himself for that. The pain of that revelation
had eaten away at him until he became someone who
avoided commitment. A man who thought love was a
fairy tale.

That was why he hadn't allowed himself fall in love
with Megan—even though he'd known that it meant
he would lose her. But having lost her, he realized the
pain he felt when Sienna betrayed him was like a paper
cut compared to the devastation he felt right now. With
her, it was his pride that was injured, not his very soul.

And he'd used the baby as an excuse—a cover for his
own fears. His love for his son would never falter. Even
though he felt as though the world was crumbling down
around him—on top of him—he could only feel joy that
he would soon be a father. Nothing could change that.

He had let his wounded pride and bitterness rule
his life. He'd let them blind him to the truth, but he
was done with hiding—done with denying the greatest
truth of his life. The reason he felt as though his heart
was being torn into shreds was because he *had* fallen
in love with Megan. He loved her with everything in
him. But he had been too stubborn and too terrified to
admit that he'd been wrong. Love was real. And maybe
if an incredible woman like Megan loved him, then he
was good enough.

What if it was too late? Fear clutched at him with its
jagged claws, but he cast it aside. He had to right this
wrong. There was no alternative. No matter what happened, he owed it to the baby to become the best man

he could be—a man who fought for his mother's love. And he would strive to be good enough for Megan. He would do anything—risk any pain—to deserve her love.

But she was hurting. He couldn't demand to see her and pour out his heart to her when she couldn't possibly be ready to listen to him. He needed to give her time. As much as he could stand, which wasn't very much at all. He would try, though. Then he would tell her everything. He hoped to God it would be enough.

Thirteen

Megan walked into her ob-gyn's office alone, blinking back tears. There was no reason for her to cry. Even at the last prenatal appointment—even when they were together—she'd told Daniel that he didn't need to come to every one of them with her. But she hadn't seen him in over three weeks and missed him so much. That was still no excuse to ugly cry while peeing into a cup, so she didn't.

Besides, she had to focus on getting up the nerve to confess her love to Daniel and to build up some serious muscles around her heart so it wouldn't break if he said he didn't feel the same way about her. Because even if he didn't love her yet, she was willing to give him all the time he needed to fall in love with her. All he had to do was stop being so stubborn and accept that love was very real. And he would have to admit that, because she intended to show him how much she loved him every chance she got.

It was a great plan. It really was. But there was still the issue of lacking courage. Where had her nerve gone? She'd always thought she had plenty of pluck. But Daniel meant everything to her, and it was so hard to be brave when everything was on the line. She sighed. She was tired of all the circular thinking. She was just…tired.

After she provided the obligatory cup of pee, she came back out to the waiting room to sit until the nurse called her name. But Megan's steps faltered as she sucked in a long, sharp breath.

"Megan," Daniel murmured as he rose from his seat. His expression was carefully blank, but his eyes skimmed every inch of her with an intensity that made her insides tremble. She wasn't sure she would be able to put one foot in front of another so she stood where she'd stopped. "I can leave if you want me to."

She released the breath she'd been holding and walked up to him. "No, I want you to stay. The whole point of our debacle was to let you be a part of our child's life, every step of the way. No matter what happens, I still want that for you and the baby."

"For me and the baby." He nodded, his mouth settling into a grim line. "I… Thank you."

"Of course." She glanced at him uncertainly, wondering what she'd said to upset him.

"You should sit." With a gentle touch on her elbow, he guided her to a chair and took the one next to her. "How…how are you?"

That was a loaded question. How would he react if she said, "Missing you? Trying to stay strong for the baby even though I want to curl up into a ball and cry most of the time?" In the end, she said what everyone always said whether it was true or not. "Fine."

He sighed and looked down at his hands, which were clenched into fists on top of his thighs. She felt like she was getting all her answers wrong. A touch of anger flared inside her. Why did he get to ask all the questions anyway?

"And how are you?" she asked, arching her eyebrow in challenge.

He raised his eyes to meet hers and the pain and longing in them took her breath away. He held her gaze as though to give her time to look inside of him—like he was laying himself bare for her. When he finally opened his mouth, she leaned toward him to hear his answer.

"Megan Han?" the nurse called from the doorway.

She wanted to snarl and tell the woman to piss off, but it wasn't the poor nurse's fault that she had shitty timing. Daniel stood first and held his hand out to her. She gingerly took it and allowed him to help her to her feet even though she could've gotten up on her own. She instinctively understood that *he* needed to help her.

"Hello, my dear." Dr. Pinkus walked into the examination room with her signature warm smile. "And Daniel."

"Hi, Dr. Pinkus," Megan said as Daniel nodded his hello.

"So, how have you been feeling?" the doctor asked.

"We felt the baby move," Megan whispered and Daniel stiffened by her side. That moment seemed like a lifetime ago. The joy and wonder that they'd shared remained crystal clear in her mind, but the memory of the sorrow that followed made her throat close up.

"Ah, the quickening." Dr. Pinkus nodded happily. "It's such a special moment."

"Yes," Daniel said thickly. "It was unforgettable."

Something in his voice made Megan turn sharply toward him, but he kept his eyes trained on the doctor as she explained the baby's growth and what to expect in the next four weeks. Megan nodded at the appropriate spots, but her mind was a mess of jumbled thoughts. Had Daniel been trying to tell her something before the nurse called her name? Was she imagining things that weren't there, because she wanted to? She didn't know. All she knew was that it hurt to see Daniel—to want him but not have him. It hurt too much.

They walked to the parking lot in silence, each lost in their own thoughts. Megan needed to get away from Daniel before she burst into tears. She didn't feel brave enough to fight for his love at the moment. She felt raw and scared.

"Thanks for coming today." She forced a stiff smile on her face. "I'll see you at the next appointment."

She'd opened the car door and moved to get inside when Daniel gripped her upper arm. "Megan."

She heard a world of emotions in that one word. He'd said her name as though his life depended on it. Her breath came in quick puffs. She couldn't… She pulled her arm out of his grasp and got inside her car.

"Bye, Daniel," she said without looking at him. He was holding the car door so she couldn't close it, and she felt panic building inside her. She was a second away from bursting when he finally let go and stepped back.

She shut the door and squealed out of the parking lot as the tears she'd been holding back rained down her cheeks.

Megan slept for three hours when she got home. She didn't feel like getting out of bed even when she woke up, but she had to get ready to meet her dad for dinner. The last thing she wanted to do was be out in public where there were people, but she couldn't refuse her dad. She had so much to make up to him.

After a long shower, she dried her hair to fall down in soft waves around her shoulders. She chose a rich yellow tunic dress to cheer herself up and added a soft pink lipstick to her light makeup. Getting herself ready for a dinner date with her dad made her feel a bit stronger, and she needed all the strength she could find.

The Italian restaurant her dad chose for dinner was one of her favorites and she found her lips curling into a smile as she walked inside. The interior was minimalistic with cream-colored walls and white linens, but the muted lights and lit candles on the tables gave the ambience a warm, inviting feeling.

"We have a reservation for two under Minsung Han," she told the host.

"Of course. Please follow me."

Her dad wasn't there yet, so she ordered herself a glass of iced tea and a basket of bread and butter. If he didn't come by the time she finished the bread, then she would text him. She was used to her dad running late for everything. Just like Daniel.

She didn't cringe away from the thought like she'd been doing for the past three weeks. She loved Daniel. Of course everything would remind her of him. It was time she accepted that and stopped trying to hide from her feelings. If she kept hiding, how was she going to win his love?

She asked for more butter as she worked her way through the bread basket. She glanced at her watch and decided to give her dad five more minutes before she texted him.

"Megan?"

She dropped the bread she was buttering on her plate and gaped at Daniel. "No."

"Pardon?" he asked, his eyebrows drawing together.

"No," she repeated. Her father has resumed his matchmaking scheme. "I can't believe he did this again."

She opened her purse and pulled out her phone to give her dad a piece of her mind. He knew she loved Daniel, and wanted to help—which was very sweet and all—but this was her life and he needed to stop meddling in it. But her dad had already texted her.

Sorry, my dear. I got detained at work. I hope you approve of your replacement date. She was so busy growling that she almost didn't hear Daniel. "Do you mind if I have a seat?"

"No, of course not. Please sit," she said, flustered. She took a deep breath through her nose and met Daniel's eyes. "I'm so sorry about my father."

"Are you kidding? Your father is amazing." He smiled sheepishly. "I'm going to buy him a drink. Well, depending on how things go tonight, I might even buy him a cellar full of drinks. Either way, I'm grateful to him."

"I'm sorry." Megan blinked. "I think I lost you."

"Never." All traces of a smile left Daniel's face. "You could never lose me."

"What?" He was staring at her with such unwavering focus that she forgot to breathe.

"You must hate me," he said with anguish in his voice.

She managed to shake her head.

"You couldn't wait to get away from me earlier today." He held up his hand. "Not that I blame you. You have every right to hate me."

"Stop saying that," she said with a confused frown. She didn't hate him. She loved him.

"Megan, I'm so sorry." He reached across the table as though he wanted to touch her but snatched his hand back at the last moment. "I'm sorry I couldn't tell you that I loved you. I'm sorry I let you walk away thinking we were finished."

She was shaking so badly that she had to clench her teeth to stop them from chattering. Hearing his apology made her realize how angry she'd been—at him and at herself. They had something special and precious, and they'd let it slip through their fingers.

"There was someone in college," he began. "I thought I was in love with her."

Her stomach dropped like rocks. She'd been right. He was in love with someone else. That was why he couldn't love her. Her nails dug into her palms.

"But she was only using me so she could get to my roommate," he stated matter-of-factly, as though it had happened to someone else.

She couldn't hold back her gasp. "That's horrible. I'm so sorry."

"She said I wasn't good enough." He paused for a second. "And I believed her. Deep down, I'd always believed that. Why else would my own mother abandon me?"

"Oh, Daniel. That's not true." She felt gutted. He didn't deserve that. Any of that. She reached for his hand and squeezed tight. "They were wrong. So very wrong. You are a good, kind man—deserving of love and loyalty."

"I know." He flipped her hand and linked his fingers through hers. "You showed me that."

"I'm not sure…"

"I… I thought that you would leave me, too." His eyes searched her face. "I was so afraid I would lose you, too."

"What are you trying to tell me?" she asked, blood pounding in her ears.

"I'm trying to tell you that… I was wrong," he said. "Love isn't a fantasy. I know you love me."

She started and tried to jerk her hand out of his, but he held on tight.

"I'm sorry it took me so long to see that." He gazed at her with heartrending tenderness. "I was a fool for not realizing how fucking lucky I was."

She nodded her agreement because she didn't think her voice would work. A crooked grin touched his lips.

"I'm sorry it took me so long to realize that *I* love you," he said, his voice cracking at the end. "I love you, Megan. More than anything."

A choked sob broke free from her and still she couldn't say anything.

"Am I…? Am I too late?" he asked with such vulnerability that her heart broke a little. "Do you not love me anymore? No, that's okay. I'll win your love back. I'll do anything for you. All I want is a chance to love you. To show you that you are everything to me."

"Stop," she whispered.

"What?" There was stark fear on his face.

"Stop talking—" she took a shuddering breath "—and listen."

He nodded, holding her hand with both of his as though she might run away if he let go.

"I'm sorry, too," she said, tears sliding down her cheeks.

"No, you have nothing…"

"Daniel, listen."

He clamped his mouth shut and a muscle jumped in his jaw. She could see the effort it took him to wait for her to finish.

"I'm sorry I didn't fight for us. I loved you, but I was too afraid to tell you. I was scared of pushing you away." She bit down on her lower lip to stop it from shaking. "I should've been braver. I should've loved you more."

"You…*loved* me?" His Adam's apple bobbed as he struggled to swallow.

"I do love you still. So much," she said. "But what I'm trying to say is I'm sorry I didn't love you harder, because you deserve to be loved—to be loved with courage. You are…"

Daniel stood so quickly that his chair scraped across the floor, and she was in his arms before she could squeak in surprise.

"Stop talking," he said in a low, growly voice before his lips crushed against hers.

She didn't waste a second before she wrapped her arms around his neck and kissed him back with everything she had—all the love, all the passion, all the regret… No. No regret. There was no room for that.

A chuckle rumbled deep in his chest, which made her kiss him harder, but he gently but firmly pushed her away. "Megan."

She frowned and tried to tug him back. This time he laughed with his head thrown back. It was beautiful.

He was beautiful. And she was going to make him do it all the time. She had a lifetime to make him laugh.

"We have to stop unless you want to be banned from this restaurant," he said. "Here, sit."

She lowered herself into the chair, but she wasn't happy about it. When Daniel sat back down across from her and pulled out his phone, she gave an outraged huff. "You dare look at your phone when you could be kissing me?"

He just smiled up at her and said, "I have to ask your father's permission for something. I'm not doing anything behind his back anymore. I really should do it in person, but I can't wait…"

"Daniel, you just confessed your undying love for me." He hadn't said anything about undying, but she was pretty sure it was implied. "I don't think now is the appropriate time for you to text with my father."

"Bear with me. It's very important." His phone buzzed right away as though her dad had been waiting for Daniel's text. He checked the message and laughed that happy laugh again. She wanted to bottle it and drink it up.

"What is going on?" she asked with a confused smile. Her eyes widened when Daniel got down on his knee and looked up at her. "Ohhh. Okay. I think I know what's going on."

"Megan Han." If she wasn't already in love with the man, she would've fallen for him when he gazed at her with such love and awe—as though it was a privilege for him to behold her. "Will you make me the happiest man alive by becoming my wife?"

"Do you love me?" she said in a shaky whisper.

"With all my heart," he answered without hesitation.

"Then, yes." She laughed even as tears spilled down her cheeks. "I'll marry you."

"Finally." He grinned as he leaned toward her.

She met him halfway but stopped a breath away from his lips. "All you needed were the magic words."

"I love you," he said as he claimed her lips and her heart.

She smiled smugly against his kiss. She knew her intuition wouldn't lead her astray. Daniel Pak was capable of love, deep and everlasting, and he was hers to love with all her heart.

*****

COMING SOON!

We really hope you enjoyed reading this book.
If you're looking for more romance, be sure to
head to the shops when new books are
available on

Thursday 5th
January

MILLS & BOON

THE HEART OF ROMANCE

A ROMANCE FOR EVERY READER

MODERN

Prepare to be swept off your feet by sophisticated, sexy and seductive heroes, in some of the world's most glamourous and romantic locations, where power and passion collide.

HISTORICAL

Escape with historical heroes from time gone by. Whether your passion is for wicked Regency Rakes, muscled Vikings or rugged Highlanders, awaken the romance of the past.

MEDICAL

Set your pulse racing with dedicated, delectable doctors in the high-pressure world of medicine, where emotions run high and passion, comfort and love are the best medicine.

True Love

Celebrate true love with tender stories of heartfelt romance, from the rush of falling in love to the joy a new baby can bring, and a focus on the emotional heart of a relationship.

Desire

Indulge in secrets and scandal, intense drama and plenty of sizzling hot action with powerful and passionate heroes who have it all: wealth, status, good looks…everything but the right woman.

HEROES

Experience all the excitement of a gripping thriller, with an intense romance at its heart. Resourceful, true-to-life women and strong, fearless men face danger and desire - a killer combination!

To see which titles are coming soon, please visit

millsandboon.co.uk/nextmonth

LET'S TALK
Romance

For exclusive extracts, competitions
and special offers, find us online:

 facebook.com/millsandboon

@MillsandBoon

@MillsandBoonUK

Get in touch on 01413 063232

For all the latest titles coming soon, visit
millsandboon.co.uk/nextmonth